"You and me, Steel̲e̲, ... ̲ ̲ ̲ ̲ ̲ ̲ ̲ ... I've ever heard of and some new ways, too. If we're going to get out of this mess, we've got to start being honest with each other. Steele, we're going to make you a star and while we're at it we're going to make me one, too."

Steele looked at Valli as if she'd lost her mind. "I see, and just how do you plan to make these miracles happen?"

"What we're going to do, Steele, is go to Hollywood. But from now on, I'm going to be the only one in your bed and I mean that, too."

The enormity of what she'd promised boggled her mind, but she was practical enough to know that they were about to take a desperate gamble, a gamble that might not work. She looked at Steele and her mind said, "He doesn't love you, Valli." She looked out at the melting Christmas snow and she knew that what she'd envisioned was just as fragile. But for this one moment, in her heart the sleighbells rang.

THE VERY BEST

Jenna Darcy

BANTAM BOOKS
TORONTO · NEW YORK · LONDON · SYDNEY · AUCKLAND

THE VERY BEST

A BANTAM BOOK
0 553 17558 0

First publication in Great Britain

PRINTING HISTORY
Bantam edition published 1988

First published in the U.S. by Ballantine Books

Bantam Books are published by Transworld Publishers Ltd.,
61–63 Uxbridge Road, Ealing, London W5 5SA,
in Australia by Transworld Publishers (Aust.) Pty. Ltd.,
15–23 Helles Avenue, Moorebank, NSW 2170, and in New
Zealand by Transworld Publishers (N.Z.) Ltd., Cnr. Moselle
and Waipareira Avenues, Henderson, Auckland.

Reproduced, printed and bound in Great Britain by
Hazell Watson & Viney Limited
Member of BPCC plc
Aylesbury Bucks

To Bob, Pepper, and the kids—
who really are the very best

PART
ONE

CHAPTER ONE

Valley Ray Turner flipped her homemade portfolio sideways and stumbled off the bus. Thirty-four hours on a Greyhound had numbed her entire body, and her wrinkled green linen sheath—the most sophisticated dress she owned—now looked more like a gunnysack than a dress.

The sweltering July heat was overwhelming as diesel fumes roiled from beneath the bus and assaulted her lungs. For a moment the blast of hot air reminded her of home, except for the strangling odor; she'd never imagined New York City would be this hot.

As she waited for the driver to open the luggage bay and remove the new Samsonite luggage that held her future, she felt the energy of the city vibrate through the thin soles of her well-worn T-strap shoes. New York City, fashion capital of the United States—she was really here.

Propping against the curb the folded piece of cardboard that protected her sketches, she carefully straightened the seams of her stockings, while she mentally reviewed her plan. It was simple: Go straight to the Lorenso Fashions Building and show them her sketches and her samples. Of course, she didn't expect to be a full designer right away; she'd work her way up.

"The blue Samsonite yours?"

"Oh, yes, sir." She stepped forward to take the heavy bag. She should have left her woolgathering, as Granny called it, back in Willacoochee, Georgia. She had graduated from high school, the class of '61, just a few short months ago. And from now on, she was Valley Ray Turner, fashion designer.

But her confidence was quickly deflated when, with a belch of air, the bus moved away from its unloading slot, and she watched helplessly as the expelled air pressure rocked the cardboard portfolio, causing it to fall directly into the path of the bus. Before she could react, her work tumbled and twisted along under the bus until it disappeared completely beneath the tires.

Choking back a sob, Valley ran into the street to pick up the mutilated piece of cardboard meant to protect the papers within. The black ribbon holding the covers together had come undone. Ruined! All of her sketches were torn and riddled with tire tracks. A honking horn startled Valley into the awareness that she was standing in the middle of a loading zone where an impatient taxi driver waited for her to either get in, or move out of his way. A sigh crept from her lips as indecision and anguish crowded in.

Suddenly the few dollars in her purse seemed insignificant now that she had reached this rumbling, impatient city of steel and concrete. The shredded portfolio had been her ticket into the fashion world. Realizing it was beyond salvaging, she dropped it into the trash can. For a second she wildly considered jumping on another bus and going home. At least she knew the demons she had to face back there. She'd been fighting them off for years. The taxi driver blew his horn again, startling her back to reality. She'd come this far, and she wasn't about to give up yet. She couldn't give up, because there really was nothing to go back to.

After tossing her precious bag into the seat and then, pushing it over to make room for herself, Valley climbed into the taxi a little more awkwardly than she wished. "Do you know the Lorenso Fashions Building?"

"Garment district? We're on our way." The yellow cab pulled away from the curb, but the driver's gaze remained on the mirror as he tried to catch her eye.

They may have been on their way, but Valley didn't realize that the distance that she had to cover was roughly the size of half of Georgia. As perspiration dribbled down her forehead and into her eyes, they sped along for short stretches, scrunched to a halt, crawled a while, and lurched forward again.

"Traffic's bad today." The driver pounded the horn and shook his fist at the car in front of them. "This your first trip?"

Valley struck a pose meant to imply disdain. "No. I'm merely a little frustrated with the way the bus driver handled my luggage."

The cabbie nodded and grinned. "Yeah, them guys don't give a damn about nothin'."

As the cab sped past streets that were numbered instead of named, Valley thought that the people in charge here must not be very creative if they didn't bother to name the streets. Through her window she saw Forty-second Street, Forty-third Street, Forty-fourth Street, and she fought very hard to keep from hanging out the window to look at the towering buildings they were passing.

Finally they reached a large park and turned in. "I didn't realize that New York City was so woodsy."

"Oh, yeah. Just in places, though."

The cab passed street vendors selling ice cream, hot dogs, and sodas as they continued on their way through the park. Valley peered at the people rowing across a small lake and marveled at the number of people who found the time to stroll through the park on a work day.

They emerged from the park onto a busy avenue, and before long Valley noticed that they were passing Forty-fifth Street, Forty-fourth Street, Forty-third Street. Her confidence sagged as she realized she'd been taken advantage of.

5

"Hey, wait a minute." She slid forward on the seat. "We just passed these streets a few minutes ago. What's going on here?"

For a second the cabbie looked stunned, but recovered quickly. "All you out-of-towners are alike. This is the West Forties. We were on the East Forties a while ago."

"Oh. Sorry, but you can't be too careful these days." Valley resumed her place by the window, still uneasy. Surely one didn't have to drive that far up to go over and back down again?

The driver was silent.

From the sidewalks throngs of people pressed forward, spreading around the stopped cars like an army of ants moving their colony to a new mound. Where could they be going in such a hurry? Through her open window the incredible volume of noise roared at her, as though everybody in the city had been thrown into the streets and given ten minutes to find their way out of a maze.

Now the cab drove through crowded streets honeycombed with droves of workers pushing metal racks of garments along the sidewalks and streets as though the cars were expected to wait for them to pass. There was constant, frantic movement, as the racks of clothing scudded back and forth and people raced through the intersections, ignoring the "Don't Walk" lights. Valley had never experienced anything like the noise and movement convulsing around her.

Eyeing the fare meter which was relentlessly clicking off her reserves, Valley realized that she'd been right to worry. When the cab finally stopped at Thirty-second and Fashion Avenue, Valley bit back her disappointment.

She'd expected a building straight out of the Hollywood musicals she'd seen at the Dixie Theatre. But this edifice, though large, was old and dirty, with only a narrow sign over the door proclaiming the name Lorenso. After paying the driver she was down to her last twenty-one dollars and twelve cents. Her head pounded and her dress felt damp. For a moment she wanted to cry. This wasn't quite what she had expected.

The interior was slightly more glamorous. The wallpaper was a shade of lavender, which Valley recognized as Lorenso's signature color. Velvet sofas and chairs in a deeper shade were placed under blown-up photographs of Lorenso's most successful designs and celebrity clients. The Chase chrome ashtray stands were placed strategically around the room.

"Yes?" The receptionist was blond, bored, and dismissive.

"I'd like to see Mr. Lorenso, please." Valley wrinkled her nose at the stale odor of cigarette smoke and tried to smile at the young woman.

The receptionist glanced appraisingly at the short, rather indistinct dark-haired girl weighed down by luggage and shook her head. Her expression said that she'd seen Valley's type before—by the dozens.

"I'm sure you would, honey. So would the rest of the people in this room." Muttering something, the receptionist returned her attention to the Italian issue of *Vogue* in front of her.

Valley looked around the foyer, seeing for the first time the odd assortment of individuals seated in the waiting area. There were tall, gaunt women heavily made up, some holding long cigarette holders, wearing a colorful rainbow of sheaths made of silken fabrics accented with scarves, and shoes with stiletto heels. Sprinkled among men in avant-garde dress clutching portfolios were a few men in business suits.

"All these?" Valley glanced down at her own dress and quickly realized that she was neither outstanding nor outrageous enough to command anybody's attention, certainly not the Great Lorenso, as the fashion editor of *Vogue* called him. Gulping deeply the smoke-laden air, she was determined to persist. She'd come this far on her wits and she'd always found there was more than one way to skin a cat, as her granny would say.

"Yes."

"Fine, I'll wait." Valley said, her eyes shrewdly searching the room for some clue as to how to distinguish herself from the mass of human flesh behind her. "Is there a ladies room, or a lounge? I . . . I feel a little strange."

Swaying slightly, she closed her eyes as she grasped for the edge of the desk and slid to the floor in as graceful a heap as she could manage in the slim skirt she was wearing.

"Oh, hell!" The receptionist came to her feet and hurried around the desk. "Damn women, trying to starve themselves to death to look like those godawful creatures Lorenso releases on the world."

Valley lay as still as she could manage. Even with her eyes closed she could feel every eye in the room piercing her body.

From somewhere behind the receptionist area two men rushed out and not very gently lifted Valley to her feet. They were obviously going to make her walk, so she managed to make herself appear to be coming out of the swoon she'd so magnificently staged.

"Come on, miss. One foot in front of the other. That's it. We're just going to take you to the ladies room and you can wash your face."

They walked her down a long corridor bustling with scurrying people, opened a door at the end of the hall, and shoved her inside. "Sit down for a minute, and then you might as well give it up and go home, kid. You got tits. Other than Verna on the reception desk, tits aren't allowed."

"Wash your face, then hit the road before the Great One gets back," she was directed, and then abandoned with a slam of the door.

Opening one eye, she saw that she and her suitcase were alone in what appeared to be a combination lounge and ladies room. The walls were lined with long racks crammed with brightly colored clothes and punctuated with hooks from which an assortment of belts, scarves, and other accessories hung. It was obviously a dressing room of some kind with mirrors and make up and every conceivable kind of garment.

The sound of approaching footsteps pushed her into action, and she fled into the adjacent toilet area, slipped into a stall, and closed the door.

"What do you think?" a tense male voice questioned.

"I think that our ass is grass, darling. Zilch, finito, capiche. When Lors finds out that Mattie's final number isn't on the rack, we're dead," another man said in a voice that was unusually high and lilting.

"Can't we shoot it over to the show without his knowing?"

"Do you want to walk in with a two-thousand-dollar Lorenso creation slung over your shoulder for all the world to see? Not me. As it stands now, he doesn't know who is responsible for its loss. If we show up there, he'll know."

A gem of an idea was beginning to form in Valley's mind. If she could just find out where the show was taking place, she'd figure a way to show him the clothes she'd brought. She didn't have her sketches, but she had the real thing, and she was sure that nobody was making anything even remotely like her sweaters. Ever since she'd been a young girl she had studied intently any fashion magazine that came her way. By the time she was fourteen she knew that she possessed a rare talent to predict the trends. At sixteen she had started to transform her mental images to paper.

"So what do we do with it? I can't stand here and hold it. Somebody just might come in and think there's something odd about my holding a bag in my hand at the same time the show-stopper disappears."

"For god's sake, stick it back here behind these tacky hostess gowns. By the time anybody finds it, we'll be on vacation and nobody will ever know."

Valley heard the rustle of fabric, the click of a closing door, and then silence. Peering cautiously out the door, she saw that the room was empty. Scanning the room until she found the rack of hostess gowns, she slid her fingers toward the back of the rack until she touched a soft velvety-finished clothing bag.

Now, if she only knew where the show was being held she could take the dress herself. That would make Lorenso appreciative, very appreciative. First, however, she needed to make a few changes; she had to make sure he noticed her designs. Quickly she skinned off her dress and T-strap shoes, exchanging them for a long, paint-splattered angora tunic. The gaudy metallic colors were carefully woven into an abstract design against a background of black and topped off with a flame-colored dickey at the neck.

She stepped into the matching short skirt, looked at herself in the mirror, and changed her mind. Without the skirt the tunic was long enough to be safe and at mid-thigh short enough to be outrageous. Besides, the short tunic made her appear taller.

Next she walked over to the makeup table and surveyed herself critically in the mirror. She had never considered herself beautiful, not even pretty. She had noticed, however, while poring through a fashion book in the library, a certain resemblance to the young Coco Chanel. But Coco came into her real beauty at a much later age. Valley had wanted to look like the glamorous Valentina, who was not only a remarkable American fashion innovator, but a scintillating beauty who had hobnobbed with society—and lost her husband to none other than Greta Garbo.

Valley's straight, shoulder-length ebony hair was thick, framing a heart-shaped face punctuated by large sapphire eyes, fringed with dark lashes, her straight brows unfashionably full. At five-foot-two, she was too short to be a model, and, as someone had just crudely pointed out, too busty. She wasn't exactly overweight, just curvacious.

She hoped that someday she would be as exalted in the world of high fashion as Valentina had been in her heyday, but she never even entertained the hope of becoming as beautiful. Yet she knew that if she were to carry out her plan, she'd have to make some kind of acceptable statement with her clothes—and her person.

Taking a deep breath and calling on the flair for the dramatic that sometimes alienated the people of Willacoochee, she took a pair of scissors from the counter and began to whack off great chunks of hair, dropping them carelessly to the floor. Shorn, she resembled that same cat her grand-mother always used as a reference point—after it had been caught in the fan blades of an automobile. At least she wasn't nondescript, now.

Before, her eyes had fluttered childlike beneath straight-edged bangs that covered her forehead and eyebrows, al-most obscuring the glitter of crystal that seemed to erupt from her eyes as she peered closely at herself in the mirror. Now they flashed back at her intensely, making her appear older than her eighteen years. Not bad, she thought, raking her fingers through the thick bob of remaining hair until it fell into a jet halo around her face.

A quick application of makeup, glittery eye shadow, and lipstick improved the face, highlighting the even pallor of her fine complexion. A quick swipe at her faithful black T-strap shoes with a damp tissue and an application of masca-ra to cover the scars on the leather, and she was ready.

But, where was she going? She stopped short and was once again assailed by doubts. Think, Valley, she chided herself. Finally, spotting a pay phone in the corner, she de-cided that she might be able to find out by phone what was a secret in person.

"Lorenso Fashions, how may we make you beautiful?"

"By telling me, darling, where Lorenso is holding court today." Valley affected a languorous northern accent.

"Holding court? He's not in court. He's at the Waldorf-As-toria showing his new line."

"Thanks." Valley hung up the phone, turned toward the mirror with a satisfied grin, and retrieved the garment bag from behind the hostess gowns. She gave a shove to her suit-case sending it under the racks.

When she reached the reception area she held the Lorenso bag close to her face as she sailed by the reception-ist, almost making it out the door before she heard a start-led, "Wait!"

She didn't. Outside the dingy building she looked about helplessly for a cab, all the while wondering where the Waldorf-Astoria was and how she was going to pay her fare when her funds were already so low.

"I said, 'wait!'" A tall man came charging through the lobby after her, grabbed her arm, and held on firmly. Valley's face dropped as she looked up at the young man, certain that he was about to accuse her of theft. "You're going to the showing, aren't you?"

"Eh, yes." Valley found herself blushing furiously.

"Fine, so am I and if we're late together, maybe the old fart won't can us."

"The old . . . You mean Lorenso?"

"Lorenso? Boy, you haven't been here long, have you? You call him Lorenso and the thunder rolls and lightning strikes. In other words, darling, you're dead." He led her around the corner of the building to the loading dock, where a pale lavender van with Lorenso Fashions scrawled in black letters across its door, was parked.

"Your taxi, kid. Jump in. I'm going over to haul everything back." A grin burst across his handsome face.

Stepping up into the van, Valley carefully folded the garment bag across her exposed legs. "I'm Valley Ray Turner, and I appreciate the lift."

"You're welcome. Sam Carr. Aren't you new here?" He peered at her from intense brown eyes and smiled again.

"Eh, yes. This is my first day." Valley's smile came more slowly, but she couldn't resist his infectious good humor.

An engaging touch of madness in his brandy-colored eyes knocked her for a loop every time he looked at her. He was certainly handsome.

"And they trust you with one of the Great One's creations?" Beneath short dark hair, his eyebrows lifted as he looked at her more closely.

"It's an emergency. It got left out of the collection. Mattie's final number," she mumbled as though she knew what that meant.

"Good lord. You've got *the* dress for the finale?" Sam's

12

foot hit the pedal, and the van lurched forward. "Old Lors must be taking those poor dressers apart. I'm glad I'm not scheduled today."

"Scheduled?" Valley couldn't imagine what he was talking about. He was only a few years older than she, and at better than six feet he towered over Valley's frame, which was a full foot shorter. His lanky physique made her feel even more dumpy than she usually did. Short black hair that might have been wavy if he'd let it grow longer exposed a strong face—a square chin jutted below high cheekbones and a straight classic nose. His lips, however, were soft and full, exposing straight white teeth.

"I'm a model. I mean, I'm not really a model, I'm an actor. But there's not much money in acting if you don't have a job—so I daylight."

"You. . .what?" Valley thrust out a hand to brace herself as the driver in front jammed on his brakes and started a shrieking chain of events behind him.

The brakes of the van joined the cacophony of squealing tires and squalling horns. "Daylight. Work as a model during the daytime while I make my rounds between assignments. I'm an actor, though I haven't done much acting yet. What about you, you got any plans?"

"Oh, yes," she said in a determined whisper, looking straight ahead of her at the snarled traffic. "This is just the beginning. I'm going to be a designer, and one day, my name will be on this van."

CHAPTER TWO

Backstage at the Waldorf was a madhouse of frenzied activity. Dozens of men and women were frantically pulling clothes on or off, cursing and tugging all the while. Other men, with face powder and brushes in hand were darting to and fro, ready to dispense their wares on anyone with a shiny nose or a hair out of place. In the midst of all this confusion a short, slim, elflike man with silver hair wearing lavender pants and a black artist's smock stood on a step stool. He held a baton in one hand and barked orders as though he were a drill sergeant on maneuvers.

"What? You say—what?" His voice rose at least two octaves and a decibel. "Quiiiet!"

You could hear a pin drop. Half-nude bodies froze and turned to stare at the red-faced designer. A thin, olive-complected woman with jet-black hair cowered at his feet. She was wearing one of the lavender smocks that appeared to separate the designers from the cast of supporting characters.

"Find it!" Through clenched teeth, the whispered words were more effective than a shout. "Now!"

Valley's and Sam's appearance in the doorway went unnoticed amidst the chaos that followed as every lavender-smocked body in the place began scurrying through the garment racks like rats in a restaurant dumpster.

"Mr. . ." Valley began, starting toward the man on the stool.

"Wait!" Sam cautioned. Just then, Valley caught her toe in the end of the garment bag and heard the sickening tear of fabric as she lurched forward. Only Sam's quick action stopped her from sprawling facedown at Lorenso's feet.

"Who are you? And where did you get that garment bag?" A thin finger, gnarled by years of delicate work, pointed accusingly at Valley, and every eye in the room focused on her.

"I brought the missing gown," she said with as much dignity as she could manage. "And, I came to talk. . ."

"What? You? You have the finale? Who told you to touch it?" he barked, his body trembling with anger, his bushy brows contracted. "You're fired!"

Motioning for the dark-haired woman to take the bag, he waited as the dress was removed. The low murmur of voices went silent again as the rip appeared in the gauzy violet fabric of the draped sequined bodice.

"You. . .you, what have you done to my creation?" He whirled at her as his thin fingers clutched at his wrinkled throat and fury leapt into watery blue eyes. "You've destroyed it!"

"Oh, dear," Valley began, aghast at the damage her stumble had caused. "I am so very sorry. I. . .I'll repair it right away. I'm very good at mending. Granny says. . ."

"Cease your chattering. Be silent and don't move. I'll deal with you in a moment." He began to bark orders to the lavender-smocked men and women who gathered around them.

"Send out the last two models with the peasant skirts, followed by the black velvet paired with the blond in the black tuxedo. Then tell Rosalind to let me have the mike. I'll simply explain that the last number has been scratched."

15

"But you can't," one of the dark-haired women protested. "What will they say? We need this number. *WWD* is holding the press until after they see the finale."

Knowing that the wrath of *Women's Wear Daily* was not something to be invoked lightly, his eyes swept the room frantically as he tried to find an acceptable solution. Finally, the sweep of his vision came to rest on Valley, still frozen in place as he had instructed. "What is that thing you're wearing, young woman?"

"I call it a tunic."

"*You* call it?"

"Yes, I knitted the fabric and made the sweater myself. I'd like to show you my samples. I'm a . . ."

"Hush!" He leaped from the stool and walked toward Valley, holding his open palm out in front of his forehead as though he were afraid of being contaminated by the bright reds and silvers in the design. He was only slightly taller than she was.

"You did this?"

"Yes."

"On what?"

"On a knitting machine. I did them all on Granny's machine. But, of course I had to leave it in Willacoochee—the machine, not the sweaters."

"You have more?"

"I have a suitcaseful . . . back at your showroom."

"You're certain that it is original, not copied?" He gazed at her for the first time, staring into her eyes as if daring her to lie. "You didn't steal this design, did you?"

"Of course not. I made this. I'm certain." Valley bristled, feeling Sam's fingers tighten on her elbow. She could sense his unspoken command to silence.

"Turn her loose, boy, and get out of the way." Lorenso walked slowly around Valley without speaking. Then, with unexpected quickness he pointed his baton at her. "Take it off."

"What?"

"I said, take it off. We'll use it. Quickly, time is money."

16

"But, what'll I wear?" she protested.

"Valley," Sam had moved in quietly behind her. "This is your chance. For god's sake take off the damned thing. Nobody here will even notice your body."

He was right. She knew it, and she knew, too, that it wasn't the nobodies that bothered her. It was the young man who took the hem of her sweater and pulled it gently over her head. In a matter of seconds Sam had removed the tunic from her body and threaded it over the head and arms of a pencil-slim, vamp-eyed woman wearing a black satin skirt with a slit three-fourths of the way up her leg. Lorenso added a satin beaded skullcap with a frothing of black net and pushed the model toward the runway entrance.

Less than a minute later the audience applauded at the unexpected entrance of Lorenso. Since the emcee knew nothing of the replacement, he intended to introduce the carefully guarded secret finale himself.

"Not fashion, darlings, but a selected, one-of-a-kind work of art that one wears on the body instead of hanging on the wall. I've used bright colors, threads of silver and gold in a special new process to produce the first evening tunic." And he paused, allowing a dramatic silence to accompany the entrance of the model. The silence continued until she strolled halfway down the runway. Then the applause began, lightly at first, finally erupting into a deafening roar of appreciation.

In the wings, Valley Ray Turner watched as her creation, the birth of her genius, and Granny's accident, received a standing ovation. It wasn't until the models and dressers backstage began to congratulate her that Valley realized she was standing in the wings wearing only her garter belt, panties, and bra. Her cheeks flamed, and she wanted to hide as she felt Sam's arm protectively around her shoulders. Someone brought a lavender smock and she slid her arms gratefully into it, buttoning it over her underwear.

"Well, Sam. Where'd you find the munchkin?" The slim, tuxedo-clad model stepped off the runway. As he approached them, his haughty demeanor fell away and his

17

green eyes flashed an open acknowledgment of interest. He was fairly tall with an athletic build and a tan that indicated time spent in the sun. His hair was a thick wavy mop of sun-bleached golden hair.

"She turned up at the showroom. First day in town and she's already made quite an impression on the fashion world, wouldn't you say?" Sam kept his arm around Valley.

"I'll say. I never saw old Lors blow his cool like that. I assume that she has a name, or did she lose that along with her clothes?"

"Sorry. Valley Ray Turner, meet Courtney McCambridge, of the filthy-rich Philadelphia McCambridges. Our Court is a would-be artist, semipro hustler, and the worst cook in the Village."

"Village?"

"Yes, Greenwich Village. You know, where all the starving artists live. And, speaking of starving"—Court sucked in his already-flat stomach and flashed a warm smile that displayed dimples and dazzling white teeth—"anybody got any money? I'm broke."

"Not me," Sam admitted, "and we won't get paid for this gig until tomorrow. Maybe Noel will earn some tips from the restaurant."

"I wouldn't count on that, but maybe he'll bring home some scraps. I'm not proud," Courtney said. "I'm hungry. When the little tyrant said he wanted skinny models, I agreed to help out. But, I didn't promise to make a career out of this."

"Speaking of the little tyrant," Sam muttered under his breath. "Here he comes."

The silver-haired designer strode across the room, arguing visibly with himself. "You don't have any choice, you must produce her. Just let them look, and that's all." He came to an abrupt stop before Valley, took an irritated look at her from her feet to her peculiar haircut, and shook his head.

"Something we can do for you, Maestro?" Court asked lightly.

18

"You"—Lorenso pointed at Valley with obvious disdain. "Come with me. Don't you have anything to wear besides that smock?"

"No," she said sweetly, "I seem to have lost my clothes."

"Never mind. Just let me introduce you to the press. I don't expect you to talk. I'll handle everything. Just smile. And, for god's sake don't start babbling about your granny."

Valley looked back at Sam, missing the comforting feel of his arm around her. She had managed to bluff her way up to this point, but stepping out on that runway was the hardest thing she'd ever done. When the lights hit her eyes she couldn't see past the glare.

Lordy, she thought, if Granny could see me now, she wouldn't believe where I am, or what I'm wearing. As she grew accustomed to the blaring lights, her eyes rested on one face after another at the seats nearest the runway. The audience was mostly made up of women. Pens poised in midair, their cold stares shot through Valley, causing her to tremble.

"And this bright young thing is the latest addition to my staff. We collaborated on this new original technique. She weaves the fabric, under my directions, of course, and I design the garment. Stunning, don't you think?"

Why that old fool. He was taking credit for her process, under his directions. . .he actually said that he had designed *her* sweater. Valley opened her mouth to protest. He couldn't get away with that.

"Lorenso, what's your new assistant's name?" One of the women in the audience asked, effectively cutting off her impending protest.

"Oh, she isn't my. . ." he began.

"His new assistant's name is Valley," Valley Ray piped up with a confident smile, linking her arm with that of the startled designer. "And we have an entire new tunic line in the works."

Valley looked up at him with as much of a conspiratorial expression as she could muster, not at all certain that he wouldn't pick her up bodily and throw her off the stage.

"Is that right, Lorenso?"

"Well, yes," he agreed uncomfortably.

"What's the metallic color in the knit?"

"That's a secret of course," Lorenso said. "It's an intricate process, and I believe I am the first to use it."

Immediate bedlam broke out within the ranks of the journalists. Always an innovator in the fashion world, Lorenso had just brought about another coup.

"About those other sweaters," Lorenso said cautiously, as they walked backstage. "Of course, I'm willing to give you a fair price for the process."

"About my new job, Mr. Lorenso, what kind of salary did you have in mind?"

"Job? Salary?" His surprise smacked of pure theater. "Surely you understood that that was for the benefit of the press."

"And my designs? You're willing to pay a fair price for my process?" Valley began to weave a web intended to catch this elusive fashion butterfly.

He began to nod in pleasure. "Yes, whatever you think is reasonable, providing of course that your work lives up to my expectations."

She had him. Oh, Granny, you can lead a horse to water, and if you pick the right horse, he'll jump in and drown. "So, I can assume from the response of the buyers and press here that they were equally pleased with my tunic."

"Yes, they were enthusiastic," Lorenso admitted more slowly now that he was beginning to worry about the direction of the conversation.

"Well, then, maybe I should let some other designers have a look, too. You never know, they might be worth more than either of us thinks."

"What?" Lorenso turned white and he caught at his heart dramatically. "How ungrateful can you be? I give you your chance, and you're ready to stick a knife in my back. I'm crushed."

"Lorenso?" Antoinette, the dark-haired assistant, walked toward them with a worried expression on her face. "How do you propose to fill. . ."

"Not now," he barked, then quickly resumed his wounded expression, waving his assistant away all the while.

Valley never knew where she got her courage, but it flowed over her and stilled the last of her uncertainties.

"I've got something you want, and you've got something I want. You get my designs—at a fair price—and I get a job as your assistant. Deal?"

He glared at her for the longest moment before allowing a smile of admiration to steal across his face. He dropped his injured pose. "All right, young lady. You've got a deal."

"Valley Originals," she whispered, reveling in the actuality of daydreams fantasized long ago as she had leaned over that old knitting machine watching Granny take the thread she'd spun throughout the winter and weave it into designs for a little girl who craved pretty colors. Who'd have thought that knocking the can of silver paint into her pot of dye would have set the pattern for Valley's life? Valley closed her eyes, picturing again the same farmhouse she'd abandoned.

The clapboard house stood alone outside the small, dusty, Georgia town that had abused the little girl with large eyes. Peering from her vantage point in the shade beneath the Chinaberry tree, five-year-old Valley Ray swept stubby fingers across the damp trail of tears coursing down dumpling cheeks and listened to the screams erupting from the open windows.

As a black sedan roared to a halt, sending clouds of dust over the clean-swept yard and Valley Ray, the screen door banged open and her mother ran down the two wooden steps and across the yard, her black-and-white polka-dot dress billowing around slim legs.

Little Valley Ray stared, not understanding the scene unfolding before her. Terror crept into her eyes as she realized that her mother was gripping her suitcase in her right hand, along with her familiar drawstring purse.

"Mama!" Valley Ray jumped to her bare feet and ran toward the car as her mother flung the suitcase into the back seat. "Mama! Stop!"

The young woman paused and stared at her wide-eyed daughter. The look bore no compassion, no invitation.

Valley slowed, not understanding the forbidding expression she read in her mother's face. Behind her, the screen door opened again and Valley Ray knew Granny stood on the porch watching the scene, but she didn't care. Mama was leaving.

"Mama." The cry came out pleadingly, the effort of a five-year-old to secure a sign of the love of her parent.

Cold blue eyes bore down on her, and the child slowed even more. If a smile touched her mother's lips, it wasn't visible.

Tears flooded across the child's face, streaking through the dust of red Georgia clay, but the woman didn't pause. Instead she plunged into the front seat of the dark sedan and slammed the door.

Valley stopped within five feet of the car, not understanding her mother's rejection, but not really expecting her to make some gesture of love. She never did.

The man peered at Valley, as if seeing her for the first time, and ducked his head inside the car to say something to the raven-haired occupant. A moment passed and he looked at the little girl again and smiled, a lopsided grin that implied, maybe next time, kiddo.

The car eased away, and then tore down the dirt road sending billows of scarlet dust in its wake.

Stunned for a moment, Valley Ray only watched. But, as the car grew smaller, she spurred herself into action and ran along the road, choking on the dust. "Mama!"

She ran and ran, chubby little legs carrying her as fast as possible, but to no avail. The car quickly left her behind, forgotten and alone on the deeply rutted road. Falling head-long onto the sun-baked clay, her knees grinding into the surface, she rose again and raced along undaunted. Her feet, cut from stray pieces of gravel and glass, ached until she col-

22

lapsed sobbing to the red dirt.

She stared through the remains of her tears for a long time at the spot where the sedan had disappeared, not caring about the spanking Granny would deliver when she returned to the porch. Her mother was gone.

Valley rubbed her knees. Tiny pieces of gravel and grit fell free as her palm crossed the tender surface several times. Her hands came away crimson-streaked with blood from the scrapes.

With resignation, Valley turned to walk the long distance back to the house. Cringing inwardly with pain at each step, she scurried along as if nothing were wrong, too proud to allow anyone to know how much each step cost in agony, not from her outward injuries alone, but from the deeper cuts inflicted by a mother who didn't love her enough to remain.

The five-year-old girl looked at the old house. Until now, it had been home. Although Mama had never really acted like other mothers, she served as the focus of the little girl's love.

And, now, the focus was gone.

CHAPTER THREE

Valley Ray watched in awe as each of the models stripped, unaffected by the contingent of men bustling around and loading the van outside. Her face was still awash with the warmth of success, buoying her to such heights that she felt as though she could float right out of the building.

She had a job. Nothing could possibly go wrong now; she was on her way to success.

"Hey, Volley," Lors called from the stool where he sagged like a wilting rose. "Be at work at eight sharp."

"It's Valley," she corrected. Why did people have such a hard time with her name?

"What?"

"Valley. My name is Valley." She propped her hands on her hips and lifted her chin. "Valley. *V* like victory. *A* like ambition."

While she spelled, Lorenso's face reddened. He obviously didn't expect to be corrected. She continued, ignoring the light tapping on the small of her back. "*L* like. . .like Lors. *L* like Lors. *E* like exquisite. *Y* like. . .yahoo."

"*Y* like yahoo?"

"That's right." She watched his face closely, half expecting him to explode at any second, but a surge of determination refused to allow her to stop once she had begun.

"*Y* like yahoo? Damnation, I love it. Funniest damn thing I ever heard. *Y* like yahoo." He burst into laughter, slapping his knee. All around her, people wearing lavender smocks and nearly nothing at all began to laugh.

"What's so funny?" Valley stepped closer to him, her determination bordering on anger. People had laughed at her for years.

He continued to laugh. "I'm laughing at the word and your use of it."

"I don't think . . ."

"Doesn't matter what you think. Not yet." The laughter lines faded from his face, and the noise in the room subsided. "Tell you what, dearest Valley yahoo. Let's perform a minor alteration to your name. From this moment, you shall be Valli."

"I am Valley." She bristled at his insinuation that he was personally naming her.

"Yes, dearest." He rolled his eyes and lifted his arms in resignation, as if he must lead her step by step. "*V* as in victory. *A* as in ambition. *L* as in Lors. *L* as in luxury. *I* as in impish little wonder. Got it?"

"Well, I . . ."

"See you in the morning." Lors dismissed her, walking out of the room, mumbling the word *yahoo* over and over. A short burst of laughter rang from the doorway where he had disappeared.

Soon, all the models were dressed and filing out the door into the fading afternoon sun. Each time someone opened the door, the twilight became more obvious. Valli watched while the boxes of accessories, shoes, and dresses were loaded into the van.

In the span of a single afternoon, she had become a part of all this—an integral part. Her creation was good enough to serve as the finale. Stardom beckoned. She wandered back to the runway, reliving the moment when Lors had introduced her to the buyers and the press. Valli Originals, now a reality. He *had* said Valli Originals, hadn't he? Well, maybe they'd talk about that tomorrow.

By now, nobody was left except Sam, Court, and Valli. She began to feel deflated. Hearing the slamming of a door, she hurried out the door and toward the van in time to see the engine roar into life, a puff of smoke bellowing out the tail pipe engulfing Valli in a cloud.

She coughed and watched as the truck moved forward into traffic. Dejected, she walked toward the corner that she thought might be in the direction of the showroom. Her new suitcase was still there. Before she could satisfy her hunger or find a place to sleep, she had to retrieve her luggage and her samples. They were all she had now that her sketches were gone.

As the lavender van disappeared in a haze of taillights of cabs, buses, and cars, all with someplace to go, driven by people who had a home, or at least a place to stay, Valli felt increasingly nervous. The smock she wore was mercifully long enough to cover her properly, but it was of little substance. She didn't relish the idea of walking all the blocks to the office in the dark, but she certainly couldn't afford a cab. Not yet. As limousines swooshed past she silently added that one day, soon, she'd be riding in one of those Cadillacs.

A horn blared—interrupting her thoughts—and she looked up. The familiar lavender van pulled over, the door opened, and out popped a blond head. "Hey! Do you need a ride? Where are you going?"

"To the showroom. My suitcase is there."

"Hop in."

Valli ran the last few steps, and with Court's help climbed into the van. He followed, and Sam again steered the vehicle into the erratic flow of traffic. "Say, why didn't you tell us you needed a lift? Where were you, anyway?"

"I didn't know you were leaving," Valli explained half-heartedly. "I sure am glad you came back, though. I don't know my way around very well."

26

"I couldn't leave you dressed like that." Sam glanced over at her and smiled in the instant before the traffic light changed.

Court rolled down the window and rested his elbow on the ledge. "You damn near got left."

"You make a wonderful model, Court." She shifted on the seat, finding the lumpy upholstery uncomfortable on her thinly clad behind. "I was very impressed."

Court stared at her a moment. "I make a lousy model. Not only lousy, but reluctant."

"Oh, no. You were terrific." His tone and denial puzzled her. Why would he be a model if he didn't enjoy it?

"Look, country mouse, I don't do it because I want to. I do it to eat."

"To eat?"

"Yeah. You know. I earn money when I do it." Court watched her bewildered expression. "Look, I'm an artist, I just work as a model to pay the rent and buy food."

"Oh, I see." She looked into his green eyes and found them sincere, not mocking. "But, why don't you paint if you're an artist?"

Sam and Court burst into laughter, and Sam answered, "You should see our apartment. The walls are covered with his paintings. Problem is, nobody wants to pay cash for them. And he's already traded one to every restaurant in New York for a meal. Even the restaurants have run out of bare walls."

"Right. So, I model to earn money until I can make money painting." Court rolled up the window as rain began to pelt his arm. "Not anymore, though. I don't like the job. Hate it, in fact. I can make more money in less time on the tennis court."

"Do you work for a tennis club, too?"

"Hell no." He grinned at her. "I play."

"He's great," Sam added. "His mother is Bitsy McCambridge. How about that?"

Bitsy McCambridge? Valli knew nothing of tennis, and the name meant even less to her. "Oh. I didn't know."

27

After a moment, Sam looked at her oddly. "Say, where are you staying?"

"I, well, I planned on staying at the YWCA. Do you know where it is?"

"You haven't been there yet?" Court asked, incredulously. "Do you realize where you are? You'll be lucky to find a vacant park bench at this hour."

"Don't you know anybody in New York you could stay with?" Sam turned the corner and swore as the driver in front suddenly applied his brakes.

"No, but—" She stopped short, not knowing what to say.

"Say, she could stay with us until she finds a place of her own." Sam pulled over to the curb and touched the van horn. "Of course you'd have to sleep on the couch, but it's not bad."

"Oh, gee. That's awfully nice of you. But I couldn't impose." Valli blushed. What would Granny think of her living with a member of the opposite sex? Before she realized it, she blurted out, "I couldn't . . . just couldn't live with two men."

Court laughed. "I suppose not. I'm sure you'll be very happy in the park with all the muggers and rapists."

Valli shivered.

"You wouldn't be living with two men, Valli. It'll be okay." Court assured her with a mischievous grin that belied his disavowals.

"What do you mean? You just said you and Sam live together."

"Right. But there are three of us," Sam replied as Court opened the door and another young man climbed in.

"Hey, guys." The thin young man tossed a paper bag into the back.

"Valli, this is Noel Gray. Noel, this is Valli—Lorenso's latest protégée, by accident." Sam laughed and launched into an explanation of the afternoon's events. "She's moving in with us temporarily."

"Oh, no. Please, I couldn't," she protested.

"Sure you can. Glad to have you." Noel offered his hand.

28

"Valli, huh? Nice name. You from the South?"

"No, retard, she talks like that because there's a spring loose in the seat," Court teased. "Of course she's from the South."

"A real-life Scarlett O'Hara, I'll bet." Noel smiled and ran his hand through a thick tousle of warm brown curls.

The van stopped at the freight entrance to the Lorenso Fashions Building, and everybody jumped out. Valli hurried in behind Sam, hoping her suitcase was still there.

She rounded the corner, headed for the dressing room where she had accomplished her transformation only a few hours ago, and stopped short when she ran into Lorenso.

"Valli. What are you doing here?" he asked.

"I left my suitcase. I . . ."

He waved her explanation aside. "I've been thinking. That was some stunt you pulled in front of those reporters. Don't think I'm so easily buffaloed." His face bore no trace of a smile, no softening wrinkle marred his stern forehead.

"No. Of course not." She gulped and eased backwards, afraid he would strike her. His glower hardly reflected the pleasure he'd shown over the word *yahoo* earlier.

"You'll learn the ropes from top to bottom. Beginning at the bottom." He started to walk away before adding snidely, "By the way, I have examined the tunic. For a first offering, it's passable."

"Just passable?" Valli was stunned. How could he say such a thing?

"Passable." He strode away, paused, and glanced back. "And, I've taken the liberty of placing the other tunics in our vault for safekeeping. Good night."

Before Valli could protest further, he was gone. She would have nothing to wear tomorrow.

For a second, she vacillated between rushing after him to demand the return of her clothes and letting sleeping dogs lie. Anger rose in her, welling and bubbling into rage over his audacity. Even more horrifying was the fact that he now possessed her designs. And, even a country girl knew the adage that possession was nine-tenths of the law.

Fury overcame her hesitation, and Valli rushed after Lorenso, ready to unleash all her ire on the little man. "You little shrimp," she muttered, jerking open the door where he had exited.

Traffic swarmed past, on the street as well as the sidewalk. Large drops of rain splattered to the ground, seemingly evaporating on the hot pavement, from which a fine mist of steam rose. A peculiar musty smell assaulted her nose. Lorenso was nowhere in sight.

Defeated, Valli slammed the heavy metal door and returned to the dressing room. Her suitcase stood in the middle of the floor with a piece of lavender paper taped to its side. She pulled the folded paper off and opened it.

"Dearest, the latest Lorenso evening wear—the tunics—are ensconced in the safe. I've placed a few items in your bag so that you won't be required to eat and sleep in your smock for the next few days. Lors."

Puzzled, Valli picked up her luggage and returned to the freight entrance. The three guys were just finishing the unloading when she found them.

"Here, I'll carry the suitcase," Court offered.

"Thanks." Valli handed it to him. He sagged under its weight.

"What's in here? Lead weights?"

"Just clothes and some sewing notions."

"Let's go." Noel skipped down the sidewalk and descended a flight of steps adjacent to the front of the building. The others followed, with Valli wondering where they were going.

They reached the bottom of the steps, each dropping in a coin until Valli reached the turnstyle. Sam fished in his pocket, pulled out a token, and flashed a smile as he dropped it in for her.

"Ever ride a subway before?" Sam asked as they walked to the edge of the concrete platform.

"No." She looked down into the tracks and saw puddles of dirty water, paper, and bottles cluttering the track. It smelled awful. Out of the corner of her eye she saw something scurry from beneath a brown paper bag and stop at the edge of a puddle. Valli shuddered.

Moments later the subway train screeched loudly to a stop in front of them, and they raced for the door, Sam dragging Valli along by the hand.

They made it in as the door slammed shut behind them, and the train sped away. Crowded into the car with countless other people, Valli watched the stations zip by at an incredible rate of speed and wondered if they'd ever stop. There were fans, but they weren't working, and Valli felt the now-familiar sweat drip down her back. Occasionally she felt a hand brush against her bottom, and she shifted uncomfortably.

The ride was shorter than she had imagined, and they emerged into a totally different New York. Here the buildings were low, narrow, and obviously quite old. The crooked streets were lined with coffee houses, small theaters, and funky boutiques. Instead of rushing for some unknown destination, people were milling around on street corners, lingering in front of display windows. Valli wanted to stop and look at some of the unusual clothing in the windows, but the men plunged ahead. The distance to the apartment was short.

Finally, they reached their destination. The building on West Tenth near Bleecker was brick and slightly run-down looking, but larger than some of the narrow town houses that surrounded it. Court ran ahead and opened the door. "Hurry, Miss Scarlett. You gonna miss the barbeque."

Laughing at his imitation of Mammy, they all stumbled into the creaky old elevator which carried them to the fourth floor.

Sam reached the door first and opened it. "Well, here it is, Valli. Home sweet home."

He switched on the light and stood aside, allowing Valli to enter first. She looked around. Sparsely furnished, the most significant item in the room was a painting which reached from floor to ceiling.

Valli could look at nothing else. The bizarre colors flowed

31

together, juxtaposing at odd angles and lines, circles and rectangles.

"Well, how do you like it?" Court moved in beside her and dropped her suitcase by the door.

She looked at him and then back at the painting. The pride in his face was unmistakable, and though Valli didn't understand anything at all about the blur of colors, she smiled. "I'm overwhelmed. I don't know much about art, but—"

"It's his mother."

Valli turned to look at Noel, to see if he was joking. The painting meant nothing at all to her. There were lots of green-and-white splotches, and along one side thousands of minidots of a variety of colors, but nowhere could she see anything that even resembled a human form.

"Valli, it's abstract. The green is the court at Wimbledon. The white area in the center is Bitsy. The smaller dots represent the crowd." Sam's sweeping gestures pointed out the areas he mentioned.

Court gazed at it reverently and quipped, "I call it, *Bitsy Wins Wimbledon*."

Valli drew her gaze from the painting and glanced at the room that appeared to serve as both sitting room and dining room. While there were none of the amenities Granny insisted upon, the room seemed homey and comfortable.

"This is just great." Valli turned around, looking at the odd assortment of mismatched furniture, overstuffed chairs, a sofa that looked more soiled than comfortable, a floor lamp with a time-darkened shade, a radio, a small bookcase, a coffee table and some scruffy-looking end tables. Nothing spectacular, but cozy and inviting to a homeless girl from Georgia.

"Great?" Court dropped into one of the chairs. "I'll be damned. Somebody actually thinks this place is great."

"It is." Sam looked around, his lips sagging momentarily before he glanced at Valli. "I think it's great."

"You have to," Noel reminded him, adjusting his tortoise-shell-frame eye glasses. "You live here."

Valli moved closer to Sam, feeling his protective gaze resting on her. "Well, it is. This place really is great. What else do you need?" she asked innocently.

"Servants. Food. Both of those would be good starters." Court grinned, stretching out his legs and laying his head on the back of the chair, staring at the ceiling. "I'll be damned. Did I say we needed servants? Boy, how soon we forget our idealistic ambitions when we get tired of washing our own socks."

"Screw that." Noel threw his shoe at Court. "Of course, you always could go home to Philadelphia."

"Cut the crap, Noel." Court sat up suddenly and looked at Valli, embarrassed. "I didn't mean that, and you know it. I wouldn't go home any more than you would."

"Yea, I know." Noel settled his tall, lanky form in the other chair.

Sam took Valli's arm. "Come on. Let me show you the rest of the place."

"Give her the nickel tour," Noel walked out of the living room and called. "I'll fix dinner. I brought spaghetti home."

Valli followed Sam through the doorway behind Noel. She felt a little uncertain about how to handle this situation. Noel couldn't have known he'd have a new roommate, so he probably didn't bring enough food. Besides, judging from what she'd heard, they hardly had enough money to support themselves.

How could she tell them her uncertainties? "Look, I think I'll go out for something. You go on and eat."

Sam stared at her for a moment. "Oh, shit, Valli. We have enough food for you, too."

"Hell, yes," Court said from behind her. "When Noel brings home spaghetti, he brings enough for the entire Salvation Army."

"I don't want to impose, so I'll. . ."

"Hey, Valli, you're lucky I have this job and can get decent food." Noel took a skillet out of the drawer in the bottom of the stove and poured in the sauce. "Mama Santini sent this to her favorite starving actor and artist."

"Yeah, he used to work at a place where all he could get was baked potatoes." Court grimaced, remembering a diet of baked potatoes that had lasted longer than he had wanted it to.

"Shit, I had to steal those." Noel turned on the gas. He put a pot of water on the back burner. "They kept your ass fed, so don't knock 'em."

"We had baked potatoes almost every night. Noel had this bag he kept tips in. He'd stuff it full of potatoes. Ain't that right, Spud?"

"Now cut that shit out, Sam." He looked at Valli for sympathy. "I feed these jerks, and what thanks do I get? They call me childish names. Can you beat that?"

"I'm sure they don't mean any harm." Valli couldn't tell from his expression whether he was sincere in his plea for understanding—or just teasing.

"Wanna bet? See how you like a steady diet of nothing but potatoes." Court grinned conspiratorially. "He could have sneaked a steak into that bag, don't you think?"

"I was lucky to get out with the potatoes. Those guys were Mafia types." Stirring the sauce, he smiled at Valli and sniffed the steam rising from the skillet. "Smells great, huh?"

"It sure does." Valli hadn't eaten since early morning when the bus had stopped to pick up passengers and she'd bought a candy bar. "If you don't mind, and if you really have enough food. . ."

"It's settled. Come on for the rest of the tour." Sam touched her elbow, and they walked toward the door of the tiny kitchen.

"Listen, I have a little money. If there's a market nearby, I can pick up some French bread and salad. I'd like to contribute something."

"Sounds great to me." Sam stopped. "We'll continue the tour later. You guys set the table. The lady and I will hit the market."

In seconds, Valli and Sam were down the street again. Steam rose from sidewalks still damp from the afternoon rain, causing the air to be muggy and oppressive. Still wearing the smock, Valli smiled as she realized no one even gave her a second glance. They walked a block past a row of townhouses and turned left. Halfway down the block, sandwiched amongst newspaper stands and florists was a tiny cramped market.

Valli picked out some lettuce and tomatoes while Sam found the bread. "How much?" she asked the grocer.

His fingers sprang up and down the cash register until he announced, "One dollar and six cents."

She handed him her last twenty-dollar bill, waited for her change, and soon they were on the way back. Fascinated by the variety of shops and people in her new neighborhood, she stumbled on the cracked sidewalk and nearly fell. Sam caught her and held her until she was standing surefooted again.

"Are you okay?"

"Yes. I'm fine." Color dotted her cheeks, and Valli smiled uneasily. "Gawking is one of my bad habits. Granny always said that curiosity would get the best of me."

They walked on in silence, Valli carefully looking in front of her.

"Say, it's too bad we don't have a bottle of wine to celebrate."

"Celebrate what?"

"Your moving in. You know, it's your first night and everything."

"Oh. I still have some money, but I don't know anything about wine." She looked at him thoughtfully. "Do you?"

"Sure. We can stop here." They entered a liquor store.

"Chianti is what we need," Sam said, taking a bottle from the shelf. "This one will be fine."

Valli paid for the wine and hurried out the door. Sam now carried one bag in each arm.

"Where's Noel from?"

"Old money," Sam quipped. "Actually, Boston."

"I see." Valli didn't really. "What is the difference between old money and new money?"

"Boy, are you a babe in the woods." Sam placed the bottle of wine in the grocery bag. "There's no difference when it comes to spending it. The difference lies in other things, for instance whether or not your ancestors arrived on the Mayflower."

"You're kidding."

"Nope." He shifted the grocery bag to his other arm and placed his hand on her elbow. "Look, in Boston, if you didn't start building your house with a plank from the Mayflower you don't get invited to *the* affairs."

"*The* affairs?" She looked at him, puzzled by his terminology.

"Yeah, you know—all the right parties." He stopped and gazed into her eyes. "Look, Valli, you and I come from the sticks. We have to work harder than Noel and Court to get anywhere. Either one of them could go home right now and live in comfort for the rest of his life. I could go home to eight brothers and sisters and raise corn for nothing the rest of my life."

Valli heard a note of envy in his voice and answered cheerfully, "And, I could go home to nothing. So, you're better off than I am. I don't even have anyone to go home to if I don't make it."

A moment of understanding passed between them, as if their mutual backgrounds bound them together against the world. Each recognized in the other someone whose ambitions transcended their past and would ensure their futures. Yet Valli sensed that Sam's bitterness was deep-rooted—and perhaps stronger than hers.

But something else held their eyes. A moment of recognition, of mutual respect, sealed a pact of friendship that buoyed their spirits.

"We'd better hurry. They'll be finished eating soon." Sam rushed her along. They entered the house, running up the stairs instead of waiting for the elevator.

At the top, Sam reached around her and opened the door. "We're home. Surprise! I brought a bottle of wine."

"Great. Dinner's ready," Noel called from the kitchen.

"I'll fix the salad in a snap." Valli stepped into the kitchen and opened the bag Sam placed on the counter. "Where can I find a bowl and knife?"

Noel provided her with the items she needed and within minutes, she had completed the salad. While Sam opened the wine, Court made a dressing.

"That was your mom on the phone a minute ago," Court remarked to Noel as he placed the cruet of dressing on the small table. "This place isn't big enough for four people to cook." Looking at Noel, Court continued. "I told her you weren't home yet."

"Thanks."

"Don't mention it. Only, you owe me for making me listen to her lecture." He propped himself against the counter, took a spoon, and tasted the sauce. "You've been invited to Martha's Vineyard for a tea honoring some jerk who probably hates tea."

"Right. Only the jerk they're honoring probably dropped a wad in the donkey's feed bag." Noel divided the pasta and poured on the sauce. "Let's eat."

"Who has a donkey?"

"Cripes. You can't be that naive." Noel stared at Valli as if he didn't believe her question.

"Well, you said. . ."

"I was speaking figuratively of the Democratic Party. You know, their party's symbol is a donkey," Noel explained. "You see. . ."

"Right. They use a picture of a donkey and put a liberal jackass in the White House," Court continued for him.

"That isn't what I was going to say at all."

"Hey, guys, no politics over dinner," Sam interrupted before the discussion became an argument. "Let's eat."

"Sure. Dig in." Noel pointed to their plates. "This is an ongoing discussion that can continue at any time."

"Here, Valli, have some wine." Sam poured some of the garnet-colored liquid into her glass and they ate in satisfied silence.

"Now, what about my share of the rent?"

"Well, all of us put in one hundred twenty-five dollars a month for rent and utilities, so if we divide it by four you could put in seventy-five dollars since you don't have a room." Noel answered. "Can you swing that?"

"I don't know. I have no idea what I'll be making." Valli's mouth went dry.

"Look, Valli, when old Lors talks to you tomorrow, demand two hundred dollars a week. He'll flip, but at least he'll understand you realize your worth." Court slid his legs over the arm of his chair and swung them easily. "I saw his face today when he looked at your tunic."

"He'll think I'm coo coo."

"He'll talk you down to a lesser amount, but at least when you talk to him, you'll have some idea of where to start bargaining," Noel added.

Court slid back from the table. "I'm stuffed. Does anyone want to go out?"

Sam looked at Court a moment. "I'm working on some lines for a part in an Off-Broadway thing. I got a script from a guy this morning. Maybe I'll get a jump on all the yo yo's reading tomorrow."

"Good luck. I've got work to do, also." Noel glanced around the table, his eyes finally resting on Valli. "Can you keep a secret?"

"Sure."

"I'm a writer. I write articles that make pin pricks in government policy. One day, though, I'll make a real dent." Noel pushed his plate away, toying with his fork.

"Oh, I think that's wonderful." Valli's eyes widened with pleasure. "I never knew a real writer before."

"Nobody knows I do it." Noel lit a cigarette. "I use a pseudonym so nobody knows who I really am."

"But why? Aren't you proud of what you write?"

"Oh, yes. The problem is that after my first article appeared, my folks got really upset."

"Why would they get mad?"

"Because the article was critical, to say the least, of the government's policy concerning the Negro."

Valli thought a moment. "But why should that upset your parents?"

"Do you know who John Kennedy is?"

"Now, look, Spu.1. . ." Sam interrupted.

"I may be from the country, but I'm aware enough of politics to know who's president." Indignation rose in Valli as she realized Noel was baiting her.

"Okay, sorry." He stubbed out the cigarette on his plate. "God, my mother hates that. Anyway, my parents were upset, to say the least, because the Kennedys are good friends. And, my father is an avid supporter."

"Oh, I see."

"Right. So one night after the article in question appeared, while we were eating and mulling over the resulting irate phone call from Father. . ."

"Keep in mind we were eating baked potatoes," Court added.

"Court and Sam suggested that the next time I wanted to bring the house down around our ears, I should use a pen name. Enter Spud Towns."

"Spud Towns. That's a wonderful name."

"Yeah, I even got a letter to the editor from Martin Luther King."

"Really?" Valli stared at him a moment, trying to ingest all he said. "Who is he?"

Valli's eyes flew open. Where was she?

After a moment's disorientation, she sat up and looked around. The room, in the darkness, was unfamiliar at first but gradually she remembered where she was.

She lay back and stretched. What an absolutely wonderful day yesterday had turned out to be, especially when everything had started out so badly. Sliding off the makeshift bed, she tiptoed down the hall to the bathroom, trying not to wake the others.

Hardly containing her glee, she established what would become her morning ritual of brushing her teeth and trying to tame her new hairstyle into something presentable. Within minutes, she hurried back to the living room to peer out the window at the city, still not believing she was really there.

Outside, everybody seemed to be still sleeping. Taxis moved along on the street below, but she saw few people, except a lone woman dressed in evening clothes obviously returning from a night out. She sat down and continued to watch the city come to life.

The sun rose and found her still watching. By now, the streets bustled with people hurrying to work or maybe to breakfast.

Breakfast. Suddenly Valli realized how hungry she was and padded barefoot into the kitchen. Humming lightly, she opened the refrigerator and found it empty except for the carton of milk Sam had bought the night before.

Pouring herself a glassful, she returned to the living room. Valli took her suitcase and placed it on the sofa, eager to see the clothes Lorenso had given her. One by one she removed the long, slender skirts feeling more and more discouraged. Surely he realized that none of these would fit her. When she pulled out a soft paisley fabric with a full skirt, she held it up to her. Several inches of the bottom ruffle lay on the floor.

Valli pulled it up further and pinned it to her bra. Though it wasn't very comfortable, the skirt struck her knees. It was still too long, but it was a start. She removed a beige shirt and held it up. It, too, hung far too long. Shrugging, she pulled it on. The effect didn't please her, so she searched through her overnight bag for a scarf. When she discovered the mauve silk that had belonged to her grandmother, Valli tied it around her waist, at once delighted with her appearance.

Now she was ready for work. But how was she going to get there? By the time the first stirrings came from down the hall, she was getting anxious.

"You awake already?" Sam asked from the doorway.

"Yes, I don't want to be late my first day." Eagerness crept into her voice.

40

"I'll be ready in a few minutes. I'll drop you by. I have a few errands to run before I audition."

Sam disappeared again, and Valli folded the blanket and sheet that had been her bed, storing them on the shelf in the closet. When he returned, she was pacing the floor in anticipation of her first day in the fashion business.

"I don't know what you're in such an all-fired hurry about. Lors won't be in until ten, at least." Sam set a brisk pace to the subway, pausing long enough for her to match his steps before continuing.

"Really?" Valli found it hard to believe that anyone came to work at ten. "He said eight. Anyway, I need to be there early. I want to get my bearings."

They got off the subway and hurried up the stairs amidst the throng of people pushing and shoving to get to street level. At the corner of Thirty-second, Sam stopped and pointed.

"Halfway down the block. Can you see the sign?"

"Sure. Thanks."

"How are you getting home? Never mind. I've got to stop in today to pick up a check, so I'll come in late this afternoon and take you." Sam smiled and confidently strode off, leaving Valli alone, feeling anything but confident.

Lifting her shoulders, she walked the short distance to the entrance and stepped into the cool interior.

Nobody sat at the desk where yesterday the receptionist had told her that seeing Lorenso would be impossible. A lot can happen in one day, she mused, wondering if she should call out to let someone know she was here.

After waiting impatiently a few minutes, she decided to look for someone who might be able to help her. "Hello," she called, barely above a whisper.

No answer. She walked through the doorway in the direction of the dressing room where she had been taken yesterday and followed the hallway to the end, entering a room with a variety of fabrics lining the shelves along the walls.

Intrigued, she walked slowly around the room, occasionally pausing to rub some particularly interesting fabric between her thumb and forefinger. After a moment, she found a soft georgette in a silver color and paused, savoring the look and feel of the luxurious silk. Since there didn't appear to be anyone around, Valli sat down on the only chair to wait.

But she was too eager to sit still, so after several minutes she took the bolt of cloth down and laid it out on the table in the center of the room. Taking a pencil and scrap of paper, she started to sketch an idea she had started before she came to New York. Before long a basic design was completed.

Carefully, Valli took the georgette and began to drape it across the mannequin, pinning it at one shoulder. Painstakingly, she formed small pleats on the diagonal across the bodice and pinned them into place. Unconscious of the noises of the design shop coming to life around her, she concentrated on the vision in her head as she backed away to examine the result with a critical eye.

Not quite satisfied, she moved closer again and repinned the pleats, this time into slightly larger folds. Her back was still to the door and her concentration deep while she folded the fabric lovingly over the mannequin's form.

Pins sticking out of her mouth, she arranged the silk in a dropped swirl skirt that opened in the front. Now she was faced with a problem. In order to complete her design, she would have to cut the fabric. She stopped. Until she and Lorenso worked out some arrangement concerning her duties and salary, she didn't dare cut the expensive silk.

She stepped back and looked again. Eyeing each detail, she nodded in satisfaction. All that needed to be done was to complete the back. On her sketch, she made a few more marks and compared them with the mock-up. Pleased, she removed a few pins from her mouth and placed them in the mannequin.

"So, I see you found us again."

Valli whirled around and saw Lorenso standing in the doorway with a few lavender-clad bodies behind him. Hands propped on his elbows, his blue eyes pierced her from a severe visage that exhibited no signs of softening.

Thus confronted, Valli found it difficult to speak.

"Well, where is the tongue that tripped so easily over the phrase 'Lorenso's assistant' to the reporters yesterday?" He stepped forward, paused, and looked back at his employees. "Do I pay you to stand at doorways gaping?"

They scattered without a word, but Valli heard the mutters of displeasure. As she did, they sensed combat. "How nice to see you again, too. I hope you rested well."

Lorenso glared at her, walked back to the doorway, and ominously pushed the glass door shut. "Spare me your Southern charm, Scarlett. This is a business. My business."

Feeling the sting of his tone, Valli glanced desperately around, her self-confidence quickly deserting her.

"If you'll show me where I'm to work, I'll begin."

"Hah," the little man snorted, "as I told you yesterday, you shall be learning Lorenso Fashions from top to bottom, beginning at the bottom."

Valli stared at him in disbelief.

"Today, you shall work on the dock, loading and unloading trucks." He tossed a lavender jump suit to her. "I'm sure you'll be a charming addition to our staff there."

"But . . ."

"After a week or so on the docks," he interrupted loudly, "you'll continue your education in the packing department. Then you'll spend some time in the cutting room, the sewing room, the. . ."

"Wait a minute." Valli stepped forward until she stood nose to nose with him. "I came here to design clothes, you have my designs."

"You'll do as I say. In fact . . ."

"You said I would be your assistant. Either you start me today as a designer's assistant or I'll go someplace else." Her ultimatum gave her a sense of superiority, bolstering her ego from the depths of shock resulting from Lorenso's pronouncement of her plebian status.

"Well, then, I see no reason to prolong this interview." Lorenso smiled complacently.

Valli was defeated. "Of course, I'll take my designs with me."

"But of course. I'll call Terrance at once." Lorenso lifted the phone—lavender, like the surroundings—from the desk. "He's been studying your little tunics all night. We shouldn't need them any longer."

Defeated, and with tears in her eyes, Valli began removing the pins from the shimmering fabric on the mannequin.

"Stop that at once." Lorenso slapped her hand as it lifted another pin. "You can't destroy other people's work simply because you're angry with me."

"Other. . . But this is mine. I have been here for hours working on this dress, and for your information. . ."

"Quiet. Quieeeet!" Lorenso ran his fingers down the bodice and around the waist. "This is a single piece of fabric." There was doubt in his voice, but a smile started appearing on his face.

"Of course it is. I wouldn't cut. . ."

"This is. . ." He cast Valli a strange look before turning to the door and bellowing, "Terrance!"

The door flew open, and a slender young man with carrot-red hair and an abundance of freckles stuck his head through the opening. "Yes, sir?"

Lorenso strode over to Terrance and whispered in his ear, occasionally turning to glance at Valli. Terrance's face turned redder, and he glared at Valli before leaving. When the door closed, Lorenso returned to her with a Cheshire Cat grin. "Now, come along, little one. We'll discuss your duties—as my assistant."

CHAPTER FOUR

"The human species is the only one that attempts to alter its appearance. Did you know that, Valli?" Lors slid down into the lavender velvet chaise that no one else in the office dared to use and motioned her to a chair.

With a sigh, Valli took a seat and lay her head back on the chair to stare at the ceiling. "Don't you think the day's been a little too hectic to start with the psychology stuff?" She'd been with Lorenso for a year now and was overly familiar with his disdain for many of his customers.

"Maybe," Lors agreed, tucking his cigarette holder between his lips. "But, you must admit it's an interesting subject. The Ford girls aren't bad, especially the younger one," he observed.

Valli witheld comment and swung one leg over the arm of the chair, totally relaxing for the first time since ten A.M.

Lors blew a smoke ring and watched it drift upward until a draft distorted it. "That old buffalo who came in after them—by the gods, that woman's impossible."

"She's a client," Valli gently chided, although she agreed with him. "And, more importantly, the old buffalo is a rich

45

and influential client. We can't afford to have her leave in a huff like she did."

"True, true. But, she takes all the pleasure out of our art." Lors snuffed out his cigarette in a tiny gold ashtray. "If that bitch stayed away from the blintzes at the Russian Tea Room, her new dress would still fit. Can you imagine? Outgrown the damn thing before it's finished."

"Well, Lors, *dahling*," Valli mocked, "if she stayed away from places like the Russian Tea Room our designs wouldn't get much publicity."

"Precisely," he conceded. "Now, what were we talking about?"

"We were talking about humans altering their appearance," Valli reminded him. "What's wrong with making ourselves more beautiful, Lorenso? That's the business we're in, beauty and illusion."

"It would take Houdini to pull off the illusion that our last client was beautiful," Lors said impatiently. "She had enough flesh on her neck to make two of them."

Placing a second Turkish cigarette in his holder, Lors lit it with a flair that would have made Valentino look clumsy.

"In Burma, the Padaung tribe places heavy metal rings around their women's necks to make them long and graceful. It eventually separates the vertebrae, and if they ever removed the rings they wouldn't be able to hold up their heads."

Valli laughed at the image.

"Valli? The receptionist said that you two were back here. May I come in?"

"Sam?" Valli found it hard to disguise the pleasure in her voice.

"Could I see you for a minute?"

"Sure, I'm about to go home early, anyway. Lors gave me the rest of the afternoon off."

"Yes. But don't be late in the morning. We have to stuff the chairman of the board's darling wife into a lovely dress."

Valli quickly locked her designs in the workroom safe,

46

ran a comb through her hair, and raced back to Sam who was waiting impatiently by the door as though he were going to bolt at any minute.

"Is something wrong, Sam?"

"Wrong? No, nothing new or different. I'd call my abysmal lack of talent and success pretty ordinary, wouldn't you? As a matter of fact, the unemployment-office ladies all know me personally by my first name. There's just one little problem."

"Oh, what's that?" Valli had grown accustomed to this same lament week after week. No matter how hard he tried, Sam didn't seem to be able to get a part, not even a non-speaking role. Over and over he went on "look-sees," with no success.

"One little problem, Val. They knew the name they were looking for, but they couldn't find a check with that name on it."

"Oh, Sam"—Valli caught his hand and clasped it tightly—"they've lost your unemployment check. I'm sure they'll find it. It's simply misplaced. Give them a day or two."

"Sure, but in the meantime the rent is due, and old Sam can't come up with his part of it. Oh, Val, maybe I ought to pack it up and make porno flicks." He glanced at her surreptitiously.

What made him say that? Valli had seen Sam depressed, but never this bad before. "Porno movies? Oh, Sam—no!"

"Well, at least it's a living. I understand it pays quite well."

"No doubt."

"Of couse, it wouldn't be that difficult. I mean, being paid to make love."

There was something almost desperate about Sam today. He was holding on, but she could see that his control was about to break. He'd come to her for help, and she needed to get him somewhere where they could talk. "Let's go to Little Italy and have pasta. I feel like splurging," she said brightly, trying to get his mind off whatever it was that was bothering him.

"I can't. I don't have any money, remember?"

"Sam, come with me." Valli led the way down to the subway and to the proper platform. She backed him against the wall and placed her arms on either side of him. "Sam, we're like family, we're closer than family, actually. Whatever is wrong with you is wrong with me. I care about you, and I'm hungry. So, it's my treat, okay?"

But nothing seemed to help. They rode the subway in silence. At their favorite restaurant, Ferrara's, Valli insisted on the most private corner with the least amount of light. Ordering without a menu, she waved the waiter away with a nod.

"Now, what's happened, Sam?"

"What's happened?" He repeated her question and bowed his head, a look of anguish ripping the contours of the face that haunted Valli's dreams.

"Yes, Sam. Tell me." She took his hand and held it tightly in silence until at last he looked up at her. The fear she saw there made her tremble. "Sam, you're like my own brother. I love and care about you. Tell me what's wrong. Please."

"It was the photographic assignment, Valli. I went down and saw Joanne—you know, that woman who handles auditions for low-budget films. I should never have gone. Noel warned me. He always knows about people. . .smart son of a bitch, Noel is." He dropped his face again.

"Sam," Valli whispered. She didn't want to hear about Noel. She knew how smart he was and how he managed to cover for Sam whenever he needed help or information. "It's all right. You went to Joanne's and registered. And then what happened? Tell me, Sam. You know you can tell me anything."

"She sent me over to Thirty-sixth Street to an abandoned warehouse where they were photographing one of those special short subjects for a guy named Scallarn. I was to play a TV repairman who. . ." This time there was the unmistakable threat of tears in his voice.

"What happened, Sam? You couldn't have been that

bad."

"I couldn't do it."

"Couldn't do what?"

"Get it up," he whispered.

"Get what up?"

"Valli"—he pulled his hands away in anguish—"they were making a porno film. I was supposed to take off my clothes and"—he stopped, turning away so she couldn't see his face—"make love to a...man."

"I see." Valli didn't see. She didn't understand anything about porno films. She'd never seen one. But right now the problem was that she couldn't tell whether Sam was more horrified at the idea of the film, or his poor performance. He couldn't get it up, he'd said in disgust, and suddenly, she understood what he meant.

"Sam, why would you want to do that kind of film?" She paused for a second, gathering her thoughts and then surging forward as if she knew everything about his experience. "It must have been awful for you."

"That's just it, Valli. I could do it! I didn't, of course. They sent me into another room with a man who was supposed to relax me and show me what was expected." Sam gulped, peeked at her, and buried his face in his hands. "By the time he got through with his preparation and explanations I got it up. Boy, did I get it up. And what's worse, Valli, what's worse was that...Oh, God, I liked it," he choked, "I didn't want to go back out in that room. I wanted to stay there and...God, I'm sick."

Mercifully the waiter brought their food at that moment, giving Valli time to collect her thoughts. Sam—tall, virile, sexy Sam—had been turned on by a man, and he was ashamed. He'd come to Valli for reassurance, Valli who was probably the only virgin left in Manhattan.

When the waiter had spread out their food and left, Valli picked up her fork and said casually, "Well, Sam, at least you've had a sexual adventure. Every man has at least one. According to Kinsey's report, that's perfectly normal. You're just a little late having yours." Oh, damn, this wasn't

49

helping. "Artists are always more emotional than ordinary people, so naturally your reaction would be more intense. Sex is an emotional outlet that allows expression, just like being on that stage." She hadn't even convinced herself.

"Oh, yeah? Well, you weren't there. There was a stage all right and a circle of people watching. I like my sex in private."

"Of course you do," she reassured him. "Any normal man would have reacted the way you did."

"You mean to have gotten up and run?"

"No, I mean"—she gulped, trying not to let Sam know how terribly inexperienced she was at even saying the words, or how shocked she really felt—"having an erection. Even normal men can be aroused by other men, particularly in exceptional situations. Look at the men in prison."

"You may be right," Sam agreed, relief stealing into his voice. "I like girls. I've always liked girls. There probably aren't many guys who've had more opportunities with women than I have." He slid around the booth and put his arm around Valli, as if that gesture proved his normality.

"Sure you do." Valli allowed herself to lean back comfortably into Sam's arm.

"You're good for me, Valli. I don't know how I'd get along without you. You make everything seem so simple." He relaxed visibly as he spoke.

The confident, in-charge Sam struggled back to the surface, and Valli realized that she had said the words he needed to hear and given evidence of the propriety of his deep fears. He shifted position and resumed eating.

Disappointment blasted across her face like the heat from a warm morning stove. For a moment she had allowed herself to imagine Sam and herself together in bed. Sam moved back to his place and began to eat.

Valli slid out her wallet and removed some bills. "Here, Sam. It's a loan until your check comes."

"Gee, Val,"—he folded the money without bothering to see how much she had offered and tucked it in his pocket—"you shouldn't do this."

50

"I have it. You need it. Simple as that," Valli assured him. "You'd do the same for me."

"Yeah, of course I would." He gave her a brotherly kiss—though by now she longed for more.

The next morning Sam slid by the kitchen door while she was making coffee.

"Bye, kid. Have to run. Thanks for the dinner last night."

Before she knew it, he was out the door. Valli tried to contain her disappointment. She'd risen early to make coffee and blueberry muffins, picturing Sam joining her for breakfast as he had so many times in the past. After yesterday, she thought, he would be sure to appreciate her, and they would become even closer.

For the next several days both Sam and Noel seemed to be away from the apartment most of the time. Court had left for a tennis tournament a few days before. She didn't know when he'd be back. For the second day in a row she had come home early and sat in the living room in the dark. Tonight was worse than usual. According to the telephone count the girls at the office kept, Valli was so low on the male thermometer that she was off the bottom. Each week the loser had to buy doughnuts. At the rate she was going, she'd be buying all the staff's doughnuts this week, too.

Outside the draped area that had been cordoned off to make Valli a private room, the shuffle of feet shattered the quiet.

"Val? You in there?"

"Court?" Valli rushed out of the living room, a smile finding her lips. She was glad to see Court. "What are you doing home this early? Did the beautiful people decide that you're too ugly to have around with them?"

"Nope. I came home to take you out for coffee. I want you to meet a couple of my friends."

"Coffee with your friends? Why?"

"Because I'm weary of bubble-headed little bimbos who can't talk about anything but Rock Hudson. I need some intellectual conversation and outside stimulation. Where's

51

everybody else?''

"Noel is out, probably with Sam. I don't know. These days, I only see Sam when there's a problem. Miss Fix-It hasn't been needed to fix anything for two or three days, so she has been ignored.'' Valli couldn't keep the bitterness and hurt from her voice. "Thanks for the invitation, Court, but I don't think I'd be very good company this evening.''

"Aha! Trouble in the camp. This is coffee. I'm not asking you for a command performance, babe. Put on your shoes and let's go.''

Reluctantly, Valli allowed herself to be lured out of the apartment and into the warm summer night. They walked for several blocks before Court spoke.

"What's wrong between you and Sam, Valli?''

"There's nothing wrong. There's nothing between Sam and me. I'm just a sounding board, a rock to cling to when the water's rough. It's Noel he prefers when things are fine.''

"Noel? Uh-huh,'' Court hesitated. "You have to remember, Val, Noel was here first. He was Sam's first rock. He needs both of you, and Sam doesn't quite realize that Noel is a threat.''

"Threat? I don't understand. Sam is smart and talented. Why is Noel a threat?''

Court stopped and looked into the window of one of the little late-night shops selling magazines and toiletries. His tone became serious as he frowned slightly. "Valli, you're still so naive. There are some things that even friends can't discuss.''

"Why not?''

"Because, there are things better left unsaid, unexplored. Doors to be kept closed and munchkins who need to remain innocent.''

"I don't want to be innocent, Court. I want...'' she stopped, clamping her teeth shut before she said she wanted Sam.

"Sam,'' he answered for her. "You want Sam. I know it, and Noel knows it. You let it show every time you look at him. The only one who doesn't know it is Sam. Don't fall for him, Valli. Sam—well—Sam's just not right for you." He took her arm and moved on down the street.

"I don't. . .I'm not. . ." Valli's heart pounded, and her breath fell in short and uneven puffs. "You don't understand, Court. Sam is having a hard time. He needs someone to talk to. I'm just there when he needs to talk."

"Sure, kid. I understand. Here we are." Court directed Valli into the darkened entrance way to Gerda's, a coffeehouse where a sign announced that this was the place where new ballad singers tried out their songs.

"This is one of the places that gave Bob Dylan a chance, Valli. Right here at Gerda's. Come in and meet the group." He saw a hand waving in the dimly lit room and led Valli over to the crowded table where several people were already drinking coffee. Two more chairs were squeezed around the circular table.

"These two are Leslie and Tom Hendon. They're married, I think. At any rate, they've been together forever. Leslie is the intelligent, pretty one. She's a psychologist, and Tom is a kept man."

"Oh, you—" Leslie wadded her napkin and pitched it harmlessly at Court. "Tom is getting his Ph.D. I'm supporting him until he graduates, then he goes to work and I go back to school. A kind of share-the-poverty program."

"And, I'm Lincoln Maxwell. And you're the famous dress designer, Valli. I hear very good things about you."

Wearing a black T-shirt and jeans, Lincoln Maxwell slouched in his chair, and yet commanded her attention. His light brown hair had the same golden highlights as his brown eyes. Although not as classically handsome as Sam, he had the same sort of presence. But whereas Sam's features were strong, Lincoln Maxwell's were soft, almost blurred. There was something strangely romantic, almost poetic, about his visage. His beauty disturbed her, and Valli might have turned away had it not been for the surge of emotion that she felt when she looked at him.

"Linc's our resident employed person. He's an actor. A star, actually. Right now he's slumming it on Broadway in

The Sound of Music. We've known each other since we were kids. His father was my stepfather—for a while. What do you think of my roommate, Linc?''

''Roommate? Surely you jest?'' Lincoln blinked his eyes in surprise, glancing from Valli to Court and then back to Valli for a second. ''I didn't realize that you were living with someone, Court. When did you get rid of the guys?''

''Oh, they're still there.''

''Wonderful.'' Lincoln said with a directness that cut straight to the point. ''Then you won't mind sharing Valli with me.''

Lincoln Maxwell's expression didn't alter. He looked at Valli as if she were the only person there. She heard Court mention several more names and nodded appropriately, but the intensity of Lincoln's gaze became a buffer between Valli and the others. She was glad she wasn't sitting next to the slim, brown-haired actor with the piercing eyes. But sitting across from him might possibly be worse. Every time she sipped her coffee, she locked eyes with him.

A light banter played back and forth, and Valli listened. Being with a new group of people was fun. Court was right. She'd become too intense lately. Seeing only the designers and clients at Lorenso's and spending time doing fashion research had narrowed the scope of her life. Lately the only time she got out for pleasure was when she, Lors, and Terrance stopped somewhere for coffee or an occasional lunch. She forced herself to listen to the conversations swirling around her.

''But how'd you avoid the draft?'' A male voice spoke from the cloud of cigarette smoke that was gradually lowering until it threatened to engulf them—a voice she didn't connect with a name.

''Got married, how else?'' Tom Hendon joked.

''Wasn't that a little drastic?'' This voice was female and equally unfamiliar.

''Sure, but it beats getting shot at in some jungle, God knows where. Take my word, making love is better than making war.''

"I'll agree to that." Lincoln's voice came out of the darkness just as the coffeehouse suddenly went dark and a spot of soft gold light encircled a young dark-haired woman seated on a stool. She held a guitar, her eyes lowered in a stillness that seemed ethereal.

"Ladies and Gentlemen, Joan Baez."

The singer lifted her head, looked off into the distance, and began to sing. Silence captured the audience, as the sweet, clear voice reached out, its purity and sincerity touching them all as she sang "Barbara Allen." As the song ended, the crowd burst into spontaneous applause and clamored for more. Valli settled back and listened to the songs.

"She's great, isn't she?" Lincoln Maxwell was now sitting next to Valli, although she hadn't been conscious of anybody moving.

"Yes."

"So are you, lady. Are you and Court and item, or am I allowed to make a move on you?"

Valli turned her back on the stage and looked at the man who was so close to her, she could have touched him by barely moving. "Make a move on me?"

"Yes? Are you and Court lovers?"

"Of course not, but I hardly see where that's any of your business. Neither Court, nor anybody else, is going to make a 'move' on me."

"Sorry. Poor choice of words. I get so involved with these flakes that I forget how a lady is spoken to. May I see you home, Miss Valli?"

"Absolutely not." She blushed. "A lady always leaves with the man who brought her. Now, please be quiet. I want to hear the singer."

But the singer was finished. The spotlight went out, and the house lights were raised.

"She's great, isn't she, Linc?" A voice came out of the darkness. Valli thought it was Tom's.

"I've seen you in *Music*," Leslie said. "And you're better, Linc. How long do you plan to go on doing that role?"

"Until something bigger comes along. I like musicals, but I'm looking for a serious role. I have a line on a new play just now. A friend of mine is doing the casting, and he wants me to come down in the morning to audition. But it's a musical, and I think I'll pass."

"New play?" Valli's ears perked up, and she leaned forward. "Are there other roles still open?"

"Yes." Lincoln leaned forward, delighted to have captured her interest at last. "Are you considering leaving fashion for the stage?"

"No, not me. But I have a friend, another roommate," she explained hastily, "an actor. And he sings as well. Do you suppose you could get your friend to audition him instead? I mean...since you've decided you're not interested? Please?"

"Sam Carr," Court explained, joining in with a sadness in his voice that was obvious to everyone but Valli. "He's very much in need of a role—any role, Linc. What about it?"

"Well, I doubt that I could get in touch with Jerry before morning. Suppose I give him a call tomorrow and get back to you?"

Valli glanced desperately around. She had to get Lincoln to agree, and she had to do it now. If he put it off until tomorrow, too many things could happen. He might change his mind. This was Sam's chance and no matter what happened, she had to get it for him. She couldn't have explained her actions, but she knew that this could be his big break.

"Write Jerry a note, Lincoln," she said. "Tell him that you couldn't make it and ask him to have a look at Sam. I'll never forget it. I'll be very grateful."

"Will you go out with me sometime if I agree?" Linc asked Valli, grinning.

"Eh, sure. Sometime. We'll all go out and celebrate...together."

"That wasn't exactly what I had in mind." Linc shook his head and reached inside his jeans pocket. He pulled out a card, scribbled on the back, and handed it to Valli. "The

56

address is on this card. Tell Sam to be there at ten-thirty in the morning. This will get him in, but he'll have to get the job himself."

"Oh, Lincoln!" Valli threw her arms around the startled actor and hugged him quickly before she stood up. She gave Court a wide smile and dropped a hurried kiss on his forehead. "This is just what Sam needs, Court. Oh, thanks for bringing me, for introducing me to your friends. I'm going to find Sam and tell him, right now."

The coffeehouse suddenly erupted into a peal of laughter, and Valli felt the buoyancy of the mood carry her down the street toward their apartment. She barely heard Court tell her that they'd still be there for a while if she didn't find Sam, and she never turned back to see the look of painful resignation on his face.

"Is he any good, this Sam Carr?"

Court watched Valli until she was out of sight before turning back to his friend. He shook himself, trying to bring the question into focus. "Sam? How the hell do I know?" he growled. "He's a good guy, I suppose. I just hope she doesn't get hurt. She's so naive."

"And she has no idea how sexy she is, does she?"

"No, I think she thinks she's ugly, actually. Damned good designer, no problem there." Court followed Lincoln back to the table. The others were leaving, heading for a party over on West Fourth Street. Lincoln and Court agreed to join them later, after they'd given Valli time to get back.

"But?" Lincoln prodded, ordering more espresso.

"But under all that tough exterior, as a woman—she has absolutely no self-confidence. And she's heading straight for disaster. All four of us are, and there's not a thing I can do to stop it."

"She's in love with Sam?"

"Yes, and he has no idea. That's not the worst part of it," Court confided. "I don't think Sam is really capable of loving anybody. Oh, I don't mean because he's conceited, or self-centered, though he's both. It's more a matter of fragmentation. Sam doesn't know who he is. He gives everybody he cares about a different Sam, depending on their needs, and he demands something different from each of them.''

"Sounds like a chameleon. How does he inspire such loyalty. Even from you?''

"I don't know. Even Leslie probably couldn't explain it. We're like a family, the four of us, and we all care a lot for one another. But Sam, Sam draws from us whatever he needs. Without Valli and Noel, he'd be nothing. *They* make him real.''

"Valli loves Sam. Sam loves you all, and you love Valli. What about Noel, who does he love?''

"That's just it. If those two ever find out who Noel loves, our family is going to be split wide open.''

CHAPTER FIVE

Clutching the business card in her hand, Valli made it from Gerda's to her building in record time. The elevator opened, and she turned the lever until the groaning lift reached the fourth floor. The slow grind upward seemed to take forever. The elevator hardly qualified as such and probably barely passed inspection, but she didn't like taking the stairs alone at night.

The apartment was completely dark. But Sam was there. She could feel it. She'd wake him. Good news couldn't keep.

"Sam?" Valli knocked on his bedroom door and called out again, "Sam? If you're not decent, you'd better cover up. I'm coming in. I have great news." Opening the door, she stepped inside, her nerve endings tingling with excitement. "You'll never guess who. . ."

The flurry of activity on Sam's bed stunned her as he untangled himself from the covers and sprang to his feet. Why was he in bed so early? A night person, he never went to bed before two or three o'clock and then he slept the best part of the morning away. Puzzled, she stood still as Sam rose beside the bed, his tall, powerful physique glistening in the half-light from the doorway.

"Valli, I . . . I mean we. . . I know this looks bad, but you see. . ."

"We?" Oh, God. He had a woman with him, and she'd come rushing in without a thought. She blushed furiously and started backing up to the door. But she couldn't resist looking at the bed to see what the woman looked like. She was curious and also jealous.

"It's all right, Valli." The second figure raised up and spoke. The words stole Valli's voice, and she felt as if she were in a dream. Desperately she tried to grasp onto something. She was Valli. She was a successful designer in New York City. She was becoming a worldly person who could handle anything. She was lying through her teeth.

"Please, Valli?" Sam started toward her, pleading with a voice that was almost petulant. "Don't be upset, Val. I can explain."

"Cut the crap, Sam. She's shocked. Put on your pants and get her a stiff drink." Noel threw back the covers and came lazily to his feet. There was genuine regret in his voice as he slid his arms into the blue terry cloth robe thrown over the back of a straight chair.

A blinking neon sign outside Sam's window shone through a crack in the drape like some kind of large pink eye. As it flashed on and off, Valli could see the desperation on Sam's face. He opened and closed his mouth, but the words seemed lodged in his throat. Valli glanced unseeingly from Noel to Sam and back again. Noel? And *Sam?* She saw, and she knew what she saw, but the scene refused to settle into perspective. She was going to be sick.

"Valli," Sam pleaded. "Please don't look like that. I need you, I . . ."

That was true. He did need her. She knew that he needed her. She was his courage, his cheering section, his confidence. But Noel was his lover. At least Noel had the guts not to try to pretend. He simply tied the robe at his waist and lit a cigarette.

"Valli," he said slowly, "I'm sorry we've embarrassed

you. We thought you were out for the evening. I wouldn't have had you find us like this for anything, but you did. The question is, can you accept it? Or does our relationship end?"

"End?" The thought of losing Sam, Court, and Noel was almost worse than witnessing the scene she'd just interrupted. They were her family, the family she'd never had, and families endured. Even though she was horrified, she couldn't let them see that. She could hear Granny's voice as clearly as if she were in the room:

We don't choose our lot, Valley Ray. The Lord sends us our trials and tribulations, and we accept 'em and go on. That's what I done when ya ma left. I mighta wanted different, but we made do with what we got.

Valli felt herself stand straighter. She looked at the two men with as much maturity as a nineteen-year-old could muster. "We give each other what we can, I guess," she said slowly, forcing herself to breathe deeply and evenly, "and we take what we need. What is between you two is between you. I have no right to judge." The words were wooden.

Relief washed over Sam's face as he started toward her.

"No!" she cried out sharply. "I know what I should say and do, but it isn't easy. You'll have to give me some time."

Noel nodded in understanding. Sam simply stood, misery drooping his body in emotional defeat. Valli watched for a moment. She truly regretted what had happened. Sam was so vulnerable, so defenseless. In spite of his bravado and good looks he was just a little boy who needed a lot of attention, maybe more than one person could give. She knew that, despite his sex appeal, women scared him to death; and the possibility of failure drove him a little crazy. Then, after what had recently happened. . . . Perhaps, only she could truly understand the scene she had just witnessed. Not even Sam understood.

"I'm all right, Sam. I'm sorry I rushed in. This is my fault. I have to go now. I've. . .I've got to get back to Court." She turned and, with as much dignity as she could manage, started toward the door.

"Wait, Valli," Sam called out. "What kind of news did you have when you came in?"

She stopped. "News? Oh, yes. I have an audition for you in the morning at ten-thirty. The information is on this card." She pitched it over her shoulder and kept on walking. As she ran into the elevator she heard Sam's exclamation of disbelief, but she shut out the sound of his voice calling her name. The flashing neon sign jeered at her as she walked down the street, not really wanting to return to Gerda's but not knowing where else to go. Suddenly she didn't want to be alone. She needed to be with Court. He'd make things right.

Damn! She shook her head, trying to clear the image of Sam and Noel from her vision. It was impossible. Slowing down, she breathed deeply and lifted her shoulders. She was angry, but that wasn't fair. Sam didn't have to answer to her. She was kidding herself when she thought of them as a family. The four of them were simply four individuals who lived together. Nobody owed anybody else anything, except the rent and an occasional attempt at housekeeping.

She realized now that she'd never heard Noel speak of having a woman friend, she'd never dreamed that he liked men—that way.

But Sam. Was he a homosexual? She couldn't accept it. She had allowed herself to believe that she was special to him. And, damn it, she was. Who did he come to when he was in trouble? Whose shoulder did he cry on? She was willing to bet that only she knew about the porno movie. And what about those lovely walks through the Village at night? Their special late-night conversations? Sam had needed affection, and Noel had been there. Probably Noel had found him alone and upset, and that's why it had all came about. But she'd been in Noel's situation before, and Sam hadn't tried to make love to *her.*

Valli couldn't know that the shock of her discovery showed on her face when she went back into Gerda's, but Court recognized her state of anxiety at once.

"Valli, you came back." Lincoln stood up and pulled out

a chair. "Did you find Sam?"

"Yes," she answered dully, sitting down without being aware that she'd done so.

"Great!" Lincoln went on in excitement. "We're all going over to the party together. You'll love this party, Valli. It's being given by a friend for this new model in town. All sorts of fashion people will be there."

"What about it, Val? You feel up to a party?" Court slid his arm around her, and his fingertips squeezed her right shoulder.

Forcing herself to respond, she nodded. Then, as if she'd made a decision, she reaffirmed her nod and answered brightly. "A party? Just what I need."

Lincoln leaned on the doorbell and almost fell inside as a tall, exotic redhead opened the door, bade them enter and led them upstairs to a room that looked like a combination music room and bordello. In fact, Valli later found out it had been exactly that in its day. The room had been left as it had been when the madame, who'd once lived there, had used it as her central room for entertaining.

Valli surveyed the room, or what she could see of it through all the people, in amazement. The scene was straight out of a movie she had recently seen with Sam: *Breakfast at Tiffany's*. But Valli couldn't possibly feel less like Holly Golightly, Capote's wacky Southern heroine.

The music of Chubby Checker blasted from the phonograph, and those who weren't dancing were twisting to the beat, while drinks and joints were passed freely around the room.

"Who are all these people?" she asked Court, who was standing behind her, very close behind her, as a drunken young man managed to spill a drink on Valli's feet.

"Who knows?" Court laughed. "Looks like theater people, mostly. And a handful of the rich and foolish. That man over there is the Crown Prince of Irara, some little kingdom in the mountains of Asia. The blond woman who is almost wearing that brocade miniskirt is the guest of honor."

63

"Oh? What's her name?" Valli turned to spot her. Here was someone she could relate to. She was an ultra-thin young woman with mannish short blond hair. She had less shape than Court, and her spiked eyelashes must have weighed a pound each from the mascara she lavished on them.

"I don't know what her real name is. Everyone calls her Twiggy. Seems to me the reason for that is fairly obvious."

"Lincoln? Darling, come over here," a voice called from the center of the room.

"Excuse me, will you?" Reluctantly Lincoln left Valli's side and moved away, only to be swallowed up by the crowd.

"This is unreal—too much," Valli murmured. "I've never seen anything like it."

"Stick with me, kid," Court whispered as he maneuvered her through the crowd. "You ain't seen nothing yet."

Court and Valli moved toward the bar, where a bartender was mixing from a concoction of bottles. "What'll you have, folks?"

"I'll have a scotch and water. What about you, Valli?"

"Me?" Valli gulped. The only thing she'd ever drunk in her life was the blackberry wine she'd swiped one summer and consumed behind the cane grove. When her grandmother found her, she'd switched her all the way back to the house. But she remembered that the high school kids in Georgia all seemed to drink one thing, and now she was going to try it.

"Bourbon and Coke," she said without hesitation. The drink wasn't bad. The sweet syrup of the Coke seemed to slide down to the pit of her stomach and, slowly, the snake of tension in her stomach began to uncoil. She lost Court in the crowd and shortly thereafter found herself talking to a gorgeous tall blond woman with a long white neck.

"What do you do?" the woman asked in a deep, sexy voice.

"I'm a designer. What do you do?"

"Oh, modeling, dancing, you know." Seeing that Valli's

64

glass was empty, the woman, who called herself Jo, ordered a refill on the vodka martini she was drinking and asked Valli if she'd care for another as well.

"Sure." If I'm ever going to fit into a group like this, she decided belligerently, I'm going to have to learn. "When in Rome," she spouted brightly, "do as the Romans do. I'll take a vodka martini, too."

Nasty, Valli decided, but wonderful, all the same. The force of the potent drink warmed her stomach, and her muscles relaxed more and more. The music changed to Charlie Parker. Court didn't return, and Valli scanned the room, anxious for a familiar face. There were none, but Valli quickly met lots of new people.

Now a stockbroker held her pinned to the wall with one arm and teased her lips with the salty rim of a margarita glass. "Mmmm, this is the best so far." Valli giggled.

"Valli?" A familiar voice broke through the pleasant haze swirling around her. "Valli, let's go."

"Court? Oh, no. I'm having a terrific time. This is a margarita; isn't it lovely? I'm going to do a dress this color, with white smeathers, no...feshers. No, hell, I'll use beads around the top." She giggled.

Court had been following Valli's progress around the room, watching her as she sampled the drink of every person she talked to. Amused in the beginning, now he was concerned. When she had come back to the coffee house he had known something was wrong, but he'd found no opportunity to ask what had happened. He pulled her through the overindulging throng that was too engrossed in loud conversation and dancing to notice the pale young woman led by the handsome man. Since they'd arrived, the size of the crowd had swelled beyond belief.

"Court," Valli called urgently. "Court, I have to go to the bathroom."

"Damn." Was she sick? No, he decided as he looked at her wide blue eyes shining with something more than excitement—some new daring he couldn't identify. He turned and began pulling her up a second set of steps to where he judged the bathroom might be. The first door at the top of the steps was locked.

"Go away, man. We're using the room."

Court tried a second door, leading Valli through a bedroom, past a couple making love on the bed, totally oblivious of their presence. Thank God the bathroom was vacant. He shoved Valli inside, closed the door, and leaned against it. It took Court a minute to realize that the man on the bed was a famous local talk-show host. The girl beneath him was probably no more than sixteen, but obviously very experienced in lovemaking.

"Court? You're going to have to help me," Valli called through the door.

Help her? Damn, the last thing he wanted to do was hold her head while she threw up. He took a deep breath, turned the knob, and went inside. The tiny bathroom was in total darkness. "Where are you? Where's the light?"

"No, Court. Don't turn on the light. Here I am."

He felt her hand on his arm, and he reached out to steady her. His hand touched her breast, her bare breast, just as she wrapped herself around him. Damn, she'd taken off her clothes. He put both hands on her shoulders in an attempt to push her away. But she was determined, sliding her hands beneath his shirt, and grinding herself against him. "Kiss me, Court. I want you to kiss me. Please."

He tried to pull away. He really did try. But when she stood on tiptoes, wound her arms around his neck, she pulled herself upright against him. He hardly breathed. Snaking her legs around his, she flattened her lower body, welding it to his, and it was too late.

Already aroused, he found her lips and maneuvered her body into exactly the right place to accommodate his erection. He hadn't known until he kissed her how much he wanted her.

Cupping his hands beneath her bare buttocks he gave himself over to the sensation and taste of her. Through his clothes he could feel the moisture seeping in to ignite the throbbing surge of his need as she rubbed herself earnestly

66

against him. Even before she began to convulse he felt himself climax, in his jeans, like some kid in the backseat of an automobile kissing his girl good night. Even more amazed was Valli. She drew back in silent wonder and in the darkness he could feel the questioning in her eyes.

"Did we do it, Court?"

"Do what," he managed thickly, still holding her against him.

"Is that what it feels like to. . .you know?"

"That's what it feels like, Valli."

"But, we didn't. . .did we?"

"No, we didn't. . ." He couldn't even say "fuck" to her. And even if he could have, that wouldn't have been accurate. What they had just done was find an explosive release, a very different explosive release, and he was still reeling from the effect she had had on him.

"Oh." She laid her head on his shoulder and began to cry. "I wanted to, Court. I wanted to know what it felt like. I wanted to understand."

"Is that why you took off your clothes?"

"Yes. I wanted you to look at me and tell me what's wrong, tell me why I'm not attractive to. . .men. Feel me here."

She unclasped her arms from his neck and slid down his body until her feet hit the floor. She took both his hands, placing them over her breasts. "I know you aren't interested in me as a woman, Court, so I want your honest opinion. What about my. . .tits? Do they feel all right? Are they attractive?"

She actually forced him to feel all of her. Already his body stirred again. What was she saying? Could she actually not know that her tits were wonderful? All he wanted to do was touch them, and she was *asking* him to do it. "Valli, your breasts are magnificent. Any man would want to touch them, to do this."

He reached down, gently took one cherry-hardened nipple in his mouth and began to draw on it.

"Oh, I didn't. . ." He heard her catch her breath, breathe

in deeply and go on. "And the rest of me. Do men like women who have lots of hair, down there. I'm pretty. . ." She gasped, as he slid his hand around her body and touched the thick thatch of curly hair between her legs. ". . . hairy."

Involuntarily she parted her legs, allowing his fingertips access to the moistness pouring from her again. "Valli, do you know what you're doing to me?"

"You?" She drew back in genuine shock. "Does touching me really affect you?"

In answer he took her hand and placed it on him, forcing her to cradle his fullness for a moment, before he found the zipper and allowed himself to spring into her hand. Valli jerked back.

"You're so big. Are all men big like this?"

"Some are even bigger, when they're aroused." Court's voice was husky as he moved against her slightly, inserting his finger inside her with the same thrusting motion until his long slim finger reached the thin membrane inside and he paused.

Court withdrew his finger slightly and massaged the tiny bud of sensation at the entrance. She fell against him, her knees of jelly refusing to hold her up under such magnificent waves of hedonistic pleasure. He placed his organ between her legs, meaning only to take advantage of the gentle rhythm of her swaying hips as his finger continued to fondle her.

With every manipulation of his finger, Valli responded in kind, and in less time than he believed possible she trembled violently, instinctively impaling herself on him as she let out a low moan of ecstasy. Too lost in his own violent explosion to understand what he'd done, he realized after a moment that even though he'd tried to withdraw to protect her virginity, he was firmly inserted inside her body.

Valli stepped back.

Court's eyes adjusted to the darkness, and he could see Valli looking at him in surprise.

"That's why your jeans were wet?"

68

"Yes. That's what you'd already done to me once. You know, twice in less than fifteen minutes must be some kind of record."

"Did I do it, too?"

"Couldn't you tell?"

"Yes," she whispered in muted wonder. "It was like I had to go to the bathroom, bad, bad. Then when I couldn't hold it any more it just burst out and it felt. . . I can't describe how it felt, Court. It was magnificent."

"You've never done that before?" Court replaced himself in his pants and zipped them, wondering briefly if the party-goers outside would be able to see what he'd done.

"No. Thank you, Court. I had to know why it was important. Now I understand." She smiled as she began replacing her clothes. She wasn't at all embarrassed. "Will you take me home now?"

Valli was very quiet on the way home. She didn't complain or discuss what had happened. It was as if, although Court was with her, she was alone. They didn't talk. They were almost back to the apartment when Valli stopped short and turned to Court with a stricken look on her face.

"Will I get pregnant, Court?"

"Pregnant?" Court stopped, suddenly aware of the possibilities. "No, of course not."

"But, we both. . ."

"Climaxed? Yes. But, we'll take care of that." He pulled her down a side street to a little store that stayed open late. "Three Cokes, please."

Valli wondered why he had bought three Cokes, but she followed him out the door without asking.

"So, I can do what we just did with anybody, and I won't get pregnant?"

"No," he answered. "Not unless you take care of yourself afterwards."

"What do you mean?"

"I'll show you."

"And it would feel the same, even if—say, even if a man did that with another man, it would feel good?"

"Feel good? Yes. Why?" He stopped Valli and forced her to face him. "Why, Valli? We're friends. I. . ." He'd been about to say "I love you," and he didn't want to think about that. "Something happened to you tonight, didn't it? Something more than all those drinks."

"Yes, Court, something happened. Something I didn't understand then. But I think I understand now."

"What happened, Valli? Tell me. You can tell me anything. I'll understand. We're friends, aren't we?"

"I saw Sam."

"So, what about Sam?" His voice sounded annoyed.

"I saw Sam and Noel together. I've never seen two men naked in bed together, and it shocked me. Did you know—about them?"

Court sighed. "I knew about Noel," he admitted. "I guessed how he felt about Sam, but I didn't think Sam had any idea. I know Sam is confused. Failure to a guy like Sam can do strange things to his thinking. I think he's just confused about his sexuality. I don't think I'd take it seriously."

"Oh, I'm not worried," Valli said confidently, with a new spring in her step. "I can see how it all works now, and I must say it's really very lovely. I don't suppose you'd like to do it again sometime?"

God, he'd like to strangle her. "Sex isn't some little pleasurable thing you do every now and then, Valli. It ought to mean something. Two people ought to care about each other."

"You sound like my home economics teacher. I thought men liked sex because it felt good. Don't they?"

"Some men do, but I—a lot of men—want more than that from. . .sex. Valli, you just can't go around doing what we did with every man you meet. Sooner or later you'll. . .get pregnant."

"But you said. . ."

"I know what I said. And I'm going to show you what to do." He searched for reasoning, something that might stop her from getting herself in serious trouble. "But this might not always work."

70

"Oh." She considered his warning. "Well, if Noel and Sam can give each other pleasure, why can't all of us do that for one another?"

"Ye gods, the woman's talking about group sex, an orgy. What have I done, awakened a monster?"

"Oh, Court, don't be silly. I didn't mean it like that. I simply mean that I care about you and I care about Sam as well. Why wouldn't he want me to do to him what I just did to you? It's the feeling that counts, isn't it?"

They'd reached the apartment. Court stopped Valli and forced her to listen to him. "I know that this is going to be hard for you to believe, Valli, but it isn't always like that. You can reach a climax and feel rotten about it, or you can do what we did and never feel what we did. It has to be special to work. Don't let yourself get hurt, kid. And to answer your question, yes, I'm always here, if you need me."

"Thank you, Court. You're a wonderful friend." She stood on tiptoe, pressed herself against him, and kissed him all the way to their floor. "And you kiss good, too," she giggled as she danced through the darkened apartment into the curtained-off area of her bedroom.

"Friend?" Court kicked the chair leg and cursed. Who the hell wants to be called a good friend by a woman who's just made him cream himself for the first time in years and left him with a hard-on that had to be taken care of before he could even take a piss.

"Vaili," he whispered through the curtain. "Come with me."

"What?"

"I said we've got to take care of you." He switched the bag of Cokes to his other hand and took her smaller one. "Come with me."

He led her to the bathroom, switched on the light, and followed her in. She turned in the small room and watched him close the door. "Now what?"

"This...this is going to be difficult to explain." He removed one of the bottles from the bag and pried the cap off on the door frame. "Take off your panties and step into the

71

shower and pull up your dress." He watched her for a moment.

He shook the Coke until the pressure threatened to explode beneath his thumb. "Okay. Now, I'm going to squirt this inside you. Understand?"

"Why?" The idea sounded stupid to her, but when he scowled she said, "Okay, okay."

She spread her legs apart and waited. Within seconds icy cold liquid erupted from the bottle and into her, surging and bubbling inside the small pocket so recently awakened to passion. "This is going to keep me from getting pregnant?" she asked doubtfully.

"They say it will." He placed the half-filled bottle on the counter and opened another one. He repeated the ritual twice more. "Here, wipe your legs with this cloth. They'll be sticky."

"What about my insides? Won't they be sticky?"

Court considered her remark. "Maybe. I think tomorrow you need to buy one of those douche things."

"What?"

"Douche. You know. One of those things a woman washes her insides with. They have them at the drugstores."

"Oh." Valli didn't know. Nobody had ever told her anything about her body or sex—except probably the preacher who had spouted hellfire and damnation, casting dark looks at the girls in church. But Valli had been too embarrassed to ask anyone the reason why. Court had said she could get one of these things at the drugstore. Tomorrow she'd find one and learn what to do with it.

Court left the bathroom while Valli showered. When she came out he was lingering in the hall. He watched her until she disappeared behind her curtain. As he had waited, he had realized that Valli did everything in high gear. And she was more naive than he'd thought. Awakening her passion might cause problems he hadn't foreseen. Tomorrow, he'd insist that she see a doctor for a diaphragm, or whatever doctors prescribed these days.

So Valli had seen Sam and Noel. He'd known about Noel,

almost from the first. They'd both tried to rent the loft apartment at the same time. Neither had the funds to swing the deal alone, but together, they decided, along with a third party they'd have to find, they could swing it. Noel had been open about his life-style, saying quietly that he was probably gay, and if that was a problem they'd better know at the start. Court had assured him that he wasn't gay, but so long as Noel didn't conduct his relationships in the apartment, he wouldn't mind. For two years he'd been discreet—until now.

For another hour Court tossed in bed, trying to erase the feel of Valli's breasts from his mind. She didn't even realize how sensual she was, or the feeling she brought out in him. He'd known she had a crush on Sam, even if she didn't know yet. First she'd appointed herself Sam's confidante, and that was fine. Everybody who knew Sam seemed to feel a need to provide something to help him. Noel became the self-appointed protector, and Valli the confidante. But after tonight he wasn't sure he wanted to be just a friend to Valli. What she'd stirred in him couldn't quite be defined—at least not aloud. Friendship, yes, but something more. . .definitely something more.

As he drifted off to sleep, he remembered her questions about Sam. And Court had the terrible feeling that he'd already lost something very special to a man who didn't even realize what he had.

CHAPTER SIX

"But, Lorenso, darling, it isn't that I don't like what you've shown me. I do. But I want something spectacular, something stunning like you created for that witch Bella Francisco. I absolutely insist."

Valli stood beside Lorenso and bit back a smile as she listened. Clarissa Thompson was one of the true coups for a New York designer. Currently married to an English duke, she was a glamorous movie star, a rare beauty, and possessed one of the finest collections of jewelry—from ex-husbands —in Hollywood *and* New York.

"I'm warning you, Lorenso, if you don't come up with something as special for me, I'll find what I want—elsewhere. Nobody must have anything like it. I refuse to walk into a ball and find a dress exactly like mine on an Italian hussy again."

"But, Miss Thompson, of course I'll find just the right gown for you." With a frown, Lorenso looked past the long-legged star at Valli. He nodded back toward the design board where Valli usually worked, and back again.

"Bring my design pad, Valli, and find that new number

I'm working on for our client. I'm sure you know the one I mean."

Why that old faker. He was telling her to give one of her designs to this woman and let her think that it was his. Well, she wouldn't do it. From now on, if she created something, it would be hers.

But before she could say anything, Miss Thompson broke in. "I'm attending the awards dinner next week and I want something absolutely smashing to wear—something long and white, I think."

"No," Valli said quietly, shaking her head.

"No? You're telling me that I don't want something long and white? Or that you don't have it?"

"Of course she isn't," Lorenso hurried stiffly to Valli's side, a frown creasing his forehead.

"No," Valli went on softly, "the way I see you is in something short, very short in the front anyway, and perhaps red, a red satin fitted dress with a gold brocade coat that is short in front and tapers to the thighs in the back." There, she'd done it. She had just given away one of her own designs.

"I'll look like some kind of idiot dressed like that," the actress protested, looking from Lorenso to Valli and back again.

"No, let me show you. Come over to the design table." Valli took the charcoal pencil and began to make swift strokes on the paper. "Let me see your legs. Lift your skirt," she instructed.

"Well, really!" Clarissa Thompson protested but complied.

"Perfect, Valli," Lorenso was quick to agree when he saw the pleased expression emerging on the actress's face. "You're right. Her legs are her best feature. Nobody else there will have such legs, and she'll be the envy of the group. That's exactly the gown I had in mind."

Shifting through a portfolio, Valli found the design she had in mind and placed it on the table. In a glance Miss Thompson could tell exactly what Valli had meant when she said that this dress would be the talk of the party. It was stunning and original.

"Red, you say? I seldom wear red. I favor blues and greens. Because of my eyes, you know."

"Absolutely, I can see why. You have wonderful eyes," Valli assured her, hoping beyond hope that she was right. The design was striking and different, and she was sure it would work. "But your coloring demands fire and passion. And, I think a small jeweled hat with a veil, something like this. And lots of jewels. What do you say, Lorenso?"

"Stunning, absolutely stunning. I knew when I created it that it would be stunning. If Miss Thompson doesn't care for this, I'm sure that Miss Lollobrigida will love it."

"Lollobrigida? Oh, Lorenso, you wouldn't. She's the cat that showed up in Moscow wearing my dress. How soon can it be ready?"

"Well," Lorenso considered, looking off into space for a few minutes, "it will take the entire staff to rush such an order. That means it will be expensive, but it could be done by Tuesday at the latest. You could come in first for a fitting on Wednesday, let us complete the fitting on Thursday, and you'll have it for Friday evening."

"Wonderful, and what will this rush job cost me?"

"Three thousand dollars for the dress and coat, and two hundred for the hat," Lorenso answered, closing his ears to the tiny gasp. He hoped it was Miss Thompson's and not Valli's shock that was so audibly expressed.

"Fine," the actress agreed, with a widening smile on her face.

After the actress had left, Lorenso let out a shout of laughter. "That will serve her right. My dress will be the hottest thing at the party."

"Your dress?" Valli muttered half under her breath. "Lorenso, how could you hold her up like that? This dress is already made. You could have let her have it today. And the price? Good heavens, that's twice what we'd anticipated."

"Valli, when are you going to learn that the easier a thing

is to get, the less desirable it is. By making her think it's designed especially for her and very expensive, she'll want it even more."

"But," she said softly, "Lorenso, it was my design—not yours."

"Valli, you have no designs here. Every dress here is a Lorenso creation, but I will see that your check reflects our good fortune. I'm not stingy."

With bitterness seeping through her, Valli watched the pompous little man leave the showroom. She didn't want more money, she wanted a little recognition. And one way or another she'd get it. She thought about the pad of new designs she had hidden in her desk and smiled. These were Designs by Valli, and all she needed was to find a way to let the world see them.

All day Valli kept waiting for Sam to come by and tell her what had happened on the interview, but when closing time came and she hadn't seen him she was filled with disappointment and excuses. Maybe he didn't know yet. Maybe they were still auditioning. Unable to concentrate on her work, Valli went straight home instead of staying late as she usually did.

He wasn't there. The apartment was empty. By ten o'clock she was still alone, and bed seemed the only choice she would have that night.

She didn't see Sam the next day. Instead, it was Noel she found in the kitchen. "Noel, have you heard from Sam?"

"Yes. He was here yesterday, came by to pick up some clothes."

"Why? Is he going somewhere?" She couldn't believe that he hadn't at least called her and told her what was happening.

"Not exactly, he's house-sitting for somebody who's out of town for a week, feeding the dog and watering the plants, that sort of thing."

"What about the part?"

"He's waiting for a call back, but I think he must have

77

done well. Valli, it was really great of you to set this up for him. Sometimes...sometimes he has a hard time saying thank you."

Noel was reading the *Village Voice*.

"What are you doing?" Valli asked curiously, walking around behind Noel to look over his shoulder.

"Just reading these articles on integration. It's coming, Valli. Sooner than people think."

"What's coming?" Valli poured herself a cup of coffee and picked up one of the papers. The article that seemed to command Noel's attention carried the byline of Spud Towns. Even the headline was controversial. CHANGE! PEACE-FUL OR WITH FORCE! "Good heavens, you're advocating taking the law into your own hands."

"Oh no, Valli. Not if people will wake up. Nobody wants violence, but sometimes you have to force people to do the right thing. It's the end result that counts, don't you see? The blacks have been second-class citizens long enough. It's morally wrong."

"Well it is, but I don't know. Somehow I can't see old Sump, the man who used to cut Granny's grass, sitting next to Mrs. Taylor or any of those other church-going women on the bus. It might be all right in New York, but the white folks in Willacoochee, Georgia aren't ready for this sort of thing and neither are the nigras."

"Not nigras, Valli, blacks. That's what they are. We're called whites; they're blacks," Noel lectured. "Shit, all you Southerners are alike."

Valli was hurt and puzzled. She'd never given much thought to it before. Most of the people in Willacoochee were poor. She hadn't even had enough money for a gradua-tion dress. Instead, she'd made one out of a tablecloth. But, she thought, pulling her mind back to the present, they were talking about civil rights.

"Noel, I'm worried. Aren't you going a little overboard in all this? What would your folks think?" Valli was beginning to get a feeling that Noel's frequent absences from the apart-ment were because he was becoming involved with these radical groups she'd heard about. She knew that some of them were violent. Even the fevered look in his eyes concerned her. He had the same wild-eyed determination as the revival minister who had come to Georgia every summer and set up in the tent.

"My folks? They're so involved in trying to maintain the social position expected of the Grays in Boston that they've closed their eyes to anything else. Who cares whether we keep up appearances? Not me. The Grays have taken from the poor long enough. I'm going to help turn the tide."

"Noel, you're crazy. If you'd been born poor and a nobody like me, you'd appreciate what your folks are trying to do. A name and position are power and that's the kind of power that moves mountains, not some lone speaker on a street corner, trying to stir up a group of nobodys."

"But don't you care about injustice, Valli?" Noel almost shouted. "What the hell's wrong with you?"

"What I care about is me and you and Sam and Court. I don't have enough energy to take on all the misfits of the world, Noel. I have to take care of myself...and my friends."

"Blacks aren't misfits, Valli." Noel spoke angrily, folding the newspapers and sliding them into his backpack. "And if I can't convert someone like you, then I'm not much of a journalist."

"Noel, isn't it dangerous? Spud Towns is becoming famous. I mean, doesn't that make you a target for the police and maybe the white press as well?"

"Maybe, but what I'm doing is morally right, Valli. It's important for man to change, willingly, not because he's forced into it." Noel stood up and headed for the door. "You're looking at it all wrong. You ought to wake up and start caring about the world."

Noel's anger hurt. Maybe she was selfish, but his intensity worried her.

"Noel"—Valli stopped him, afraid suddenly as she knew with certainty what Noel was doing—"be careful."

"Just consider what I've said and open your mind."

"Be careful, Noel," she repeated in a whisper, remembering as he left the apartment that last summer when the revival preacher had come. He'd brought snakes, and he'd held them in his hand, caressing them, daring them to bite him, professing that his faith would protect him from the wickedness of the devil. That the snake didn't bite him was proof that though he faced the danger again and again, he would always be safe. On that last night, when the snake lunged for his neck, he'd died with a look of disbelief and terror on his face. Valli was afraid that Noel's devotion to his cause was like the preacher handling that snake.

Court walked into the kitchen some time after Noel slammed the door. He watched her and smiled. "How about a movie tonight? Just you and me."

Scarlet splotches sprang to her cheeks. Lately, every time she saw him she recalled his hands on her body, caressing her. She was less embarrassed than afraid it would happen again. She hadn't yet decided where she was going with her life, but an affair with Court could only complicate things— since she was in love with Sam. "I can't make it. I . . . I'm working on a project."

His smile wavered. "Too bad. See you later."

Noel was angry with her, and Court was hurt. She was glad Sam wasn't around. This didn't seem to be her day for diplomacy.

It was a week later before Sam came bursting into Lorenso's waving a script in his hand. "I got it, Valli. Valli! The script. I got the part." He lifted her up and whirled her around before a startled Clarissa Thompson.

"Oh, Sam. You really got the part?"

"Yes. Jerry—you know, he's the director—loved me. We start reading the lines tomorrow, and rehearsal beings in full next week. I'm going to be a star. How soon can you leave?"

"Leave?"

"Yes, we're going out to celebrate. The four of us are going to paint this town red, white, and blue."

"Before you leave, Valli, dear," Miss Thompson interrupt-

80

ed, "would you mind terribly if we finished?"

Valli returned her attention to the woman standing in front of the mirror. "Oh, I'm sorry."

With her regal carriage, the dress fit perfectly. Even Miss Thompson couldn't find a single fault with its fit. Overnight, Valli had created a new style predating Courrèges and Paris couture by almost a year. And the actress—though an unsuspecting candidate—became the harbinger of the miniskirt among society's elite.

"Now, the coat." Valli stepped up on the platform and slipped it over her client's arms. "And the hat." She added the tiny pillbox and stepped back. "What do you think?"

Sam walked around the actress critically, examining her from all sides. His minute perusal of the woman closed off any comment.

"Exquisite," he said seriously, "absolutely exquisite. And," he added with a wicked grin, "your legs are wonderful, too. Madam, you're a grace to your profession."

This was Sam at his best, playing the role of connoisseur and expert on female beauty. When he took the lady's hand and kissed it elegantly, his gesture seemed not at all affected. "What do you think, Madam? I believe this very talented lady has created a masterpiece."

"Oh, I agree." She warmed under the glow of Sam's attention. "Except it was that genius Lorenso who created this gown." She turned to Valli, not noticing her slight frown. "I'll take it with me, as is."

"Thank you, Miss Thompson," Valli said simply. "I'll have the dresser remove the garment and pack it for you. It was a pleasure serving you, and when you need another dress, we hope you'll remember us."

"And me, too, Miss Thompson," Sam injected. "I'm Sam Carr, and I just landed my first Broadway part."

The green-eyed beauty stared at him a moment. "I'll remember you."

Sam took her hand and kissed it once again, more passionately and with a smack of his lips. "You do that. Our next meeting, dearest lady, will be recorded on celluloid for posterity.''

"Why'd you let that old fart claim the credit for your dress, Valli? I know that you designed it." Sam slid his hands into his jeans pockets. "Did you see the way Miss Thompson looked at me?"

"Unfortunately, if I want to keep on working, I have no choice. Everything here is designed by Lorenso, whether it is or not. But that will change, Sam. I'm only keeping quiet long enough to learn how everything is done. Then things will change. I promise you. Do the others know about the part?" She ignored his remarks about Clarissa Thompson.

"No, you're the first. You set it up, my dear, sweet Valli, and you're the one I wanted to share the news with first. Oh, Valli." To the pedestrians watching, the two of them were any other happy couple striding down the sidewalk. When Sam lifted her into the air and whirled her once again, only a few noticed and smiled. When he let her back down and continued to hold her, they simply made a path around them and kept moving.

"Sam, I'm so happy for you. You're on your way. Nobody can stop you now."

"So are you, Valli. After Clarissa Thompson goes to the ball wearing that red dress, you'll have to beat off the society matrons and stars with Lorenso's cigarette holder. We're both on our way, Valli. You're my good-luck piece." He leaned down and kissed her, a gentle, nonpassionate kiss that was more a thank-you than anything else. But Valli felt the bottom of her legs grow weak, and she swayed into Sam, unwilling to have it end. She wanted to stay in his arms, wanted him to sweep her up and take her away like some caveman reeking with primitive passion. When he pulled back and gave her fanny a sharp pat, she forced herself to let go of the fantasy that had become almost second nature to her by now.

Ferrara's, their favorite little Italian restaurant, was crowded with regulars. Many of the customers recognized the four friends celebrating at the boisterous table in the center of the room. Two empty wine bottles sat on the table, and a third was already half-gone.

"A toast," Court proposed, holding up his glass.

"You've already made four," Sam grinned. "It's my turn. Sit down." He raised his own glass and leaned into the center of the table. "Here's to success for all of us. Valli's own label; Noel, as Spud Towns, the satirical political writer, or Noel Gray of the Boston Grays; and Court, as a famous artist, or the next Rod Laver."

"No," Court overruled dramatically. "This toast is to Sam, for tonight." He raised his voice. "Here in this city, at this table, a star is born. Ladies and gentlemen, I give you . . .wait a minute, what the hell kind of name is Sam Carr? We've got to find you another name, a name with star quality. *Uno momento,*" he said to the diners who were listening with smiles to his speech.

"What's wrong with Sam Carr?" Noel inquired. "There isn't another Sam Carr in the actors' guild. I checked."

"Court's right," Sam agreed. "My name needs to represent the proper image to the world. I need a macho name with sex appeal. Something the men will identify with and the women will swoon over. . . . How about John Coal?"

They all groaned.

"No, not enough zip," Valli agreed. "We want you to be hard as nails and soft as butter. Nails, something like Copper, Iron, Steel, that's it. You'll be Steele. S-t-e-e-l-e," she spelled it out. "But Steele who?"

"I like it," Sam agreed. "Nothing wimpy about a name like Steele. Am I Steele somebody, or somebody Steele?"

For the next hour two dozen names were bantered around between toasts. Later nobody could have said who thought up Colton, or exactly when Sam Carr became Steele Colton, but the final toast of the evening was offered to the new man among them, rising Broadway star, Steele Colton.

Arms linked, the four friends started home.

"Hey, what time is it, anyway?" Steele was walking, but his feet were still a foot off the ground.

"Somewhere about two o'clock, I think." Noel yawned. "Hell, I've got to get to bed, I've got an important meeting."

"And I've got a tennis date at eight o'clock with a pro who's scouting for the circuit," Court added reluctantly.

"Well, I'm not ready to turn in yet. Valli and I are going to take a carriage ride in Central Park. We've never done that before, and we're entitled—now that we're both residents who are self-supporting and employed. You two bums go to bed, Valli and I are off to the moon."

"Good night, then, Sam, Valli." Court and Noel turned in the direction of the Village, and Steele, holding Valli pulled tightly against him, started for the subway.

"Don't call me Sam," he yelled out to the two men. "From now on, I'm Steele. Steele Colton says good night, world. You may not know that name now, but you will one day."

They reached the subway station and started down the steps.

"Valli, do you have any money? I seem to be out."

"Aren't you always." She laughed. "When you get your first check I expect you to buy me champagne and caviar."

"Most definitely." He stumbled and made an attempt to get on the wrong train.

"No, Sam. . .Steele," she corrected herself and grabbed Steele, turning him to the other platform. "This way."

Central Park was quiet and lovely, and the open horse-drawn carriage floated through the night in a romantic blur. Valli leaned agianst Steele with her head in the crook of his arm. Steele, a silly smile pasted across his face, hummed a wordless tune and stared up into the star-flecked night.

"Steele, do you believe in God?"

"No," Steele said quietly. "I don't think so. At least not the God I was taught about, a God filled with kindness, forgiveness, and love. No, I don't think that kind of God would stuff eleven people into one tarpaper shack with no food or clothes. Or give a kid parents who beat him." He shook his head and shifted his body uneasily. "Naw, I only believe in myself, in me, Sam—I mean Steele Colton."

Valli heard the bitterness in Steele's voice, and she recognized the determination as well. She knew she'd heard something profound, and she wanted to let Steele know how sorry she was that he'd been that child. She hadn't had a mother, but she'd had Granny, even if Granny had only seen her as a cross to bear. Valli understood that, in her own way, Granny had loved her, even if her coldness and the constant criticism were hard to take. More than ever she understood how much alike she and Steele were. And the resulting bond drew them closer. Impulsively she reached up and pulled his head down to hers.

"You can believe in me, Steele. I promise that I'll never hurt you. No matter what happens, I'll always be here for you."

Her need for Steele drew him to her like a magnet. His needs were strong as well, and he responded to her directions. It was only natural that he kiss her. His lips met hers, almost hesitantly, and even though she'd waited and wished for this moment, when it finally happened and she felt herself surrendering, her emotions became a confused tangle of fear and resistance. She wanted him, but now, in this, she wanted him to take charge and lead the way. She wanted the man Steele as strong as the name she'd given him.

"Ah, Valli," Steele cooed in her ear. "I think we should make love tonight."

His eyes softened in the moonlight, and together with the sweet-smelling night and the warm touch of his body against hers, Valli felt her worries melt away. When she felt the touch of his hand against her neck, she moaned with pleasure. This was what she'd waited for, what she'd wanted when she and Court had made love that night, what she wanted for the rest of her life. Her body tingled with her desire and needs, yet the desire was a conscious one, not the swept-away feeling she'd experienced with Court. Even as Steele kissed her now she recognized that something was not quite right. Of course, that night with Court she'd been pleasantly drunk, while tonight she was suddenly much too sober.

Steele was hungry for success, and she'd make him hungry for her. They were a team; they understood each other as neither of the others could because they were both desperate for fame and fortune. They shared the same past—and future. It didn't matter about Noel or any of the other women in Steele's life. She was the source of his confidence, and she'd make it happen for both of them—no matter what it took. When Steele's hand slid down the open neck of her shirt, she leaned back to make it easy for him.

"Ahem. . .I'm sorry, folks, but this is it."

A thoroughly shaken Valli and a fully aroused Steele sat up sheepishly and looked around. They'd traversed the park and were back where they'd started.

"Well, just go around again," Steele directed happily. "The lady and I don't seem to be quite ready to stop."

"Not tonight, buddy. It's quitting time for me. Why don't you and the lady find some nice, quiet private place and finish. . .whatever it is you aren't ready to stop." He stepped down from the carriage and held out his hand to help Valli.

Embarrassed, Valli pulled together her shirt front and allowed herself to be assisted from the carriage. Steele, sullen and apparently spoiling for a confrontation, was ready to take on the driver physically.

"Come on, Steele," Valli protested. "You don't need any bad publicity now. How would it look if the newspapers ran a story of Broadway's newest star landing in jail the day he gets his first big part? Let's go, we'll find someplace else."

"I know. How about behind this bush?" Steele laughed and pulled her off into the shadows, clasping her to him roughly.

"Steele! Suppose someone comes by?"

"Don't worry, Val, this won't take long."

Horrified, Valli watched Steele zip open his fly. This wasn't what she wanted, what she'd envisioned. Angrily, she took Steele by the shoulders and shook him.

"Not on your life, Steele Colton. If, and when, we make love it won't be behind some bush in Central Park. It will be in a bed, with soft music and romance. Now put yourself back together and let's go home."

"Ah, Valli," Steele said with chagrin, "I'm not that dumb. I was just kidding. Hold on a minute, I've got to. . ."

Valli heard the stream of water hit the ground as Steele relieved himself in the darkness. She sighed a false sigh of relief. He hadn't been serious. He wasn't really in the habit of having sex in the park behind a bush.

Steele stumbled out of the shadows and grinned at her apologetically. "Sorry, Val. Call of nature, you know. Didn't mean to embarrass you."

"You idiot." She laughed.

He flung his arm around her shoulders and they started down the sidewalk. Walking beside him, Valli felt all the emotions she'd kept so carefully locked in for the last months loosen and flow all over them. Steele was just an overgrown kid, covering his insecurities with a veneer of sophistication. Steele was no more sure of himself than she was, and now she knew that his background was even worse than hers. He genuinely needed her. Unlike most women, who want somebody to take care of them, Valli's lifelong independence had promoted a different need. Afraid of acknowledging her own dependence on someone else, she had deliberately chosen a man who needed her.

Taking care of Steele would ease her own insecurities. Together they'd nourish each other.

And Court? In a way she loved him, too. How could she help it? But she wasn't sure he returned the feeling. After they had made love he'd acted slightly hurt when she rejected his advances, but in a short time he seemed to have accepted it completely. Now, they were good friends; Court seemed content to keep it that way.

Court had been born to money and society, and Valli had a suspicion that right now he was just marking time. He didn't possess the fierce ambition that drove Steele and Valli. Lately he didn't even seem that dedicated to his art. Valli couldn't understand this, and it made her wonder whether Court was capable of being much more than an amiable dilettante.

"You don't mind taking care of me, do you, Val?" Steele interrupted her thoughts, hugging her unsteadily and planting a wet kiss against her forehead.

"Gee, thanks," she said sarcastically. "That really makes me feel special."

Steele stopped and turned toward her, a serious expression on his face. "You are special, you're very special to me. You're the only one I can really be myself around. I don't have to pretend with you, Val. Don't ever forget that, no matter what happens."

If the kiss that followed wasn't exactly what Valli had dreamed of, her imagination supplied enough of the details to make her heart take wing.

Steele pulled back and let out a whoop. "Hot damn," he called out to a passerby, "this is one lovely lady. Let's stop and get a beer."

"Not on your life, Sam . . . Steele," she corrected herself. "If you have another beer we'll never get home, and it's late. Isn't there something you'd rather do?"

Steele became heavier and heavier as he slumped against her. "Oops." He stumbled and caught himself, pulling himself upright with concentrated effort. "Valli, my dear, I must feed the fish. I promised."

"Feed the fish? Steele, you're drunk. We don't own any fish."

"Not our fish, my darling—Ted Corran's. And water the plants, too."

"Oh, the house you're sitting. Do you want me to take you there?"

"I'm very much afraid that we won't get there if you don't take me. I'm tired of subways, Val. Couldn't we just call a cab?"

As if on command a cab suddenly appeared and slowed at Valli's raised hand. An aura of melancholy settled over Valli as they rode through the empty city streets, and Steele seemed to withdraw into himself.

By the time she inserted the key in the apartment door, Steele had begun to swallow hard. "Oh, Valli, I'm sick." He barely made it to the bathroom and stumbled to his knees in front of the toilet. Valli held his head as he threw up. When he finally leaned back and looked up at her with chagrin in his eyes, she smiled in return.

"Sorry, Val. I didn't intend to do that. I think we celebrated too much. But I've never landed a real Broadway role before." He had to be helped from the floor and led to his bed where Valli undressed him. The shirt and jeans were no big deal, but the underwear was something else. Should she leave it on, or remove it? Steele cracked one eye and watched her indecision.

"I sleep raw, Valli. The shorts go, too."

Looping a finger in each side of his briefs, she pulled them down. He was big and limp, his penis curling over the thatch of dark hair and flat stomach.

"Come here, woman. Take off those clothes and get in this bed."

"What about Court and Noel? Won't they wonder where we are?"

"Not enough room." He grinned foolishly. "Let them get their own girl. Valli's mine."

Slowly Valli began to unbutton the blouse she was wearing. She slipped it over her head and peeled off her skirt before sitting down on the bed to unzip and remove her knee-length white boots.

"Now, the slip and bra, Valli. Let me see those tits."

This wasn't working out as she'd hoped. Instead of feeling romantic, she felt nervous. There was something cold about sitting there beside Steele, taking off her clothes. The desire was all gone and had been replaced by fear. Steele might not have been conscious of her anxiety, but he should have at least noticed her reticence.

But she and Steele were here, and Steele was what she wanted. Resolutely, she stood up and stripped the remaining clothes from her body, turning to face him with fright clearly reflected in her eyes.

"Come here, Valli. I'm not going to hurt you." Steele spoke gently and held out his arms as Valli crawled into bed.

"I'm sorry, Steele. It's just that . . ."

"Don't worry, I'm just as scared as you."

When he put his arms around her and pulled her into the warmth of his body, she gave a deep sigh of relief. There was nothing to be afraid of. He wasn't laughing at her. His touch on her skin was light and experimental, almost as though he really didn't know what was expected. She reached up and kissed him shyly, sliding her leg across his thighs.

As the kiss deepened she felt the uncertain touch of his fingertips inching toward her breast. When he feathered the nipples with his fingertips, she shuddered and moved her body against his hip. It was going to be all right. For the last year she'd waited for this, and now it was within her reach.

Steele's hand on her breast moved more slowly until at last it stopped altogether. He was lying beside her, very still, almost stiff. What had happened? She raised herself up on one elbow. "Steele? What's wrong?"

"Nothing, nothing at all," he managed as he began a mechanical examination of her body once more.

"Steele, you don't have to make love to me. We're friends. Just let me hold you close while you tell me what's wrong. Don't worry," she said patiently rubbing his chest and shoulders in a gesture of comfort. "It will be all right."

"Oh, Valli," he said with a groan, turning toward her in a move that placed Valli on her back and Steele's head resting on her breast. "Valli, suppose I can't do it? I'm scared I'll flop in front of all those people."

"All those people?" It took an instant before she realized that he was talking about the play, not making love to her.

"Steele," she murmured, applying light, warm kisses to his forehead while her fingertips threaded through his dark hair and ran down his neck in a soothing touch of reassurance. She pulled him closer, lifting the side of his body over hers so that she held him clasped to her, like a child.

"Don't worry, darling. You'll be wonderful. You're talented and handsome. You have what it takes. They wouldn't have chosen you if you weren't capable. This is only the first step. Someday soon you're going to be a star, Steele Colton."

Valli was startled to feel Steele's fingertips circling her breast again. This time he seemed merely curious as he touched her, rimming the hardened nipple and forging out to the edge of the dusky areolas.

"I'm so scared," he whispered.

Was he talking about making love or the musical?

The warmth of his breath moved closer to the nipple and she had to hold herself still when she felt his lips nuzzle her lightly. She almost felt that he was asking for her permission, not sure, but needing her to tell him. Valli knew at that moment that Steele was no more experienced than she. He didn't really know how to make love to a woman. He was reaching out to her on the only level he understood. He was the child, waiting to be led. She was the mother, who turned slightly, and lifted her breast to the lips that opened automatically to receive.

The wave of heat that swept through Valli was a threat that she held back. She sensed instinctively that Steele mustn't be rushed or frightened. She must move slowly and gently, building him to the ultimate union. She wasn't sure what might happen, but she'd wait and let whatever natural instincts she possessed take over. Her experience with Court had offered her little tutelage in the art of foreplay.

When she felt Steele's breathing begin to shorten, she forged lower, pushing him onto his back as she applied light, feathery kisses across his chest, nipples and down the thick mat of chest hair below. Slowly but steadily, her hands and her mouth covered his body. When she came to the part of his body that had once hung limply, she couldn't suppress a gasp at the rigid protrusion that met her lips.

"Oh, Valli," he sighed, "that's so good. Don't stop. I want . . . I need . . ."

She wasn't sure what was happening, but she knew that her own body was crying out with its own needs. If she wanted to stay in control she'd have to force Steele to turn to her for release, the kind of release only a woman could give him. Taking a calculated risk she turned onto her back

91

and pulled his face back to her breasts. He responded eagerly, arching himself against her. Urging him to the other breast she pulled his body upon hers until his penis was edging into her body in delicious spasms.

"Oh, Steele, you're wonderful," she whispered. "You feel so good against me. You'll feel so good inside of me." She opened her legs and felt him increase the rhythm, each movement sending waves of pleasure through her body, until he plunged unexpectedly deep inside of her in a rage of sensation that made her cry out with the force of her response.

The next thing she heard was the sound of heavy breathing and a muffled snore. He was asleep, and they were still together. She didn't move. This was what she'd wanted. She and Steele. They were two halves of a whole. She pushed aside her own still-aching desire as he went limp inside of her and thought about this man she loved so much. He was like a child—trusting and scared, sometimes sweet and then suddenly belligerent. Once he got the security he'd never known as a child, Valli was sure that he would grow and their love would ripen to maturity. So used to creating from her imagination at work, Valli felt that he was a child to be molded and she would see that he became the man she envisioned. She never doubted her ability to do so, nor questioned her own motives. For Valli, it was love—pure and simple.

If her body still clamored restlessly, she put it down to nerves on her first time with Steele. It would be better the next time, she told herself. Making love always became better with experience, or so she had read.

Later in the night she felt him move away, and her attempt to recapture the closeness was met with a mumbled rejection. And when she woke the next morning, Steele seemed embarrassed as she hurried back to the apartment so that she could dress for work.

"Valli, about last night . . ." he stammered. "I was drunk on wine and success. I needed you, and you were there for me. I . . . thanks." His kiss was hurried and unsatisfactory.

92

The next time she'd looked forward to seemed to be swallowed up in rehearsals and late-night gatherings with the other members of the cast. As Steele's self-confidence grew with every rehearsal, Valli's confusion deepened. Steele needed her; she knew he did. When things went wrong she was the one he turned to, and she was sure he'd turn back to her once he'd worked his way through the fear of failure.

Six months later, opening night found Valli, Noel and Court in the audience at the Majestic Theatre, applauding furiously at the final curtain. Steele was good. His portrayal of Lancelot was refreshing, and the audience loved him. Once he stepped onto the stage he became the errant knight and lover who tempted the loyal wife to run away. At the end of his brief but emotional love scene the audience applauded wildly. The woman sitting next to Valli commented to her girl friend that if Guinevere wouldn't go with Lancelot—she would. Steele's magnetism reached out to the sexual fantasy of every woman in the audience and made the dream seem vividly real.

Valli watched with envy. As she remembered the touch of Steele's body, she felt desire grow inside her body. She'd waited long enough. Steele had mastered his role, and the world would quickly know who he was. Now it was time that he came back to her. She wanted him, God how she wanted him.

She didn't know that Noel was thinking the same thing.

Court watched his two companions, each caught up in their own secret thoughts as they watched Steele perform. He watched their parted lips and short intakes of breath. In despair he watched, knowing that they were both going to be hurt. Steele wouldn't mean to do it, but he would hurt them both and he'd never even know he'd done it. And they'd both forgive him and keep hoping.

Court cleared his throat, managing a series of short unbelievable coughs, stood up and whispered. "Excuse me, Val, I'll meet you in the lobby." He slid past them into the aisle, and neither of them noticed he'd gone.

CHAPTER SEVEN

During the next few weeks Valli felt that she'd somehow lost her three best friends. Not only was Steele continually absent, but Court was spending less time painting and more time traveling the circuit. Valli often found herself dining alone.

Recently she had run into Lincoln Maxwell again, and he had started calling her at the studio. But she delayed going out with him and then berated herself for doing so. As her portfolio gradually filled up with sexy new lingerie and dress designs that she hadn't shared with Lorenso, her determination to have her name on the label inside became an obsession. She knew that her designs were light years ahead of Lorenso's more traditional evening clothes.

Valli's clothes were designed for women who were rich, fashion-conscious, and wanted to demonstrate their youth. Being young was in. Mary Quant's clothes reflected the new age, and so did Valli's. But Valli's clothes weren't exclusively for the young. Mod, impish, and offbeat, they were creations that the jet set—under and *over* twenty—could wear; they looked expensive.

The shop bristled with anticipation this morning. Lady Emily Spencer was coming in for the first time. Briefed earlier, Valli knew that Lady Spencer wanted a special gown to wear to a party being given by a famous writer. When the young Englishwoman came in, a clerk ran to notify Valli, who slipped into a fresh smock and waited quietly in the showroom while Lorenso made his usual fawning welcome to the sharp-nosed English beauty.

Valli knew what Lorenso expected of her and she went through the motions of standing quietly in the background until the buyer made her preferences known.

This morning Valli was drawn to the Englishwoman. She was slim, clear-eyed, and elegant without the least indication of fuss. She'd be perfect for Valli's own private collection of gowns. As Lady Emily and Lorenso exchanged information, Valli envisioned the English beauty wearing the green chiffon dress she'd sketched last night. It would be stunning with the woman's pale silver-blond hair and lightly suntanned skin.

"At the Waldorf," she was saying. "It's a masked ball for five hundred of his most intimate friends." She laughed gaily.

"Well, most of Halliday's friends are 'intimate.'" Lorenso snickered. "Friends of both sexes." He arched his eyebrows.

"Yes, he certainly has some interesting friends. Please, Lorenso, design something exciting for me to wear."

It took most of the morning to find a gown that satisfied Lady Spencer's exquisite eye for the dramatic. She left with the promise that the black dress she'd chosen would be complemented by Valli's suggestion of an exquisite beaded headdress with a mask built into the headpiece.

The next day was Sunday, and when Valli stumbled sleepily into the kitchen she was surprised to find all three men sitting glumly around the table.

"What's wrong?"

"Nothing really," Noel said.

"Just a major catastrophe," Steele corrected.

"Valli!" Court exclaimed, causing Valli to flinch at the

emphasis on her name.

"Yes? I'm standing right here, Court. Why are you yelling?"

"I'm not yelling, Country Mouse. You're the answer."

"You're tired, Court." Noel stood up and refilled his cup from the pot simmering on the stove. "Want coffee, Valli?"

"Yes. What's going on?"

"I've been invited to a party," Steele explained glumly. "An important party at the Waldorf."

"The masked ball? I know about it. I'm designing a dress for Lady Spencer to wear. We've been going crazy filling orders for it. Everybody who is anybody is going."

"That's exactly what I mean," Court insisted excitedly. "Valli is perfect. She's a designer, and she knows all those people. It would be perfect for you, Steele, and you'll be able to put on a good show because you won't have to worry about trying to please your date."

"Gee, thanks," Valli said sarcastically. "I take it you're supposed to bring a date, and you're looking for somebody cheap."

"That's partially right. I'm supposed to bring a date. And at the moment everybody who is anybody is already going. And I want to make an entrance that will be spectacular."

"As spectacular as you can make without a chauffeur and limousine," Noel explained. "Though why this kind of thing is so important to you, I don't understand. You're a good enough actor to allow your talent to speak for itself, Steele."

"Maybe, but there are a lot of unemployed 'good' actors in New York City, and I don't ever intend to be one of those again."

"You dummies, think about it for a moment," Court insisted. "Valli will be perfect. A lot of the women there already know her. And she'll fit right in with Courrèges, Beaton, Yves Saint Laurent, and all those others. And you'll have the scoop on them by bringing her first. What a coup for you. I'll even design your masks."

"Great," Valli interjected, looking at Court's latest work

of art hanging on the bathroom door. "We'll go as blobs, or whatever those things are."

As she saw the wince flash across Court's face she wished she could call back her words. He was painting less and less these days, and now she'd said something uncomplimentary about one of his few efforts. She felt like an ass.

"Valli?" Steele looked at Valli with an incredulous expression on his face. "Are you sure that's a good idea, Court? I mean, will that impress anyone?" The skepticism obvious in his voice showed in the lines around his mouth.

"Trust me, Steele. George Halliday likes women, particularly women in fashion. He's probably the most available escort to the fashion industry in New York," Court said with a shake of his head. "When I get through with the munchkin here, her own mother wouldn't recognize her, and you're going to have to fight off every man at the party, particularly the press."

"The press?"

They were talking about her as if she weren't even there, arranging, deciding for her without considering that she might object.

"Now just a minute," Valli interrupted. "It might be nice if somebody asked me if I'd like to go to this party before you all go getting yourself into a tizzy." She put down the coffee cup and left the room with as much affected dignity as she could manage.

"No," Court said softly. "Let her go. She's right. We do tend to arrange things for her as though she were the child and we were the parents." He held out a restraining hand as she reappeared in the hallway dressed in red bell-bottom pants and a tight purple knit vest. They watched her in silence as she left the apartment and started down the steps without her customary wave. "Valli is a lot smarter than any of us give her credit for. And she's a lot better-looking than you guys think. You'll see." He rose, following her with a lanky, disjointed stride that belied the grace he showed on the tennis court.

"You know it's your chance," Court said as he caught up

97

with her and walked down the street. They stopped at a café and sat outdoors, ordering juice and thick black coffee. In the background someone was playing a guitar, and the sound of a barking dog blended into the warmth of the morning.

"I mean, so far everything you have done is as Lorenso's underling. You can go to the ball as Cinderella wearing your own dress, and when everyone there sees you, there'll be no holding Valli, the designer, back."

"Maybe," she agreed, "but I'd rather die than force Steele to take me and be ashamed."

"Ashamed? Valli, don't you have any idea of how you look? With the right makeup and clothing and a decent hairstyle you'll be a knockout." He leaned across the tiny table and peered intently into her eyes, and an expression that she didn't quite recognize began to warm her skin and bring an unexplained tingle to its surface. "Let me show you how beautiful you really are."

During the next week, Court spent almost every moment attending to Valli. He even went down to the salon and met with Lorenso, explaining what they were doing and why. Lorenso, immediately ready to take credit for any good impression Valli might make, put the seamstresses to work full-time on Valli's gown and turned the workshop over to Court as he went to work on the masks.

For once Valli was allowed to design with no over-the-shoulder comments from Lorenso. She followed Court's suggestions, and the final product was ready when he brought a mass of white, downy feathers edged with silver glitter. They were to be attached to the shoulder, Court directed, and held in place at the top of the neckline with a silver clasp. He refused to allow Valli to view the accompanying mask until the night of the party. Steele was directed to come to the salon after the show, and they would be dressed in the workroom.

Valli showered, slipped her arms into one of the models' robes, and reported to the dressing room where Lorenso had brought in the hot new hair designer to do Valli's hair. Vidal Sassoon had already created a geometric cut that had immediately become the rage. Now he immediately went to work with the scissors, modifying Valli's dark locks into a slightly different five-point cut.

Afterwards a makeup artist went to work on her face. Already over-large, her eyes seemed to grow into intense orbs that reached out with a mystical allure. As he applied a silvery eyeshadow and blackened her lashes to long feathery spikes, Valli began to feel a strange excitement as she watched. Looking at her face in the mirror, she felt more like Cinderella than she had ever thought possible.

"Now, Valli," Lorenso intruded into her thoughts, "remove the robe."

"But, Lorenso," she protested, "I'm not wearing anything beneath it."

"I know. We're going to make you a Lorenso beauty from the skin out. Start with these."

Valli started. He was holding out a pair of sheer silver stockings, a garter belt, a lacy bra, and brief underwear. It was her design, the new panties made to hug the hipline without extending to the waist. How had he done it? He'd stolen her design and obviously was going to claim it for his own.

"My new lingerie designs. How, where?"

"Yes." Lorenso beamed with an expression that dared her to correct him. "When I found the designs in your desk, I knew they'd be perfect for tonight. I had them made up especially for you. Now, quickly, slip into them."

Too angry to reply, Valli grabbed the wispy piece of material and stepped into the panties. Under the robe she fastened the strapless chiffonlike bra and garter belt. Sitting down on the work stool, she pulled on the silver stockings, dropped the robe to the floor behind her, and stood. If Court and Lorenso intended to exhibit her like some kind of mannequin, she'd let them.

Valli stepped back onto the platform before the mirrors standing stiffly like a china doll, porcelain, and petite and almost fragile in her beauty. She was so angry that she noticed neither Court's intake of breath nor the naked desire in his eyes as he gazed at the woman who never knew he was there.

"Perfect," Lorenso decided, clapping his hands in glee. "Terrance, bring the gown."

From out of the shadows, Terrance appeared, knelt before Valli, and held the dress for her to step into. The gown was exquisite. It fell freely from the left shoulder in a whisper of silvery white. A slit in one side exposed the silver stockings and made it possible for her to walk without effort, exposing her thigh as she moved. Stepping into the silver stiletto-heeled shoes, the illusion of height was complete.

"Perfect," Court echoed. "Now, if Noel has Steele ready, we'll bring him in and then I'll show you both the masks."

Terrance appeared with Steele. He walked up to the platform and stood beside Valli, his eyes filled with pleasure when he saw the woman in the mirror beside him. Whereas Valli was white, Steele was black. His tux was as unadorned as Valli's dress. Beneath the black tux, he wore a plain pleated white shirt and silver cummerbund. At his neck he wore a black bow tie, and in the pocket the silver tip of a handkerchief peeked out. Diamond studs held the shirtfront and cuffs, and in the mirror the light seemed to reflect the flint of the stones in his black eyes.

"Damn, Court, you were right. We're dynamite. Where are our masks?"

"I'll bring Valli's, but Lorenso, I'd like you to help me put it on her. Terrance, you bring Steele's."

The three men reappeared with the masks, feathery creations that appeared almost human. First Steele's mask was placed over his head. Sleek black feathers had been delicately stitched into a soft netlike hood. Holes were cut for the eyes, and a tuft of feathers built up like brows gleamed with a deep blue-black tint. An appendage shaped like a silver beak covered Steele's nose. The head covering was magnificent, beautiful with a hint of power and cruelty in the shape of the beak that extended almost to the base of Steele's chin.

"I'll be damned," Steele said in awe. "You can hardly tell it's there, and yet it's almost real. I'll have to hand it to you, Court. You're all right as an artist. I think you ought to stop painting and make masks."

"Now," Court said softly, "let's bring in Valli's mask."

If Steele's was hard-edged masculinity, Valli's was definitely all femininity. The soft white of her headdress was pure and gentle. Her sapphire eyes beneath the mask showed through, wide-eyed with wonder and surprise. She looked like a gentle white bird, caught in a moment of wonder or fear. Her beak was silver-blue, ending in a curve at the bottom of her lips. The chin below was exposed, adding a desirable touch of vulnerability.

"When you remove the mask later in the evening," the young English hairdresser said from behind, "your hairstyle won't need any attention. You'll still look lovely."

"Thank you. I'm more beautiful than I ever realized. Thank you all."

"And now for the final touches," Lorenso said with his usual pompous flair. He handed Steele an ebony cane with a silver head shaped like an eagle. For Valli he produced a cape made completely of white feathers. It covered her shoulders and fell in a curve to her knees.

"Oh, Lorenso, it's beautiful. I don't know why I didn't think about something like this. It's magnificent."

"Of course it is, Valli. I'm still a designer and a very good one, even if you do seem to conveniently forget that."

With Lorenso's rebuke still ringing in her ears, Valli took the arm Steele offered and stepped out into the night, wondering if she was about to step into a pumpkin pulled by white mice. Waiting at the curb was the black limousine she'd promised herself she'd ride in that first day she came to New York. "If Granny, if Willacoochee, Georgia, could see me now."

From the minute they stepped into the Waldorf ballroom Steele suddenly became a star. The hesitant, uncertain boy whom she'd once held in her arms to comfort had been replaced by a suave, sophisticated man-about-town who

101

seemed to know everyone there. Most of the masks were masks in name only, and outside of the feathery masks they wore, most of the face coverings were simply appendages to be removed as soon as possible by the wearers. Attached to lorgnettes, quite a few of the masks were so elaborate and unwieldy that they were abandoned almost immediately. When Steele suggested that they remove their masks, Valli quickly convinced him that the aura of mystery was far more exciting than the knowledge of who was behind the feathers.

Realizing that they were the center of interest, Steele agreed and seized on playing up the intrigue by being even more mysterious. He introduced Valli to one celebrity after another but refused to reveal his identity or that of the enchanting woman behind the mask.

From Lauren Bacall to Norman Mailer, from Yves Saint Laurent to Cecil Beaton, Valli met them all. When their energetic host claimed Valli for a dance, Steele was forced to let her go.

"My dear, Noel said I should invite Steele, but I never expected you as a bonus."

"Noel? Noel is responsible for the invitation?"

"Why, yes. I wanted him to come, but he refused—something about publicity, or something. He said that I should send his invitation to Steele. Now your charming escort won't give me your name, and I'm sure you weren't on my invitation list or I'd recognize you. Let me try and guess. I've heard you speak, so I know you're from the South. Alabama?"

"No."

"Georgia?"

"Yes."

"You're small, Southern, and altogether the most exquisite creation at my party. You must be Valli."

"Oh, how did you know?"

"I know all the ladies—the important ones, naturally—and I've heard them talking about a new designer in town. She's also short and Southern. Voilà! Valli! I think that after tonight, my dear, everyone will know who you are."

"Do you really think so?"

"After tonight, my dear, your name will be quite famous. You'll see."

The waltz ended and Valli was claimed by a tall, slim masked man.

"So, you're the hit of the evening," her partner said as he pulled her closer. "And I'm finally going to have a moment with you."

"Lincoln! I didn't know you'd be here."

"I couldn't miss this, and you, my little chickadee. Or are you an owl tonight? Yes, a gorgeous snowy white owl. Why haven't you answered my calls? You're never in."

"Oh, didn't you know? Owls never come out in the daytime. We're creatures of the night." Valli shivered, remembering the favor she owed Lincoln. If it hadn't been for him, Steele wouldn't be on Broadway and they wouldn't be here tonight. She'd been rude and ungrateful. She blushed beneath her mask and was glad that Lincoln couldn't see.

"Relax, babe," Lincoln whispered. "I'm not going to carry you off. I know that you're here with Steele. But, given a little time, I'd like to think I could earn a night like this for me."

She finally spotted Steele, hemmed in by two portly men not even pretending to wear masks. Steele looked uncomfortable. With a flick of his finger behind one of the men's backs, Steele motioned for Valli to rescue him. Without a thought she excused herself from Lincoln and made her way to Steele's side, sliding her arm around him as she felt him sag against her in relief.

"I'm so sorry, gentlemen, but I've come to claim my mate. You will excuse me?" She deftly turned Steele around and pulled him back onto the dance floor.

"Oh, Valli, don't leave me alone anymore tonight." There was an odd desperation in his voice, and his grip around her waist was like iron.

"I don't like being away from you either, Steele. I'm not comfortable with all these strangers."

"I know what you mean, Val. Stick close. That way neither of us can, will, mess up. Would you like something to drink?"

Valli didn't really want Steele to take his arms from around her, but the music ended temporarily and she allowed him to escort her to the bar. Several champagne cocktails later, both of them began truly to relax. As the evening turned into a lovely blur of famous names—Mary Martin, Tammy Grimes, Dick Van Dyke, Kitty Carlisle, Bennett Cerf —Valli allowed herself to remember another evening with Steele, an evening of triumphant celebration that had ended in bed.

Not once, since that evening, had Steele made any reference to their making love, and not once had he indicated any inclination to repeat the experience. Yet, as the night wore on, Valli felt the sexual tension grow between them. She wanted Steele and, somewhere after midnight when the music was romantic and slow and the lights on the dance floor were dimmed, Valli slid her arms around Steele's neck and pulled his face down to hers. He wanted to kiss her. She felt it in the sudden bulge pressing against her.

Suddenly the soft music turned into a drum roll, and a spotlight flashed on the bandstand. The mood was lost, and Steele turned the frustrated Valli toward the band, clasping his arms in front of her. In the darkness, one hand slid across and rested on her breast while the other pulled her against him, revealing without question that the bulge she'd thought she'd felt was most definitely still there.

"Steele!" she protested as he made an unmistakable arch against her rear. "Someone will see."

"Damn, Val, you've got great tits. Be still now. Everyone's watching the stage."

Vaguely she saw someone standing by the microphone about to speak. "Ladies and gentlemen. In honor of the occasion, we've selected one couple to receive special recognition for the most spectacular costumes of the evening. I have managed, during the time we've been judging, to identify this couple." He paused dramatically. "Will the newest

104

sensation of the Broadway stage, Mr. Steele Colton and his guest, the lovely Valli, please come forward."

"God, Steele, that's us."

"You're right, Valli. That's us. Let's go claim our fame."

As the spotlight fell on the couple, Steele straightened up and took Valli's hand, leading her down the opening pathway created as the crowd stepped back before them. Their private moment was gone, and suddenly they were standing on the platform and bowing to cheers and applause.

The announcer held up his hand to arrest the applause. "The award is given for the most spectacular costume and mask. Thanks to another famous personality in our midst, I can tell you that the couple is wearing Lorenso Originals designed especially for this occasion. Steele Colton, of course, is appearing in the Broadway musical *Camelot* with Richard Burton and the lovely Julie Andrews. And the beautiful Valli is Lorenso's protégée, one of New York's up-and-coming designers. Ladies and gentlemen, I give you Valli and Steele."

Standing behind the couple were two men who stepped forward and lifted the masks, revealing their faces. With the spotlight on them, Valli could do nothing but bite back the anger she felt at Lorenso's latest deceit.

"Smile, Val, the world is watching."

"But Steele, that old cheat stole my credit," Valli said between clenched teeth. "This is my dress and my night. I'm not going to let him get away with it."

Steele turned Valli toward him, clasping her with both arms in a display of love. "Don't, Valli. Please. Don't ruin this for me—us."

Valli looked up into Steele's eyes, saw the pleading desperation reflected there, and felt herself begin to relax. She couldn't spoil this night for him. She couldn't.

Steele felt the change in her body and knew she'd given in. This time he did kiss her, but she knew as he kissed her that the kiss was for the world that was watching, and she wished for a moment that they were back on the dance floor hidden in the dim light where they'd been before.

From that moment on, they were whirled from one famous person to another. By the time they finally stepped back into the waiting limousine at three A.M., Valli was drained. Her moment had been jerked from her. And though she suspected she'd become an overnight sensation, it was not her design that had gotten her there, it was her fame as Lorenso's protégée and Steele's date. When Steele pulled her close, she didn't resist, but what she had wanted so badly before suddenly became an expected duty, and she knew that the Steele kissing her was only acting from a script he'd written for the evening.

CHAPTER EIGHT

"Valli, love, Lincoln Maxwell is on the phone. Are you in?"

Terrance waited in the doorway expecting a repeat of the refusal she'd given every day for the last two weeks since the ball. Lincoln Maxwell—handsome, successful, and persistent—pursued Valli relentlessly.

"Tell him that I'm with a client," she began as she pushed herself away from her table and stretched muscles that were screaming from being hunched over the design board.

"If you say so, sweet, but going out with Lincoln is good press and good press is good for business."

She knew he was right, but she didn't want to make a name for herself in the society columns. She wouldn't know how to act around Lincoln. Still, she knew she owed him for Steele's audition. And she'd never been one to be ungrateful.

Lincoln Maxwell. Valli shook her head wondering why he continued to ask her out. Just yesterday she'd seen his picture in *Variety*. And she'd read in the papers that the week before he'd been at Elaine's with Rita Moreno. He dated beautiful actresses, celebrity debutantes, and models. He was one of the most successful young actors in New York and a favorite of the jet set. He couldn't be interested in Valli. But he was.

"I'll talk to him," she decided impulsively.

"Hello?."

"Valli? I don't believe it. Do you have any idea how many times I've tried to reach you?"

His voice was polished and surprisingly pleasant. He sounded delighted, and Valli felt herself warm to his words.

"I have a vague idea. The girls keep a running count of how many men call and so far I've managed a very respectable score, thanks to you. As a matter of fact, you've earned me a doughnut every morning for a week."

"I see. Well, if my calls get you a doughnut, let's really go for broke. How about dinner? That ought to be good for a couple of imported Danish at the very least."

"Dinner?" She knew the alarm was evident in her voice, and she fought back an impulse to hang up the phone and pretend she'd never agreed to talk to Lincoln Maxwell.

"Yes? We could go out, somewhere special after the show. How about the Oak Room at the Plaza? Or Sardi's. Or maybe you'd rather catch Frank's late show at the Copa."

"Frank? As in Sinatra?"

"Yes. Frank. What about meeting me at the theater? I'll have a ticket for you at the box office, and after the show we'll put on our dancing shoes."

"But I don't dance."

"To tell the truth, I'm pretty bad myself. But women usually expect anybody in a musical to be a combination of Fred Astaire and Gene Kelly. We can always watch. Will you come, Valli?"

"I . . ."

"The show begins at eight. Just tell the ticket agent who you are. I'll arrange a seat in the front row. See you, babe."

"So? What is it on the ceiling that you're looking at?"

"Oh, Lorenso. I'm sorry. I don't seem to be doing very well today. I guess I'm preoccupied."

"Preoccupied is okay. It's the unoccupied that worries.

108

Your hands, they aren't moving. They always move, as if you're touching something that nobody else can see. What's wrong, Volli?"

"Valli," she corrected absently. Lorenso knew very well how to pronounce her name. This was one of his little attention-getting affectations, cultivated because his public expected it. "Look, Lors, I just can't seem to make my mind and my fingers join forces today. What would you think of giving me the afternoon off?"

Lorenso's astonishment was real. Valli arrived first in the salon each day and left last each evening. "Afternoon off?"

"Yes. I promise that I'll make it up. I won't take a lunch for the next week. I'm . . ." she stammered, "I'm going out to dinner, and I don't have a thing to wear."

"Yahoo! Yahoo!" Lorenso chortled. He didn't seem to understand that the word wasn't an expletive. "Valli, the city's smartest new fashion darling is going out to dinner, and she hasn't a thing to wear. Hurry! Go home."

All the way down to Greenwich Village, Valli worried. What would she wear? What was she getting herself into? Lincoln Maxwell was a star. What could he see in her? Why had she ever agreed to go out with him? If she knew how to contact Lincoln, she'd cancel the date.

Letting herself into the steamy, quiet apartment, Valli went straight to her part of the living room. Apparently she was alone.

She took a quick shower and donned plain black panties, a black garter belt, patterned Balenciaga tights, and her laciest half slip. Dressing for work or going out with the fellows was simple. A date? That was something else.

Dinner, he'd said casually, as though she'd known what that meant. Valli looked into the mirror. Hair. She wanted to do something different with the heavy shock of dark hair. With fierce determination she began to back-comb, one hank of a hair at a time. When she'd combed the mass into a frenzied halo about her head, she took a brush and began to fashion the fringe into the fluffy bouffant style that was all the rage.

Well, she thought critically as she surveyed the finished product, you've created a style that falls somewhere between Elizabeth Taylor and a poodle. Linc won't know whether to pat you on the head or scratch your ears. Briefly she considered trying to get an appointment with Kenneth. His new salon on East Fifty-fourth was all the rage, and most of Valli's clients went there. She probably couldn't get an appointment. Besides, it was definitely too expensive.

Fumbling through her underwear drawer looking for her black bra, she heard someone behind her.

"Fetching, but a little risqué, even for you."

"Court."

He grinned appreciatively at her bare breasts and the simple black-lace slip she was wearing. "Why didn't you knock?" She turned her back to him.

"We seem to have a small problem with knocking, Valli. You have no walls, and drapes just don't make any noise. Maybe I'll just stamp my feet next time. What's with the new look?"

"Oh, Court. Please help me. I'm going out to dinner, and I don't know what to wear."

"Don't you ever listen to your own advice? My telling you what to wear would be like your giving me tennis lessons. If Katharine Hepburn came into the salon and asked for a dinner dress, what would you recommend?"

"Oh, but that's different. Katharine wouldn't come, and if she did, she'd wear pants. And the most important thing is that she'd know where she was going—and what she was doing. I don't know why I accepted his invitation, and I can't find my bra. I'm just not going, that's all there is to it. Oh, here it is." Valli pulled out the bra and put it on, stuck her petite stockinged feet into a pair of fuzzy scuffs, and began poking at her hair.

"Perfect! Now, turn around and let me have a look at you."

Court took the brush from Valli's hand, caught her chin with his fingertips, and twisted her around to face him.

"Listen, babe, you're Valli. You set trends. You don't follow them—ever. For God's sake, untangle your hair. You're going out to dinner, right?"

His eyes traveled down from her face to her breasts. God, he'd wanted his hands on those breasts for ages, ever since that night. Now Valli looked at him wide-eyed and expectant, and it was all he could do not to rip the offending garment from her body and bury his face in her cleavage.

"You need," Court said with a grimace and a swat on her rear, "to get dressed."

"I know"—she stamped her foot—"but I don't know what to wear."

"Oh, where are you going? And who are you going with that invokes such concern?"

"Lincoln Maxwell."

"Linc?" Court whirled around, rare lines of displeasure marring his face.

"Yes. What's the matter?" Valli bristled.

"I know him, Valli. He's a nice guy, but he's not going to take you to dinner and bring you straight home afterwards. Trust me; he's not your type."

"And who is, Court?" Valli shrieked. "You aren't my father. I'm twenty years old. And I'll go out with whomever I damn well please."

"Who are you going out with?" Sam and Noel had come into the bedroom behind them.

"Do come in," Valli said sweetly. "I suppose you may as well put your two cents in."

"What are you talking about, Valli?" Noel straddled a straight-back chair and rested his chin on folded hands.

"She's got a dinner date," Court explained.

"What dinner date?" Steele lost his light tone and walked over to the mirror, peering in with displeasure at Valli.

"I'm going out to dinner," Valli said calmly.

"With whom?"

Noel and Court faded into the shadows as Valli contemplated the stern set of Steele's lips.

Valli's first reaction was one of anger. What right did he

111

have to question her? It wasn't any of his business.

"With Lincoln Maxwell," she answered as she turned back to the rack which held her clothes.

"It's a damn poor idea, and you're not going." Steele grabbed the dress she'd been holding and shoved it back on the metal rod.

"I certainly am." Valli grabbed the dress. "Lincoln is holding a ticket for me to the play, and he's taking me to dinner afterwards. He's the first man to ask me out to dinner in a month. You guys have your own lives. I have to have mine, too."

"We haven't meant to neglect you, Valli," Noel protested, genuinely hurt by her accusation.

"Don't you understand? I have to find my own way. I don't expect you to entertain me. I'm an adult, and I'm going to dinner with Lincoln Maxwell. Now get out of here, all of you," she said sternly.

Dismissing them, Valli turned back to the rack, reached in, and caught the first garment her fingers touched. She pulled it out and slid it over her head. The dress was one of the few designs she'd actually found time to have made for herself. She'd designed it several months ago but hadn't yet had an opportunity to wear it. It was a short black satin skirt with a matching ultra-sheer silk blouse. Her breasts were spared exposure by a snug-fitting gold vest that was clasped together with baroque costume jewelry.

She added some Kenneth Lane bangles—one of her few extravagant purchases—and the look was complete. By the time she'd combed her hair out and applied a light dusting of makeup, she was nearly ready. After she'd added a beaded satin clutch bag she'd bought in a used-clothing store over on Third Avenue, she left the area cordoned off as her bedroom.

Lincoln pinned a spray of white gardenias in her hair and stepped back to survey his date in his dressing-room mirror. "Beautiful, absolutely beautiful. Just have a look at us, Valli."

Valli turned and glanced in the mirror. He was right. The couple in the mirror complemented each other perfectly. Lincoln wasn't tall, yet Valli's petite size accentuated his height. Her dark hair and blue eyes played perfectly against the softer golden brown of his eyes and the blond streaks in his brown hair. His traditional black tuxedo with white pleated shirt and silk handkerchief was the perfect foil for her more wild black outfit.

"We do match in a funny way, don't we?"

"Absolutely. I knew we would. Shall we go?" He executed a jaunty little dance step, offered her his arm with a debonair gesture of elegance, and led her toward the door, pausing to pick up a silver-handled ebony cane before they stepped into the empty corridor backstage.

They decided on the more sedate Oak Room, rather than fighting the crowds at the Copa, or the inevitable intrusions of theater people at Sardi's. The evening was fun. Rather than the strain she'd feared, Valli found herself laughing at Lincoln's little stories, appreciating the trials and tribulations he'd endured in landing his various roles.

"John Huston was in the audience last week. We went out afterwards and he tried to talk me into going to Hollywood, but I don't know."

The waiter removed the remains of Lincoln's steak as a second waiter wheeled a small cart over to the table, and poured some liqueur over the contents in the pan, set it on fire and poured a second liquid into the pan. Valli caught her breath as he poured the flaming red liquid over a dish of ice cream and placed the dish before her.

Lincoln observed her delighted reactions with pleasure. God, she was so open. Unlike the women he was used to, she didn't hide her feelings behind a mask of boredom or sophistication.

"Do I eat it, or pour water on it?" She giggled, raising her eyes to look at Lincoln who had suddenly dropped the smooth patter of entertaining stories he'd regaled her with all evening.

"You eat it," he said quietly, watching as she took a

spoonful of the sweet red-and-white concoction and slipped it between her lips.

"Tell me about Hollywood and the movies," she said, trying to relieve a tension for which she had no explanation. Why was he staring at her that way?

"Oh, well, I don't know. Performing before a live audience is wonderful. I don't know that I'd like a camera. It's too cold, too impersonal . . . ."

He looked at her intently as his voice trailed off, and Valli felt a shiver course through her. "What's wrong, Lincoln? Have I done something wrong?"

"No. I'm not sure how to say this, Valli. I just realized how much I like you, how much I enjoy being with you." He paused as if he didn't understand exactly what he meant. Disbelief crept into his voice when he continued, the idea too incredible for him to fathom. "I don't have to impress you, and you aren't trying to impress me. That's something pretty special."

"Please, Lincoln. I'd rather you didn't talk like that. We've simply had dinner together, that's all. And I do like you. We've had fun."

And they had, Valli thought later as they rode through the brightly lit city back to the Village. Lincoln was a gentleman, and the evening had been even better than she'd expected. But, already she was looking forward to the safe haven of her apartment—and Steele. Lincoln moved in a glamorous world—one she wanted to be a part of but wasn't quite comfortable with yet.

Lincoln directed the driver to wait, and he walked Valli inside.

"That's all right, Lincoln. You don't need to come up. One of the boys will be there."

"I insist." He pushed the elevator button, and the door opened instantly. When he stepped inside, Valli felt the chamber shrink. When Lincoln turned her gently into his arms she resisted for a moment, then remembering the feeling of assurance she had felt when she'd entered Lincoln's dressing room, she lifted her lips to his. His kiss was gentle

114

for a moment, and she relaxed and gave herself over to it.

The elevator door slid open, and over Lincoln's shoulder she saw the disapproving glare of Steele's eyes as he stood, arms folded, leaning against the post in the entrance.

"Evening, Lincoln," Steele said in a voice that Valli recognized as dangerously low. "Valli?"

"Hello, Steele. Just get in, did you?"

"Me? No, Lincoln. I've been here for quite a long time. You must have had a leisurely dinner. It's two A.M."

"Yes we did, any problem with that?"

"Not at all. We do appreciate your bringing Valli home, Lincoln. Good night."

"Good night? Now wait a minute, Steele. I'll tell Lincoln good night when I'm ready. . . in my own way, privately, or in front of you, if you insist on standing there like some irate parent."

She turned back to Lincoln Maxwell, slid her arms around his neck, and tilted her head provocatively. "Thanks for a lovely evening, Linc. It was very special." She pulled his head down so that she could reach his lips and ground her body unmistakably against him. The startled Lincoln took a few seconds to respond, but his body responded eagerly.

The slow, rhythmic clapping that filtered through to Valli finally forced her to draw back. Steele grinned and nodded his head in perfect accompaniment to his clapping.

"Beautiful, Valli, just like in the movies. Lincoln, you're very good, but Valli's better. This show is a real smash." He saluted the two of them and turned away. "Better think about that for a minute, Valli. What are you planning for a curtain call?"

"I think I'd better go, Valli," Lincoln began. "I don't relish being ripped apart by your three protectors, and I have the feeling that they're just waiting for the command to attack. Next time we go to my place, okay?"

Valli watched him step into the elevator, her heart clamoring in protest. Next time? The idea of a next time both excited and frightened her. But even more exciting was Steele's obvious jealousy.

CHAPTER NINE

They watched the procession down Pennsylvania Avenue; the horse with the empty boot reversed in the stirrup and the solemn beat of the drum, signifying the death of the nation's leader.

A tear rolled unashamedly down Noel's face. His fists were clenched and his expression grim. Court watched his friends as they watched the screen, and a deep sorrow cut through him. President John F. Kennedy had been assassinated, a tragedy beyond understanding, and within minutes Lyndon Baines Johnson took the oath of office. And yet, a simpler understanding came to him. Everything was changing. A different world was emerging. After two and a half years, the four of them were beginning to separate, finding different paths. The assassination signaled the end of an era. It was an end they hadn't expected, couldn't quite accept . . . and yet now it was a reality.

The effect of Kennedy's death on Noel was particularly poignant. Early in the administration, Noel had been a vocal critic of the youngest elected president of the United States. But as Kennedy matured in office, insisting on equality for all, Noel's articles of stinging criticism had evolved into praise. He had gotten caught up in the dream of Camelot.

Noel seemed to have isolated himself from the foursome, spending almost all his time with his activist friends. Last August he had attended the massive march in Washington, D.C., where 200,000 people had congregated and heard the already immortal words of Dr. Martin Luther King: "I have a dream. . . ." Now just four months later, another of Noel's dreams was dead.

Court watched as Valli glanced at Steele periodically as she always did. All her thoughts were directed toward Steele —and probably always would be. It was no secret to anyone, except perhaps Steele. Even since Valli had become a part of the Manhattan society scene, she still seemed obsessed with Steele. Suzy Knickerbocker's column frequently noted her dates with Lincoln Maxwell. After ten months of dating, they were an "item," and Valli was rapidly gaining fame in her own right as Lorenso's protégée.

Steele? There Court had even more worries. On the surface he'd become the darling of society, escorting a new starlet or model every night. But privately Court heard other reports—some from Lincoln Maxwell—about his activities that both worried and alarmed him. Everyone was taking drugs these days, but knowing Steele's personality Court felt that Steele was heading for trouble. And if there were numerous girls, there were also a lot of pretty young men and influential older ones in the picture. But without Noel's help—and Noel seemed to have concentrated all of his energies on his private causes—Court didn't know how to deflect Steele from his present course.

Court worried about the three of them. He'd resigned himself at last to the fact that he was not an artist. He'd decided to join the Navy. He didn't exactly want to shoulder arms, but he didn't want to stay in New York any longer. He didn't want to witness Steele's downfall, and he could no longer sit back and watch Valli's growing need for a man who didn't deserve her. Shit, Valli had no idea how he felt. But even if she did, she'd probably only feel sorry for him.

117

He couldn't fight it so he chose another battleground. He sprang to his feet and strode from the room.

"Court?" Valli called after him. "Where are you going?"

He didn't answer. There was no answer.

Court joined the Navy and left for England to spend Christmas with his mother before reporting for duty.

Noel made a startling announcement; he was going home to Boston to enter law school. He had become convinced that the way to fight injustice was within the legal system. In order to be accepted at Harvard, he'd enter undergraduate school for his last two quarters. He left shortly before Christmas. They didn't even have a farewell party. The defection had begun and ended without any one of the four understanding what they were losing until it had happened.

The apartment was empty. Waiting for Lincoln, Valli was drawn back to the night—almost a year ago—when Steele had waited for Lincoln to bring her home. He had acted jealous—and attentive for weeks afterward. But then, in the flurry of activities with his new friends, he had accepted the relationship. There was an ache in her that seemed to be permanently present now that both Court and Noel were gone. She rarely saw Steele, and when she did there was an unhealthy glint in his eyes that worried her. Once he'd needed her. Once he'd even loved her—a little. She was sure of that. And yet, even at their closest there was a part of him that she'd never reached. . .that part that first Noel, then other men, seemed to satisfy.

But Valli had not been able to appease the sleeping need that Steele had awakened in her. At party after party she had fought off the advances of bodies, bodies obvious in their desire to possess hers. Even Lincoln, who never pressed her, was clearly becoming less and less able to hide his physical desire. Simple good-night kisses had turned into a kind of passion that she could no longer reject.

He had waited a long time for Valli to return his ardor. At first she had insisted on no ties, and he'd continued to go out with other women. But one by one he'd dropped them from his life, and Valli knew he'd fallen deeply in love. Tonight, if he asked her, she would go to his apartment. This time, she would stay overnight. If her plan worked, they'd either celebrate, or she'd need his comfort.

Lincoln Maxwell was a handsome man, a man who promised to give her as much as he demanded, and her long-starved body seemed to come alive as she waited. She hadn't given up on Steele, but she had finally realized the futility of waiting.

The doorbell rang.

Valli opened the door and was greeted by a laughing Lincoln, covered with glistening drops of water where snowflakes had hung on his overcoat and hat, his hands thrust awkwardly behind him.

"Guess what, babe? It's snowing. We're going to the Winter Ball in real snow." He drew back and looked at her. "I've seen that dress before, haven't I? Oh, I remember, it's the dress you wore to the party at the Waldorf, isn't it?"

"Yes. I thought it would be appropriate to wear it tonight —though I don't have the feathered cape that matched it. Lorenso sold it to some overweight matron from Queens."

"That couldn't be more perfect. Open this." He drew out a large, gaily wrapped box with a bright red bow from behind his back. "My Christmas gift for you."

"Oh, Linc. I don't have a gift for you. I've been so busy, I haven't even thought about shopping."

"You, my darling Valli, are all I want for Christmas." Lincoln swore as he unwrapped the box himself and let the contents fall out across his arm. Like a child he stood back and waited for her reaction.

"Oh, Linc. . .I don't know what to say." She slid into the ermine cape, relishing the cool feel of the satin lining and the tickle of fur on her arms. "It's beautiful, but you shouldn't have. This is much too expensive. I can't accept it."

"Ummm. . ." Lincoln straightened the cape around Valli's shoulders, ignoring her protests. "Valli, when are you going to understand that just because your granny didn't accept expensive gifts from men doesn't mean that you can't. Besides''—he turned her to face him and added solemnly— ''I'm not 'just a friend,' you're very special, and before this night is over, you're going to know how special.''

On the way to the ball Valli thought about his words; and she thought, too, about her earlier decision to sleep with Lincoln. She was even more determined now. This would be her gift to him: She'd give him Valli, if not forever, at least for now.

The festive crowd at dinner, gaily turned out in greens and reds and silvers glittered and glimmered, sequins flashing from the lights. From the table where she and Lincoln were seated, she saw Jacqueline Susann wearing one of her creations. At the next table, in another of her gowns, was the new editor of *Cosmopolitan,* Helen Gurley Brown. She was sitting with a man Lincoln identified as Edward Albee, the author of the shocking play *Who's Afraid Of Virginia Woolf.* Although they were wearing her gowns, each one carried Lorenso's label. She picked at the food on her plate, wondering if the $500 Lincoln had paid for their tickets could have possibly been rewarded with a more unappreciative appetite. Periodically she fingered the long, slim evening bag holding the sheet of paper she so carefully concealed inside.

For days Valli had planned her move. When the script for the annual Winter Ball fashion show to benefit the Metropolitan Opera had been submitted to be coordinated with the dresses being shown by Lorenso, Valli had taken it to a secretarial service and had a copy made. For the next few days she had edited the copy and had it reproduced by the same secretarial service and tucked it away. Before she had been uncertain as to how she would accomplish her goal, but finally she had found a way.

A runway had been built to extend between the dinner tables out into the center of the ballroom. As the dinner progressed toward its conclusion, Valli excused herself to go to

120

the powder room. Instead she moved backstage, skirting the models and the dressing room until she reached the celebrity opera soprano who would introduce the gowns from a podium beside the runway.

"Good evening, Ingrid," Valli said, catching the woman's attention.

"Oh, Valli. Isn't the turn-out wonderful, and don't you look lovely!"

"Yes, the crowd is very festive tonight. I'm sure that it's going to be a financial success. I've brought a new sheet to be inserted in the Lorenso Fashions' portion of the show."

"Oh, dear." The soprano's voice fell. "I've already rehearsed the copy as it was."

"Don't worry," Valli added quickly. The last thing she wanted to do was call attention to the changes. "We've simply changed a few words, nothing major. You probably won't even notice the difference." She held out the copy and waited for Ingrid to replace the old copy with her altered version.

"Don't tell Lorenso," she cautioned as she breathed a sigh of relief and tucked the old copy in her bag. "You know what an old fuss-budget he is if he gets upset before show time. By the way, we have an absolutely heavenly number in the show that would be perfect for your hair and coloring. See what you think about number three when it comes out. It would be just divine on you."

"All right. Oh, my goodness—that's my cue. I'm more nervous about this than I was singing *Aida*."

As the lights dimmed and the music began Valli slid back into her seat, her heart pounding erratically as the first model strode rapidly down the runway.

The audience's applause after her first three offerings supported her thoughts. Two of the five presentations were miniskirts with matching long jackets, brightly patterned leotards, and white calf-high boots. The third was a pair of tunic-topped trousers. All in white, the accents were in reds and silvers with fanciful jewelry by David Webb. Each model sported what was now considered to be Valli's personal trademark, the five-point haircut given to her by Sassoon.

The fourth ensemble was a winter-white geometrically cut knit outfit, with an ultra-short skirt and small vest over an all-knit cat suit of the same color. The model wore Mary Janes, giving her the appearance of a space-age schoolgirl. But when the last model stepped into the light, a collective gasp swept the audience. The model's body stocking gave her the appearance of total nudity beneath a see-through shimmering silvery fabric that clung to her body as she moved. Her face had been made up by Pablo, the Italian wunderkind: A transparent dusting of silver sparkles was topped off with geometric ice-blue eye paint.

After the audience had a moment to accept the vision of ice and silver, Ingrid read Valli's new copy—giving full credit for the five presentations to the outstanding young designer, Valli.

The final model paused at the exit for a moment as instructed, then disappeared into the wings in a roar of applause from the audience.

"Valli"—Lincoln turned to her with a look of pride—"I had no idea that that old fox had finally decided to give you credit for your work."

"He didn't," Valli whispered, excited and flushed with the feeling of success.

The other guests sitting at the table with Valli motioned the spotlight toward Valli, forcing her to stand. For more than a few minutes the show came to a halt while the audience showed their appreciation for Valli's original creations. She hadn't anticipated this. When the light left her and found Lorenso she could see him fighting to hold on to his control as he smiled and bowed for the public. When he moved toward Valli, taking her hand in a painful grip, she knew she'd made a dreadful mistake.

"I hope you know that you've designed your last dress under the Lorenso label," he whispered between clenched teeth.

"I hope you know that you've shown your last design by

122

Valli under the Lorenso label," she returned, trying unsuccessfully to pull her hand from his.

When the light finally moved back to the stage, Lorenso dragged Valli from the table into the alcove leading into the kitchen. "You ungrateful little bitch. I take you in and give you a job without forcing you to work your way up and you stab me in the back."

"Let me go, Lorenso. You could have acknowledged my work. I didn't ask for full credit. But, you didn't. You preferred to take all the credit. Well, you can't do that anymore. And you can't get along without me now."

"No?" He let her go. A smile curved his lips as he spoke. "Replacements are a dime a dozen, kid. There's all sorts of new talent begging to be let in. There are ten new applicants every day, just waiting for your spot. When I get through letting the other houses know that you are nothing more than a thief, devious and untrustworthy, that you stole all those designs from me and pulled off this stunt to force me into making you a partner, the only job you'll get is as a seamstress in a mattress factory. We designers stick together and you're out, Valli. Why do you suppose none of my assistants have ever gone on to make their own place in the world of fashion? You aren't the first to try to worm your way past my name, and you won't be the last." He strode off, leaving Valli trembling against the wall. She'd expected him to be angry, but nothing had prepared her for this.

Lincoln found her huddled in a dark corner, facing the fact that Lorenso was probably right. She'd forced him to give her credit, but credit wasn't enough. She had to have her own salon. She had to be one of them in order to survive. But she didn't have the backing to support her yet. She'd moved too quickly. Besides maybe he really could ruin her name, her reputation.

"What's wrong, babe? Why aren't you out there celebrating your success?"

"Oh, Linc, I just got fired." Valli threw herself in his arms, finally letting the tears fall.

"Fired? What do you mean *fired*? That doesn't make any

123

sense. Why would Lorenso fire the goose that laid the golden egg?"

"Because the goose underestimated the lack of talent of her employer. I don't think he's been designing any of the Lorenso Fashions. He's stolen them all from hopeful young designers. He already has my replacement waiting in the wings. He's done this before. He never had any intention of putting my name on anything."

"Well, you've already taken care of that, my pet. Now, dry your eyes and let's take in a few night spots. Mustn't let the world know that Valli isn't on top of it."

He was right, she told herself at Twenty-one as he led her into the exclusive horseshoe ring of tables. By the time they'd reached their favorite late-night supper club she had stopped thinking about Lorenso and given herself over to the feelings of success she'd felt earlier. Several people dropped by their table to congratulate Valli. Evidently Lorenso hadn't spread the word yet. Well, if she could do it tonight, she could do it again. And next time neither Lorenso nor anyone else would be able to claim her designs weren't hers. After Lincoln had devoured his plate of hash and she had finished picking at hers, she drained the last of her Manhattan.

"Take me home with you, Linc. I don't want to stay by myself tonight," she whispered, her voice breathless.

His apartment was decorated for Christmas. In the corner, an artificial silver tree, a foot shorter than Valli, was decorated with metallic clusters of ornaments. At the base of the tree a small light flashed red, then green, then blue and started over again.

"Want another drink?" Lincoln took her fur cape and laid it across the back of a chair. He didn't turn on the lights, and Valli didn't answer his question. When he looked up again she was standing in the flickering Christmas tree light wearing nothing but her bra, garter belt, and silver stockings.

Walking slowly toward her, Lincoln shed his own clothes until he was totally nude. When he lifted her into his arms Valli held him tightly, swallowing back the rush of bitter fear that swept over her. As though he sensed her uncertainty Lincoln began to kiss her gently, whispering loving words in her ear, words that began to filter through to her as he guided her gently to the bedroom, laid her across the bed, and buried his face against her breasts.

"I love you, Valli. I want to marry you, my darling. That old crook doesn't deserve you. I'm going to Hollywood. I've already signed a contract, and we're going into production the day after New Year's. Come with me, darling, and you'll never have to work again."

She began to squirm in resistance. Marriage? No. She couldn't leave New York, leave her career, leave. . ."No, Linc, please."

What he'd held back for so long now raged out of control, and as he parted her legs and found the warmth and moistness Valli screamed out. Suddenly it didn't seem so right, but there was no stopping. As he plunged relentlessly into her, her inner resistance melted into a rush of desire that shocked Valli into becoming more than a willing accomplice. It wasn't love. It wasn't gentle and good. Their coming together was a physical passion that they rode to a tumultuous climax, sweaty and exhausting. And Valli learned that there was lovemaking without love and that her body didn't care how it reached the pinnacle, as long as it did.

Later, Lincoln lay smoking a cigarette. The glow of the tip was the only light in the darkness. Valli lay where he'd left her, stunned and uncertain as to what had happened.

"I'm sorry, Valli. I never meant it to be like that."

She didn't respond. She couldn't tell him that she was having trouble understanding what had happened. When Steele had made love to her, it had seemed beautiful and loving. But nothing had prepared her for what it meant to reach a climax of the magnitude she'd just experienced, and she didn't want it to happen with Lincoln.

"Did you hear my proposal? At least I think I proposed. Somewhere, in my pants pocket, wherever my pants are, I have a ring. I bought it first—for your Christmas present.

125

Then—" he hesitated, "I was afraid you'd say no so I went out and bought the coat to give you in case you turned me down."

"I can't marry you, Linc. I don't love you." Valli whispered quickly.

Lincoln seemed to anticipate her answer. "After what happened tonight, I think we could both live with that. I love you, Valli. You need me. Come to Los Angeles with me, and I'll make you happy." He stubbed out the cigarette and lay in the darkness waiting.

Valli listened to his breathing for a moment, then sat up on the side of the bed. "Please understand, Linc. You're right. What we just shared was special. You're special and if I were looking for a husband, I'd say yes. But, I'm not the kind of woman for you. I'm ambitious, selfish and. . ." She searched for the right word. "I'm driven." She stood up and put on her underclothes. "I'm going to be somebody, Lincoln, and I have to do it on my own. Thank you for the offer, but I can't accept your ring."

"It's Steele, isn't it?"

"Yes. In a way it's Steele. But it's also me."

"Does he know?"

"No. I'll miss you, Linc," she said more softly.

"You know he'll hurt you, Valli. Oh, he won't mean to, but he's wrong for you, and someday you'll be sorry."

"You're probably right, but that doesn't change anything. If I went with you you'd always know you were second choice, and I can't do that to you. I care too much."

She paused in the darkness and looked back at the figure on the bed, knowing that she'd lost something she might never find again.

"If you ever need me, Valli, I'll be there for you." She wasn't sure, but she thought she heard tears in his voice.

Valli whirled around, opened the bedroom door, went down the steps into the living room. She knelt and picked up the white dress she'd dropped so carelessly on the floor just a few hours before and stepped back into it. Her purse was on the table beside the door. At the last minute she paused and picked up the fur, remembering Lincoln's words. He had wanted her to have it even if she turned down his offer of marriage. She had. She was sure she wasn't making a mistake, but it hurt nonetheless. First she'd lost Court, then Noel, and now Lincoln.

Valli let herself into the apartment and kicked off her shoes, listening intently to the silence as she gauged the feel of the apartment.

Steele was there. She could feel his presence. Running to his room, Valli knocked lightly on the closed door.

"Come in."

He was standing, naked, by the window looking down into the street and smoking a joint. She'd never seen Steele smoking marijuana before, but it didn't surprise her. His silence and lack of interest in her entrance did.

"What's wrong, Steele?"

He didn't answer. Only the movement of his hand, sliding absently up and down the hemmed edge of the curtain, gave away his inner tension.

She tried again. "Steele, what's happened?"

"I'm ruined, Valli. My career is over. I'll never act on the stage again."

"You're on the stage now, aren't you?" Valli stepped inside the room and moved quietly to Steele's side.

"Tonight was my last performance."

Something about his monotone voice and defeated stance began to frighten Valli. Something had happened, something that had rocked Steele and sucked the life from him. He wasn't even reaching out for help. She wished Noel were there. He'd know how to handle Steele. But Noel was in Boston with his parents, and Steele was here with her.

"I might as well be dead." His voice was flat, expressionless.

He was serious. Valli began to search her mind for some way to reach him. Always before, no matter how bad the situation, he'd been ready to let her straighten things out. Finally she gave up and just told him about herself. "I don't

127

know what happened to you tonight, but it couldn't be any worse than what happened to me."

He took another drag from the joint as though she weren't even there.

"Steele, damn you! For once in your life, listen to me. *I* have a problem. I need help. You owe it to me, Steele Colton. Lorenso fired me. Fired me, Steele! Do you hear me!" She began to beat on his bare back, letting the tears fall and her voice rise hysterically. "Oh, Steele, listen to me, or so help me God, I'll kill myself before you've even figured out a way to do it."

Her outburst had started out as a way to get through to him, but as she began to cry and flail out at the silent man she realized that everything she was saying was true. She'd held back her fears and frustrations for so long because everybody expected her to be tough and strong, but she wasn't. She needed somebody, too, and for once in his life Steele was going to be there for *her.*

He turned around, recognition slowly dawning as her words cut through the hazy fog. Dropping the joint into an ashtray, he placed his hands on her shoulders. "That asshole fired you?"

"Yes. I did a stupid thing, and he fired me."

"You never did a stupid thing in your life."

"Well, there's always a first time," she wailed. "I substituted new copy for the show and had the announcer give me credit for my designs. I was a hit, Steele. They loved my clothes. New York City, half of Hollywood, and part of the rest of the world saw my clothes tonight and they knew that I did them. But Lorenso fired me."

He didn't understand. "So? Every firm in New York will be ready to hire you tomorrow."

"No. Lorenso fixed that. He's telling them that I stole the designs from him, along with the credit. He's turned them against me, Steele. They'll be afraid to take a chance. I'm ruined."

"I'm sorry, Valli." Steele pulled her into his arms and held her close, caressing her shoulders and the back of her neck with a desperation that communicated itself to Valli's body. She felt her nipples harden and the heat between her legs.

"Oh, Steele," she whispered urgently. "Please make love to me. I need you. I need to be close to you, to have you inside me." She pulled herself away and slipped out of her dress, leaving it and her underwear in a heap at her feet until she was nude, too.

"Valli, I can't." Steele turned, walked around, and sat down on the other side of the bed facing away from her. "You don't know what I've done. You'll hate me. Everyone will hate me."

Valli knelt on the bed and moved behind him, massaging the muscles in his neck and down his back, rubbing herself against him as she nuzzled his ear and the side of his chin with her lips.

"Lie down, Steele. Forget what happened for now. I love you. I'll make you want me."

Obediently he complied, closing his eyes and lying back in the semi-darkness as she'd directed. With an instinct born of her own need, Valli began her assault on Steele's body. With her hands and her lips she touched, kissed, and tasted every part of him beginning at his face and traveling down.

When he reached out to guide her lips she followed his directions, taking his erection into her mouth. She felt his gasp and the throb of him and knew that she'd finally reached him. When he began to arch himself against her she pulled back and swung her body over him, spearing herself with the huge organ. He was big and she was tiny, but she felt herself opening up and he filled every part of her with a white-hot heat that began to culminate in an explosion greater than anything she'd every expected. The moaning and cries she was hearing were her own. And then she felt him stiffen and groan, and he became still beneath her.

Valli slid down beside him, laying her head in the crook of his arm, and waited. Sooner or later he'd tell her what had happened. He always did. Just as she'd almost given up, she heard him swallow.

"I was with a man tonight, Valli, before I came home. I

129

went home with him after the show. It wasn't the first time, of course. But then you know that.''

''Yes,'' she acknowledged. She didn't want to hear it, but she knew that if she were to ever really be close to Steele he had to know that she wouldn't condemn him. ''I don't understand, but I care about you, Steele, and I'll try not to judge you.''

''He's a director, not my director. At the moment he isn't working, but he's one of the best, and he likes me, Valli.''

''Everybody likes you, Steele.'' She didn't understand Steele's desire to have everyone like him, but she knew that it was a deep-seated need that drove him.

''Yes, but this man could make me a star. He knows all the right people, travels in all the right circles, and he's got more money and power than you and I ever dreamed of. He's taken me places and bought me things, and I've been with him now for nearly a month. Do you understand what I mean?''

''Yes.'' She understood too well. She understood that the man had been buying Steele's trust and affection with toys and things. She reached across his chest and held him, feeling the moisture of their coming together still wet between her legs. ''What happened?''

''It was wonderful. At least I thought it was. He showed me new things, and I pleased him—I know I did.'' Steele's voice dropped into a low whisper as though he were talking only to himself.

Valli slid back from him and lay quietly for a moment, feeling her body cool away from him. She didn't know what to say. ''It felt good being close, didn't it, Steele? And now we're apart, and my body doesn't like it. My body is shivering. It wants your body close again. Do you feel it, too?''

He shifted in bed, turning toward her. ''Yes. I like being close to you, Valli. I like the way you make me feel.''

''Then come back to me, Steele.'' Valli opened her arms and he came willingly into them, laying his head across her breast, his lips a hair's breadth away from one nipple. This time his leg draped across her, and she felt him limp against her hip, warm and damp. "Now, tell me what happened."

"He took pictures, Valli. I didn't know what he was doing until the door opened and another man came in, a man I didn't know. He wanted me to make love to him, too."

"And did you?"

"God, no. I didn't even know that man. I couldn't do anything. I went all cold and limp, and they laughed at me. I couldn't do anything. Valli, do you know how that made me feel? I couldn't do it."

"I think you reacted the way any—normal—man would have acted, Steele. You liked the director, and you were showing affection. The other man didn't mean anything to you, and you aren't some kind of prostitute."

"That's what I tried to tell him," Steele said with the hint of a sob in his voice. His hand crept across Valli's body and grasped the other breast, holding it like a security blanket as he rubbed his cheek against her body. "And then he told me that if I didn't do it he'd show the photos to every director in New York. He said that nobody would let a fairy have a leading role on Broadway. He said that I'd be finished, they'd see to it."

"Oh, Steele. The bastards."

"I tried, Valli," he said in a tight little voice. "I tried, but I couldn't do it. I ran away. I'm ruined."

"Steele. . ."

"I'll never work again."

She felt moisture on his cheek. His grip on her breast was painful, and she knew he wouldn't hear her. She had to quiet him. Remembering the last time they'd made love, she turned slightly and with her hand she fed her other breast into his mouth. For a second he resisted, then took it eagerly. For a while there was nothing but the sound of his suckling, then slowly but surely she felt the swell against her hip.

This time it was Steele who crawled over Valli and entered her. It was Steele whose body responded with an urgency that erased the ugly pictures that had been engraved in his mind and swept him into a noisy, surprising

131

release before he collapsed against her and slept.

Dawn crept through the crack in the drapes over Steele's window as Valli made her plans. She didn't know how yet, she only knew what and where.

"Valli, I'm sorry. I've been drinking and smoking hashish for the last two days. I'm not sure what I said or what we've done." Steele was sitting at the table, trying desperately not to look at Valli.

"Steele, cut the crap. You know what you told me, and you know what happened. We've spent most of the last two days in bed. You and me, Steele. We've made love every way I've ever heard of and some new ways, too, and you've come back from the dead. If we're going to get out of this mess and make you a star, we've got to start being honest with each other."

Steele was startled by this new side of Valli.

"Make me a star?"

He hadn't heard another word she'd said. Well, maybe that was better. "Yes, Steele, we're going to make you a star. And while we're about it, we're going to make me one, too."

"How? You must know that those men are powerful enough to see that those photos are released. I'll have to go back and try to make them give me another chance."

"Absolutely not! Steele Colton doesn't make love to anybody unless he wants to, and from now on the only person in his bed is me," Valli said, as much to convince herself as Steele. "I told you, Steele—honesty. You can't be a star and fool around with men. Sooner or later it'll hit the papers, and that will really be the end. I'll take care of your body, Steele. I'll do whatever it is that satisfies you."

Now Steele looked at Valli as if she'd lost her mind. "I see, and just how do you plan to make miracles happen?" His sarcasm was cutting.

"Don't be an ass." Valli poured coffee for the two of them and sat down. "Steele, that old fart can't release any photos. He's on the film, too," she said triumphantly.

"You're right." He looked at Valli with wonder. "I don't

132

know why I didn't think of that. I'll just go on doing what I'm doing and tell them to. . ."

". . .go to the grass and eat mullet," Valli finished.

"What the hell does that mean?"

"I don't know. Granny always said it." Valli waved off his next question. "What we're going to do, Steele, is go to Hollywood. We're going to make you a movie star. You're talented all right, but your most obvious talent is your looks. Every woman in America will come in her pants looking at you." She was startled by her own language.

"Valli, just because you and I. . .I mean really, now. There's no way I can possibly service every woman in America." He grinned and Valli knew that he was coming back to life.

"You'd damn well better not, either. I don't expect you to go from men to women, Steele Colton. I said I was going to make you a star, and I will. But I also said that I was going to be the only one in your bed and I meant that, too. Go get dressed. We're going to go out and find the biggest turkey in the Village."

"Turkey? Are you cracking up?"

"Turkey," she said happily. "Don't you remember, Steele? It's Christmas. And if it hasn't melted, there's a brand-new white world outside waiting for us."

As they stepped out into the bright ermine-covered world, Steele stopped and in the fresh snow beside the walk, drew a large heart. Inside he wrote "Steele loves Valli" and turned to Valli flashing that big smile that melted her heart. A single snowflake fell and hung in the blackness of his hair.

The enormity of what she'd promised boggled her mind, but she was practical enough to know that they were about to take a desperate gamble, a gamble that might not work. She looked at Steele, and her mind said, "He doesn't love you, Valli." She looked at the heart, already melting in the snow, and she knew that what she'd envisioned was just as fragile. But for this one moment, in her heart the sleigh bells rang.

133

PART
TWO

CHAPTER TEN

Driving down Sunset Boulevard in her secondhand red Volkswagen Beetle, Valli accelerated past the traffic. She had an appointment—ten minutes ago, to be exact—with Asa Winslow, Lincoln Maxwell's agent, and she was already hopelessly lost. Try as hard as she could, after nearly six months in Los Angeles she still didn't know her way around. To make matters worse, she had gotten a late start because the delivery she had been expecting had not arrived—and she wasn't about to trust this package to anyone else. Finally, two men had shown up and unloaded the long, oblong parcel; it was the silver-and-gold sign for her new boutique, VALLI'S. It was perfect.

While Steele grudgingly supervised the placement, she had run off for a "hair appointment." Hopefully if the meeting went as planned, she'd be able to tell Steele the truth when she got home and at last remove some of the despair in his eyes. And if all went well, she would be ready to open her boutique in only two weeks. Then she would be able to start making money, instead of spending it at the alarming rate she had been.

At last she was there. She pulled up and parked the car in front of a small Spanish-style office building, resplendent in blooming pink flowers and vines. She wasn't sure she'd ever get used to the pink buildings, palm trees, and vivid blue skies.

Taking a deep breath, she opened the front door. The receptionist's desk was vacant.

"Hello?"

"Hello. Valli, is it? Come on in." She hesitated briefly before bypassing the reception area and following the sound of the voice into an office that appeared to be more of a sunroom than a place of business. "Mr. Winslow?"

"Yes. I'm Asa Winslow. And you're Valli, right? Recognized the accent. Linc warned me about that, but he didn't tell me you were such a doll."

Asa Winslow was, to Valli, typically Californian. Tall, slender, and deeply tanned, he would be considered attractive except for a slightly receding chin which he tried to conceal with a beard. Blue-eyed and blond, he wore a tapered white jacket over a pale blue shirt, gray trousers, and white leather basket-weave shoes.

He walked around and around Valli several times as though he were sizing her up for a role, then took her hand and led her through a second door.

"This is a lovely office, Mr. Winslow. So many plants," Valli said brightly. Damn, she was nervous. "You should see the apartment where Steele—" She broke off. This would never do. She was chattering nervously like some ignorant schoolgirl. This man was Steele's ticket, and she'd better not blow this chance.

"Call me Asa. I know all about Steele. And I know that you wouldn't come to me in his place unless you were making the decisions. That's fine. I told Linc last night that I'd be glad to help you out, and I meant it."

"I know, but I feel so bad for trading on my friendship with Lincoln. I don't know what we expected, but we didn't realize that it would be so difficult for Steele to make contacts."

138

"Oh, I'm sure that we can work out something." He ran his finger up Valli's arm around the collar of her dress and down the *V* to the top button. "Nice dress. Did you design it?"

"Yes. Linc must have told you. I'm opening a boutique off Rodeo Drive."

Asa Winslow's finger began a slow, questioning examination along the top of her breasts, feathered across the buttons, and circled a nipple, bringing an immediate hardening response that was obvious even beneath the fabric of her dress. She heard her own gasp, and she felt the answering shiver of anticipation.

"I'm sorry, Mr. Winslow," she whispered hoarsely. "I shouldn't have come here. I'd better leave."

"No!" Asa reached out and caught Valli's arm. "Don't be foolish. Let me see if I can explain. Out here everything is a trade-off, you know. Linc gives up a role in *The Sound of Music* to the nephew of the casting director for Metro. In return, I cast Linc in a movie. Now, you want something I can do for you, and if you're smart you can exchange something you have for favors from me. Understood?"

"Yes." Valli had allowed the man to direct her steps while she'd listened to his soliloquy. Now she realized she was in his bedroom. She looked around, comprehending what he was saying. She knew what he wanted. He wanted her, and in exchange he'd help Steele. Cold, hard facts that she either understood or accepted—or rejected. It was up to her. He released her arm and waited.

They'd been in Los Angeles for six months now. Without a job, Steele's spirits were low, alternating between despair and anger. He was beginning to blame Valli for the move. After all, he could have stayed in New York, with a job on Broadway.

The cost of setting up the boutique had been tremendous. Valli had come to Los Angeles with a substantial savings account, bolstered by the unexpected "loan" Court had secured for her from an English businessman. But now they only had a couple of hundred dollars left, certainly not

139

enough to pay the next month's rent or a salary for help in the store. And there were outstanding bills to seamstresses, delivery men, tradesman—not to mention Steele's extravagant purchases at department stores. Let's face it, Valli, she thought to herself, if Steele doesn't get a job soon, you might end up in debtor's prison.

She had no choice. Unbuttoning her dress swiftly, Valli stepped out of it and faced Asa, completely nude.

"Good," he said with a nod of approval. "I like a woman who knows what she wants and what it takes to get it."

She thought that it wouldn't be easy, but she cooperated, giving Asa Winslow a lesson in the unexpected. Asa Winslow was not only skilled, but surprisingly tender. He never knew that she was acting on sheer instinct and determination. If she was earning a beginning for Steele, he'd start at the top.

Valli stopped several times on the way home, picking up Dungeness crab and sourdough French bread, a bottle of Fetzer fumé blanc, Telamé jack cheese, and finally, a tin of Beluga caviar that cost more than all the rest put together. Steele would be so happy. He was finally going to get his chance. They'd celebrate with a California-style feast, and tonight he'd make love to her, and everything would be as she'd envisioned it.

They were living in an apartment above the boutique. A Beverly Hills address but definitely not a Beverly Hills–style residence. She paused to look at the new sign, with a grin of satisfaction, before going in.

"Steele? Steele." The sound of her voice echoed through the salon. He wasn't here. She could tell without looking that he was gone. Valli looked at her watch. It was early yet. He had probably gone out for a walk. After putting away her purchases, she draped a sheet across the table and arranged the silverware, fresh flowers, and candles. Next she straightened the bedcovers where Steele had lain earlier, took a long hot bath and slipped into her sexiest negligee. Arranging herself on the bed she lay back to wait. He'd be here soon, she told herself as she waited and waited and waited.

The clock read 3 A.M. when she finally heard his uncertain step on the stairs below. Sitting up quickly, Valli pulled on her robe and walked through the bedroom door into the half-empty apartment.

Steele was standing openmouthed, staring at the burned-down candles and flowers.

"Valli?" Steele turned toward her and lifted his arm in empty apology. "I'm sorry, love. I went down to the pub to have a drink, and one thing led to another. I'm sorry, Val." By now he saw what she was wearing and realized that he'd made a grave error. He eyes fell, and his lower lip began to tremble. "Oh, Val, I didn't mean for this to happen. I swear I didn't." He stumbled toward her and put both arms around her.

"Come to bed, darling. Don't worry." She helped him into the bedroom and began to undress him tenderly.

She kissed him and rubbed away her own fears as she began to talk. "It doesn't matter, Steele. Listen, I've got great news. I've arranged an appointment for you in the morning with Asa Winslow."

"Asa Winslow?" Steele opened his eyes in disbelief. "The Asa Winslow who represents. . ."

"Yes, darling." Valli stood up and removed her gown. "He has a movie in mind for you. You're going to make a movie, Steele Colton." She laughed as she slid into bed and began to kiss his body. She took his hands and placed them on her so that as she began to arouse him he responded by caressing her. By the time she took him into her mouth he was stiff and undulating beneath her.

"Oh, Valli, Ummmmm. God, you're going to make me come. Uhhhh. . .Uhhhh. . ." And he released his fluids into her with a cry of joy that filled her completely. She'd satisfied him, and that was all that mattered.

Steele took her into his arms and began to talk. For nearly an hour they discussed the coming day and the future. With every caress, he fed Valli's need and she nearly cried out in pure frustration when he finally fell asleep, his head on her

141

chest.

The faint touch of dawn colored the sky when Valli finally slid out of bed and onto the tiny second-story balcony that looked out over Beverly Hills. The soft beauty of the California dawn and the absolute stillness in the streets below were at odds with her jumbled emotions. She was still keyed up, aroused and frustrated. Only when she saw a blue Volkswagen pull to a stop and a red head emerge from the window did she realize that she was stark naked. Embarrassed, she returned to bed. She had managed to avoid thoughts of the afternoon with Asa Winslow. She felt guilty, not for what she'd done, but because part of her hadn't hated it—a coupling with no love, no emotional passion, no meaning.

The next time she got up, she followed Steele downstairs to see him off for his appointment with Asa Winslow. Steele was keyed up but confident. This time *he* returned with the fixings for a feast, and they celebrated by making love on the plushly carpeted floor of Valli's boutique.

The next week Steele landed a small but important part in a movie. Soon afterward, an invitation to a party being given by the producer, Hal Wallis arrived. Steele and Valli were on their way.

To say that Steele liked being in Hollywood was an understatement. Since he'd found work he was absolutely smitten with the city and its people. After the first minor part, Universal Studios took him in hand and started grooming him for stardom.

Tonight, Valli looked at him and smiled in appreciation. These last ten months, he had seemed truly happy, and that delighted her.

"Steele, darling, Asa says John Huston will be at the party. He's about to cast a movie that has a perfect part for you."

"Asa? When did you see him?"

"Today. He brought Monica Coleman into the boutique. She bought a dress for the party. If everything goes well, Asa thinks this dress and this party might get me the design contract on her new movie." Valli smiled at Steele, thrilled at

142

the prospect of embarking on a new phase of her own career.

"Good. Then maybe we can move out of this apartment." Steele retied his tie and refolded the red silk handkerchief Valli had provided. He was on edge and trying not to show it. Grimacing at his unsuccessful effort, she deftly redid both.

"Maybe." Valli looked around the small apartment. She'd been happy here. She was fond of the three small rooms. For the first time in her life she felt truly at home. Leaving was something she didn't want to contemplate. She and Steele had lived here for more than six months, almost as husband and wife. Here they were committed to each other and insulated from the world. Well, as insulated as they could be in Los Angeles.

"What do you think, darling? Come and stand beside me and let's see how we look."

Steele looked down at her and smiled. The deep-red silk sequined dress she wore clung to her softly, whispering a sassy invitation when she moved.

"You look sexy as hell." Steele placed his hands on her shoulders and turned her to face him. Bending down he touched a gentle kiss to her lips.

Valli closed her eyes and felt a flame ignite inside her. Moving into his arms, she waited for Steele to deepen his kiss. When he didn't, she opened her eyes with resignation.

Drawing back, she peered at their reflection. She'd selected Steele's black tux with the red tie and handkerchief to complement her dress. With their dark hair, they both reeked of fire and sensuality.

Steele grinned, and she felt an unexpected weakness in her knees as she always did.

"I'd say that we're going to make quite a splash. Old John Huston will be panting around you all evening if what I hear is true."

"What do you hear?" Valli reached for her bag and flipped out the lights.

"Oh, just that he likes the ladies."

143

"And I hear the ladies like him, too."

"Well, if it gets me a part in his next movie I don't care if you show him your etchings," Steele said with a flippant tone in his voice as he followed Valli outside to their Rolls. Steele had insisted on leasing it for the evening, refusing to show up in a Volkswagen. After all, in Hollywood the appearance of success begat success.

Valli bit back the desire to tell him that she'd already done enough to launch his career. She wondered how much he suspected and decided that he probably didn't know. Right now New York and Steele's crisis seemed a million years ago. Valli intended to keep it that way.

"Remember, Steele," she cautioned, "a part for you isn't the only thing we're going for. I'm also out to get the design contract for the movie. The boutique pays its way, but Valli Originals isn't launched yet."

"You're just scared, Valli." Steele braked the car at a traffic light, then eased past a restored Stutz Bearcat. "Between Lincoln Maxwell and Asa Winslow, half the stars in Beverly Hills have already been to VALLI'S We're on a roll, babe. Quit being such a pessimist."

He was right. VALLI'S was doing very well. Her connections to the film industry had ensured the right clientele, and news of her New York "treachery" had never filtered out to the West Coast. They could afford to move to a better address.

Steele found the Hollywood Hills address with ease, pulled the Rolls into the long curved drive, and handed the keys with a flourish to one of the red-jacketed attendants. Assuming his place in the spotlight, Steele took Valli's arm and escorted her inside, as though he were onstage.

For over an hour they moved from one group to another. Valli felt as though she were on a carousel. Steele knew a great many more people than she realized. Spotting someone else he knew, Steele steered her toward a small knot of people standing by the bar.

"Good evening, sir. Nice to see you." He nodded at a portly silver-haired man who seemed momentarily nonplussed at Steele's greeting. "Have you met my. . .friend Valli?"

At the silent shake of the man's head, Steele plunged on, oozing charm. "If you don't know her name now, you will when you get your wife's bills next month. Valli designed Monica's dress for this evening."

Valli understood now. This was Monica Coleman's husband, Richard Cobel—who with two Oscar winners in the last four years just happened to be producing and directing her film. He was the man who would get her the contract. He didn't appear to recognize Steele, but Valli's name caught his attention, and he turned to her with a smile.

"Of course, Valli. My dear, you don't have a drink. Here, let me."

He took Valli's arm, turning her neatly away from Steele with an intimate leer as he signaled to the bartender. "What would you like, my dear?"

"A ginger ale, please." Valli tried to turn around, wishing that Steele had picked a different group of people to invade, but she knew that she needed this contact—and probably Steele did, too.

"Very sensible, my dear. Never did have much respect for empty-headed little ditzes who mix pleasure with business."

Valli took her drink and lifted an eyebrow in surprise. "What do you mean 'mix pleasure with business'? Aren't we here to have a good time?"

"Maybe, depends on what you consider a good time. Now me, I have the very best times when my business deals are conducted satisfactorily." He gazed directly at her, gauging her with the acuity of one talented in the art of evaluating people quickly. "I suspect that you and that cardboard hero escorting you are here for one thing, too. He'll make the women's hearts flutter and their pussies juicy. And you? What will you do?"

Valli gasped. He was both vulgar and tactless, and as he drew her closer the hand that directed her movement slid dangerously low. She felt his fingertips stroke the swell of

145

her breasts as he awaited her response. His smirk effectively told her that he never got slapped and didn't expect to this time.

"I'm not sure what you mean." Valli's voice was much steadier than her pulse, and her accent deepened in an attempt to sound truly naive. Repulsed by his invitation, she struggled to rein in her anger. She wasn't quite sure how she should act. She couldn't risk offending him, but she damn sure wasn't going to sleep with this lech.

"Oh, I think you do," he answered. "You're built for loving, doll, and I appreciate any woman who knows how to market her skills."

"And, I'm a woman," Valli whispered without a hint of anger in her voice, "who knows what kind of price to set for them." She lifted her chin, turned, and slid gracefully by the director, stopping only to turn back and look at him boldly for a minute. She was furious but knew she couldn't afford to show it. She smiled.

Suddenly, Steele appeared out of nowhere. "I can't believe he went for you. The hottest producer in Hollywood has the hots for my woman." Steele slid an arm around her and hugged her gleefully as he leaned down to hear her reply. "What'd he say?"

"He wants to screw me, Steele. If I play my cards right I can probably get the costume design for his movie and a part for you as well. Is that what you wanted to hear?" Valli hissed as she pulled back and wove her way through the crowd of people and out the sliding glass door onto a patio. She didn't turn back to see Steele's quizzical look.

At the end of the patio, steps led up to a deck that wrapped around the second floor of the house. As Valli climbed the steps she couldn't think clearly. She should be pleased that they were even invited to such a star-studded gathering; that she was able to make contacts that would secure Steele's future as well as her own. But the methods were cheap and shoddy. Work ought to earn its own rewards. Gazing over the patio below she caught back a sob as she realized that she wasn't alone.

146

"Valli?"

"Linc? What are you doing up here?"

"Same thing you are, I bet. Escaping from all those phonies down there."

"Oh, Linc, what are we doing here? I don't understand all these people and their. . ." She cut herself off as she moved closer to Lincoln.

"What's wrong, Valli?" Lincoln pitched the cigarette he'd been smoking out into the night and put his arm around her shoulder.

"Oh, I don't know." She hesitated, hardly able to find the words to describe her experience. "I've just met Monica Coleman's husband."

"Richard Cobel? Well, you've met the cream of the crop so far as who's important in Hollywood at the moment. What did he do, rip off your clothes. . .?"

"Go ahead, Lincoln, say it. . . rip off my clothes and screw me."

Lincoln was surprised and concerned about the anger in her voice. As she stepped out of his arms and turned to gaze out over the hills, she gripped the rail for support. "Oh, Lincoln. I'm not sure I belong here. I'm not sure I'm tough enough to be successful here."

"You may not belong here, but you're tough enough, my love. You're probably tougher than Steele; you're probably tougher than me."

"No, I'm not, Linc." She lifted her head and faced him, her eyes shining with tears. "I just want someone to hold me and look out for me. . . Is that so hard to find?"

"Not if you're looking in the right place." Lincoln leaned down and kissed her, knowing as he was doing so that the kiss she returned so passionately wasn't a sign of love. All the pent up rage and emotion she'd held in so tightly exploded, and she desperately pulled him closer. He could barely contain his feelings.

His fingers slid beneath the strapless top and encountered bare skin, hot to the touch and rippling beneath his hands.

"God, Valli. You're burning up. Are you sick?"

147

"I'm burning up from desire, need. Oh, Linc, I'm so tired of scheming and bargaining. Everybody is for sale and it seems that I'm at the top of the list. I want something for me. I want. . ."

"Let's get out of here, love, and I'll give you what you want."

Why, she thought crazily, when I love Steele as I do, why can't he make me feel like this? With Steele she always felt in charge, responsible for their passion and their reaching a climax. More and more often she took care of herself after Steele slept. But it wasn't the same. She couldn't arouse her body to the pitch it had reached just from Lincoln's touch. How could love and sex be so separate? Even as he kissed her, she knew that this wasn't love. She didn't love him as she loved Steele.

"Oh, Lincoln, we can't. This isn't right. I'd better get back to the party. I don't want Steele to be. . .upset."

Lincoln took a deep breath and pulled away, looking straight into her eyes. She looked away, afraid that he might read there the intensity of her aroused state.

"I'll go on downstairs. You wait a minute and then come. We wouldn't want anyone to think that we'd been. . ."

"We haven't been, Valli," Lincoln said soberly, "but sooner or later we're going to. You need me, and I want you."

"But Steele loves me, and we're going to make this relationship work." Oh, God, if only she were as confident as she sounded.

She left Lincoln standing on the deck and strode purposefully through the doors and down the hallway, trying to close her ears to the sounds of those others inside the bedrooms who hadn't been as reluctant as she. Valli hurried toward the sounds of the Beatles' "Norwegian Wood."

Pausing midway down the steps, she scanned the room for Steele and spotted him with his arm around a curvacious blonde in a tight black dress slit up the side to mid-thigh. Fishnet hose and stiletto heels made her almost as tall as Steele, and she leaned against him with an open invitation on her face.

148

Valli made her way toward him, touching Steele on the shoulder from behind. When he turned and found her behind him, he rewarded her with a gorgeous smile of relief.

"Valli! Where've you been?"

Sliding between Steele and the blonde, Valli linked her hand with his and gave him a quick kiss. "Darling, I've been talking to Lincoln. Have you seen him?"

"No, but I do want to say hello."

"Do excuse us." Valli smiled at the blonde and turned Steele neatly away and into the crowd.

"Thanks, Val, I thought she was going to rape me right there on the floor."

"You could always refuse." Valli smiled, but the words she spoke under her breath were less cordial. "Have we circulated long enough, Steele? I'm ready to go."

"Go? But it's barely midnight. I really want to talk to Richard Cobel."

Valli stopped and turned slowly toward Steele. "I really don't care." Her words were fierce.

"But I thought you wanted to be the costume designer for Cobel's movie." Steele was genuinely puzzled.

"I've changed my mind, Steele. I'm beginning to wonder if coming here was the right thing, after all. Maybe I'd be better off staying in the boutique and designing dresses."

"And me? What do you expect me to do? Stand there and hand you the pins?" Deep anger flashed in Steele's eyes, turning them from brandy to the color of coal. "You may not need this kind of exposure, Valley Ray Turner, but I do. I haven't even seen Huston yet. If you want to leave, go right ahead. I'll find a way home."

"Never mind, Steele. I'll take a cab." Valli turned and plunged into the crowd, leaving Steele standing there.

Outside the house she stood on the huge terrazzo patio inhaling the cool night air and wondering how she expected to carry out her threat. This wasn't New York, there weren't any cabs unless they were called. How could she have let this happen? She'd have to learn to control her temper. Steele didn't need to be left in there alone, not with the blond rapist on the loose. Maybe if she went back . . .

"Valli? I'm sorry." A figure emerged from the shadows.

"Steele?"

He took her in his arms and held her, and Valli felt herself go weak with relief. He'd come after her. He did love her. Everything would be all right.

All the way home a feeling of warmth enveloped them like a protective bubble. When they arrived at the salon, Steele parked the Rolls and follwed Valli up the narrow stairs. By the time they reached the bedroom both were nude, and when Steele took her this time he was a savage who demanded everything she had to give.

For the first time, Valli slept peacefully, and Steele stood in the window smoking as he watched the sun rise over the mountains in the distance. Later, he pulled on jogging shoes and shorts and ran for miles before he'd exhausted his body and felt he could return home.

Sunday morning was quiet and peaceful. Valli woke in a state of blissful satisfaction. Curled up like a contented cat, she lay in the silence remembering the night of passion. The same aura of warmth still hovered over the apartment.

A month later Valli signed the design contract for Monica Coleman's movie with Universal, *Darkened Dreams*. In a city where the selling of flesh was an accepted method of exchange, she had succeeded on her merit alone. For a few days, she held the world—the glittery, glitzy world of Beverly Hills and Hollywood, of film and fashion—in her hand. Nothing could stop her now.

CHAPTER ELEVEN

Pregnant.

The churning inside Valli's stomach as she drove back to the boutique made her glad that she had no appointments scheduled for the afternoon. The doctor's news that she was pregnant had shaken her more than she wanted to admit.

A baby. She couldn't have a baby—or could she? Valli considered the implications. How much of a strain would it place on her business? Not much. How much of a strain would it place on her relationship with Steele? Quite a bit—probably.

Her own pudgy, sweet-smelling baby. Valli knew nothing about babies. Unlike most teenage girls, Valli had never baby-sat.

She felt awed, reverent. The cycle of life was repeating itself. When her mother had left Valli, she had been heart-broken, but life had gone on and the years had passed. Still, for the first of those years, she had sat on the top step every evening and wished on the first star she saw, wished that her mother loved her, wished that her mother would return. But there'd only been Granny, and Granny had tried, but the void had remained—until now. This baby would have everything she had never had.

They'd marry now. Mrs. Steele Colton, Valli Colton, Valley Ray Colton. Like the high school girls back in Georgia, she practiced the sound of her new name, hugging herself slightly as she thought how proud she'd be when those old crows back in Willacoochee found out she was married to the movie star Steele Colton. More important, she was going to marry the man she loved—finally.

Striding through the showroom, she paused and stared at herself in the mirror. She didn't look any different. Her hair hung a bit longer now—as was the style. Her eyelids, artfully brushed with a silvery blue, gave her already-large blue eyes a frosty look of surprise. She'd lost weight over the last two years, and her petite figure lent itself well to the new styles. The changes in her life had been unexpected and drastic. The boutique was successful—although she missed the intense competition of the New York couturiers —and she had Steele. Now everything in their lives must change again. Steele, she'd have to tell Steele. They were going to have a child. She had no idea what he'd say. Valli prepared herself for Steele as if he were a customer she needed to impress and cajole into accepting a new style.

Though he spent less and less time in their bed, Valli had forced herself to understand that he must follow the studio's directions in escorting the starlets to Hollywood functions. He was supposed to be a handsome bachelor—a leading man. High visibility meant publicity, and publicity translated into box-office dollars. Publicity pictures and dates were arranged. They meant nothing. Besides, he had to have some friends besides Valli. She knew Steele missed Noel and Court as much as she did. They'd given him an outlet she couldn't provide. Now all that would have to stop.

She sat down and waited. Hours later Valli stood on the tiny balcony overlooking the sprawling city watching impatiently for Steele to come home. She'd hoped that tonight would be one of those rare ones when he'd head straight for home, but she'd been disappointed. She shrugged her shoulders and retied the belt of her blue bathrobe.

"You're *what*?"

Steele's voice was shot with incredulity. "God, not now, not this, just when I'm about to get the best role of my life." The anguish in Steele's voice turned into a desperation that shocked Valli with its depth. He was almost hysterical, pacing wildly back and forth.

Valli felt her heart rip. It lay for a moment in her chest and took one last flutter, as though it were a wounded bird beating its wings on the ground in the final anguish of death, and lay still.

"What about the baby, Steele? Our baby?"

He shot her a bitter look, then blinked as if he didn't understand why she was even there. "Baby? Oh, Val. I'm sorry," he managed, the look of blank horror he bestowed on her more devastating than his words.

"I'm sorry," he whispered again. When he straightened his shoulders and took her in his arms she allowed him to hold her, sagging against him in relief. But even as they held each other she knew that the embrace didn't change matters. He didn't want a baby. He didn't want her. She was no longer an aid to his career. She was a hindrance. Yet she was sure he loved her. He simply wasn't prepared for commitment—and fatherhood.

"We could get married," she ventured hesitantly. "We'll say that we've been married for months."

"Mexico," Steele whispered, his mind on alternative solutions. "Of course. You can go to Mexico and fix it." He drew back, a smile of relief washing across his face. "That's it, Val. There are doctors in Mexico who don't ask any questions. I've heard that it isn't hard. We'll go down together. . . ." Steele's voice faded away.

Fix it? He wanted her to fix the problem? Why not? She always had. She couldn't expect him to react any other way, could she? A shudder rippled through her body as she

153

thought of the reality of fixing it. She couldn't do that. Give up her baby in an even worse way than her mother had given her up? "No! I won't let anything happen to this baby."

Even in her state of anxiety Valli could tell that Steele understood the finality in her voice. She pulled herself free and looked at him. "I'm going to have this baby, Steele, with or without your help."

"I see." He looked grim—and angry. "How do you know that I'm the father, Valli? How do I know that this baby's mine?"

This couldn't be Steele talking, Valli told herself. He didn't mean the words that hurt her far worse than his suggestion that she consider an abortion. He was just desperate, striking out in the fear that he'd have to accept the responsibility he'd avoided for so long.

"We've been sleeping together for over two years, and you've never been pregnant before. For that matter, I've slept with other women, and none of them ever got knocked up. Why now? Why have you done this?"

She felt hard and cold. He was confirming her worst fears. There had been other women.

"At least you've switched from men to women," Valli lashed out. "I suppose I should feel thankful for that." Steele's expression turned from anger to guilt. At that moment she realized that in a way he did truly love her—but not enough.

Steele stared out the window for a moment before responding. "No, there aren't any men. . . . And, I'll marry you, if that's what you want."

"Steele, I . . ."

"Don't interrupt. I gotta say this now or I'll never get it out. We'll keep it a secret for now. Then later when I'm a success we can tell the world. You know that I love you. Hell, you're probably the only one I do love." He stopped his rush of words, facing her with naked honesty. "But, I don't know that I can be what you want in a husband, and you deserve better than me, Val. I've tried. God, I've tried." He dropped to the bed and hung his head.

154

"You're right, Steele. It would be wrong for us to marry. I guess I've known all along. Maybe you should get your own place for a while."

He didn't disagree. "But the baby? What will you do?"

"It's my baby, Steele, and my choice to have it. And you're right. The baby would be a bad move for your career."

"And your career, Valli? What will everyone think? How will you manage?"

"They'll just think I'm an eccentric designer. And this is Beverly Hills where anything goes, doesn't it?"

"I'll help you. As soon as I get this new movie under my belt I'll be making big bucks. And I'll look after you, Valli. You won't have to worry about a thing."

"I know you will, Steele, but I don't need it. My clientele is growing, and so is my bank account. I'll send to New York for Terrance. He'll be a big help. He's been scared to death of Lorenso for years. He'd love it out here."

"Sure, Valli." Steele willingly let Valli make the decisions. He always did, confident that whatever she said was the right direction to move. Yet, even as he packed he was subdued, and every move he made showed that he was torn between the need to go and the desire to stay.

"Valli, I . . ."

"Just go, Steele. I'll see what I can do about finding a place for you. Call me in a few days."

"That won't be necessary. I'll manage, Val. For once, I'll do it myself. Call me at the studio if you need me. I do love you, you know."

He attempted to kiss her. His lips almost caught her cheek, and then he was gone. She felt the warmth of his breath on her face, and the tingle left behind seemed to grow. As the silence swelled around her, smothering her with a thick nothingness that took away her breath, she slumped to the floor, drained and unable to move. She wondered if this was the way Granny had felt when she was dying. She sat for hours in a state of suspension.

Suddenly Valli shivered. It had been a long time since she'd felt the power, the warm glow that caught fire somewhere deep inside her and spread through her body unexpectedly. It had come back to her. Unsure that she'd made the right decision until now, she reveled in the knowledge that she was still on the right path. As a euphoric sense of well-being hovered over like a soft mist, the uncertainties disappeared. She still hurt, but she was going to be okay.

"Well, Scarlett," she whispered as she stood on the little balcony overlooking Rodeo Drive, "tomorrow is still another day."

The next day Valli spent the entire morning on the phone. A week later Terrance arrived, bringing an unexpected bonus, his friend Zack who was not only an expert cutter, but also willing to work for room and board. Both were eager to live and work in Los Angeles, the land of sunshine and stars. With Terrance to answer the phone, set up appointments, and help charm the clientele, and Zack to oversee the seamstresses, all she had to do was create. Not only did their presence lighten her workload, but they also gave Valli the kind of emotional support she needed. Their lively antics and friendship kept her mind off her problems.

Dividing her time between the boutique and her work on the movie, for the next month she was so busy that she rarely found time to think about Steele, or the child, during the day. By bedtime, she tumbled exhausted into bed and dozed off easily, sleeping more soundly than she had in years.

Terrance and Zack had left the shop to make Friday-afternoon deliveries when Valli heard the melodious tone of the doorbell. With a weary groan she ran her fingers through her hair, stretched her neck, and got up to answer.

"Valli?"

All she could see was a silhouette, as the light shone behind the figure standing in the doorway.

"Country Mouse, is that you?"

"Court?" Valli gasped in disbelief. She hadn't seen him since she'd left New York. "I can't believe it. What are you doing here?"

Holding a bunch of yellow daisies, the slim, sandy-haired

156

man standing before her in dress blues and a snappy officer's cap seemed a grown-up version of the man she'd roomed with in the Village.

"I'm still in the Navy, Val, stationed right here in the state of California. San Diego, to be specific."

"You look so. . .so. . .incredibly sexy. Your uniform is wonderful." Valli looked down at the slacks she was wearing, wrinkled and covered with short threads and fuzz. "I didn't expect anyone. I'm afraid I'm a mess."

For a moment they both waited awkwardly, looking at each other.

"Valli, this is Court, remember?" He handed her the daisies, as his face lit up with a grin. "And you're always beautiful to me."

He held out his arms, and Valli rushed willingly into them. "Oh, Court, I'm so glad to see you. You'll never know how glad I am to see you. Come on up." She linked her arm around his waist and led him up the stairs.

As they reached the top of the steps, Valli felt awkward again. She'd have to tell Court about Steele and the baby. "Thanks for the flowers, Court. This is where I live, for now. Later on after. . .I mean, I'm going to find a larger apartment soon."

"It looks like you, all warm and welcoming."

"It does?" Valli glanced around. Gradually, without realizing it, she had added little touches here and there until the apartment had taken on a personality that she'd never noticed before—her personality. Eclectic, but comfortable, the furnishings reflected her flair for dramatic color without jarring the beholder's eye. The furniture was overstuffed, with dozens of throw cushions scattered everywhere.

"Would you like some tea?" She arranged the daisies in a clay vase on the countertop.

"Tea? You're asking a sailor if he wants tea?" Court laughed and sat down on the red-and-black pin-striped couch, swinging his leg over the arm.

"I guess that does seem pretty lame," Valli admitted and sat down opposite him. "I'm afraid I don't have anything stronger. I tried to keep Steele from. . .I mean, there were times, in the beginning when everything was very difficult for Steele. . . .''

"But not anymore?"

"No." She struggled to sound enthusiastic. "He's doing very well, Court."

"And Valli seems to be doing very well, too, from the looks of your salon." Court stopped. He knew he had to cheer her up. "Are you free this afternoon?"

"As a matter of fact, I am. What do you have in mind?"

"A little bread, a little wine, and a whole lot of thee. Get your dancing shoes on, the Country Mouse is taking the sailor boy out on the town."

"Oh, Court, what fun! It's been so long since I've been out just for fun. In Beverly Hills you go to the right places for the right reasons, never just for fun."

And fun it was. They walked down Rodeo Drive, window-shopping like two children in fairyland, and then climbed into Valli's car and headed for Bel Air. Later, they dined at the Brown Derby and enjoyed after-dinner drinks at the Polo Lounge. By the time they were back on Sunset Boulevard, Valli was pleasantly high. Court was driving.

"Oh, Court, what's this?"

Court pulled up and parked the car in Westwood.

"A coffeehouse. Do you know how few coffeehouses there are in Los Angeles? I have an insatiable urge for cappucino."

Over tall glasses of dark, rich coffee with frothy whipped cream spilling over the edges of the cups, Valli finally got up the courage to tell Court about Steele's leaving and her pregnancy. "And I'm having my child, Court, so don't try to talk me out of it," she concluded. "I've got it all worked out. For the time being I'll stay over the shop. After the baby comes, I'll find a larger place and raise her all by myself. I'll hire a nanny to help."

"I see. And how do you know it's a girl?" Court hadn't appeared surprised, just a bit worried.

"Because, I can feel it. It completes the circle, and that's how it's going to be, I just know."

"Hmm, and what does Noel say about it?"

"Noel? Why would he say anything? He doesn't even know about it."

"Oh, I thought you'd seen him. He was just out here in June I think." He stopped short. Noel had already told him about the situation between Valli and Steele.

"That's funny that Noel should come and not let me know he was here. But if he and Steele, well, Steele doesn't . . .didn't say much about his activities." She and Noel were never especially close, but his visit without seeing her hurt more than she wanted to believe.

"Well, I'm probably wrong. He could have said that he was on his way out here and not made it. You know Spud, always was better with words on paper than words from his mouth. But I do know that he's kept up with Steele—and you. That's how I knew that you needed a little R and R."

"Oh? What's a little R and R?"

"Military talk for rest and relaxation after a time of heavy stress and battle. And speaking of rest, I think it's time to get you home. Expectant mothers need plenty of sleep, and it's after midnight."

"Good heavens, I had no idea." Valli stood up, feeling the room shift slightly. "I think I might still be just a little high, Court. I feel wonderful. I can't remember when I've felt so wonderful." She leaned into him as they left the coffee-house, feeling his arm slide around her in steadying comfort.

The air was warm, filled with the scent of blooming flowers. The streets were thick with automobiles, but the sidewalks were virtually empty.

"How do you like being out here, Valli?"

"I like it, Court, but I miss New York. It's rude and dirty and loud, but there's something about it that's alive. Out here everything's so perfect, so clean, but there's a different kind of power and drive. It's under the surface. It's who you are, who you've been seen with, and who you screw that's important, not what you've accomplished."

"From the looks of your boutique, though, you're doing all right."

"Yes, business is good, but it's not exactly what I want. New York is where the challenge is in my work. Someday I'm going to go back there and make the world sit up and take notice."

"After you have the baby," Court whispered as they reached the store once more.

"Maybe," Valli conceded, handing Court the key.

He opened the door and locked it behind him, still holding Valli protectively as they climbed the stairs. "Careful," Court cautioned as she stumbled slightly, her step carrying her into Court's arms again.

He hadn't intended to touch her. He'd told himself sternly to make certain that she was all right and leave as soon as possible. Once he'd seen Valli earlier in the day, all disheveled and vulnerable, he had forced himself to keep his distance—until now. Closing his eyes to the flush of warmth in her cheeks, he tried to keep his mind off what he truly wanted.

Valli raised her eyes, puzzled by the iron grip of Court's extended arms. She felt him trembling. His body seemed tense, but his eyes were hungry, and she remembered the last time she had felt like this—the first time anyone had made love to her, and it had been Court. How he'd loved her! She remembered the rush of feeling he'd given her, feelings that neither Steele nor Lincoln could achieve. She wanted Court now, tonight, and she thought he wanted her, too. For a moment she forgot her pregnancy. All that mattered was that she was with Court. There was no past; there were no feelings except those of their bodies close together. Very deliberately, just as she had the first time, she reached up and pulled his head down to meet the fire in her lips.

Court stiffened for a moment, then lost himself in the feel and taste of the woman whose memory he'd carried with him over so many miles of squalling or mirror-calm sea. Steele was a fool to have left her, and he was perhaps a fool to have come back. But he hadn't been able to resist.

160

And then, he pulled her away. Slowly reaching around her neck, he found the zipper beneath her hair. As he slid it open, the soft whispery sound crawled along his spine. He took the top of her dress and peeled it down, staring at Valli in mute wonder.

As she wiggled, the dress fell in a swirl around her feet. She stood there in a filmy satin slip for a second, before he pulled it over her shoulders and threw it into the shadows.

"Do you remember that you once asked me if your breasts were attractive?" His lips touched them lightly, leaving little spots of moisture on the filmy bra she was wearing, tiny spots that hardened with the cool touch of the air. She felt a fluttering response as his tongue touched and moved away, leaving a trail of heat behind. She breathed rapidly.

"No. Did I?"

"Yes. And you wanted to know if men liked women who had a lot of hair here?" His fingers slid down inside her panties between her legs and pressed against her without moving.

"I did?" Her voice shook, and he felt her tremble beneath him, but she held back, waiting for him to lead the way.

"You did. You were wonderfully high that night, and you wanted to sample everything. You must have tried every drink at that party, and that still wasn't enough. You wanted to touch all of life. You wanted this." He inserted his finger inside her and felt her stiffen, tightening herself around him for a moment before she moaned and moved against him.

"And, how did you answer me, Court? How do men feel about women with big tits and lots of hair?" The words came out hoarse and jerky as Valli caught her breath.

"I don't remember my answer, darling Valli. I only remember that I came in my pants just holding you, and I'm going to do the same thing again if I don't get out of them."

"Oh?" She pulled back her head and opened her eyes wide. "Please, let me undress you."

"All right, but what are you doing?"

"I'm turning on the lamp. I want to see. I don't remember much about that, that night." She walked back toward him,

161

openly without shame or embarrassment. He examined her body but could see little sign of her pregnancy. Her breasts were full, but they'd been full before. There was a soft curve at her stomach, but otherwise her body was still lush and beautiful.

"I only remember feelings, and touch, and wonderful waves of sensation." Valli unbuttoned and removed his jacket, hanging it carefully on the back of a chair. Next she slowly unbuttoned his shirt, running her fingers beneath in curious little forays of motion that set off ripples of heat. By the time she reached his belt he took her hands away, unzipped, and removed his slacks himself, kicking them away impatiently.

"And do you remembering asking me if all men were this big?"

"Oh Court, did I actually say that?" she giggled.

"Yes. I don't think you'd ever seen a man before."

"I hadn't, and I remember thinking that you took more time than I expected," she teased, running one fingertip back and forth along the length of his erection. "I remember I'd always thought that men were only interested in sticking it in right away, and you seemed to be trying to keep from doing it."

She stepped backwards against the bed, reached up, and clasped her arms around his neck, and threaded her legs around his hips. "If I remember right, you just wanted to put it between my legs, like this."

Back and forth, she rubbed against him, almost, but not quite letting him enter her. Pulling away became more difficult, and the readiness of her body to receive him grew into exquisite torture.

"I remember, you little witch," he panted, clasping her rear in his hands. "And I remember that you wouldn't let me stop until I'd done this." He pulled her body toward his, holding her buttocks until he pressed the head of his penis against her, holding her immobile for a second before plunging inside her.

"Oh, God, Court. You feel so good." She turned into a

wild creature, thrashing against him until he unclasped her legs and physically forced her to lay back on the bed, away from him.

"What's wrong, Court?"

"Wrong? Nothing. Absolutely nothing, you vixen. But I'd like this to last. I've waited too long to be burned by pure desire. Now be still. I'm going to make love to you, slow, passionate, beautiful love. Be still, you'll see."

And Valli tried. Court could tell how badly she wanted to reach out and rake his body with passion, but she lay there and let him explore every inch of her. Then she pushed him over on his back and began the same minute investigation of his body with her lips and fingers.

When at last he entered her again they'd both passed the point where they could move slowly. From the moment he slid over her she arched herself to meet him in a rush of contractions surging through her with an intensity so great that the bed seemed to vibrate beneath them.

Afterwards, lying sweaty and sated in each other's arms, they talked.

"You're an incredibly sexy woman, even more now than before, if that's possible." He cupped her breasts and ran his fingertips across her stomach and into the hair below.

"I've heard that women are the most passionate when they're pregnant. Maybe because they don't have to worry about getting pregnant anymore. That's probably a good thing, Court McCambridge, because I don't have any Cokes in the house." She laughed softly, brushing his forehead with her lips.

"Valli, I want to talk to you. You know that I care for you. I always have. Now since Steele has left you, I want to take care of you. I mean will you. . ."

"Don't, Court. I love making love with you. I need you, but I've seen what happens when one person loves and the other doesn't. It hurts too bad, Court, and. . .I don't love you the way I love Steele. I wish I could, but I refuse to hurt you. Steele will come back. He needs me to survive and, God help me, Court, I need him too."

They lay in the darkness. Court lit a cigarette and drew on it deeply as he tried to figure out some way to reach Valli. He couldn't believe she didn't love him. She was so blind, so intent on one course of action that nothing else was even a possibility. He put out the cigarette and hugged her to him. He'd wait. Someday soon she'd see where she belonged.

"How about your painting, Court? Have you sold anything?"

"Hah! You know what the world thinks about my art. It's just a silly dream. Forget it, Valli. I have. When I get out of this mess, I'm going to concentrate on tennis."

"Oh no, Court. It takes years to become recognized. I've been noticing the paintings out here, and I don't think any of them are as good as yours. You mustn't stop. I didn't understand that before, but I didn't understand anything else either. Noel said you were good, and I trust Noel's judgment. You should keep at it. Tennis is fine for recreation."

"Valli, you're good for me. You believe in me when nobody else does."

"Oh, Court, I do care for you and believe in you. I feel closer to you than Steele. Isn't that odd?" She switched the subject abruptly. "Would I really not let you stop that night?"

She reached down and found him, throwing her knee across his thighs so she lay against his hip. Between her legs she was warm, sticky and very damp. The sweet smell of their body fluids inflamed him, and as quickly as she touched him he sprang to life and wanted her again.

I'll always want her, Court thought, with a mixture of despair and joy. But what will she want, he wondered. He was afraid that she might never know.

In the weeks that followed, Valli's life settled into a curiously restful routine. Steele still called occasionally, but she wasn't ready to talk to him. Valli didn't spend much time in the boutique. Instead, she was on the set, designing costumes. Business at the boutique continued to improve as well. Noel called to tell her that he had joined the Peace

164

Corps and would be spending a year in India. Court was stuck on base, but she talked to him frequently.

Outside Beverly Hills and Valli's safe little world the chaos grew. The war escalated in Vietnam; civil rights marches spread across the country; and even close to home ten thousand blacks burned and looted hundreds of square blocks in a section of Los Angeles called Watts. Valli—dividing her time between the boutique and studio—hardly noticed.

Once the frantic rush to design and fit the costumes was finished, Valli withdrew completely from the outside world. Hollywood had been exhilarating, but it was only a means to an end. She'd tackled costume design for one reason only—fame and contacts. Once her name was established in Hollywood, her label would do better. Meanwhile, the men around her kept life serene, and while Valli's pregnancy was no secret to the world, they zealously isolated her from any conflict or unpleasantness. She knew what they were doing and let them do it; for the first time in her life she was cared for and protected. The only outsider who broke the barrier was Lincoln who came by at regular intervals, refused to take no for an answer, and swept her out for a trip up the coast to a charming new restaurant at Malibu, to the premiere of *Dr. Zhivago,* and sometimes to a quiet dinner in his apartment.

Tonight they'd been dining at Le Bistro when Valli became so uncomfortable that Lincoln insisted on taking her home where she could stretch out.

"Dear Lincoln," Valli said, kicking off her shoes and stretching her toes as she tried to find a position that allowed her to breathe. "I don't know why you'd want to be seen with me when I look like a lumpy sack of flour. It can't be good for your image."

"I don't care about my image, Valli. I'm an actor, but I'll never be the kind of star Steele is. So those kinds of restrictions don't concern me." He lifted one of Valli's stockinged feet and began to massage it. "It's pretty bad now, isn't it?"

"Short women definitely shouldn't have children.

165

There's just not enough room to expand,'' she agreed with a laugh.

"Here, put this pillow behind you." She did look like a little sausage, a warm little dumpling that he wanted to comfort and care for. He'd proposed to her a dozen times at least, but she always smiled and turned him down. By now he knew she wouldn't accept, but he kept asking to cheer her up and in the vain hope that she might surprise him.

"Valli, why don't you let me get us a snack? You didn't eat enough to say you'd been to dinner."

"Lincoln, the way this child is plastered against my backbone there isn't room for any food." She stretched again and grimaced. "She simply won't allow me to be still."

"All right then, we'll see what we can do to make you comfortable." He stood up, gathered the startled Valli in his arms and started up the stairs.

"What are you doing, Lincoln? Don't you think I'm a little out of shape for a seduction scene?"

"Actually, I find you incredibly sexy, but that isn't what I have in mind. Just hush." He let her feet drop and started to undress her.

"Please, Lincoln. I'm embarrassed. Have you ever seen a nude woman eight months pregnant? It's bad enough if you've watched the development, but to be hit in the eyes with it all at once will gross you out."

"Hush woman, this is purely medicinal, and nothing about you could gross me out."

Valli allowed him to disrobe her completely. Lincoln was a friend and she trusted his actions, even if she didn't understand them. He took off his own clothes and kissed her gently and led her to the bed.

"The doctor said no lovemaking from now on, Lincoln."

"Just lie down, Val, on your side I think. Isn't that more comfortable for you?"

"Yes." She followed his directions and lay on the oversized bed with her knees bent and her body totally exposed. She felt the bed move as he sat down beside her. His fingertips touched her back with an iciness that made her jump.

166

"Sorry, my hands are cold. Just give me a second and this will feel fantastic." Lincoln massaged her neck and shoulders with a cold liquid that warmed up with the gentle manipulations of his hands. He worked her muscles and nerves until they slowly stretched out and untied themselves. Down her backbone, across the pelvis, and down her thighs his hands slowly probed, caressed and soothed.

"Turn over, Valli. Can you lie on your back?"

"Yes, I think so—now." She turned over and tried to relax as she felt the child kick out in displeasure.

"Goodness, he's a little tyrant, isn't he?" Lincoln began a slow, gentle exploration of her stomach, touching her warily as the determined assault inside continued.

"She. Her name is Valley Rae, but I'm going to call her Rae. She's got a mind of her own already, and if she doesn't like me to lie on my back she won't stop until I turn over."

"All right, Rae, you little spitfire, you just settle down while I help your mama feel better." He continued to talk to the baby as his hands kneaded and pulled and gently rubbed Valli's legs and arms and the muscles beneath her stomach and breasts heavy with readiness for the child. Valli knew that Lincoln's touch was spiritual rather than sexual. But after the tension evaporated, Valli started responding in a different way.

She became aware of a growing physical response that was difficult to conceal as Lincoln continued to caress her. Her body hadn't known a man's touch since that night with Court five months ago.

Court. He'd been looking after her, too. Once he'd come up and whisked her off to a quiet weekend at Big Sur. They'd taken in the dramatic landscape and enjoyed a delicious dinner at a cliffside restaurant. But when they retired to the Pinetree Inn Valli had been surprised to discover Court had reserved two rooms.

What was wrong with her that she couldn't love either of the two men who loved her? Maybe, deep down inside, she wasn't sure that she was good enough for either Court or Lincoln. They both came from wealthy families. More important, they were both talented yet didn't seem to feel the need to prove it to the world. Lincoln was one of the most low-key stars in Hollywood—and also one of the most respected. Only Steele pushed hard—like Valli—to be the very best. Only Steele could understand that same need in her. And only with Steele was that fierce need replaced by her desire to take care of and protect somebody. Maybe little Rae would fill that spot.

"Lincoln, I think you'd better stop," she whispered, aware that her voice sounded embarrassingly breathless.

"Why? Don't you like it?" His lips were close to her. So close that she could feel the warmth of his breath on her chest.

"I like it very much—too much, I'm afraid. Lincoln, please. . ."

"Just be still, Valli. I think I understand what you need, and I'll take care of it." Two lips caught her breasts and Valli felt her body churn into liquid heat that exploded through her.

His lips and fingers continued their exploration until she was no longer able to be still. Every nerve ending in her body begged for release, and she knew that her response to Lincoln's mouth was shameful. When he reached inside of her legs Valli rolled beneath his touch, arching herself against him.

"Maybe, if you could just put it in a little," she said. "Oh, Lincoln. I can't stand it."

"No way. If I put it in, Valli, I could never do it just a little." When he shifted around, his body lay parallel with hers, his feet near her head. And then he fastened onto the tiny bud of sensation that seemed to burst into a kaleidoscope of feeling at the touch of his tongue.

Reaching between them he took her hand and placed it on his swollen penis. As she grasped him he continued the assault on her with his mouth. Almost as soon as he began again her body responded with a violent shudder that shook her all over. It happened so quickly that she didn't recognize his own rapid response until he rolled away and

168

sighed.

They lay beside each other, and Valli seemed embarrassed. It occured unexpectedly, and she was shocked. She reached down to pull up the sheet to cover her body which suddenly seemed swollen, ugly, and distorted, and she felt the threat of tears in her eyes.

"Don't, Valli, Don't. Please don't cry. There's no reason to be ashamed." He lay there in the darkness without touching her.

"Why, Lincoln? Why do you put up with me? I'm nothing special. I'm definitely not good for your image, no matter what you say, and I'm certainly no clever, fun-filled date."

He raised up on one elbow and looked down at her. "Because you're real, Valli. Do you realize how rare that is? In the middle of all of this tinsel and glitz you're constant. And somehow you keep me from becoming one of 'them.'"

He turned her on her side and pulled her close to him. She bent her legs and felt Lincoln's legs bend too. Like two spoons they lay close together and slept.

Two weeks later, when Valli was down on her knees pinning the hem of a green brocade satin evening coat, her water broke. The sticky warm liquid gushed down her leg, and she gaped at the evidence in wonder, too stunned at first to move. "Terrance!"

"Yes, love?" Something about Valli's voice must have alerted Terrance for he was beside her instantly, staring at the circle of soaked carpet beneath her knees. "Oh, shit. Hold on. . .you can't. . .Zack!"

"Calm down. We have plenty of time. Zack," she said to her assistants as Zack ran into the room, "finish this hem. Terrance, help me upstairs." She walked stiffly up the steps with Terrance's assistance and into her bathroom where she removed her damp and sticky clothes.

"Do you want me to help, Valli?"

"No, not yet. Just wait there." She finished bathing as the first pain cut through to her back and she cried out with the unexpectedness of its severity.

169

"Valli!" Terrance rushed inside and saw Valli clutching onto the sink as she waited for the pain to pass. "Put this on, Val. I'll have Zack get the car."

"Not yet. It takes a long time for the baby to come, Terrance. The doctor said to time my contractions first." Another pain wracked her body, leaving her white faced and panting.

"Valli, I have a feeling this child is not going to give you time to count anything." He tied the terry-cloth robe around her, lifted her in arms muscular enough to have belonged to Gorgeous George the wrestler, and started downstairs, yelling at Zack to start the car.

By the time they reached the hospital Valli was rolling in one long pain that refused to stop. She never dreamed that giving birth could hurt this badly. She gripped Terrance's hand as they laid her on the gurney and screamed as she felt the movement inside her. Her daughter seemed to be trying to tear through her very skin to escape.

"Now, now, mother," the nurse said soothingly, "You can't be hurting that bad. You've got hours ahead of you, just relax."

"Ah—ah—ah—," Valli spread her legs and began to pant. "I don't think so, nurse. You'd better get your ass in gear. This baby...oh, shit, Terrance, I'm ...ah...sorry I'm squeezing so hard, but..."

Terrance laid his fingers across her lips. "Relax, Val. They'll take care of everything."

The nurse laid her hand on Valli's abdomen and felt the prolonged contraction. She looked back at Valli's face and panicked.

"Oh, no! You're not having this baby in the elevator, lady. You can't."

"Help me, Terrance," Valli pleaded, leaning up as she spread her legs, felt one final heave and saw the tip of dark hair between her legs.

As the elevator door opened, the delivery room nursing staff watched in amazement as the nurse caught the child being born.

170

"Let me have her," Valli demanded as the baby began to cry lustily. Covered with blood and other stuff Valli couldn't name, the wrinkled, red-faced baby clenched its fist and wailed.

"It's a girl, Val." Terrance stared in wonder at the scene he had just witnessed.

"But, the cord. She needs cleaning," the young nurse protested, though she laid the child in Valli's outstretched arms.

"She needs me," Valli said, "and I need her." Valli held her until the nurses wheeled her into delivery and wrenched the child from her arms.

Valli Ray Turner gave birth to her baby. Lincoln came the next day. There were flowers and a card from Noel. Court was confined to base but must have called a dozen times. And Steele, on location, was the last to respond to the birth of his child, sending two dozen red roses and a fancy layette from one of Beverly Hills' most exclusive shops.

CHAPTER TWELVE

Two years later in January Valli was prepared to spend her twenty-fifth birthday alone.

Shortly after Rae had been born, Valli had found a house in Laurel Canyon and moved Rae and a housekeeper in. She had tried to seclude herself there, but Lincoln and Court had refused to allow this. They participated not only in Valli's life but her daughter's as well. They were there to witness Rae's first words, her first stumbling steps. But no matter how hard they tried to pique Valli's interest in the world outside her home and boutique, little Rae was the focus of Valli's existence.

Occasionally Valli shared Lincoln's life and his bed, but with Court she was more careful. She had known that falling in love with Court might be all too easy, and she had protected herself against those kind of feelings.

Court visited every chance he got. He loved to play with Rae, and the baby responded to him. But he soon realized that Valli's devotion lay with Steele, however misplaced Court thought it was. He never gave up hoping that she'd see the futility of loving Steele.

172

No matter what happened, Valli remained devoted to Steele. Perhaps only the child of an upbringing such as hers could understand her deep needs. First, she needed constancy, to feel that she belonged to one man. Her mother's numerous affairs had impacted strongly on the little girl, Valley Ray Turner. Even though Steele seemed to reject her outwardly, she never doubted that he loved her and would one day marry her. This thought kept her going.

Her second need was easily attainable. She craved physical affection. Both Lincoln and Court provided her with that amply, but she still held something back—commitment.

Too long ago, she'd committed herself to Steele. Too much time had passed for her to loosen her grasp on that commitment.

Tonight, on her birthday, Valli had refused invitations from both men. She had felt that what she needed was to be alone, although she wasn't quite sure why. When the phone rang, she knew why. It was Steele.

"I need to see you, Valli. I . . . I need to see Rae."

"Why?"

"Damn it, Val. She is my child. What's wrong with me wanting to see her?"

"Nothing. But she's almost two years old, and you haven't wanted to see her before. Why now?" Valli asked warily.

"I heard you were with Lincoln, and I thought it would be best."

"I don't suppose it mattered what *I* thought?"

"Don't be hard, Valli. You've never been like this before."

There was a calm insistence in his voice that Valli couldn't ignore. Still, she tried. "What is it, Steele? Don't give me any crap about sudden fatherly urges."

"Val, I just want to see you . . . both of you. I think I've changed. I don't know. It's just important. Please!"

It was late when he arrived. Valli had fed Rae, then put her to bed, sitting for a while as she often did watching her as she slept. Standing on the slate patio in the darkness, Valli felt Steele's presence. A breeze rippled across the pool, and she shivered, whether from a chill or Steele's arrival, she wasn't sure.

"Hello, Valli."

She took a deep breath and turned around. She would wait for him to speak, to explain why he was here. But she hadn't counted on the look of honest joy in his eyes, the warmth of emotion when he smiled, or the rush of happiness she felt in return when she saw him.

"You look good," she said, knowing how inadequate those words were. The fragrance of bougainvillea wafted across the patio.

Magnificent, tanned, and casual, he wore charcoal slacks and a sweater made by designers whose names he couldn't have pronounced five years before. He face was stronger, more chiseled. Quite simply—he looked like a star. "Would you like a drink?"

"No thanks. You look good, too," he said, and his voice couldn't mask his feelings any longer. "Oh, Valli! I'm so glad to see you."

And they were in each other's arms, both crying, both comforting, both ashamed of the depth of the emotional need they felt for each other.

"Valli, Valli," he whispered again. "It's been awful. I've missed you. I'm such a fool."

"Yes, you are." Valli allowed herself to lean against him for a long moment, feeling the heat of him warm her skin where they touched. She inhaled the familiar spicy smell of his after-shave and sighed before she forced herself to pull away.

"What's wrong?" His look was wary, almost uncertain as she moved back several steps and crossed her arms over her breasts.

"That's what I want to know, Steele. What's wrong?"

"Wrong? Aside from the fact that I miss you and that I have a child I've never seen, nothing's wrong. Where is she, Valli, the baby?"

174

"She's not a baby anymore." Then she softened. "She's in bed, Steele. Would you like to see her?"

The eagerness in his eyes assuaged her anxiety for a moment, and he nodded. He followed her inside and up the heavily carpeted steps past two of Court's paintings that accented the peach tones of the carpet.

"I like your house, Valli. It has a good feeling about it."

Valli smiled. At Rae's bedroom door Valli paused and placed her finger across her lips. "Shhhh."

Rae lay sprawled in a sea of stuffed animals across the bed, her covers kicked wildly to the floor. Her head was turned slightly, and a trace of a smile wrinkled one corner of her mouth. One chubby hand was threaded through a mass of dark curly hair.

He stood for a long time at the foot of her bed looking down at the child before he spoke. "She looks like you, Valli," he said simply, too devastated to speak further. He hadn't realized how much emotion the first sight of his daughter would bring.

The child turned on her side and pulled a stuffed pink bear close.

"We'd better go before we wake her."

Steele followed Valli down the stairs and into the den. "I was such a fool, Valli, about Rae. I was afraid that my career would be ended before it started if they thought I was married with a child."

"And you don't feel that way anymore?"

"No."

"Cut the crap, Steele. This is me, Valli." She propped her arms on her hips, adopting the stern visage she used when Rae was naughty. But seeing the sincerity in his eyes, her voice softened. "Let's go into the kitchen. I'll make coffee and we can talk."

She found the coffee maker ready. Leona, the housekeeper, always left it ready for her to plug in. Valli took two mugs from the cabinet and placed them on the breakfast table. By the time she found the sugar bowl and took the cream from the refrigerator, the smell of perking coffee had filled the room.

"I hear that the boutique is doing fine." Steele sat down and took his mug in his hand. "I'm proud of you, Valli. Coming to California was good for both of us, wasn't it?"

"I suppose," Valli admitted and sat down across the table from him, watching as he turned the mug back and forth in his hands without drinking. She gazed at him. He looked so tough, so handsome, so sure of himself.

"Steele," she said carefully, praying that he'd say the right words. "Why have you come? Let's hear the truth."

She watched him twirl the mug, his eyes hypnotically drawn to the black liquid. Finally he spoke. "I'm—different, Valli. But, I'm not . . . I mean . . ." He stood and walked over to the window.

Hope surged within her. Maybe he was growing up.

"Oh, Valli." He turned and took her in his arms, clinging to her as if he were afraid that he'd whirl off into space if he let her go. "I'm sorry, so very sorry. You know that I do love you. I really do. Please . . ."

He slid a tear-dampened cheek across her face and kissed her.

Don't let him do this to you, Valli. Just because you've waited for this day is no reason to melt into his arms like a schoolgirl. Dizzy with the reality of his body next to hers, Valli dug her fingernails into his back as she tried to push him away. Too many times her hopes had been dashed.

"Oh, Valli, I want to grab onto you, hold you close to me, take a carriage ride through Central Park and talk for hours the way we used to before. I'm lonely, Val. I never know whether people are around me because they like me, or because they want to use me. Oh, Valli, I don't think I knew what I had then, but I do now. I need you and Rae!"

"You don't love me, Steele," she said. "You only think you do. You can't . . ."

Before she could say it, his mouth covered hers, kissing her urgently, with such desire that she felt all her resolve melting, and she kissed him back.

He lifted her in his arms and carried her back up the

stairs, releasing her mouth long enough to ask, "Where's our bedroom, Valli?"

When she nodded her head he kicked open the door she had indicated and fell across the king-sized bed still holding her in his arms and kissing her as he tore away her clothes. He continued to hold her with one hand while he ripped off his own clothes and then he was on her, burying himself inside her with a desperate need that ripped through both of them. She felt him inside her, felt his heart pounding as if it were in her chest, felt the tide of churning release sweep over them and shoot them with spears of exquisite rapture. And then it was over, and they were both stunned at the unexpected depth of their experience.

"God, Valli, I'd forgotten how good it was between us."

"It was never that good before, Steele."

He lay, still joined to her, supporting himself over her with his elbows. In the half-darkness he looked down at her, planting little kisses across her face and down her neck.

They had been married for almost four years, and she had never been so happy except when Rae had been born.

From a wary beginning, Rae had fallen in love with her daddy, and the two had soon become inseparable. They were more than father and daughter; they were friends, and instinctively Steele seemed to understand how to reach the child in a way that Valli never had. Soon it was Steele who put Rae to bed and read her a bedtime story. At first Valli had almost been jealous of their closeness, yet somehow Steele filled the space that Rae had once occupied.

Court was doing well on the tennis circuit. Noel's fledgling political career was coming along. Life was good, better than she'd ever expected it to be. Steele was a better husband than she'd ever imagined. If there were occasional times when she felt his restlessness, she pushed those feelings to the back of her mind.

"I think we stand a chance of the awards this year, Valli. But then again, I don't know. You never know what the academy will do. We really need to get some young, fresh blood into the voting."

They were decorating a small evergreen pine tree Valli had set up in the bay window of the house where they still lived. The colored lights had already been strung, and they twinkled brightly. Valli was having a hard time unwrapping ornaments and adding the wire hooks quickly enough. Rae, chattering happily, was being allowed to place the balls around the tree wherever she wanted to.

"You need something red up high, on the right, by that green light. Steele, I wish you'd quit worrying. Even if you don't win, you'll get a nomination. You were wonderful."

"You're only as good as your last picture, Val, and Hollywood has a short memory. I have to keep my name before the public."

"Your picture is on the front page of every magazine in the checkout line of the grocery store. If the world doesn't know who you are by now, they never will."

"I suppose, but I get antsy waiting around for that phone to ring. Damn, Val, I just can't get used to Christmas trees and summertime weather. Look out, Rae."

Valli watched as Steele caught Rae up in his arms and helped her hang the ball she was holding on the end of a limb. The bottom half of the tree was definitely well covered with ornaments, at least as far as a six-year-old could reach.

"Oh, Daddy, it's the most beautiful tree in the whole world. Don't you think so?"

"Well. . ." Steele took an exaggerated walk examining the tiny tree and pretending to consider his answer. "Maybe not the absolute, most beautiful, but it's probably at the top of Santa's list."

"Santa's list?" Rae's tiny voice would someday be the female equivalent of her father's deep, rich timbre. She'd never spoken like a child. From the time she'd first opened her mouth, she sounded like an adult in miniature.

"Oh, yes. Santa has a list of all the children and their parents. He keeps an eye on them year round, and on Christmas Eve he gets out his list and packs his sled. You *have* sent in your Christmas requests, haven't you?''

Rae's face fell. "Oh, Daddy. I didn't know. Was I supposed to?''

Steele took on a worried look. "Oh, dear. I should have asked earlier. I just assumed you'd written to him and told him what you wanted for Christmas."

"Steele," Valli interjected. "You'll drive that child to tears.''

"Well," he said, "I guess what we will have to do is give him a call, or better still, what do you say we go down and visit him tomorrow and tell him in person.''

"Oh, could we Daddy? Could we really go and see Santa Claus?''

"What about it, Mommy? Could we take a little trip downtown tomorrow and visit old Saint Nick?''

"Oh, honey, I can't. I have two fittings and a consultation tomorrow. Last-minute requests for holiday gowns.''

"Oh!" Steele's mouth tightened for a moment before spreading into a smile that made Rae's frown waver.

Valli tried not to see the look of disappointment on her daughter's face. She'd been so busy lately, but she hadn't had a choice. Business was just now hitting a dependable volume, and she was afraid to say no to anything or anybody. "I'm sorry, darling, but why don't you and Daddy go? You could have a nice day together, just the two of you.''

"Sure, kitten," Steele said. "We'll have lunch and go to see Santa.''

It wasn't what Rae wanted. And it wasn't what Steele wanted either, and Valli began some mental rearranging to try to change her schedule. Terrance could handle the fitting, but Dyan Cannon wasn't going to let anybody but Valli make a decision on a dress for New Year's Eve. Valli shook her head. She'd do something, she just didn't know what.

To liven up the mood that had suddenly gone serious Valli brought out hot chocolate and cookies and they sat around the tree in the darkness, watching Bing Crosby's Christmas special on the television. Later after they'd put Rae to bed, Valli sat with her head on Steele's arm, content and happy, just the two of them, like a normal family.

December, Valli thought, letting the rich, sad sounds of Elvis singing "Blue Christmas" flow through her. December is my month. Rae was born six Christmasses ago, and now it was Christmas again, Christmas, 1971, and life was very good.

"What are you thinking, Val?"

"I'm thinking about Christmas. After my mother left we never had a tree. As a child, I always hated December. But," she added in a whisper, "not anymore. There's nothing blue about Christmas for me now."

"I know," he answered softly. "I never had a tree, either. On Christmas Eve some well-meaning soul would come by with a basket of goodies for the kids. I hated it. I never want Rae to know that kind of life."

"She won't. Thank you, Steele. Thank you for December. Merry Christmas, darling."

Steele lifted Valli's chin and kissed her with agonizing slowness, forcing her back into the thick cushions of the couch.

Valli's fingers clung to Steele, deliberately teasing her fingernails against his skin as she slid his shirt up over his head. Joyfully she joined his disrobing until they were both exploring each other. The longings she'd felt all night became a lovely reality as they gave themselves to each other.

"Valli," he whispered later as they lay languid in the aftermath of their love, "I want you to know that I was afraid before, afraid that the world wouldn't accept me as a husband and father. I was wrong. I've been doing a lot of thinking about us. Val?"

"Yes, Steele?"

"You won't laugh if I tell you what I'd really like?"

"Laugh? Of course not. What would you like?"

"I'd . . ." he hesitated and she felt him tense for a moment before reaching out and pulling her across him, curling his arms around her tightly. "I'd like us to have another baby, right away."

"Another child?" Valli sat up, staring at Steele in confusion. "You can't be serious. The boutique is only just now beginning to make a real name for itself, and you expect me to take time out to have another child? Besides, designing *Starlight* took a lot of my time. It's the last movie I'm going to do. I need to devote my energy to the boutique. Surely you understand that?"

"Yes, I guess it's not a good idea," he agreed quickly. "I'm just being silly. You have your career, and I have mine. And you never know, you might have to support us again. What if I don't get another picture?"

Valli lay back down. Steele wasn't serious. He couldn't be serious. She loved Rae dearly. She would never regret having Steele's child, but another baby? No, not now. How could he even ask her to do that, knowing how much she'd given up to come out here with him, and how long it had taken her to achieve the success she'd only just now begun to enjoy.

He pulled her back into his arms, but she could tell that the mood was different. Mentally she cursed herself for her outburst. She hadn't even thought about another child. It wasn't such a dumb idea. She'd love to give Steele a son, but something had made her reject the idea. What was wrong with her?

Valli was with a client in the boutique when Rae and Steele left the next morning. She'd intended to call and have them stop by and pick her up, but one thing after another had happened, and it was one o'clock before she'd noticed the time. The last client was dressing and discussing the gown she'd ordered for New Year's Eve when she heard them in the reception area.

"Mommy, Mommy. We saw Santa." Rae bubbled with excitement. "And he's going to bring me a pony, a real pony I can ride."

"Nonsense, Steele. How could you promise her that?" Valli said without thinking as she boxed up the gown.

"I didn't, Valli," Steele corrected sharply. "Santa did. That's what Rae asked for. Don't spoil her fun."

Valli looked up at the tiny face all screwed into tight little

181

lines as she tried not to cry. "I'm sorry, darling, but where would we keep a pony? He'd be very unhappy in the house, and we don't have a big enough yard."

"But Daddy. . .Daddy said that we could keep him in a barn with hay to eat and a pas. . .pasture to live in. You said I could ask Santa."

Lordy, Steele, how he could stir things up. Listening to the enthusiasm in Rae's voice she realized that she couldn't pour cold water on her happiness. But a pony? He could really complicate things sometimes.

"Of course, Rae. If Santa brings you a pony we'll find a place for it. I'm sorry. Mommy is just disappointed because she couldn't go with you and Daddy. Did you have a nice day?"

"Oh yes. We had pizza for lunch and we went shopping, but we can't tell what we bought, can we, Daddy?"

Looking at Rae and Steele beaming all over from the secret they were sharing, Valli felt a pang of jealousy and busied herself with adding a bright red ribbon to the box she was wrapping.

The customer, a famous writer's wife, had dressed and was waiting for the package. "Steele, will you and Valli be attending Sam Guccione's New Year's Eve party?"

"No," Valli answered for Steele, "we're going to Aspen skiing. The three of us."

"We're going skiing?" Rae began clapping her hands. "Can we take my pony, Daddy?"

"No, sweetheart, but they'll have some horses up there that pull a sled through the snow, and we'll take a ride. We'll have fun, I promise," Valli answered, giving Steele an embarrassingly open look of promise.

"We missed you today, Valli," Steele said, hoisting Rae onto his shoulders. "Are you done here?"

On the way home Valli held the overtired child in her arms. She was too big to sit on her mother's lap, but she seemed fidgety and unusually quiet. Just tired, Valli thought. She's had a long day. Pushing a lock of raven-colored hair away from her flushed cheek, Valli realized with a start that Rae was unusally warm, hot in fact. She laid her palm across her forehead.

"Steele, I think Rae may be coming down with something."

"You mean she's sick?" His alarm was genuine.

"Yes, probably just a cold, but, I'd rather get her straight to bed."

Valli and the housekeeper quickly undressed Rae. As she prepared to slip a cotton nightgown over the child's head Valli saw them, the small telltale red spots that signified the beginning of the childhood disease chicken pox.

Rae spent Christmas in bed, with Steele anxiously beside her. The pony Santa had left waiting in its stall and Rae's patience wore thin before the itching stopped.

"Sorry, darling," Steele said as he and Valli stood over their child's bed. "Wouldn't you like to slip into something, darling? We could still make the party."

"I'd rather stay here with you, Steele, if you don't mind. We've never spent New Year's Eve at home, have we?"

"No. I could run downtown and pick up some Chinese food and a bottle of champagne."

"And bring party hats and streamers," Valli encouraged. "I'll shower and change while you're gone, if you're sure you don't mind missing the crowd."

"Not a bit," Steele said with certainty. "The only thing we need is Central Park and some snow."

All the time Steele was gone, Valli felt a warm veil of happiness wash over her. She wished there were snow. She wouldn't have told Steele, but she wished they were back in New York. She could see Rockefeller Center, with the winter ice skaters in their brightly colored costumes and the enormous lit-up tree.

After a quick shower she splashed herself with Chanel No. 5, humming as she watched the woman in the mirror without acknowledging that it was herself. One day she'd have a fragrance named for her. Val, she'd call it, just Val. Carefully stepping into the long flowing red velvet pants dress, she zipped it up.

183

From the drawer she took the present that Rae and Steele had shopped for on their trip into town. It was a ruby, a two-carat stone set in a filigreed setting of leafy gold. Fastening it around her neck, she felt very elegant. It was the most beautiful thing she'd ever seen. With the feel of the stone on her throat and the velvet gown on her bare body, Valli had forgotten about food by the time Steele returned. From the look on his face when he saw her, she thought that his hunger might be for something else, too. She was glad she'd closed the windows. Otherwise she'd have floated straight out into the velvety blue-black sky of Southern California.

CHAPTER THIRTEEN

"Hey, Valli. Look at this." Steele was holding a creamy antique-white envelope addressed in a precise black pen. "It's a wedding invitation. Noel's getting married in April. What about that heathen, getting married and he didn't even mention it when he...when I talked to him the other day."

"Who's he marrying?" Valli was lying beside the pool, enjoying a sense of pure relaxation, basking in the sunshine that was strong even for Los Angeles in February.

"I don't know the girl, probably one of the Boston blue-bloods dear Celeste kept pushing at him. The way his career's going, who knows, one of these days we may be able to say we're personal friends of the President."

Valli slid her sunglasses back over her eyes and lay back on the lounge. "We'll go, won't we?"

"I don't think we'll be able to, Val. It's the same week as the Academy Awards ceremony. I missed out once on the Best Supporting Actor, but I think I'm going to get it this time."

"I think we ought to be there for Noel, even if its only for the wedding and back. He's always been there for you."

"I said *no*, Valli. I can't. We'll send a silver service. I'll call Noel and explain how important it is that we be here."

There was a coldness in his voice that startled Valli. She'd never heard Steele quite so vehement about anything. He'd bypass his oldest friend for the sake of his Hollywood crowd? Valli pushed her hands against the chair arm, forcing the back to move up, and threw her feet over the side of the lounge. Was it Steele's career, or was it something more?

"The truth, Steele. Why don't you want to go?"

"The truth, Val? Who knows which truth is the real truth? Let's just say that I don't think it would be right for me to be there and overshadow the bride's day. We want the press's mind where it ought to be." He laughed lightly. "And it would be. . .well, it would be hard on others, too. Besides, if we aren't at the ceremony, people might talk about us, and we don't want Hollywood to think we aren't happy, would we?"

There was a sinking feeling in the pit of her stomach. Was it that he didn't want to spoil Noel's wedding? No, he was concerned about something else. She'd thought everything was fine. Had she been wrong about Steele? Is there something I don't know?

"When's dinner?" Steele interrupted her thoughts.

"I asked cook to wait until you'd said good night to Rae."

"Fine, I won't be long."

Valli sat staring at the doorway after he'd gone. The sinking feeling in her stomach persisted. Something wasn't right, and she didn't know what it was.

"Valli, have you heard?" Chris Ross's voice was filled with excitement.

Valli spit out the mouthful of pins she was holding and said, "Heard what?" Valli hadn't made up her mind yet about Chris Ross, the publicist Steele had hired last year. Determined to involve Valli in Steele's day-to-day activities, Chris was forever calling with some kind of information that he wanted to pass on. Stop it Valli, she told herself, his intentions are good.

"Hurry, Valli. My back is killing me." Clarissa Thompson was now not only one of Valli's best customers, but the two had become friends.

"What is it, Chris? I'm very busy."

"It's Steele, he's finally made it. He's been nominated for an Academy Award for *Into The Wind*. I knew it, I knew it!"

"I'm so glad, Chris." Valli was truly excited, but she'd rather have heard the news from Steele.

After talking to Chris for a few more minutes, she hung up and turned to Clarissa.

"Steele has just been nominated for an Academy Award."

"Well, it's about time." Clarissa smiled. "He should have been nominated for *Winter*. I never understood that. I thought it was all set and then zilch, the studio pulled back, killed the publicity, and the press played like he had leprosy."

"That's the movie he made with you just before we were married. I didn't know anything had happened. Why do you think they did that?" Valli knelt to adjust the hem of the lime green one shouldered dress.

"Oh, some foolish gossip of some kind. I never paid any attention to it because I knew better. After all, I was in a movie with Steele, and it didn't mean anything. I know that he's definitely a real man. It's too bad that you weren't married sooner, then there would have been none of this gossip and he would probably have gotten the Oscar back then. Of course, Best Actor is better, and he's a cinch to get it this time."

Valli finished Clarissa's fitting in a trance. "Some foolish gossip. . .too bad you weren't married sooner. . .the studio. . .killed the publicity. . ." It finally became clear to her why Steele had returned so suddenly, insisted on the marriage, and formally announced that Rae was his child. Steele had been lying to her. Their whole marriage was a lie. It couldn't be. Steele loved her. He made love to her regularly and with enthusiasm. It couldn't be true, yet she knew it was. And now. . .he was tiring of her again. He didn't need

187

her any longer.

For the first time Valli left the salon with a customer still pinned in her gown. "Terrance, I don't feel very well, please finish with Clarissa. I'm going home."

"But Valli . . ."

She didn't even hear the rest of his sentence. There was a loud ringing in her ears, and she felt her heart palpitate wildly as she drove. She didn't want to think about Steele and what Clarissa's words might mean. Thoughts charged in relentlessly, and she knew that she had to face it—but not now. From the boutique, she drove aimlessly around until she found herself back on Wilshire Boulevard near the high-rise where Lincoln lived. She turned into the parking area, handed the keys to the valet, and moved woodenly inside.

"Yes ma'am? Ma'am?"

The guard behind the security desk raised his voice before she realized that he was talking to her. "Oh, I'm sorry, I'm here to see Lincoln Maxwell."

"And who may I say is calling?"

"Valli. Just tell him Valli."

Lincoln opened the door, took one look at Valli's ashen face, and knew that she was in trouble. "Darling, come in. Let me fix you a drink." He led her inside the library and hurriedly poured a large amount of brandy into a glass. "Here, drink this."

Dutifully she swallowed, choking for a moment, then emptying the glass before she began to talk.

"Linc, Steele was been nominated for an Academy Award. He would have had one before if he'd married me sooner. Did you know that?"

He knew immediately what she was talking about, and he knew he needed to be very careful. He filled her glass again and watched as she emptied it without even being aware that she had. "Val, that was a long time ago."

"Have you heard anything, Linc, about Steele and . . . someone else?" She couldn't bring herself to put a name to her fears.

"No." Lincoln looked away, unable to meet Valli's eyes.

She turned at last and looked at him. "You loved me once. Do you still?"

"Yes."

"Then love me now, Lincoln. I need you to love me now." She began removing her clothes.

Lincoln watched her as she methodically stripped, one article at a time, until she stood defiantly nude before him.

"Take me, Lincoln. I want you to fuck me until I forget, forget everything."

It was all wrong, Lincoln knew as she tore his clothes away and rubbed against him as though she were on fire. He wanted to stop her, to tell her to put her clothes back on and go home where she belonged. This wasn't Valli. This was some anguished creature, lost in the depths of desire and despair. The only problem, Lincoln thought as he felt himself respond, is that I'm the wrong man.

Their coming together was violent and abusive and instantaneous, the first time. Afterward Valli paced back and forth, still fraught with an inner agitation that refused to be quieted. He'd never seen Valli drink, yet now she finished almost an entire bottle of brandy without any apparent effect. Valli came back to the bed where Lincoln lay watching, stretching herself over him with no pretense at hiding her desire. She arched herself against him.

"Valli, are you sure this is what you want?"

"Yes." She took his hand and placed it on her breast while she fondled him shamelessly.

"Just a minute, love. I have something here." He reached in the drawer and removed a small pastic bag of white powder. "Just lie back and let me show you."

"No, Lincoln. I don't do drugs. You know that I don't do drugs. What are you doing? Ahhhh. . ."

Lincoln sprinkled the white powder across her clitoris and deftly began to rub it with his fingertips. Almost instantly she felt the explosion of tingling heat ripple through her and she shifted her body so that she could pull him over her. "Please, Lincoln, now!"

"No, not yet. I'm going to show you how it feels to be

alive with sex." He pulled back and inserted his phallus into the plastic bag, feeling the jolt of cocaine clear into his brain as he absorbed it through the open skin at the tip. He felt himself begin to swell.

When he entered her, he had to move slowly in order to push it in. He seemed to have grown so large that he wasn't sure that she could take him. And then he was inside her, and dimly he heard her scream, as orgasm after orgasm seemed to rip her apart. The feeling wasn't new to Lincoln, but this was Valli sharing it with him and that magnified his climax immeasurably. When the effects of the drug finally dissipated and he was limp once more, he fell across her in sheer exhaustion, the smell of sweat and semen permeating the air. And they slept.

Valli had come to Lincoln on a Friday. On Saturday morning Lincoln called Leona to let her know that Valli was all right. On Monday morning Valli finally put on her clothes and went home. For the first time in her life she'd been drunk, drugged, and screwed out of her mind, and she still felt dead inside.

On the night of the Academy Awards ceremony, Valli wore a red satin dress she had designed especially for the occasion. It clung to her generous bosom, revealing enough to be naughty but not indecent, and kisssed her tiny waist. Long drop diamond earrings sparkled in her ears. As she moved, the satin whispered luxuriously around her feet and fell just short of the matching satin heels with the Austrian crystal-studded bows. The earrings were Steele's gift to her in celebration of his nomination. The necklace she wore, a collar of diamonds, was her gift to herself for being nominated for the best costume design on *Starlight*. Her own nomination had come as a complete surprise—surprising Steele the most. He had tried to be excited for her, but she knew it bothered him.

This was supposed to be his night, the night Steele had waited for for so long. Valli fit in as a wife but not as a fellow nominee. Numb, Valli went through the motions that Oscar night as she had for the past three months. For several weeks there'd been interviews, pictures, and publicity; the Colton candidates, Hollywood's most prominent couple.

Since that weekend with Lincoln, Valli had turned most of her work at the boutique over to Terrance and Zack as she spent all her time with Rae. But that hadn't been enough. It wasn't Valli that Rae wanted, it was Steele, but in the great rush of hype over the Oscar he seemed to have shoved his feelings for his daughter into the background. Valli saw Rae turn accusing eyes on her, as though she held her mother responsible for her father's defection.

"We're invited to three parties afterwards, Val," Steele said as she entered the library where he was waiting. "There's Swifty's party at Le Bistro, of course. You aren't invited there unless you're a cinch to win. Of course, we're not invited to dinner, but we'll be at the awards dinner anyway. Then there's Lincoln's party, and of course the party at Ronnie's. I've been trying to decide how we should work it."

Steele stood behind the desk nervously shuffling through envelopes as he spoke.

"What does Chris say about it, Steele? You pay him to get you publicity and give you advice. Why ask me?"

"Don't be an ass, Valli. I'm only asking you for an opinion."

"The only opinion I have is that you'd better not pour another drink or you'll be in the men's room when they call your name—if they call your name."

"Thanks, Val. My kidneys could make a perfect topic of conversation at the ceremony."

A flash of anger flushed Steele's face even more. She knew she had jabbed him too much. He was nervous, and only she knew how nervous. She watched him as he tossed off the last of the scotch he was drinking and picked up the bottle.

"No, Steele. You don't need that," she said quietly and laid her hand on his arm. "You're a star, Steele Colton, hard as nails. You don't need this."

191

He raised his eyes and looked at her, a sad smile touching his lips. "If I remember the rest of your words, Valli, they were as hard as nails and as soft as butter. Tonight, I seem to be remembering the softer comparison. God, I'm scared."

She took his hand and squeezed it. "Of course you are, Steele. Haven't you always been?" He was so preoccupied that he didn't notice the contempt in her voice.

"Not when you're with me, Val. Are you with me?"

She couldn't refuse him, not when he looked at her like that. Of course she was with him. Hadn't she always been?

"Yes, Steele, I'm with you . . . tonight."

Valli and Steele stepped from the white limousine onto a wide red carpet and were suddenly bathed in the blazing spotlights. It was still daylight, and, for a second, Valli was stunned. Her first thought was that their attire—black and red—would be marvelous on television.

Steele's fans roared when they recognized him and pressed closer to reach out for him over the satin cord strung just far enough away from the carpet to prevent them from touching him. Valli smiled and waved as he spoke briefly to a television interviewer. He's got to win. He'll be devastated if he doesn't, she thought as she smiled.

Basking in the fans' electric response, Valli took Steele's arm, and they entered the mass of glitter, gems, and gold flashing in the lobby. Clarissa Thompson hugged Valli and pressed a kiss on Steele's cheek before whispering congratulations and moving on. Valli watched the graceful swish of violet satin and lace as the actress strode off to greet Cary Grant.

They took their seats and waited. Palms damp with excitement, Valli squeezed Steele's hand. To anyone watching, they appeared to be a couple deeply in love, and the brief meeting of their eyes confirmed it. Time crept on, and the evening seemed endless. Will he win? kept pulsing through her in time with her heartbeat.

When they called Valli's name, Steele looked at her in surprise. Jealousy flushed his face for a moment before he realized that the whole world was watching. With a plastered smiled he reached over and kissed Valli's white cheek, lifted her to her feet, and gave her a little shove to the stage.

The applause sifted through to her, and she realized that they were handing her the gold statuette and standing back for her to speak.

"Thank you," she mumbled. "This is wonderful. . . ." What was she going to say? She hadn't prepared a speech. "My granny once said that no matter what happened in life, the only way anybody ever amounted to a hill of beans was to work like a dog, accept what came, and be the best you could be—the very best. That's what I've tried to do," she said, her voice growing stronger. "I have a lot of people to thank. Granny, Noel, Court . . . and my husband. Thank you for this honor."

She was whisked backstage to the awaiting press, and so she missed the announcements for Best Actor. Steele won. A reporter from the *Times* informed her, and she rushed to the wings of the stage. Steele's dazzling smile was painful to watch. She'd wanted to rush out onto the stage and throw herself into his arms. But fear of Steele's reception, more than of embarrassment at the audience's reaction, checked her impulsive action. She knew he was excited, filled with success and the glory of achievement, and she knew that this was his moment alone.

For the rest of the evening there were congratulations from people who'd never known her name before. *Into The Wind* didn't win the Best Picture award, but that only intensified the focus on Steele. It wasn't the picture that was hot, it was Steele, and he gloried in the adoration.

Other invitations for parties were pressed on them, and it was very late when they finally left the Academy's Governors Ball, picked up Steele's Corniche, and reached Swifty's. A mass of diamond-encrusted women and tuxedo-clad men filled every inch of space. The noise was deafening, and Valli clung to Steele's arm to keep from becoming separated.

"There's Raquel Welch, over in the corner talking to that

193

talk-show host. You know, Dick Cavett."

"Fernando, your wife is still as beautiful as she was the first time I saw her in a swimsuit. How do you manage to stay so slim?"

"Boy, wouldn't I like to be a fly and light on shoulders here tonight," Steele said, excitement coloring his voice.

"Why?" What Valli wanted to do was make an appearance and go home. Her head was splitting, and she didn't like the way Steele kept excusing himself all night to go to the men's room. From every trip he returned brighter and wittier, and she worried. Whatever Steele did, he went at it full-speed-ahead, and she was sure that right now he was high on cocaine. She was definitely concerned.

"Because, I'd like to hear what they're saying about Steele Colton now, those sanctimonious bastards."

"What do you mean, Steele? What would they be saying now?"

"They know I should have won before, but they wouldn't let me have it. Thought they were smart, they did. But we showed them, didn't we, Val? We showed them."

"Yes, darling. We won tonight, and the world knows it."

"Let's go, Val, there's one more party I want to look in on."

"Oh, Steele, no more. I'm out on my feet. My head is splitting, and we've both had too much to drink."

"Shove it, Val. This is my night. You can just take that headache and sit on it. We're not going home until every person in the whole fucking town has gone to bed." Steele strode off and Valli, fighting back tears, followed.

Steele drove recklessly and much too fast, up the canyon into the hills overlooking the city. He parked the car in a small driveway filled with Mercedes and Jaguars. From the moment they stepped inside, there was a peculiar feeling about this party, and it took Valli only a few minutes to figure out what was bothering her. The laughter was shrill and loud, much too loud. It was almost dawn, but everyone was still drinking, eating, and dancing. The party was going strong, but Valli didn't recognize many of the people.

194

"Oh, look, Valli, there's Max Barr. Hang on a minute—I just want a word with him."

Steele strode off and was immediately swallowed up by the crowd. For the next hour Valli searched for him, but he was nowhere to be found. Every once in a while she'd glimpse a nude figure running outside the house and around the swimming pool. A lot of sweet smoke filtered through the air, and simply taking a breath made Valli feel high.

"You're just the one I've been looking for," a tall, deep-voiced woman said behind her, spinning her around.

"I'm sorry, I don't believe I know you." Valli whispered.

"Strictly an oversight on my part," she whispered, swaying with the slow beat of Roberta Flack's "Where Is the Love?" blaring from speakers placed throughout the house.

Horrified, Valli jerked away and ran out onto the balcony, determined to find Steele and get out of there. Where could he be? She reached the end of the wraparound deck and leaned against the rail for a moment, breathing heavily.

"I told you it would work. And it did. Now we don't have to worry anymore."

"You were right all along. Now, I've got it made. Did you bring what I asked for?"

It was Steele. Quietly Valli tiptoed toward the window and peered in. Steele was lying naked on an oversized bed. Beside him lay another man. Steele was with a man, in bed with another man. She caught her breath. It felt as if her heart had stopped. And she closed her eyes, forcing herself to breathe before she opened them and looked back inside. It was happening all over again.

The stranger got up, handed Steele a pair of silver holders in which a tiny stub of a cigarette glowed brightly, and left the room. In a moment the doorway was filled with another man, young, blond and muscular with a huge erection. He swaggered over to the bed and stood over Steele with his hands on his hips. Steele, equally aroused, crushed out the rest of the cigarette and shifted his body. When the boy knelt down before him and lowered his head Valli gave a cry of anguish and ran away, swallowing her revulsion.

She swerved the car wildly down the canyon road, barely able to keep it out of the ditch. How she reached her own house on the opposite hillside she never knew. By the time she had parked the car her eyes were dry, and Valli knew what she had to do. She called Terrance and told him what she wanted to do, changed her clothes, stuffed some clothes into her suitcase, and moved on to Rae's room. In thirty minutes she had packed every article of clothing and stuffed animal that belonged to Rae and thrown the suitcases in the trunk of her Mercedes. Finally, she woke Rae and dressed her.

"We're going on a trip, darling. Let Mama put on your shoes."

"Daddy, too?"

"Not this time," Valli said resolutely. "This time it's just you and me."

"No. I don't want to go if Daddy isn't coming with us."

"Daddy isn't coming, Rae. He has something else he wants to do."

Valli was halfway to New York before she remembered she'd left her Oscar on the hall table. So be it. It was time she went back to where she had intended to go and pursued the goals she had set so long ago.

PART
THREE

CHAPTER FOURTEEN

The silver limousine moved like silk among the battered taxis until it pulled in to a side street and glided to a halt at the curb. A doorman rushed to the limo's door and opened it. Valli peered up at the young man, slid her legs around until her feet touched the concrete, and helped Rae out.

"Welcome to the Waldorf, ma'am."

"Thank you." She stepped across the walk and waited for the driver to unload no fewer than six Hermès bags. When he approached her, she removed some bills from her wallet and paid him. Marveling at the difference time made, Valli thought back eleven years to 1961—when her bus fare all the way from Willacoochee had cost less than this limousine ride from the airport, and when she had arrived with one piece of Samsonite luggage.

Touching his fingers to his cap, the driver hurried around the limo and got in. Catching Rae's hand in hers, Valli followed a bellhop to the desk and picked up her luggage receipts.

"Follow the stairs up to the lobby, and by the time you register your luggage will be in your room." He slipped elastic-banded tags on her bags and placed them on a cart.

Valli led Rae up a flight of curving stairs to the lobby. Energy surged through her, billowing her sagging spirits into a bravado that would carry her for a while. I'm back, she thought, back where I belong. And, this time, I've arrived in style.

"Mommy, I'm hungry."

"I know you are, darling." Valli looked down at her daughter. Her long black braid was unraveling, and her blue eyes were smudged with black shadows. The poor child was bewildered, but Valli didn't know how to comfort her. They stopped at the desk and registered.

She reached a bank of elevators and pressed the up button. Brass doors slid open, and she stepped inside with a throng of others.

Rae looked around. "Where is Daddy? Why didn't he come with us?"

"Shhh. We'll see your daddy soon," Valli reassured her. "How would you like to call Uncle Court? He lives here."

"Can we?" The little girl's voice lifted with pleasure. "Now?" Court wasn't Daddy, but he was close.

"In a few minutes."

After several stops and starts, the elevator doors opened to the tenth floor, and Valli stepped into the corridor. The waiting area by the elevators was plushly decorated with gilt-framed chairs and a love seat which stood on graceful legs on a lush carpet. The heavy satin draperies, caught with a golden cord, complemented the colors of the print in the wallpaper.

"Okay, we're just around the corner." Valli hurried down the hallway, beginning to feel the fatigue in the backs of her legs from wearing high heels all night, the strain of the awards ceremony, and the parties. At the moment, all she wanted to do was fling off her shoes, collapse in a chair, and sob.

Of course, she couldn't. Rae would never understand such conduct from her mother, and the child was upset enough by their hasty departure. Valli didn't have time to indulge herself by giving in to her emotions.

Once inside the suite, Valli looked around. Satisfied that she and Rae could live comfortably there temporarily, she hurried to the phone to call the concierge. The first order of the day was finding a nanny for Rae. Perhaps the concierge could recommend a service.

The call took several minutes, but the voice on the phone provided her with the names of two reliable services. Valli slid her aching feet out of her black sling-back shoes and wriggled her toes. She felt better already. Her second call cheered her considerably. A candidate for the position would arrive at the hotel shortly for an interview.

Valli laid her head back and closed her eyes. She was exhausted. In less than twenty-four hours she'd won an Oscar, left her husband, and moved three thousand miles.

When she opened her eyes again, an hour had passed. She sat up with a start. Where was Rae? She looked around the large sitting room and in the bathroom without finding her.

"Rae? Where are you, baby?"

No answer. She searched the little girl's bedroom and found nothing. Beginning to worry, she crossed the sitting room and entered the second bedroom. Rae was lying across the king-size bed. Beside her lay Court, and both were sleeping soundly.

"Court," she whispered and touched his arm.

His green eyes opened sleepily, and a smile teased the corners of his mouth. Sliding his arm from beneath the little girl's head, he tiptoed out of the room after Valli.

"Hi, Country Mouse." After hugging her he sat down in a chair opposite Valli on the sofa. "Sorry you caught me napping."

"What are you doing here?"

"I'm hurt." He held his hand over his heart. "I thought you'd be glad to see me."

"To be truthful, I'm delighted." Valli tucked one foot beneath her and flexed her other foot gingerly. "I was just going to call you, when I missed Rae. I wonder why she didn't tell me you were here?"

"Beats me, but I'm glad she's asleep." Court hung his leg over the arm of the chair and began swinging his foot back and forth. "Terrance called me. He's worried about you, Val."

Valli stood and walked to the window, recalling the scene of her leaving. From her vantage point, she could see Park Avenue below. "I know."

She swung around to face Court. Why did he have to bring this up immediately? She wasn't ready to talk about it yet.

"Look, Val," he said as he moved across the room to her. "We don't have to talk about this at all, if you don't want to."

She watched his fluid, athletic movement and smiled. "That's what I hate about you."

"Hate?"

"Yes, you're always so damned understanding about everything." Her eyes softened. "But, I don't really hate you. I never could."

"You can't know how happy I am to hear that." He reached out to her and rubbed her arm gently.

His arm around her waist, Court led her to the sofa, and they sat down. Valli rested her head in the crook of his arm, saying nothing for a few minutes. "I'm moving to New York, Court."

"Moving?"

"Yes. I've left Steele." Her voice quavered, and she paused.

"Look, let's order a pot of coffee. And something for Rae. She won't sleep long." He strode to the phone and dialed room service. "Send a pot of coffee, some milk, a platter of sandwiches, and something sweet, enough for three people. . .Room 1026."

"Thanks, Court. I'm really starving now that I think about it." Valli closed her eyes and rested her head on the back of the sofa.

"From the looks of you, you've been starving for some time."

"What?" She peered at Court through a fringe of dark lashes, "Oh. I've been dieting."

"You don't have to look like a pole, Valli. Those models are bad enough." He gazed at her and then walked over to her. "You need to find a place to live."

Valli filled Court in on her plans to hire a nanny. "And then we need to look for a place, of course. And I've got to find a job."

"Say, Val, you and Rae can live with me in Connecticut until you get a place. When you need to stay in the city, the nanny will be there."

"That sounds wonderful, Court." Valli felt relief flood over her. The idea of leaving Rae alone in the hotel day after day—even with a nanny—bothered her tremendously. "I think I'll take you up on that."

Just then the waiter knocked on the door with the coffee and sandwiches. Court took care of everything while Valli called Rae into the room.

Court removed the silver lids and smiled warmly at Valli and Rae. "A feast."

He poured two coffees and handed Rae a glass of milk, while Valli put three tiny finger sandwiches on a plate. "Here you are, honey. Why don't you take this to your room and watch some TV?" Rae scampered out of the room. Valli leaned back, sipped the dark brew, and smiled. "This could be habit forming. It's the best coffee I've ever had."

"Are you ready to talk?"

"No, I don't think so. Give me time, Court."

"You have all the time in the world, Val. You know I'd never pressure you into anything." He sat down beside her on the sofa.

"No, you never have."

"What are your plans?"

"Plans? I haven't any. That damn Steele. Court, he promised me. Promised. And, he just can't stay out of trouble." Valli fought back the tears.

Court said nothing but sipped his coffee and nibbled on a salmon-and-cream-cheese sandwich.

"I decided that I wanted to come back here, to New York, to the pulse of the fashion industry. I'm going to open my own house."

"I see." Court put down his cup. "Have you talked to Lorenso?"

"Lors? Why would I talk to that old fool? After what he did to me?" Valli stared at Court. "I hope I never have to see him again." A flash of life came back into her eyes.

"Come on, Val. He was just protecting his image. You know, he hasn't done very much since you left."

"Don't I know it? And I have. But designing for movies was not what I wanted to do, or run a boutique—no matter how successful." Valli studied the hem of her white linen skirt, not daring to allow Court to see the tears of frustration that stung her eyes.

"Well, I think an Academy Award is pretty special. And it's helped make you famous. Look at you." Court lifted her chin with his fingers. "You're one of a kind. All you've been doing these past years is. . .is building. Now you have a solid base of clients and the Oscar to prove it. Use them."

"Use them?"

"Yes."

"I suppose I could. You know I've been thinking. . .that fashion may be ready to follow the movies. *Dr. Zhivago* single-handedly created the Russian craze. And women have always wanted to look like the stars. We could show a whole line of the most beautiful designs ever filmed. Sort of a retrospective, but updated. New, but old. Hollywood Classics. I think people will love it."

"I'll do whatever I can to help. I'm going to be in town for a couple of weeks."

"No tournaments?"

Court's dimples showed. "Oh, I gave that up long ago. I've got other plans in the works." He kissed her on the cheek, his lips lingering a moment as his hand touched her shoulder. "Look, I've got a couple of things to do this afternoon, but I'll be back later."

"Court, I apologize. I've been so wrapped up in my problems that I haven't even asked about you."

"Hey, I came to see you. I wanted to make sure you settled in okay." He took her hand and squeezed it gently. "There's plenty of time for me later." Damn, he hoped that was true.

"Well, what brings you to the garment district, Court?" Lors pointed to a chair. "Have a seat. Don't tell me you're looking for designer tennis shorts."

"No, just dropping in on an old friend."

"'Old' is right." Lors lit a Turkish cigarette, leaned back, and blew a smoke ring. "Now. What's on your mind?"

"Nothing much. Just in the neighborhood."

"Scouting for a new escort? None of our models are in this afternoon. Besides, from what I read, you've been dating some starlet barely out of rompers."

"Okay, she's a little young."

"A little? Come on, this is Lors. I doubt you're looking for a part-time modeling job." Stubbing out his cigarette, Lors propped his elbows on the mahogany desk. "So tell me what you want."

"Just visiting, honest."

"This visit have anything to do with Valli?"

Court looked around the office. The area around the desk appeared to have been devastated by a recent tornado, but a small area to the left of the desk was neatly decorated with a thick carpet and velvet love seats in Lors's signature color. "Not really. She's in town—or had you heard?"

The gray-haired man's blue eyes brightened. "No. But since you haven't graced my office since she left, I could only surmise that this visit must be related to her."

Court gazed at Lors a few seconds, trying to decide how best to approach him. "Look, Lors, I'm going to level with you. Top secret, huh?"

"Top secret?" Lors stood up. "Let's move to my sitting room."

Following Lors, Court moved into the lushly carpeted sitting area. The velvet love seat faced a painting of a woman dressed in lavender chiffon, her breasts and pubic hair barely visible through the transparent fabric.

"Well, I'm waiting."

"Just admiring your painting."

"Ah, yes, my painting. Which reminds me, what in hell happened to you?"

"Economics. One day, maybe, I'll get back to my art, if you can call it that."

"Don't deny your talent. But all of us must make concessions to the mighty dollar." He smiled at Court, inviting confidences. "I've made enough concessions in my lifetime."

"We all do," Court agreed. "But that has nothing to do with Valli."

"Oh? Is she above economics?"

"I'm not certain of her financial status, but she's done very well in California." Court recollected her demeanor, her suite, and her past successes. "In fact, she's probably in very sound financial condition and, of course, her prospects are excellent after winning the Oscar. It's her personal life I'm concerned about. She's moving back to New York."

"And pray why did she send you around to see *moi*?"

"Damn it, she didn't send me. In fact, if she knew I was here, she'd probably never speak to me again."

Lors looked stunned. "She didn't ask you to come?"

"Hell, no."

"Well, then why are you here?"

"I don't know, really." Court watched the designer's expression change to one of interest. "I just feel it's time to mend fences. You and Valli need to. . ."

"Are you mad?" Lors jumped out of his seat. "After what she did to me?"

"Come on, Lors. Save your injured-designer routine for someone else." Court stared directly into Lors's heavy-lidded eyes. "I know who kept you afloat when she was here. And I also know that the reports on Lorenso Fashions are getting worse."

"I resent. . ."

206

"Let's see, I can quote a few. 'Uninspired,' 'below par,' 'flagrantly disorganized' shows..."

"So what's your point?" Lors chewed on his ebony cigarette holder.

"Why not go to see Valli? She's at the Waldorf until she gets a permanent place."

"Over my dead body. Do you think for one...never. Let *her* come crawling back to me!"

CHAPTER FIFTEEN

Roses. Reflected in the gold-framed mirror were a dozen red roses, half-open and fragrant. They had arrived from Court that morning. Valli touched the deep red velvety petal of the nearest bud, fingering it lightly, lingering over its lushness a moment before turning to face Lors. "Why are you here?"

He gazed at her a second, tired lines framing his eyes. At twenty-nine she was far more beautiful than at nineteen, he thought. In her crimson silk pants suit, she looked like an American Beauty Rose herself, almost but not quite in full bloom. "No reason. Just welcoming a competitor. . . .a comrade in the industry."

His voice faded to silence. Stunned by the changed shrunken man the great Lorenso had become, Valli waited. This Lors was very different from the in-charge, go-get-'em Lors of the early days. He was probably in his late fifties, but he looked much older.

"Volley," he teased, his eyes brightening briefly before his lips trembled and the smile disappeared.

"*V* as in Victory," she bgan, hoping to draw him from his doldrums. Even though she still felt cheated, Valli hated to ee Lors looking so pathetic. "*A* as. . ."

". . .as in Ambition. I know. How well I know." His shoulders straightened. "I'm simply here for a friendly visit."

"I doubt it. But tell me about yourself, anyway."

"What's to tell? I'm making a fortune." Wrinkles fanned away from the shrunken corners of his mouth as he grinned conspiratorially. "The fashion industry is at its finest hour, and Lorenso is riding the crest of the wave."

"Crest of the wave, huh?" Valli watched him with renewed interest. She knew better, and despite his bragging she sensed a desperation that refused to be quelled by his bravado. "I'm delighted for you."

"And you?" His smile widened. "How are you doing?"

"Lors, you know very well how I'm doing." Valli drew a satin throw-pillow into her lap and leaned against it, studying him carefully. Without a doubt, Lors was up to something.

"Come on, haven't you learned to be civil during the past few years?" He held his hands to his chest. "I'm wounded that you would think I'd be so underhanded as to come here with an ulterior motive. You were like a daughter to me until you chose to cut my heart out and cast it beneath the feet of the heathen press."

"I. . .Now, look Lors," Valli sputtered. "Let's not. . ."

"Right, let's not fight." He closed his eyes wearily.

"And, to answer your question, yes, I've not only learned to be civil, but I've also learned to speak properly, apply makeup, and I've learned where and what to spend my money on—everything a girl needs to know in order to get along in Beverly Hills."

"Do tell."

"Damn, Lors. You're so. . .I serve dinner on Sevres china so fine that you can see a broom straw through it, adorn my beds with Porthault linens, sip Chateau Lafitte Rothschild from fluted Baccarat crystal, this little bauble on my finger is a black diamond, and what's more, I know a fish fork from a salad fork. What else would you like to know?" Valli's eyes flashed fire.

Lors laughed gently. "Of course you do, darling. Like every little Beverly Hills bitch. But, I merely wanted to know how you're doing."

"Simmering. Lors, why are you here?"

"Ah, calm down. You must admit that we got on well once upon a time." He slid forward on the chair and reached for her hand. "Truce?"

Reluctantly, she grasped his feather-light hand. "Truce. I'm fine. No, not so fine. You probably heard that Steele and I separated."

"I heard." He released her hand and leaned back in the chair. "He was never good enough for you, Valli. He'll never understand how to tame the vixen in you."

"And who could, if not Steele?"

"Now that shows how naive you still are, Valli."

Valli didn't understand. Her mind wandered back to her lovely home in Laurel Canyon, to the elegance of its Spanish architecture, the lacy wrought-iron trim, and her landscaped pool, artfully designed to appear as if it cascaded naturally from the ground into a pond. And, then, her memory drew up Steele's image before her—full and sensual and disloyal.

"Ahem, are you listening?"

"What?" Scarlet flashed into her cheeks as he called her back to the present. "I apologize, Lors. It's not you. I'm so distracted with the separation and the. . .I, eh, with everything."

His eyes widened. "Not telling me something? Come on, darling. What's going on in your devious little mind?"

"Nothing, really." She looked at him. She certainly wasn't going to tell him about her career plans. "Nothing. Now what were you saying?"

"I was saying that your success might be directly associated with your connection with me. Lorenso Fash—"

"What? Of all the nerve. Damn you, Lors. You. . .''

"Now, hold on. I didn't mean to. . .''

"Didn't mean to what? To insult me? To insinuate that you are responsible for my success? Just what is your game, ors?" She jumped angrily to her feet, strode to the silver coffee service, and poured herself another cup. "I'm tiring of this cat-and-mouse game. Get to your point."

"The lady's still a vixen," he chided. "Look, Valli, I'm a successful designer with a reputation that extends over three decades, under my own signature. You're. . ."

"A successful designer whose reputation spans over a decade. What's a few years?" She spun around to face him. "Don't try to intimidate me, Lors. You'll find I'm not easily cowed."

"So the lady's got moxy." He moved to her side and poured himself a second cup of coffee. "Truce, remember?"

Lors returned to his chair, avoiding her gaze. "Come, sit down. I want to discuss something serious with you."

"What is it?" Valli sat down on the corner of the sofa across from him and drew her feet under her.

"I'm tired, Valli. I want to rest, relax, take a vacation, anything." He rubbed the brocade of the chair. "I want to sell a significant part of Lorenso Fashions. You boosted us to prominence with your crazy, wonderful tunics, so I'm offering you the majority partnership in Lorenso Fashions."

Valli's mouth opened, but no words came out.

"Don't stop me. I have to get this out." He waved her unspoken comment aside. "Hear me out. I want to remain in an advisory capacity, to work with a few select clients."

"But Lors, how. . ."

"How? Lorenso/Valli Fashions. That's how."

"I can't imagine. . ."

"Look, you want a way to break back into fashion in this town. Now you know you can't do it without backing. And even then, a new venture could fail. You need an established house, and I'm offering it to you"—his eyes seemed glazed tired, as if they'd seen too much of the competition, the glare of footlights on the runway and stages of fashion shows, and the fierce cutthroat industry magnates—"on a silver platter, Valli, dear."

"No. I can't. . ."

"Don't say no, yet. Think about it." Lors placed his cup

on the Louis XIV-style table and moved toward the door.
"You know. . .I need you, Valli."

Valli studied the roses once again, hardly seeing them after a time. Lors's unexpected proposal kept filling her mind, swirling about with possibilities, probabilities, and eventualities that she considered satisfactory if she could buy at the price she expected. Her dreams were coming true.

Years ago, on her first day in New York, a scrawny kid from Willacoochee had stood on the curb looking at the famous signature across the lavender van. Vowing that one day she would own Lorenso Fashions, she'd climbed inside with Steele. Now, she was thirty-two and her dream was about to come true.

Time softens the blows dealt by fate, she thought. The deal would be struck, if for nothing else, then for sentimentality and for the fulfillment of her dreams. She'd have to go into debt to do it, but she knew that when she finished, she could turn Lorenso/Valli Fashions into the brightest star in the sky. Slipping a rose from the vase, she carried it with her, holding its soft petals close to her nostrils.

A knock on the door startled her momentarily, but she strode across the room to open it, knowing it would be Court. The card attached to the roses had invited her to dinner at nine o'clock. "Who is it?" she called out.

"Court."

Swinging the door open, she gazed into the familiar green eyes sprinkled with gold. "Hi."

"Hi." His gaze swept the room and he turned to face her. "Alone?"

"Just me and Rae. Were you expecting someone else?" She sniffed the rose gently, then lifted her eyes to face him.

"No. You just mentioned that you might have an appointment."

"Oh, I canceled my appointment."

"You look lovely, especially lovely this evening." His gaze raked across her body, taking in every detail. "How about dinner?"

Valli smiled, delighted that he seemed so pleased with her gown. It was one she'd designed for herself before she'd first learned about Steele's problems with the first Academy Award nomination. "Let's have room service. I don't want to leave Rae with a sitter. She's asleep now."

"Fine by me." He placed his hand on the small of her back and followed her across the room, dropping onto the sofa beside her. "Bad day?"

"Sort of. Lors came by." Twirling the rose between her fingers, Valli kicked off her shoes and propped her feet on the dainty coffee table, careful not to wrinkle the Chinese watered silk that floated around her. The cerise-colored fabric complemented her dark hair, and when she stood, she knew she looked like a delicate doll. "He looks awful. Oh, shit! I pricked my finger."

She sucked her finger for a second, watching Court beneath velvety lashes. Despite all the hell she'd gone through in the past months, Valli felt flushed, passionate, and her passion was directed toward Court. Perhaps only Court could make her feel that way again.

"Be more careful. You can't afford to be out of commission with an infected finger," Court teased. "And, I'd hate to think I caused an injury to you. What did Lors want?"

"To make me a partner in Lorenso Fashions." She idly fingered the collar of diamonds around her neck.

"You're kidding." He watched her perfectly manicured nails a moment, not noticing her minute examination of his face and body, then reached out, lifted her hand to his lips, and kissed her fingers.

"No," Valli said too quickly and looked into his eyes, feeling all her apprehensions and tensions melt away with her earlier resolve to avoid intimacy while she sorted through her problems with Steele. "I don't want to talk about it, not yet. You know, I think my daughter's in love with you."

"Right. Children fall helplessly and hoplessly in love with me immediately." He cupped her chin in his hand and touched her lips with a kiss. "I wish I could be as successful with their mothers. One in particular."

"Court, now. . ." His touch burned into her skin, fueling the passion that she held in too tightly for fear of starting something that would only complicate matters. She knew Court's feelings and didn't want to toy with them.

"Don't give me your lecture. I promise not to pressure you, but we could be so happy." He wrapped his arms around her. "Rae would be happy. You could be, too, and if you were happy, then I would be."

"Court. . ." She twisted the rose absently. His lips silenced her protest, and Valli felt fire course through her, liquid, lunging through veins to inflame every cell until her body burned with the desire that captured her each time Court embraced her. Fully aware that surrender meant scalding, passionate lovemaking, she allowed herself to melt into his arms.

Her nipples hardened, and her fingers sought the fullness of Court's hair as he wound his fingers into her ebony mane. His tongue, plunging into her mouth, teased hers and explored as the pressure increased and drew her further toward the lip of a volcano.

With the ease of an athlete, Court lifted her and carried her to the bedroom, not stopping until he reached the king-size bed. Placing her on the edge, he felt along her shoulders until his fingers touched the zipper at the nape of her neck. Beneath the sheer silk float, she wore a matching satin slip appliquéd with roses of a slightly darker shade so that when someone first looked at the dress, they saw only the filmy cerise silk. On second glance, they caught the real mood of the dress—roses and romance.

Cursing the complexity of her gown, Court could hardly keep from tearing it off her body. His fingers caressed her back as it came free of the fabric, and he pulled her to him, kissing her lips with a vigor that belied his carefully paced disrobing.

He pressed her back into the bed, nearly collapsing beside her. "God, if you only knew what you do to me."

Like a whisper of spring, his fingers swept down her body, teasing her skin as it burned beneath his touch, and

214

she thrust her body nearer his. She welcomed his lean frame against hers, reveled in the throbbing erection against her thigh.

Still clutching the rose, she drew it lightly down his back until he paused and stared at her, puzzled by the feathery sensation. She took the opportunity and pushed him onto his back. "Shhh. Lie still."

In the dimly lit room, she played with the rose, caressing his body until he twitched beneath her touch. Valli smiled, as she teased his skin with the velvety petals, delighted that her play enhanced his pleasure as evidenced by his heightened arousal.

"Enough." Court took the rose from her hand and tossed it across the room.

"Love me, Court." The sound of her voice was barely audible as he slid between her legs, needing no further encouragement.

He set a steady pace, thrusting against her, meeting her hips in a joyful celebration as his lips claimed hers again.

Valli peered out the window and then back at Court, lying on a bed lit only by the light of the rising sun, slanting through the angle of the curtain where she stood. His caresses had thrilled her, brought her to heights attained with no other man, but still something held her back.

Steele. Though the marriage had failed, the ties remained. Substituting Court wasn't the answer. It was too easy—and too complicated. As she watched him, Court stirred. His hand moved across the bed, searching for her as he mumbled her name in his sleep. The innocence portrayed in his face fascinated her. He was a worldly, powerful man, especially since he'd inherited his father's fortune, but he lacked direction.

Valli knew it was perverse, but she couldn't understand his lack of amibtion. He had a talent—a rare one, but he didn't use it. He wasn't the type of man to seek fame. That was fine. She'd seen what fame could do to a man. But why didn't he paint? That, she could never understand. In many ways he seemed to exist only for her. And she wasn't sure if she could live up to his expectations. What kind of woman had she become? In love with one man and aroused to passion by another.

"Damn!" Jumping up and down on one foot, she removed the offending thorn from her foot. The rose lay where Court had tossed it. "From my bed of roses into the streets of thorns." A movement behind her reminded her that Court was still asleep, or had been until her outburst.

Valli smiled as his eyes opened. In the dim light, she could only see that they were open, but she knew that the startling green beneath the mass of honey-colored hair had captured many unwary women's hearts. Yet few women knew the real Court. If they did, they would probably all fall in love with him.

CHAPTER SIXTEEN

Valli heard the loud music before she opened the door to the apartment. Closing the door behind her, she strode down the hall toward Rae's bedroom. Thank goodness they had good insulation. And thank goodness their neighbors were in Europe.

"Turn off that noise, Rae, and get off that phone. I want to talk to you." Valli opened the door to see her lanky thirteen-year-old daughter lounging on the bed, telephone in hand.

Rae looked up at her mother with scorn and continued to talk into the phone. Valli caught the petulant curl of her lips, full sensual lips exactly like her father's, and she winced. She could almost feel the touch of those lips, even now after all this time. After six-and-a-half years of separation she still wondered whom he was kissing now. She wondered if he ever thought about her. But then he didn't have a constant reminder around to make him remember.

Valli shook her head and backed out of Rae's room, trying to ignore the mess. A splitting headache sent arrows of pain into the back side of her eyes.

She knew that she was hard on Rae sometimes. She knew

that it was because of Steele and her anger at him that she couldn't handle her own teenager without yelling like some kind of banshee. She'd wait until after dinner to talk to her. Perhaps by then she would feel calmer. Since Valli had bought Lorenso Fashions over six years ago, her life had been turbulent and satisfying.

From a company on the brink of bankruptcy, Lorenso/ Valli Fashions had become a shrewd competitor in the fashion world. Lorenso remained in the background, advising when asked and designing a few gowns for the older matriarchs who had long insisted on his services. To Valli, he seemed a perfect partner—never around to get in her way, and seemingly content to hand over the reins of power. Others would say that Valli had grabbed the reins and not let go. Most would admit that her designs had renewed the house's place in the spotlight. Valli herself would readily admit that Terrance's newfound business acumen and Lorenso's old connections had helped a great deal.

"Mrs. Colton?" Mrs. Hill, the housekeeper, stood quietly in the open doorway, interrupting her thoughts.

"Yes?"

"Will you want dinner soon?"

"Yes, let me take a quick shower, and I'll be right in. Please tell Rae when it's ready."

After a shower and two aspirins, she felt better. Sometime during the time she was being pelted with the hot water, Rae had turned off the stereo, and now blessed silence graced their twentieth-floor penthouse apartment.

Valli waited until they'd finished eating before she broached the subject she'd been preparing herself for all day. "Mrs. Hill tells me that your teacher called, Rae. She said that you skipped school again."

"So?" Rae's voice was sullen, her eyes lowered.

"So, you've been told not to do that anymore." Valli looked across at her daughter. At thirteen, Rae was already five feet seven—five inches taller than her mother and quite developed. Even her uniform of tattered jeans and sweatshirts couldn't hide her blossoming figure. She wore her black hair in a messy shag, which emphasized her over-large blue eyes. "Oh, Rae, what am I going to do with you? I know that it's hard, just the two of us."

Rae's knife clattered on the edge of the plate, but that was the only sign she gave that she might be concerned about her mother's words.

"Where were you?"

"Just goofing off, Mother. Down in the Village, You know about the Village, don't you, Mother? Where you met my father?"

Valli looked up, startled at Rae's vehemence, then quickly masked her feelings. "Yes, that's where I met your father. But besides the fact that you're supposed to be in school, I don't want you going down there alone, Rae. It isn't safe."

"I can look after myself, Mother. I've been doing it for a long time. As a matter of fact"—she paused and glanced from beneath half-closed eyelids—"I've been thinking of moving back to Hollywood with Dad."

"Absolutely not!" Valli sputtered furiously. "You aren't going anywhere. There'll be no discussion of that, young lady. Let's stick to the facts. You will go to school every day, and you'll come straight home from school, and you're not to go off with anybody without checking in with me first."

"And how am I supposed to do that, Mother? Do you have a phone in your purse? You're never there when I call and you're hardly ever at home at night. I think you'd better clean up your act, Mother. This conversation looks suspiciously like the pot calling the kettle black. At least I won't sleep with other men when I'm married."

"Don't talk to me like that, Rae." Valli did go out with other men, of course, but really most of the time it was for business. Valli's devotion to her company was absolute, and there was no room in her life for a man. More important, she had wanted to make it on her own this time—without a man. Even Court hadn't understood that.

After she had come back to New York, she'd thought that Court might accept a relationship without commitment. But soon she'd seen how much more he wanted and how much he was hurting. After a few months she'd rented an apartment and brought Rae back to New York as soon as she could, but even that hadn't been soon enough. Rae at seven hadn't understood why they'd left her darling daddy in California and moved to New York. Then to leave Court in Connecticut and move into their first tiny apartment had been too much for the child. Even now, six years later, she still held Valli responsible for Steele's absence.

"I don't go out with other men, not like that, Rae." It was true. She'd completely submerged her sexual nature.

"Oh? And how is it that you're still Mrs. Steele Colton and yet you live here and my father lives all the way across the country? I'm the only girl in my group whose parents aren't divorced, and you don't live together. Why is that, Mother? We had a good life together as a family."

"You don't know everything, Rae." Valli took a deep breath to steady herself. "You wouldn't understand if you did."

"What was it? Sex? Drugs? I'm thirteen years old, Mother, and I'm tired of your bullshit." Rae's voice rose shrilly. "I've got a father, and I want to live with him. At least he'll be around occasionally, and maybe, just maybe, we might have dinner without it turning into a fight."

"Rae, there are things you just wouldn't understand. I love your father, and he loves me. We just can't live together. But remember, we both love you and want what's best for you, darling. I'll call him tonight and see if he'll let you come for a visit before school begins. I can't promise, but I'll talk to him. In the meantime, young lady, no more cutting school."

"You'll talk to him? I don't believe it. You've told me that before."

Valli watched Rae storm away from the table with that melodramatic dare that said, you can talk 'til hell freezes over, but you aren't telling me what to do. She sighed as a tide of frustration engulfed her. The last thing she wanted to do was come home to a confrontation with Rae every night. But she knew that they were heading for disaster. Last year

Rae had been kicked out of school. Her teachers couldn't handle her frequent outbursts in class. Rae, they informed Valli, had a severe behavior problem. Now Rae had it in her head that she could go and live with her father, and Valli knew that it just wouldn't work.

Chris had moved into Steele's house, and they lived a quiet life. But if Rae were there, Steele mightn't be able to conceal his activities from the daughter who still shadowed every step he took on the few occasions when he did come to see her. No, they'd decided that it was best for Rae if she lived with her mother. Heaven knows, sometimes the idea of shipping her difficult daughter off to Steele had been tempting.

As Valli lay in bed reading the latest report from her accountant, she heard a light knock at her door.

"I'm sorry I'm such a disappointment to you, Mother," Rae said in a throaty whisper. "I just get so lonely. And it's very hard—you don't know how hard it really is."

"I'm sure I don't," Valli agreed mutely. "You're a good girl, Rae. I worry about you more than you could possibly understand. Come here and give me a hug." Valli held on to her daughter in a rare moment of conciliation. Sometimes Rae could be so sweet.

A week later Valli got a telephone call from the police department. Rae had been arrested for shoplifting, and they'd found three joints in her purse.

"Why, Rae? Why would you do a dumb thing like that? You know I'd have bought it for you."

"Oh, I didn't intend to wear it. I was going to sell it."

"Sell it, what for? What could you possibly need money for?"

"Oh, grow up, Mother. I wanted to buy pot. It doesn't grow on trees you know, at least not in the city."

"Pot?" There was incredulity in Valli's voice. She'd heard the lieutenant say they'd found pot in Rae's purse, and she'd been alarmed, but pot smoking was so common that she'd actually gotten used to it. But now her daughter had been arrested for stealing a necklace that she intended to sell to buy drugs? Something was seriously wrong, and Valli couldn't handle it anymore.

"Mrs. Colton?"

It was Mrs. Hill. Valli waved Terrance away with a shush and answered with a sense of dread. Mrs. Hill never called unless there was a problem. "Yes?"

"I can't be sure, Mrs. Colton, but I think Rae has run away. When I went in to wake her this morning she was gone, and her bed hadn't been slept in. Did you see her last night?"

"No." Valli's heart fell. She'd gotten home so late that she'd gone straight to bed. Then a breakfast appointment had taken her away from the house earlier than usual. She tried to think when she'd last seen Rae. It had been the evening before, or maybe the day before that. Trying to get the fall line ready was turning into a nightmare of complications. She'd simply let time get away from her. "I'll call the police. I'm sure they'll find her."

But they didn't. And Valli had nearly collapsed from fear and anguish. After four days, it had been Steele who called. "Rae turned up at my front door last night, Valli. She said she'd hitched a ride from New York. How the hell could you let that happen and not even let me know?"

Thank goodness, she was safe. "You're right, Steele. I should have called you at once. I should have known that she was going to you. Is she all right?"

"Yes, no thanks to you. I'm going to let her stay for a few days before I'm due in New York. I'll bring her along with me, and we'll talk."

"Maybe I ought to just let her stay with you for a while, Steele. She seems to want to be there, more than she wants to be here."

"And I'd keep her in a minute, Val, but I'm off to Australia to do a film. You know how unstable my life is. I can't keep her, even though I'd like to."

The next week Valli consulted Court and made arrangements for Rae to go to boarding school in Switzerland. Although she hadn't seen him in over a year, Court and Valli talked frequently. Recently he'd bought a tennis resort in the Cayman Islands and had spent the last year promoting the resort. He lived there now year-round. Rae had visited him there recently.

Valli wanted to get Rae as far away from New York City and Los Angeles as she could, and Steele agreed with her. The ticket and a new wardrobe were ready when a subdued Rae returned. For the first time in a long time she and Steele put her on a plane together. Valli had expected protests, and she wasn't sure she would be able to go through with it, if Rae had been genuinely unhappy. But Rae had received the news with stony silence. That night Valli invited Steele back to the apartment. He could stay with her while he was in town, but he declined. Outside of dinner and a play, he had other plans which he couldn't, or wouldn't, alter.

When he dropped her at the door, she made one last open plea for his company. Already, she missed Rae. "Wouldn't you like to come in for a drink, Steele?"

"No thanks, Val. I don't think that's a good idea. I hope we've done the right thing about Rae. But I don't know. I don't seem to know much about anything anymore. It's hell to realize that I'm almost forty."

"You're a long way from being over the hill, at least according to the stories I hear." She felt a stab of jealousy cut through her. He was her husband, damn it, and she'd stuck with him for a long time.

"It was your choice to leave me, Valli."

"Yes," she rasped, "and it was your choices that made me do it."

"Damn it, Valli, I still love you. You know that I do."

"Yes." Her voice was suddenly sad. "I think you do, and I still love you, Steele. But I can't live with you, not knowing that I have to share you. . . .I want a divorce, Steele. Maybe if we settle our marriage, Rae won't be so unsettled."

"No, Valli. I won't give you a divorce. You're my wife, and I want you to continue to be my wife. No divorce."

"You can't stop me, Steele. I believe I have more than

enough evidence to prove just about anything I want.''

"And if you use it, it will destroy Rae." He slammed the door and left the apartment, burning with shame at the challenge he'd just flung at Valli. He didn't know why he'd refused the divorce. She deserved to be allowed to live the kind of life she wanted to, remarry, even have more children. . . . And yet, confusion was tearing him apart.

He loved Rae, and he wanted her to have a mother and a father. No step-parents for his daughter. This was better. Val had never seemed interested in remarrying. If it ever came to that, he'd reconsider. Until then, Valli was Mrs. Steele Colton, and he liked the security that gave him. He and Val belonged together and, someday, maybe they'd be together again.

In the penthouse apartment where Valli Colton lived, there was no noise, only a blank silence. Stepping out onto the terrace, Valli looked down at Central Park. The city below was quiet and dull; the trees were bare. Valli shivered and went back inside. Opening the door to her daughter's now-empty bedroom, she lay across the bed and allowed the tears to fall. Life with Rae had been difficult—more so than Valli had ever expected—but they had had each other. Now Valli felt alone, and she hoped she'd done the right thing.

In a plane, flying through a sky so black that even the stars were absent, Rae Colton allowed the hatred inside her to begin to grow. For the first three hours of her flight she'd cried, and now the tears were gone. She wouldn't cry again. All right, so neither of her parents wanted her. Neither of them had enough time to spend with a thirteen-year-old. So? Fine! She'd do without them. They wanted to get rid of her. Fine! She'd give them their wish. Rae Colton had no intention of ever going home again.

CHAPTER SEVENTEEN

"You must go to Los Angeles. He's sick, Valli, very sick."

"But, Noel, I don't understand. I haven't heard a word, and you know he always calls me if there's anything wrong."

"Not this time, Val, and that's what scares me. He's holed himself up in that house in the canyon with his publicity agent, and nobody is allowed inside. Nobody."

"What do you want me to do?"

Valli glanced around her Park Avenue apartment and considered Noel's words. She hadn't seen Steele since the night four years ago when they had put Rae on the plane. She'd hardly seen her daughter since then either.

She'd kept in touch with Noel since he'd become a congressman, but this was the first time in nearly five years that he'd come to see her. He was graying about the temples, older with a strained look about his eyes. At forty-seven he'd seen much of his dream of equality come true, but he was still a maverick on the issue—only now he fought for women, homosexuals, and any other downtrodden group.

Valli sighed. "Do you ever think about the Village, Noel,

and the beginning? I mean, did you ever dream that Steele would really be a Hollywood superstar, that I'd buy Lorenso's salon, and that you'd end up a congressman from Boston?"

"No, I guess even my wildest dreams never went that far. And Court's done all right, too. His resort in the Caymans is the 'in' place to go, isn't it?"

"Yes, Court is—doing well. How about writing, Noel? Is Spud Towns dead and gone?"

"I still do a little writing, nothing for publication I'm afraid. I've been playing around with the idea of writing a screenplay or novel someday."

"Oh, Noel, how wonderful. You know Rae thought she might want to write. She's been working with a little magazine in Paris."

"I thought she was in school at the Sorbonne."

"She is, or was. To tell the truth, I'm not quite sure. At eighteen they resent any questions at all, and she's such a poor correspondent. The only way I know she's still there is because she cashes her allowance check every month. Court sees more of her than I do."

Noel looked up in surprise at the bitterness in her voice. "Court?"

"I don't think she's ever forgiven me for leaving Steele. Court was patient and kind, and he was there for her. She's been much closer to Court in the last few years."

"Then she doesn't know why you left?" Noel rose and walked over to the window, looking down at the traffic below.

"No. I didn't want her to know. He is her father, and I thought the truth would be too much."

"So you let her hate you in order to protect Steele. Why haven't you divorced him, Valli? There must have been other men in your life."

"Yes, but it never seemed right. After all is said and done, Steele and I belong together, even if there have been— others. Why did you go to see him, Noel? You're married. It was a risk, a big risk."

226

"Yes, it was a risk, a risk I had to take. I understand well what you mean about you and Steele, even if there are others. I've seen Steele frequently. I never told my wife, though."

"Oh." Valli was surprised. Steele had never told her, but she no longer felt hurt or jealous of Noel.

The two friends stared at each other, both knowing and accepting the fact that loving Steele Colton was a risk they'd both taken.

"All right," she agreed, "I'll go. But, what makes you think that he'll see me if he wouldn't see you?"

"Because, in spite of all that has happened and in spite of what Steele is, he loves you the best."

Valli placed a call to Paris. She thought that Rae should know about her father, although she didn't expect her to respond. After the first few years at boarding school and of asking Steele to come and get her, Rae never asked again. She had seen him on occasion, of course. But during the last few years he'd been even less attentive than usual.

"Rae's not here, Mrs. Colton. She's in the Cayman Islands at her uncle's tennis resort."

"Oh, I see. How long has she been gone?"

"This time she's been there a week, but I never know how long she'll stay," her Parisian roommate answered. "You know how she is when she gets down there with 'him.'"

"Him?"

"Court. She's absolutely crazy about him, you know."

"Yes, I know."

The second call took longer.

"And you're going, of course." Court's voice was resigned.

"Of course. Noel thought I should. I tried to call Rae, I thought she should know that her father isn't well. I understand she's there with you."

"Yes. She came down for a few days, but she isn't here just now. I'll tell her when she returns."

"Please do." Valli didn't know how she knew, but she was

227

certain that Rae was there standing close by the phone with Court, and he'd protected her.

Valli had learned not to feel hurt. Hurt was destructive and was in itself a kind of vengeance wrought by the other person. She knew that Rae had transferred all her affection to Court, and she could understand why. Court was a very special man. Valli hadn't been a very special mother. She'd meant to be, but somehow there hadn't been enough time to break through Rae's shell. She should have tried harder; now it was too late. Court, she thought, hugging herself with her arms, why aren't you here holding me. I want to lie in your arms, just once more before I go back.

The sky was smoggy and the air heavy with pollution when Valli stepped off the plane at LAX, the Los Angeles airport. She rented a yellow convertible and drove toward her old home with apprehension. She hadn't seen it in nearly eleven years. Every time she had visited, she'd stayed in a hotel.

At the door she looked around a minute at the house where they'd lived. The same gardener planted the same kind of flowers along the drive—only the trees were larger. She felt a lump in her throat as she thought about the happy years she'd spent here with Steele. They had been too brief.

"Valli!"

"Hello, Chris. Where is he?"

"He doesn't want to see you, Valli." Steele's friend held the door half-closed, blocking her entrance with his body.

"Move out of the way, Chris. This is still my house, and I'm coming in, with or without your permission."

"All right," he said in resignation, "but please don't let him know how awful he looks. I haven't let him see himself in a mirror since he got so bad."

Valli swept past Chris and grimly climbed the stairs, softly opening the door to their bedroom. She stopped short and had to suppress a gasp. The man lying in Steele's bed wasn't Steele. He was a skeleton of a man with sallow skin that hung in loose folds beneath his eyes. He seemed to have

228

shrunk. Even from where Valli was standing she could see the perspiration on his forehead.

"Steele?"

His eyes opened in panic. "Valli?" Valli trembled like a leaf. She held every muscle in her body rigid in order to remain upright. The big smile she gave Steele was the hardest thing she'd ever had to do. All she wanted to do was turn and run away. Bile crept out of her stomach and up her throat, lodging there in a lump that burned and choked her.

"Yes, it's me. What's wrong, Steele? Why haven't you called me?" She walked toward the bed.

"No! Stay away, Val. Don't come any closer."

"When have I ever done what I was told?" Valli forced cheerfulness into her voice. She sat on the edge of Steele's bed and took his hand. "I'm here to help you. Tell me what's wrong; I'm not leaving until you do."

"How'd you know anything was wrong?"

"Noel told me."

"That nosey bastard. I thought if I didn't meet him he'd be protected. And then he sends you instead. God knows, I've ruined enough lives; I don't need to add any more to the slaughter. Go back to New York, Val. This is one thing I'll have to do alone."

Valli began to panic. This certainly was not Steele. He'd clearly given up. Steele had done many things during the past twenty years, but never once had he given up.

"How's Rae?" he finally asked.

"Rae is fine. She's in the Caymans with Court."

"What's she doing there?"

"Punishing me, as always. She doesn't come home, she goes to Court, or her girl friend, or her lover, God knows, I don't."

"Still blaming you for my problem. I'm sorry, Val. I never intended to hurt you. I thought. . ."

His voice was weak and thready, and she knew that speaking was an effort. As she held his hand she realized that she was seeing death, cruel and superior, and she wanted to strike out at him, to demand that he rise and be Steele Colton, vivacious, sensual, the heartthrob of America once again.

"Don't talk, Steele, I'm here. We'll fight whatever this is together." She stood up, removed her coat, and opened the closet door for a hanger. "I've arranged to turn my business over to Terrance for as long as it takes for me to get you up and going again."

"Valli, this is one fight we can't win." Steele turned away. "I have AIDS."

Valli dropped the coat where she stood. "I don't care what it is." The smile she forced to her lips belied her terror. This disease was something beyond her power. "We'll find someone. A doctor. . .a clinic. There must be somebody in the world who. . ."

"No."

The single word stopped her in mid-sentence. The finality of his simple statement arrested her, and a quivering that she couldn't control welled up in her. "We'll. . ."

"No, Munchkin." Steele raised himself slightly so he could look at her. "There's nobody. Nothing. No cure, no help."

Somewhere in the house a phone rang, and a door closed.

In the silence, Steele began to cry.

The end did not come quickly. They spent Thanksgiving, Christmas, New Year's and Valli's fortieth birthday together. Between them, Valli and Chris changed Steele's bed, bathed his body with soothing ointments, and talked to him for hours. There were times when he was lucid, and a shadow of the old confident, almost gallant Steele would emerge.

"Valli, I didn't have this thing when I was with you. You're safe."

There were days when Valli cried with Steele and there were nights when she cried alone. Noel called weekly. Still, he wouldn't allow Noel to come.

"Noel is an important public figure, Val," he said with finality. "What would happen if someone found out?"

"What about Noel's wife, Steele? Doesn't she know?"

230

"His wife is an alcoholic. Know about Noel? No, I don't think she really knows. She just knows that Noel doesn't love her. He never has."

That was Steele's last good day. He took Valli's hand and held it into the cool twilight. "I want to sit on the balcony, Val, and watch the sun set over the ocean and the moon come up over the water. There are some things I need to say."

Chris helped him into the chair, pushed him to the porch, and lifted him onto the chaise lounge so that he could stretch out in comfort. The night air was crisp and clear, and Steele smiled a sad smile as he held Chris's hand for a long moment. "You've been a good friend, Chris. I'm lucky to have you."

There were tears in Chris's eyes as he backed away, leaving Steele and Valli alone in the balmy evening.

"It's just not fair. I couldn't bear it if the world, if everyone found out how I died. I've spent my whole life trying to keep it a secret. Don't let anybody know, Valli. I couldn't stand if if the world knew."

"I won't tell them, Steele. Nobody will know except the four of us, and Chris."

"About Chris. I've left him the house in Malibu, Valli. He's been with me all the years since you left, and I care about him."

"I understand. I don't need anything. I've already got more money than I could ever need.

"This house goes to Rae. She may hate me, Val, but I want her to have this house and all the movies in my film room. Maybe someday she'll understand."

Valli offered no comment to the man who now accepted the inevitability of his death with a calmness he had never exhibited in his life.

"And this is for you." He handed her a key. It was an ordinary house key with no identifying marks.

"I don't understand, Steele. What does the key fit?"

"The door to our first apartment, Valli, back in the Village. I guess I've always been a sentimental fool, but we were happy there. I bought that building for you a long time ago. I'd like to think that you might want to keep it."

Until that moment, Valli had managed to suppress her tears. But now, the tears streamed down her face. She moved over and lay on the lounge beside Steele, taking him into her arms and cuddling him against her breast as she had done so many times before.

"I've done a lot of wrong things, Val, mostly cheating you out of the love you deserve. I've used you."

Valli wiped at her tears. "We've used each other, Steele. I tried to mold you into something you could never be."

"I wanted to be what you wanted. That's the image I gave to my fans, Val. They never saw the real me—only your vision of me."

"It worked." Valli hugged him. "They adore you still."

"I've wronged you. God, I wish I could have been different." Steele's voice quavered.

"I know."

"You achieved success so easily. You always came through. I was so scared to death I'd be the only one to fail. Maybe things would have been different if you'd needed me."

"We can't take back the past, Steele. Never did two people love each other more who were so unsuited." Valli laughed softly.

"Val, Court loves you." Steele paused as if he couldn't continue. "You love him, too."

"I can't, Steele. I can't. . . I can't stand another broken relationship. I can't hurt anybody else."

"Look, you remained married to me all these years. And, for what? A bunch of wagging tongues?" He sat up slightly. "Do something for yourself. Marry Court."

In the days that followed, nothing the doctor prescribed relieved the pain for more than a few hours. Now Valli's tears weren't the only ones shed openly and often. At last the sedative was administered by injection, and both Valli and Chris were given instructions in giving the shots.

For days Steele fought the pain, trying stoically to hide his

232

feelings. Then one day he lapsed into a kind of semiconsciousness and didn't feel anything at all. Chris stood by the bed for hours, waiting for Steele to rouse. Valli tried to rest, but every minute she stayed away seemed to take more out of her, and finally both she and Chris simply sat by Steele's bed and waited.

"He really ought to be in the hospital," the doctor said before leaving.

"No! Anything he needs, we'll have brought here."

Both Valli and Chris were absolutely determined. Steele would die with his dignity, in his own home.

"Valli?"

He was awake. She hurried to his side and leaned down to hear the labored words. "Yes, love?"

"Valli, I can't stand it anymore. I'm ready to die."

"Oh, Steele, I can't give you any more shots yet. It hasn't been an hour."

"You don't understand, I want to die—now. . . . How many morphine tablets are left?"

"I'm not sure, but they're much weaker than the injections. You said they don't help anymore."

"Get me the bottle, Val. And bring me all those other things that quit working."

"Why? What are you going to do?" Valli knew.

"Just get them," he whispered raggedly, drawing breath painfully inside lungs that seemed more closed than open.

Valli looked through the medicine cabinet and found three other partial bottles of pain killers.

"Good. Bring the vial of medication and your needle."

Valli placed them on the table along with the tablets and waited, knowing fully what he was going to do.

"That ought to be enough. Now you and Chris go for a walk. Get out of here. Go someplace."

"No way, pal," Chris said emphatically. "I'm not leaving you alone to do whatever it is you have in mind. We've been together too long—I'm with you all the way."

"No. Please, just go, both of you, now." He breathed heavily, gasping between each word as he pleaded with eyes that

233

already burned with the disease that ravaged his body. "I love. . .you, both."

"And, we love you, Steele," Valli finally managed to whisper as she hugged him fiercely. "We'll go."

She turned and walked toward the door. Chris, with a feeling of helplessness ripping him apart, gave in and followed Valli.

"Valli?" Steele stopped her with a whisper. "Remember that ride through Central Park when we made love afterwards? We were good together, weren't we Valli? There's only one thing I regret, Val—I didn't love you enough."

"It doesn't matter, Sam. I love you, and that's enough."

Valli walked for a long time in the garden, watching the light fade into a night sky sealed by a mass of clouds. She felt numb, almost catatonic in her weary state. How long had she been here? She wasn't sure. Time ran together in a blur of smells and pain and remembering.

Steele was amost a physical part of her, and suddenly the pain was gone. He was dead. She knew he was dead before she walked back into the house and entered the room to find Chris wracked with sobs at Steele's side.

After a generous bribe the doctor signed the death certificate, without mentioning AIDS. Steele's body was quickly cremated, according to his wishes. Steele and Chris had made all the plans soon after they learned that the simple skin problem was one of the harbingers of the dreaded disease. His ashes were scattered through the Hollywood hills and into the sea.

Valli knew that soon she'd have to face the press and the outside world, but she seemed unable to function. She'd gotten through the ordeal of death and now she sat on the balcony, unable to force herself to move. She was truly alone, just as she had been in the beginning.

The day of the funeral was unusually warm for February. Chris had made all the arrangements and notified the members of the press as well as Steele's friends. Lincoln arrived

234

immediately, making arrangements and holding Valli together.

"Rae will come with Noel, Valli. She's pretty upset about all this happening without her being here."

"Steele wouldn't allow it."

"I know, but she's only nineteen years old, and she's still a child. Right now she's hurt, and you're taking the brunt of her grief."

"My God, look at that crowd."

Rows of limousines ringed the block around the chapel where the ceremony was being held. Beyond the building great ropes of thick black braid cordoned off the area holding the crowds back as police directed traffic around the area. Valli, Chris, and Lincoln were taken into a back door and ushered into a private room.

"Valli, are you all right?" It was Noel, sad and strained but concerned about Valli.

"Noel, it was bad, very bad, and now he's gone."

"Yes, I know. I would have come, but. . ."

"He didn't want that. And it might have caused problems for you. He understood. It was right for me to be there."

"Too bad you weren't there earlier." Rae's voice, filled with venom, rang through the room.

"Rae! Oh, darling, I know you don't understand, but this was the way your father wanted it."

"You're damn right I don't understand. You leave my father for eleven years with no explanation that makes any sense to anybody, then you rush back to his bedside to nurse him like a dutiful wife. What a hypocrite!"

"Rae!" Noel's stern voice cut off Rae's tirade. "Don't judge something you don't understand. It was the same distance between California and New York as it was from New York to California. Your father could have made the first move any time he wanted."

Rae stared at Noel for a moment, bit her lip, and whirled away, lighting a cigarette as she paced jerkily back and forth. She had grown into a stunning young woman. Taller than her mother, her black hair was fashionably short and had the same satiny sheen as her black Chanel dress. Since the last time her mother had seen her, she had been transformed from young bohemian to Paris chic.

She glanced at her mother. Why, if she loved Daddy so much, had they lived apart? It was because of her career, Rae had decided. She was so damn selfish.

Where was Court? He should be here with her, comforting her. She needed him, and he wasn't here. She wished she'd been at the tennis center when her mother had called about her father's death. But she'd been in Paris, working, and she'd learned of his death through the newspaper headlines, *"Steele Colton, 'Star' Cheri de Hollywood, meurt du cancer."*

Her own father had cancer, had killed himself, and she hadn't even known. Then she had had to fly to New York alone. Noel had met her there and insisted on accompanying her, but she'd never been that fond of Noel. He was stuffy and cold and she wished Court would hurry. She didn't know why everybody was so concerned about her mother. Nobody understood that she was the one who truly loved her father.

As the music began to play, the murmur of voices in the room beyond quietened. Lincoln stood on one side of Valli and Noel on the other. They were treating her as if she were the one with the great loss, her mother who had never loved her father, only her career.

Rae's fury bubbled under the surface. She drew on her Gauloise cigarette and wished she could find something stronger to get her through what was coming. And then the door opened and the minister who was to conduct the services motioned for them to come into the chapel.

They got through the service, the testimonials, and the final music, and Valli stood, a cocoon of blessed numbness protecting her as she started down the aisle. Flanked by Lincoln and Noel with Rae following sullenly behind, she left the chapel. There were so many people. She hadn't expected that, though from the number of times the phone rang she should have guessed.

236

And then Court was by her side, and she felt a great sense of calm settle over her. She hadn't realized how much she needed him until he was there. Court, Noel, she, and Rae made their way to the limousine, and the driver drove slowly through the mourning throngs of people lining the street.

"Where did they all come from? Why?" Valli asked.

"He was a star. Maybe he was the last of the real movie stars," Court answered, holding her hand.

"He was more than that," Noel added. "He was everyone's dream. He had it all."

"Except his family," Rae said bitterly. She didn't speak again on the long drive to the house.

The drapes were open, and the sun streamed into the house where Steele had lived in secret for the last year. Tables of food were laid out. Rae took one horrified look and turned back to Valli. "Surely they won't come here."

"Look behind you, Rae." Court pointed to the chain of black limos threading their way up the canyon road.

"It's indecent, obscene. Why are they coming here? We have no right to be comforted, we should be tortured for what we've done. I won't have any part of it."

Rae ran from the room and up the stairs. A door slammed, and the house was quiet again.

Court said, "Do you want me to talk to her, Valli?"

"No, let her go, Court. I think she's hurting so much that she can't face anyone or she'll come apart. It's up to the three of us to handle this last thing, isn't it?"

"It was always the four of us," Noel said, oblivious of the presence of Steele's manager who stood quietly in the back of the room. "This is how it started and this is how it will end. The others never mattered anyway."

Court and Valli stared at each other, recognizing the truth in his words.

CHAPTER EIGHTEEN

For nearly two hours Valli, Court, and Noel circulated among the mourners. They weren't crows wearing pearls and short gloves like the women at Granny's funeral, Valli thought, but the difference was slight. Aside from Lincoln, who hovered quietly in the background, the others were simply a blur of faces with an unending barrage of questions.

"I don't understand," she said wearily to Noel. "They don't even go through the motions of grief. They just come right out and ask how bad off he was. They want all the gory details, and they expect me to tell them."

"Human nature, Val—a bunch of vultures gathering at the side of the road, hoping to pick up a tasty morsel. It's the reporters you have to watch. They're shrewder."

"Reporters?" She was shocked. "They've come here?"

"Only as bereaved friends of the deceased, but they're here, and two of them have already made discreet offers to pay for your story of Steele and his death."

"Oh, God." She'd been tough up to now. With the help of one of the tranquilizers from Steele's medicine cabinet, she'd managed to operate in a calm state of detachment. But the medicine had worn off too quickly, and stark reality overwhelmed her. "How much longer, Noel?"

"I'll ask Lincoln to announce that he's leaving. He'll make a production of telling you good-bye, and you can announce to the others that you're very tired and excuse yourself. Without you, they'll soon give up and go. Let's make our way over to the foyer. You can stand on the steps and make your apologies."

"Will that be all right? I mean is it respectful? I couldn't leave after Granny's funeral until everyone else did. I would have been tarred and feathered."

"God, Val, after twenty-three years you're still dredging up Granny when you're nervous. Do now what you should have done then, tell them all to go to hell."

"Congressman Gray, is it true that you shared an apartment with Steele and Valli in New York in the sixties?"

"Yes," he said coldly to the female reporter who made no secret of the fact that she wrote down his reply. "We've been friends a long time."

"Do your constituents know that you were one of the original flower children, that you lived with an unmarried woman and two other men?" She brushed a stray blond curl from her eyes and adjusted her steel-framed glasses.

"Madam, your questions are in poor taste here. If you'd care to make an appointment with me next week, I'll be glad to discuss our past in detail." He turned Valli neatly away, leaving the nonplussed reporter surrounded by silence.

A step later Valli was interrupted by an actor whom Steele had admired. "Yes, I'll let you know if there's anything you can do, thank you." Valli moved toward the foyer. "She can't hurt you, can she, Noel?"

"Probably. I suppose. I have too many skeletons in my closet. I'm up for election next year. But don't worry. I can handle it," Noel went on as they made their way around small clusters of people. "And you and I both know it could be much worse."

239

"Cancer," she repeated for the hundredth time this morning to someone else. "We're setting up a research fund in his name."

"I'm sure he'd appreciate a contribution to the fund. Thank you, that's a very generous pledge," she said to a woman she knew to be only one step away from bankruptcy.

"Oh, Noel," she managed to say under her breath. "I'm sorry about that reporter. You shouldn't have come. You're too vulnerable here."

Conversation swirled all around them. Business, gossip, it was almost like one of the cocktail parties she'd hated so when she lived here. Disjointed snatches of conversation jumped out at her as they crossed the room.

". . .yes, I've read the script, Luther. It's a bitch. You can't really expect me to let that over-the-hill asshole blackmail me into playing a woman that old."

"That's his wife's picture over the fireplace. She's very striking, isn't she?"

"Sure, I knew him, never understood his marrying her," a deeper voice confided. "There was a time when . . ."

"Here's Court," Noel said eagerly, drowning out the rest of the conversation behind them. "Stay with him while I find Lincoln and tell him what we'd like him to do." Noel turned Valli over to Court and slipped away.

"How are you, Country Mouse?"

Court's hand held her arm firmly, and she felt a curious sense of well-being wash over her. His presence always made her feel so cared-for.

"I don't know, Court. I seem to be operating on automatic pilot. Is the food holding out?"

"Leona is doing fine. I've just been up to see Rae. She's very angry right now, and she doesn't know how to get rid of the hurt. She always loved Steele with such blind eyes."

"Didn't we all," Valli murmured.

"Mr. McCambridge?" The same woman reporter was back again. "I saw one of your paintings in George Hamilton's home last week, one of your earlier works. He tells me

240

that you've amassed rather a unique cult following in recent years. Do you still paint?"

"Only for my own pleasure," Court said briskly. "Please excuse us."

"Valli . . ." Lincoln came up behind her, took her hand and held it with both of his, raising his voice as he said, "I must go now. I'm sure you're exhausted." Under his breath he added, "I'd like to see you when you're ready. Will you call me?"

"Thank you, Lincoln, you've been very kind. I am tired," she agreed. "And, yes, I'll call," she promised as he touched his lips to her cheek. "Thank you."

"No you won't, but you're welcome. And I won't let that stop me. I'll see you next week. Chin up, Mrs. Colton, you're doing fine."

"Thank you, Lincoln. Thank you for being there so many times before." She squeezed his hand and watched him make his way through the door, pausing once to speak sharply to the reporter who seemed intent on pursuing her story no matter what.

Valli stepped up to the third stair and surveyed the crowd for a long silent moment. "Thank you all for coming," she said softly, letting her voice quiet the crowd. "My husband would have written a different script for. . .this day. He'd have wanted a dark rainy day with umbrellas and black raincoats. He'd have ordered a single red rose for drama, and a set of bagpipes to play in the background. And he would have been very pleased at your expressions of respect. Thank you again for being here."

With Court in front of her and Noel behind her, Valli moved quickly up the steps, leaving the hum of conversation behind. Noel stopped to confer with Chris and unexpectedly put his arm around the man who seemed near the end of his ability to cope with the events of the day.

"I'm going to take Chris to his room and sit with him for a while, Court. Stay with Valli."

"Poor Chris," Valli said stoically. "He's the real widow, you know. Steele lived more years with Chris than he ever lived with me. Chris shared his life and his success. Now he's lost part of himself, and he can't let the world know how he feels."

Valli opened the door to the bedroom she'd shared with Steele long ago during their marriage and then recently during his illness. And then finally the tears came—great, wet, noisy tears that rolled unchecked down her cheeks.

"Valli," Court's voice startled her. For a moment she'd forgotten he was there. "Valli, don't worry. I'm here."

It seemed natural to step into his arms and rest her head on his shoulder. Everything about the feel of him against her was good. She'd missed him fiercely during the last few years. After he'd first stopped coming to New York so often, she'd been too busy to miss him. When she finally realized how much she needed and depended on him, she didn't know how to bring him back. Now he was here. Steele's death had done what she hadn't had the courage to do.

The next day Court and Noel were still there. They stood in the library after the reading of the will. Rae had heard the lawyer out. Once he'd gathered his papers and departed, she rose and walked over behind her father's desk.

"Please feel free to stay as long as you feel that you need to. I have decided that I will be moving into my house immediately, but I wouldn't want you to cut short your stay on my account. You were my father's friends, and he loved you. I thank you for that." She smiled at each of the men individually and then left the room, making her avoidance of her mother more real than any spoken words could have.

"Rae, just a minute. We need to talk," Valli called after her.

Rae stiffened for a moment and jutted her chin forward. She didn't stop, and she didn't look back.

"What am I going to do?" Valli looked helplessly at the three men watching Rae's performance.

"She holds you responsible, Country Mouse. You're going to have to tell her the truth."

"No. Steele didn't want that. He kept her at arm's length because he didn't want her to know. It was very important to him that she think he was the man he pretended to be. He wanted her to think he was strong, not weak."

"He drank too much and loved too much. He was afraid to say no, afraid if he turned anything down it wouldn't be there anymore. Except for you, Valli, he never believed in anything permanent in his life," Noel observed.

"Except for me, and you, Noel," she said quietly.

"Perhaps, and perhaps the time has come for me to go home and clear up this mess with my wife."

"Oh, Noel, do you think that's wise?"

"Isn't honesty the best policy?"

"Not necessarily."

"Maybe it's time I stopped hiding behind secrets and fear and took old Spud out of hiding. I don't think I have the energy to hide him any more. And I still think you should tell Rae the truth."

"Poor Noel," Court said sadly after Lincoln and Chris left the room. "He's more like Steele than he knows. They're both dreamers. They just dreamed different dreams."

"Aren't we all?" Valli turned out the lamp and stood for a moment in the darkness. There was no wind tonight, only the heat and the everlasting sound of the hard rock music that Rae had been playing ever since her father died. From Led Zeppelin to AC/DC the beat reverberated through the house like a cheap presence that didn't belong there.

"I suppose we are. And in a weird sort of way, our dreams came true, most of them." He came and stood beside her, content to watch the evening settle over the valley.

"Steele wanted to be a star and he was, even bigger than he'd ever planned. Four nominations and two Oscars and a dozen smashes at the box office. He made it. As for me, my label is finally worth more than money. I could never expect more than I have right now. But what about you, Court? Is it true that you're painting again?"

"Yes, I've been fooling around with some still lifes and a few portraits, watercolors, nothing like the abstracts I started out with."

"Oh, I kind of liked those. You must come to the Village

when I've moved in and see my special plans for the original works of Courtney McCambridge."

"You're moving back to the Village? Why would you
want to give up that lovely apartment and move back?"

"Because that lovely apartment is cold and empty, too
empty of memories to go there. Besides, Steele bought our
old apartment for me as a sentimental gesture. I want to go
back where we started."

"Valli, don't get your hopes up. I think it is true that we
can't go home again."

"Oh, I hope not, Court, because I'm just beginning to
understand about home and what that means." She hesitated. "I'd like to think that you aren't leaving me, too."

She was tired, and she wanted Court's arms around her,
comforting her, telling her that everything would be all
right. She wanted the truth between her and Court. She
sighed deeply and turned to face the man who Court had
become. Lines crinkled his green eyes, but his dimples were
still there.

He simply looked at her for a moment, and she felt the
years slip away. And suddenly it was back, the power that
seemed to come during special times in her life. Surely
Court must feel it, too. But Court only stood and waited,
uncertain of Valli's words. He was accustomed to years of
discipline, of refusing to recognize and accept the strong
feelings she evoked in him. For so long he had not allowed
himself to believe he had a chance. Indeed, having con-
trolled his feelings for Valli for so many years, he was no
longer certain they existed.

Overhead sounds of recorded thunder rolled and lightning cracked and the beat of the drums accelerated. Valli
winced at the constant noise and wondered how Rae could
stand the frantic sounds.

"Let's walk in the garden before we turn in, Country
Mouse."

Gratefully she opened the door and stepped outside.
Shivering, she wished she'd brought a sweater. Court
removed his jacket and draped it around her shoulders, and

Valli breathed in the smell of him. Slowly, they walked through the garden.

In a shaft of moonlight where they were standing he could see what she'd managed to conceal before. She wanted him, and the honesty of her need rocked his composure. As he took her in his arms, Valli leaned against him softly. This is wrong, he told himself. Steele just died, and she doesn't know what she's doing. She just needs someone to comfort her, to depend on. She's tired. She's always turned to me, he finally admitted, and I want her as much as I always have. And he held her, stroking her hair gently.

She pressed against him, giving way to the need to be held, and began to weep.

"Don't cry, Valli. I'm here with you."

"But you'll go away again."

"No, not this time."

She felt his quiet strength flowing into her, and her tears subsided. She lifted her face and accepted his kiss.

From the upstairs window Rae watched her mother with horror. Bitterness swept over her. Court was kissing her mother, and her father was barely in the ground. Court—her Court—was in love with her mother.

There'd been a time when her mother was her whole world. Then her father had come into her life, and she'd loved him dearly. When her mother packed her off in the middle of the night—with no explanations—she'd hated her. And her mother had been too busy to care.

But then Court had come along, and after a while he'd taken the place of her father. He'd loved her, too. But when the love of a child turned into the love of a woman, he hadn't noticed. Now she knew why. Her mother. Her mother had always stood between her and everything she loved.

Lighting a cigarette, she sucked in the smoke while hatred enveloped her, and she planned her revenge.

"Valli, we ought to go inside. It's late, and you've had a bad time. I know you're exhausted."

Valli pulled away and looked at Court. "Yes, I've had a bad time, but it has nothing to do with you and me, Court. And later, when this is over, we need to talk."

Court read the promise in her eyes and nodded. He wanted to talk now, to dispel any doubts that finally Valli was ready to accept his love, to return it. Instead, they turned and walked slowly into the house and up the stairs. At Valli's door he stopped, took his jacket in his hands, and started to remove it from her shoulders. When she reached up and drew his head down to hers, it seemed only natural for him to kiss her again. There was passion in his kiss, but also a deeper feeling, an affirmation of what they both understood would come—in time.

"Good night, my love," she whispered. "I know how very lucky I am."

"And I. Good night, Country Mouse." He kissed her lightly again, pulled the jacket from her shoulders, and moved down the hall toward his room.

Down the corridor Rae closed her door and smiled. She'd find an answer. She wasn't her father's daughter for nothing.

It took the better part of the night to formulate her plan, but by morning Rae was ready. Valli, Chris, and Court were seated at the breakfast table when she came into the room. Valli looked up with a hopeful expression on her face. Court gazed anxiously at Rae and back again at Valli. Chris sipped his coffee and made no attempt to speak.

Rae stared at her mother for a long time. She was, as always, perfectly dressed for the occasion. Her black dress had been exchanged for dark gray slacks, a tailored cobalt-blue blouse, and a pale gray cashmere vest left unbuttoned. Her full shoulder-length hair, streaked with slivers of gray, was combed straight back into an old-fashioned pageboy held in place by a print scarf that complemented both her eyes and the blue of her blouse. Valli may have never been beautiful, but today, except for the shadows beneath her eyes, nobody would ever notice.

"Good morning," Rae said with a sharp clip in her voice. "I have something I'd like to say. Uncle Court, I apologize for my behavior yesterday." She managed a recalcitrant sniff. "I know that I've behaved badly, and I'm sorry."

With a smile of relief Court acknowledged her apology. "We understand, Rae. This has been a shock to all of us and you most of all."

"And, Chris," she continued sweetly, "I know how difficult it must be for you to stay on here with my father gone. Under the circumstances, please feel free to pack your things today and move into your beach house. I'll be staying here with Leona."

"But . . ." Chris started to protest.

"Mother," Rae went on smoothly, ignoring Chris, but not looking into her mother's eyes, "you're right. We do need to talk. In fact, I'd like to see you alone, in the library, after breakfast." Rae gave what she considered to be a very brave smile, lifted her head regally, and left the room without looking back.

"Shades of Grace Kelly," Court observed with amusement. "She isn't Steele Colton's daughter for nothing."

"Oh, Chris," Valli said awkwardly. "I'm sorry. I don't want you to leave here until you're ready. I'm sure that Rae only meant to let you know that she understands how difficult this is. Obviously she doesn't know that this house is mine."

"No, she meant it," he said stiffly. "And I don't think you should tell her. Steele wanted her to have the house. He could have bought it long ago, but for some reason he didn't want to. I think he always believed that you would live here again someday. It will be better if I go." He stood up, then looked around as if he were memorizing the room. "If you need me, Valli, just let me know. I realize that we were never very close, but somehow I feel . . . I feel I know you very well." Chris exited the room quickly.

"He's a nice man," Valli said. "Steele was very lucky."

"Steele was always lucky. Do you want me to come with you to talk to Rae?" Court slid his half-finished plate away

247

and lit a cigarette. "I have the feeling that she's up to something."

"No. She's my daughter, Court. It's time that we had a real mother-and-daughter talk. But thanks." Valli felt tired and drained this morning, certainly not up to the mother-and-daughter talk she anticipated. She'd been here nearly four months, and for the last few weeks, she'd operated on the last of her reserves. But it was now or never.

"No," she repeated, "I need to go alone. But thanks, Court. You'll be here when I'm done?"

He walked around the table and lifted her chin with his fingertips. "I'll be here, Country Mouse. I don't intend to leave you again." His light kiss stirred something inside her that she suppressed. She wanted Court's strength, his caring, his arms, but that was all, for now.

"Well." Valli stood up, squared her shoulders, and said, "No sense in waiting." She no longer felt empty. There was a sense of urgency about her now, and she quickened her step. The time had come for her to be frank with Rae, or at least lay the groundwork. They had the rest of their lives to close up the distance that she'd allowed to arise between them, and Valli wanted to make a start. And then, well, there was Court. She couldn't be positive what he meant by being there, but she was ready to find out. She knocked firmly on the library door.

"Come in."

The drapes were pulled, leaving the room dusky. Rae sat behind Steele's desk with a curious smile on her face.

"Rae, darling," Valli began.

"Cut the crap, Mother, and close the door." Rae's voice was harsh.

Too shocked to do otherwise, Valli complied and strode into the room. Rae obviously wasn't going to make this easy, but Valli vowed to stay calm and not allow Rae to force her into losing her temper.

"All right, Rae. You wanted to talk, I'm ready. I think the time has come for me to be honest with you."

"Oh? And why now?"

248

"Because you're old enough to understand."

"Oh, I understand all right. I understand more than you know. I understand that you were more concerned about yourself—the famous Valli—than you ever were about your husband and your child. You cheated me, Mother, cheated me out of a father who loved me, and a home."

"Maybe I did, Rae, but I never meant to hurt you. I was only trying to protect you."

"Protect me? Protect *me*?" Rae's voice rose as she jumped up. "That really sucks. All my life I've wondered what *I* did wrong, to be taken from my father, sent away to school, not even in this country. I had to go to Switzerland. No one wanted me. Not my mother. Not my father. Only Court cared for me." There was a softening in Rae's voice as she spoke of Court, and Valli seized on this softening to plead her case.

"Court thought I should have been honest with you from the start, but I couldn't do it, Rae. I wanted you to *have* a father, the father I never had. And, in spite of everything that happened, your father loved you the best way he could."

"Then why did you keep him from me?"

"I didn't keep Steele from you, Rae. He loved you, but he wanted to protect you from . . ."

"I don't believe you." Rae cut off her mother. "You kept him away. Somehow, you kept him away. You didn't want me to have anything you couldn't have."

Dear God, what was she going to do? How could she possibly make a nineteen-year-old understand that her parents had done what they thought was best for the child they both had loved. But they'd been wrong—very wrong—and she wasn't sure how to rectify the mistake. But she had to try, otherwise Rae would carry this great load of hate around with her and sooner or later, she'd be consumed by it.

"Rae, back in the sixties, the world was becoming much more liberal, but even then there were certain things that were unacceptable. Rather than expose you to . . . certain

249

things, your father and I decided that boarding school was best. Rae, you have to understand. Your father was a wonderful man, but his career was very demanding. I had to make a living. I had to start over for the third time. . ."

"Oh, I understand all right. You thought that Court would marry you, but he didn't. That's why we moved to New York. I don't blame him. He was content to share your bed. But he wouldn't take you away from my father."

Valli was beginning to lose patience. Obviously Rae had no intention of allowing her to explain. Somehow she had formed her own opinions about what had happened, and nothing Valli could say would alter that. "No matter what happened to either of us during our marriage, Rae Colton, your father and I always loved each other. And if he were here, he'd be the first to tell you that. And I've heard just about enough of your crudeness."

"In all the years you were separated my father never cared about another woman. Tell me, how many women were there in my father's life before you deserted him?"

"None," Valli said tiredly.

Rae sat down, sent a malevolent icy blue glare across the desk, and spoke. "Once you took my father from me. Then you tried to take Court. But what you don't know, Mother, is that *I* got Court."

"Court always loved you, Rae. He spent so much time with you as a child. . ."

"Oh, it's not the child we're discussing, Mother. I'm a woman, or haven't you noticed? And Court's mine. I saw you last night in the garden, and it won't work."

Valli rose swiftly to her feet, worried now about the tight fury in Rae's voice. Something was wrong, and Valli was afraid. She erased all emotion from her voice. "What isn't going to work, darling?"

"Court. He's mine. I won't let you have him."

"Rae, don't be silly. I don't know what you're thinking, but Court is old enough to be your father."

"Father? Court is much more to me than a father. You took my father. You killed him. You aren't going to take my

250

lover."

"Lover?" The wind whooshed from Valli's lungs in one great surge. Her heart lurched and left her unsteady on her feet as she reached forward to catch the edge of the desk for support. "Don't be foolish, Rae. I don't believe that Court is your lover." But her voice trembled.

"Oh no? I thought you'd say that. That's why I want you to see this."

Rae reached back and flicked a switch, bathing the portrait over the fireplace with light.

Valli gasped. For a long moment she simply stood and looked. The portrait of herself was gone, and in its place was another, a portrait of a young nude woman standing on the beach gazing shyly at the artist. Her deep blue eyes were filled with liquid desire. Behind her ear was a delicate orchid set against long, flowing, jet-black hair.

All the sensual feel of the islands, of man and woman and the passion between them, were portrayed in the girl's flushed face, the soft curves of her tanned body. Behind her the ocean crashed on the beach and the sun, a swollen orange ball, hung precariously on the horizon. The artist had caught the sexual promise in her eyes, the virginal quality of her pose, and you knew beyond any imagining that once the dark had come, the woman would be ready for love. The artist had demonstrated his love for her in every stroke of his brush.

The girl, young, slim, unbelievably beautiful, was Rae. And even from where she stood, Valli could read the artist's signature—Court.

"Now you know, Mother. I love Court. And he loves me. We've been lovers for more than a year. You've already cheated me of my father. Don't"—her voice broke just enough for Valli to realize that she was very serious—"don't take the man I love."

Valli gazed at the portrait for a long time. Oh, Court. Her heart contracted. Just as she had begun to acknowledge her feelings for him, she'd been shown that they could never be. Did he truly love Rae? She didn't know. But it didn't matter.

251

Rae was right. For whatever reason, she'd separated Rae from her father. She couldn't hurt her again. Maybe if she stayed away, Court would find in the daughter what he'd wanted from the mother.

Valli turned and walked slowly and silently out of the library, out the door, and climbed into her car. Tears were streaming down her cheeks as she realized that once more she was leaving everything she cared about behind.

CHAPTER NINETEEN

"Where's Valli?"

"She's gone, Court. There's only you and me now."

The dark-haired beauty straightened up and stood waiting, her chin jutting forward, her eyes blazing with triumph.

Court stared at her for a long, puzzled moment before his eyes focused on the portrait over the mantel. The painting of Valli, long-ago commissioned by Steele, had been changed for one of Court's more recent works. How had Steele gotten that painting? Shit, nobody was supposed to see this series of paintings.

"Where did you find it, Rae?"

"My father had it, Court. Don't you remember?"

Court covered the distance between the door and the portrait in four giant strides. "No. I didn't give it to him. Did you?" Court looked furious.

"No, I showed it to mother. She couldn't believe you had painted me. I think it gave her quite a shock." Rae couldn't help a small, triumphant smile.

A peculiar feeling gnawed at the pit of his stomach, as if

he'd been violated somehow. His paintings were a secret part of him, never intended to be viewed by anyone else. He resented Steele's theft, his secretive intrusion into Court's dreams. Always Steele had taken what he wanted and always he'd been forgiven, but this time he'd gone too far. For the first time, Court realized he hated Steele Colton.

"I wasn't sure myself how you felt about me, until I saw it," Rae went on hesitantly. "I knew how I felt about you, but you never responded to me. Never once did you let me know how you really felt. And then when I saw this, I knew." She flung herself against him. "Oh, Court, please, don't you see how much I want you, how much I've always loved you." And she wrenched his face down to meet her lips.

Court pulled away and looked at her. He knew that all the horror he felt was reflected in his face. The knowledge washed over Rae's face, and she realized that she'd been wrong, very wrong. "I see," she said finally in a small voice.

"No, you don't, Rae. There's so much you don't see."

"From the time I was a little girl you were there, Court, whenever I needed you. You were the only one who cared. And I loved you for it. Later, I realized that my love was no longer that of a child for a father; it was the love of a woman for a man. Take a good look at me, Court. I'm a woman, a woman. I'm the woman you painted in that picture."

His tone was sad. "Yes, you're a woman. But I'm not the one for you, kid, and someday there will be a man for you. You've built me into some kind of superhero who fills all your dreams. You were lonely, and I was there."

"Oh God, Court. Next you're going to bring in a gypsy with a violin. I know how you feel about me. I can see it in the painting, even if you deny it until hell freezes over."

"That's not you." Court grabbed her shoulders. He had painted Valli. Valli as he remembered her, as she looked to him in a thousand different poses. Looking at the woman standing beside him now, he saw the resemblance to Rae. Did Rae really think this was she? Of course she did. How could she know that he still saw her as a child and her mother as a young girl on the brink of womanhood?

"Take a good look at the painting, Rae. It's your mother, over twenty years ago, as I remember her, as I see her, even now. I painted that same portrait or one like it a hundred times in the last ten years. That's what changed my style, trying to capture on canvas what I couldn't capture in real life. I didn't know your father took it. He shouldn't have. Believe me. It isn't you, Rae. It's your mother."

"No. It can't be. It's me! You love me. That portrait is of me. I look like that."

"You look like your mother, Rae. You're Valli as I first saw her and she's the woman I love. I've always loved. You must accept that. You have your entire life ahead of you, Rae. You've got to stop this hate and make peace with her. Don't make her suffer any more."

"*Her* suffer? What about me? What about the way she cheated me out of my father? She was never home. She never truly cared about me. All she cared about was being famous. What about being sent away to school so that she could have other men without a teenager around? Don't I count?"

"Of course you count, Rae. Your mother may not have always made wise choices, but she did what she thought was best for you. It's been difficult for her. She couldn't have known how you would misunderstand."

"Go away, Court," Rae said, suddenly deflated and showing her youth in a way that made Court's heart contract with pity. "I've always been alone. I don't need you. I'll manage."

He couldn't leave her like this. She had to be told, to be made to understand. She wasn't his child, but she could have been and she was right, he did love her. Like a daughter. Maybe he had subconsciously used this love to fill the emptiness Valli had left. "No, Rae, it doesn't end like this. You wouldn't allow your mother to talk to you, but I'm going to. Come, let's go into the kitchen and have some coffee."

"Coffee? No, thanks, Court. I think I'd like something a

little stronger." Rae reached into her pocket and pulled out
a crudely rolled joint and cupped it in the palm of her hand
as she struck a match.

"Rae, throw out that stuff." He had to get her attention.
"You've got decisions to make, important decisions, and
you've got to keep your head on straight. The last thing you
want to do is allow anything to come between you and your
father's wishes. He wanted you to have this house, but
you've got to figure out how to earn a living to keep it up."

"I don't know how I'll keep the house, not yet, but I will.
One way or another, I'll find a way. My father wanted me to
have this house, and I'm going to live here." She was petulant and spoiled—a child, really, and clearly not capable of
taking care of herself right now.

All right, he'd stay for a few days and help Rae get everything in order. Valli would do the same if she were here.
After all, he'd waited twenty years for Valli, a few more days
wouldn't make any difference.

But the few days turned into weeks. He'd tried calling
Valli, but she wasn't in New York, and she didn't return his
calls. Court was worried.

At first Rae wandered around the house, restless, unable
to focus in any direction. Then, after he suggested she
watch some of her father's movies, she became obsessed.
She decided she wanted to be an actress, and for days she
stayed holed up in the screening room, watching her
father's films over and over again. The watching became a
compulsion, as if in watching his movies she had finally
found the father she had sought. Court had to do something
to help her, and he had to find Valli. Finally he called
Lincoln.

"Where's Valli? I knew she wouldn't call me," Lincoln
inquired.

"She and Rae had some kind of a big fight, and she went
back to New York, or somewhere. That's what I'm calling
about. Rae."

"What about Rae?"

"She isn't taking this well at all, Linc. And I wondered, do you think you might arrange it for her to have a screen test. She's got it into her head that she's going to follow in her father's footsteps."

"That doesn't sound like a bad idea, if she has half the talent Steele had."

"I think she does, Linc, but she's. . .well, right now she's a bit unstable, and I want to get her out of this house and involved in something other than her grief for Steele."

"Let me see what I can do. Her father's name ought to be good for something in this town."

A few days later, Steele's agent, Asa, called. "Court, let me speak to Rae. I may have something for her."

Court knocked on the screening-room door. There was no answer. He knocked again, opened the door and went in. The room was dark. Rae was sitting on the edge of the sofa, gazing hypnotically at the screen. Steele's film *Winter* was playing. "Rae, you have a phone call." She didn't seem to hear him. Reaching over her inert form, he switched off the projector and turned on an overhead lamp.

"What are you doing?" Rae came to her feet and turned to him in fury. "What are you doing in here?"

"Rae, Asa is on the phone. He wants to talk to you."

"Asa?"

"Your father's agent."

"Tell him to leave me alone."

"No, Rae. I won't tell him to leave you alone. You are coming out of this room and into the sunlight, one way or another." He took the projector and smashed it to the floor. "Talk to Asa, now!"

For a moment she stared at him blankly, then with a move that would have made her father proud she lifted her chin and swept from the room. As Court opened the windows and turned on lights, he heard her lift the phone in the hall. "Yes? This is Rae Colton speaking." Her voice was steady, firm.

She would be all right. Asa would take her in hand in the same way he had Steele. Court wondered sadly if what he'd done was wise. He was throwing her into the fire, but he

257

hadn't any real choice.

In his room he packed his bags and prepared to leave. Choices? He shook his head as he started back down the stairs. Had any of them ever had a real choice? No, a man might fool himself into thinking he was deciding, but somewhere up there was something, or somebody, writing the script, letting them get close, then jerking them away again. You just had to take what came and learn to live with it. You're getting plumb maudlin, Court McCambridge, he silently scolded himself with a wry smile. You're beginning to sound like Granny.

In June of 1984 Rae Colton began work on her first movie. It was only a small part, but she was noticed by the press.

Court flew first to his resort and then to New York to find Valli, only to discover that she'd gone to Ireland. When she came back several months later she called him. She had already convinced herself that Rae had lied, but as long as her daughter loved him, she could not marry Court.

Noel separated from his wife, and in so doing they became better friends. He decided not to run for reelection and retired to write.

"Terrance, these figures look fine." Valli folded the last report and tapped it absently.

"Then what's the problem? Why do you look so unhappy? We can hardly keep up with the demand for *Hollywood Classics* evening wear. Nineteen eighty-five will be our best year."

For the better part of the year before, nothing had held Valli's interest. She was a woman torn between the past she'd been forced to cut loose from and a future not yet defined.

Rae had refused all her mother's calls, but Valli had kept up with her daughter's progress through Lincoln.

At Christmas Lincoln had told her Rae was to be his costar in his next movie. It was daring and new and, with the exception of Lincoln, everyone in it, from the writer to the

producer, was a virtual unknown. They were pushing filming and production ahead in order to get it out in time for
next year's Academy Award nominations.

She had not heard from Court since the previous spring
and didn't expect to. He had been very angry. Valli recalled
his words now. "Hasn't it ever occurred to you, Val, that I
might be tired of being some kind of ship in the night. I'm
ready for a wife and home. Damn it, Val, I won't wait forever. I'm not letting you push me aside this time. It's now or
never."

Damn it, Court, Valli thought now, I'm tired of it, too, but
what can I do?

"I don't know what else you want, Valli," Terrance persisted, drawing her back to the present. "We simply can't
handle any more work without going into some kind of
mass-market production line."

"I know, Terrance, that's why we're going to expand.
Keep an eye on things this afternoon. I'm going shopping."

Terrance shook his head and followed Valli from the office through the salon, watching as she donned coat and hat
along the way. "If I need you, where will you be?"

"Where? I'll be at Bloomingdale's, Bergdorf's, Saks,
Bonwit's, Lord & Taylor, and Bendel's, of course."

"Of course," he agreed in complete bewilderment.
"Where else would you go shopping?"

For the rest of the afternoon, Valli covered the New York
department stores with a magnifying glass. She knew that
people who had never valued the couture's high-toned
image were now buying Halston and Mary McFadden at J. C.
Penney, Jaclyn Smith creations at K-Mart, Cheryl Tiegs at
Sears, and Gloria Vanderbilt and Pierre Cardin on every
corner. In Paris, couturiers were lending their name to a
variety of products. And if the Parisian "artistes" could do
it without losing prestige, so could she.

Until now, she had refused to dilute the power of her
name by mass producing her clothes or assigning licenses.
Even her highly successful Hollywood Classics were mar-
keted under a different label, although most of the world

knew who designed the line. It was time, she decided, fo
Valli to return to Willacoochee, Georgia, and this was th
way to do it.

Over the next few days she conferred with fellow de
signer Pauline Trigere about her licensing arrangement
consulted with the marketing directors of every majo
department store, and set up appointments with Joa
Hansen, the licensing expert who had engineered contract
for some of the top names in the fashion world, Vanderbil
Dior, Jhane Barnes, and Michael Jackson.

Three months later, Valli was ready to announce he
plans.

"Come in, Terrance, I'd like you to hear what I have i
mind." Valli indicated a seat to the assistant she'd long ag
promoted to vice-president. Lorenso's boudoir decor ha
been replaced with simple but elegant furnishings that re
flected Valli's opinion that the surroundings should no
overwhelm the gowns being created. Inside the room wer
Joan Hansen, her attorney, and a few other chief execs. Vall
was seated behind a Louis XIV library table she used for
desk.

"Gentlemen, Ms. Hansen, I'll get straight to the point
What I propose is that we market a new line of evening wea
to be called 'Val.' The fabrics will be imported, but the man
ufacture will be strictly American-made. It will look like a
couture line, but the prices will be such that small-town
mayors' wives will rush out to buy them. I want every hole
in-the-road in this country to have somebody wearing a 'Va
dress.' And I've arranged a sample of what I have in mind."

Valli touched a button on her desk. The curtains at the
end of the room parted, revealing a model.

Terrance did a double take, looked at the model, back at
Valli, and at the others, who were smiling broadly. "Is
that . . .?"

"Yes, Terrance, that's the very first Valli Original. And I
propose to expand that concept to cover the newest metal-
lics and glittery fabrics and go into the mass market. We will

launch the first fall line next spring in conjunction with a new fragrance of the same name. From what you see there, I intend to market this." And the first model, wearing the original brightly-hued knit tunic, was replaced by a new one wearing a modified version of the tunic. It had lost very little in the translation and could be produced for one-tenth the cost.

"Now, that is what I want to do, and you are the people I want to handle it. Val will be the sassy, in-charge liberated woman that all of us would like to be, yet she'll be sexy, feminine, and desirable. Val will represent the ultimate success in a woman's life. I leave the details to all of you. The only thing I insist on is that the arrangements be fair and that the initial launch of our line be the most extravagant production campaign that the fashion world has ever seen.

"We'll invite celebrities to model our garments. We'll invite the locals, the librarian, and the fresh young hopefuls who have never modeled before. We'll present the press with samples of the perfume at press parties in all the major cities. *Bazaar, Glamour, Vogue,* and *Women's Wear,* of course, will be our special guests, and we want to overwhelm them with the possibilities. Understood?"

The men and women gathered around her desk and could only nod in amazement as they watched her stand and walk to the door. This was an enormous, exciting task.

"Where are you going?" Terrance managed as he hurried after her, opening the door.

"I'm off to Ireland, to begin searching for manufacturers of our fabrics."

"But you don't know if it's going to go, Valli."

"Oh, yes, it's going over, Terrance. I'll leave all that to you and Joan Hansen. You set it up and I'll design the line. I'll keep in touch."

And during the next six months Valli arranged a contract for fabrics woven in Ireland and went to Paris to absorb the couture at the heart of the fashion world. Like her, many of the finest couturiers were diversifying. She saw Spain, Germany, even dipping into the Orient for inspiration and

the latest in production methods employed by Hong Kong
and the Japanese. She was so busy working—and absorb
ing—that she didn't have time to feel lonely.

CHAPTER TWENTY

"Oh, hell," a voice said in disgust. "Where'd she get this stuff?"

Rae tried unsuccessfully to concentrate on her lines. "You can't do this," she finally managed. "I'm not interested in you or your body."

"Anybody watching will certainly believe that," the man opposite her said through lips clenched into a garish smile, as he abandoned his script.

"Linc," Rae whispered. "Don't be mad at me."

"Mad is not the word, Rae. I'm livid. This is only a walk-through, but you're about to blow it wide open." He ad-libbed his own movements, making his way to her side as though it had been written into the script. "You said that you weren't feeling well, let me help you to the trailer."

Before a furious director, the entire crew, and her mentor and senior star-in-residence, Rae Colton was propelled from the set, practically held upright by Lincoln Maxwell until they reached the motor home.

Inside he laid her across one of the beds and applied a damp towel to her forehead.

"Why, Rae? Why are you doing this? They aren't going to put up with this much longer. You're going to be thrown of the picture, and then what will you do?"

But Rae was flying too high to hear. Lincoln had worried about her for days. He'd known how afraid she was of failure, of not living up to her father's name, but he didn't know how to help her. He didn't know how much longer he could cover for her, and this time she wasn't in any shape to make it back to the set.

There was a knock on the door. Lincoln glanced back at Rae, then stepped outside the trailer. She didn't appear to have heard the knock.

"Well?" Mark Flemming, the director, was not going to be soft-soaped. He'd been around long enough to know that Rae was on something, so there was no point in trying to fool him.

"I don't know, Mark. She's high on something. We'll have to shoot around her this afternoon."

"I'm thinking that we may have to shoot around her permanently, Linc. She's good, she's very good, but she's not worth a budget overrun to me."

"I know, but please, let's just get through this afternoon—then we're scheduled for two days off while you shoot the war scenes. Let me have a couple of days with her, please?"

"All right, but this is it. Either she gets her act together or she's out. Her father might have been a flaming queer, but he never fucked up like this. He was always a pro."

Lincoln walked over to a phone and dialed a number. "Noel? I'm sorry to bother you, but I need you to come to Virginia. You know where we're filming. Rae is . . . she's bad, Noel. I need help."

"I'll be there in two hours. Have someone meet me at the airport."

After Lincoln had arranged for someone to meet Noel, he stationed one of the security guards outside Rae's trailer with instructions not to let her leave, or allow anybody else to come inside.

When Noel arrived he'd already made up his mind that Rae Colton had to have the truth, the entire truth, both good and bad about her father and mother. She had to stop blaming everybody in the world for her problems and start facing them, or she would be finished in the movie business before she even got started.

The trailer was dark, and it took Noel a few minutes to see Rae huddled cross-legged in the middle of the bed.

"Rae? It's Noel. I hear you're in a bit of trouble."

"Noel? Hell, who called you? I suppose I can expect Court to show up any minute now." Rae's voice was belligerent.

"No, just me." He reached for the light switch.

"No, don't. If we must have this little discussion, I'd rather talk in the dark if you don't mind. I don't think I can stand too much light right now."

"I think you need a spotlight on you, Rae, so that you can see what you're doing to yourself. But if you want to sit here in the dark, that's fine. Either way, you're going to listen to a few hard truths."

"I already know the hardest one, Noel. I heard Mark outside the trailer earlier today discussing my father's preferences. I've heard little innuendos before, but I refused to believe them. I've been sitting here all afternoon thinking about what I heard. I want you to tell me the rest."

"Well, it goes back a long way, Rae, and I don't know all of the story. But I do know that when I met your father, he'd run away from a terrible childhood. Poverty, and I think his parents beat him. They certainly neglected him. He never talked much about his family, but it was pretty bad. His mother worked two jobs and left an older sister to ride herd on the younger kids.

"Anyway, he and I ended up sharing an apartment with Court. For as long as I knew Steele, he was some kind of emotional pack rat, trying to store up everything he had never had before. He collected love and adoration from everyone he came in contact with. It was as if these relationships represented power and security to him, and he was afraid that if he didn't constantly recharge that power source, he'd die.''

''I can understand that,'' Rae said softly, ''I just don't understand why everybody gave him what he needed.''

''Well now, I can't answer you there. All I can say is, it worked both ways. Steele seemed to recognize our need and respond to it in turn. He gave me the courage to reach out and be the kind of man I wanted to be when in actuality, away from Steele, I was never what I appeared to be.''

''And Court? What did he do for Court?''

''I suppose Court was the only one who never really asked anything of Steele; and yet in a strange kind of way he was the adhesive factor that held us all together, so I suppose Steele was responsible for giving Court the one thing he wanted most in his life, your mother.''

''Hah, that's some kind of double entendre, isn't it? My father was responsible for giving my mother to Court?'' Rae ripped back the covers, sprang to her feet, and began searching through the tangle of makeup and hair products on the dressing table. He waited until she found a cigarette and lit it before he answered her.

''You don't understand your mother, Rae. You never have, and that's the real problem. In many ways, you're just like Valli, and it's tearing you apart. I know you don't want to hear that, but it's true.''

''I'm not like her. I can't be like her. I'm like my father. Everyone says I've got his mannerisms, his talent, his fire. I'm not like my mother!''

''You're Valli all right, Rae, and believe me, that's a much better thing to be. Because your mother has purpose and direction. She's always been a survivor. And she's been able to do what Steele never could: earn the respect of the world, without destroying love in the process.''

''Damn you, Noel, why should I believe anything you say? You're probably her lover, too. You're as blind as everybody else. And you're prejudiced against my father.'' But Rae's words lacked conviction.

''No, Rae, I wasn't your mother's lover.'' He looked her

straight in the eye. "Listen carefully. I was your father's lover. For twenty years we were together a part of every year. There was never really anybody else I wanted. I loved your father, but he was a spoiled little boy who never grew up. He had to have everything, and he never learned how to judge what was good and what was not. He was terribly insecure, and he allowed himself to be manipulated by the people he was trying to impress. If it hadn't been for your mother in the beginning, Steele would never have been more than some two-bit actor making porno films."

Rae's eyes widened in disbelief. "Don't expect me to believe that. My mother latched onto my father and used him until she became successful and then she dropped him like a—"

"Your mother," Noel thundered, "arranged Steele's first audition for his first role on Broadway. When he got into some trouble that threatened his career on the stage, she used all her savings and brought him out here to start over."

"But she became a success, too. Interesting coincidence, isn't it?" Rae bit on a strand of hair she was twirling between two fingers.

"Only after she arranged for Steele to audition for a movie part, found him an agent, and kept him convinced of his talent until he believed it himself. Even then she didn't get what she wanted. Why do you think they got married?"

"Because of me. Daddy explained it all when I was little. He wanted me to have a family and a name, not grow up like he did."

"Then why did it take him two years after you were born to get around to it? Oh, Rae, I don't want to kill all your illusions about Steele. He was your father, and Valli truly loved him. With Steele she was an equal, and he made her feel that she was as good as anybody else. He needed her, and she needed him. He just couldn't stop loving everybody else. And for twenty years every time he called her she sacrificed herself and her career and went to him."

"Sure she did. I lived with her, remember. At least until she sent me off to boarding school halfway around the

267

world."

"Rae, she sent you out of the country partly so that you wouldn't learn about your father's homosexuality. You wanted to live with him. He loved you, but he didn't want you to know, and Valli went along with him because she wanted to keep his image for you, because she loved you both. You've got to accept what I'm saying, Rae. To Steele, Valli was a mother, a friend, and at times a lover, but she was never the only love in his life."

Rae was silent, eyes downcast, and then said finally, "I know."

This time Rae switched on the light and turned to face Noel. Her lips trembled for a moment while she seemed to prepare herself.

"For all these years I thought that he was the most wonderful man on Earth. I was sure that my mother kept me from him, that she was some kind of wicked witch who wanted to punish me. And I hated her. I guess even when I started to know the truth I couldn't let go of those feelings."

"But, Rae, she never stopped loving you. And she never stopped loving Steele. He was what he was, and she forgave him for every sin he committed. She is a woman with a great capacity for love, understanding, and forgiveness and I happen to think that you're just like her, Rae."

"I don't know, Noel. Maybe I'm not that good. At any rate, it's time for me to put up or shut up, isn't it?"

"I'd say it is. Maybe you're neither your mother, nor your father. Maybe you're a combination. Maybe you're the best of both."

Noel kissed her gently on the forehead and left the room. He didn't know that he'd accomplished anything, yet he went away with a sense that Rae had grown up before his eyes, and perhaps, he'd defined a part of himself as well.

"Bye, Noel, tell mother. . . No, never mind. I'll simply have to show her, won't I?"

"What about it, Rae? Are you alright?" Lincoln appeared at her elbow, motioning the security guard away with a nod of his head.

"I'm not sure, Linc, but I'm working on it."

Six months later Valli slipped unnoticed into the back row of a movie theater in Times Square to watch the movie *Don't Cry For Me.*

As Valli watched Rae move across the wide screen, she felt her heart swell in pride. Not Grace Kelly this time, but an intense, emotional young Nicaraguan woman who was the partner and lover of the last Contra hiding out in the mountains. She was exciting, sad, a woman in love with a man who was both her idol and a hero, and Valli felt every raw emotion with an intensity she hadn't expected.

Ironically the woman in the film was forever drawn to the fanatical leader, a handsome, dark-haired older man who ruthlessly used everyone he came in contact with to further the cause he supported. In the end, rather than face defeat, he died from a self-inflicted gunshot wound, leaving the loyal young woman alone. Vivien Leigh's final words in *Gone With the Wind* were no more poignant than Rae's as she stood on the side of a mountain jungle and said, "Don't cry for me. I will survive all this and more."

When the movie ended Valli was drained and very proud. Rae was the young woman and she, too, would survive.

Valli's trained gaze panned over the banquet hall. Once, a long time ago, she'd bribed the announcer to substitute her copy for Lorenso's. She'd gained the credit for her designs and lost her job at the same time. Now twenty-two years later, she was standing in the same place about to introduce her new line—"Val."

The tables were laden with hors d'oeuvres, cheeses imported from Finland and Sweden, pasta from Bologna, French wine and champagne, Beluga caviar, baskets of fresh fruits and breads. At one end of the room was a rock 'n' roll band ready to accompany the entries planned for the teens. At the other end of the room a string quartet was preparing to back the remaining presentations.

The last few months had been such hard work. Valli had

269

thrown herself into it wholeheartedly, and now they were ready to launch both the fragrance and the collection of metallic knits and evening wear.

Backstage ultra-thin models were sliding into body stockings and leotards designed to be worn beneath the gowns. As the models and dressers scurried about making last-minute corrections to their eye shadow and their hairstyles, Valli watched calmly. They were as nervous as racehorses at the starting line waiting for the bell. Valli was tense, she admitted, but no longer frenetic. Everything that could be done had been. Now the true test would come.

On Valli's signal, the doors were opened and the guests swept in. They didn't have to be urged to sample the feast, choose a wine, or a glass of champagne. They did have to be urged to have a seat while ten men wearing Spanish matador costumes and capes passed through the crowd bestowing small sample ebony flasks of perfume on the women guests and miniature golden flagons of cologne for the men. Clouds of "Val" cologne were released into the air from pressurized red-and-gold flagons built into black onyx columns along the models' runway that extended into the audience. The buyers and the press seated themselves on black straight-backed chairs for which Valli had thoughtfully provided red satin cushions.

"Good evening, Valli. It's been a long time."

"Yes." The speaker was a reporter from *Women's Wear Daily*.

"Have you heard the news?"

"No, I guess not. What news?"

"Your daughter has been nominated for an Academy Award. Everyone's comparing her with her father. She's sure to win," the woman gushed.

"Yes." Valli smiled. "I always knew that she was very good. She had a very good teacher. Please excuse me."

Rae. She had suddenly intruded into Valli's evening. As she checked the models, rearranging a ruffle here, an inappropriate pair of earrings there, she suddenly realized that every garment she'd designed would be perfect for Rae.

270

All the colors were Rae's colors, and the models she'd chosen even looked like her daughter.

And now she was thinking of a day twenty-five years ago when she'd witnessed the backstage hustle and bustle for the first time. For a long time, it had been the best day of her life, and today would be another best—but not the very best. That day seemed unattainable now.

She'd promised herself that she would leave Rae alone. But she couldn't do it. Somehow she had to make her daughter understand, and in so doing, clear the way for her and Court. Valli couldn't live without her daughter in her life—or Court. For the last few months she'd promised herself she'd confront Rae. But she kept putting it off.

"Coward, that's what you are." Valli admonished herself.

Now, on her second picture Rae was already following in Steele's footsteps. He had won the award on his first nomination, and Rae would, too. Valli was convinced of it, and she was very proud.

The rest of the evening passed in a blur of excitement. The launch of "Val" was a resounding success, and from this showing alone they'd generated enough excitement to practically guarantee—in a world where there were no guarantees—that the new marketing venture would be a smash. Every hamlet in the country would have access to an original "Val," even Willacoochee, Georgia.

Later that night, back in her apartment, Valley Ray Turner Colton paced the empty apartment. Twice she picked up the phone and twice she replaced it in the receiver. She was forty-three years old and for the first time in her career, she had no more mountains to climb. There was only Rae —and Court, and she was scared to death to face either one.

CHAPTER TWENTY-ONE

Valli opened the special-delivery envelope and examined its contents, including the note with something akin to shock.

Linc, Lincoln Maxwell, had done this. Well, it wasn't going to work. She had no intention of using this invitation. The last place in the world she belonged was at the Awards ceremony. She didn't have time to get a plane reservation to L.A. anyway. If Rae wanted her there, she'd have invited her. Her offer—by letter—to design a gown for Rae to wear to the ceremony had been declined. Politely, but still declined.

Valli raked her fingers through her thick hair and pushed her new bifocal glasses back on top of her head while she examined the invitation more carefully. Pinned to the envelope was a second folder—an airline folder—containing a round-trip ticket. So Lincoln had covered that problem, too. The departure time was one o'clock today. Even if she could make the flight, she'd barely have time to get to the hotel and change her clothes without being late to the ceremony.

No, she couldn't go. She wouldn't subject herself to unforeseen humiliations. Rae had made it perfectly clear that she wanted no part of her mother.

But Rae didn't have to know she was there. Valli dialed the phone.

"Noel? Am I disturbing you?"

"Not at all, Val. What's wrong?."

"Nothing, at least I'm not sure. I got a ticket in the mail, an invitation to the Academy Awards ceremony tonight, and I don't know what to do."

"Don't know? Go. You don't want to miss seeing Rae pick up her first Oscar, do you?"

"No, but there's only the invitation, an airplane ticket, and a note. It just says come. And it's signed Linc."

"So? Why aren't you on the plane halfway to L.A.?"

"I'm scared, Noel."

All the way to the airport Valli fingered the ticket and wondered what she would say to Rae if they came face-to-face. She hadn't had time to make a hotel reservation; she'd just have to take care of that when she got there.

But when she stepped off the plane, she heard her name being paged. "Valli, passenger Valli, please meet your party at the baggage counter."

So she was being met. She hadn't considered that, but Lincoln's being here certainly made everything simpler. Glancing at the sleek gold Piaget on her wrist, she quickened her step. Even if she didn't do more than take a quick shower, she still might not make the opening ceremony on time.

"Ms. Colton?" The uniformed chauffeur stepped up, doffed his hat, and took her suitcases from her. "I'm to take you to your hotel. I'll wait for you to dress and drive you to the awards ceremony." Valli was surprised but happy to let someone else take over.

Valli sat back and let the flavor of California wash over her. She hadn't been back since the funeral, though she'd meant to come several times. Somehow she couldn't face any more failures with Rae. As long as she didn't force a confrontation, she could still believe that things could be different. Even though her career had been tackled with unwavering purpose, Rae was different. In that area, Valli was afraid.

When the limo stopped at the Beverly Hills Hotel and the doorman opened the door, Valli gracefully stepped out and allowed herself to be swept into the lobby. The reservation clerk summoned a bellhop, and Valli was led to a cabaña where the door was opened and her baggage placed in the bedroom.

Bewildered by the day's events, Valli took a quick shower. From her own collection of Hollywood Classics, she selected a cobalt-blue gown of clinging silk that swirled about her body without the benefit of obvious seams or buttons. Quickly she made up her face, dusting a sprinkling of silver across her eyelids and down her neck. Catching her hair just behind one ear, she sprayed it as she brushed it straight back and across her head, allowing the fullness to swing across her cheekbone on the other side.

Sapphire earrings and a pendant, encircled with diamonds, completed the ensemble and she was ready. Not bad for an old lady, she thought. Satisfied with her appearance, she stepped back into the parlor and gasped.

Entering from the door opposite was a man, a tall sun-kissed man with green eyes, an equally startled smile, and two very familiar dimples.

"Valli?"

"Court?"

They met in the middle of the rug and simply stared at each other hungrily.

At forty-eight, Court was more handsome than ever. Years of playing tennis had kept him trim and given his body a golden glow of color. Tiny lines crinkled around green eyes that had softened over the years from emerald to moss. The flash of his smile seemed to reach down inside Valli and touch a fiery response in her body. She stretched out her hand to touch the ever-present dimples, and Court captured her hand, then kissed it softly.

"He sent you a ticket, too?" Valli felt her heart pound like some schoolgirl at her first prom.

"Yes. I only got it at the last minute and I almost didn't come. . . But I did," he faltered.

"Yes, you did," Valli laughed nervously. "I guess we'd better hurry. We're already late, aren't we?"

"Yes, we'd better." But neither made a move to go.

"God, I've missed you, Valli. I thought it was bad before, but since our last conversation it's been awful."

"I know," she agreed breathlessly and took a half-step toward him.

His lips tightened for a moment. Then he sighed and looked at his watch. "We're going to be dreadfully late. Linc went to a great deal of trouble to arrange this. We'd better go."

Valli nodded and turned toward the door.

A smattering of applause died down as they found their seats and the Dorothy Chandler Pavilion went dark. The lights on the stage were brought up, and the first of many tributes began to the old-timers who had forged the path for the current nominees to follow.

A film clip of Gene Kelly's and Leslie Caron's dance scene from *An American In Paris*, the Best Film of 1951, gave way to the two performers who finished the number live. Immediately the orchestra swung into the music from *Cabaret* and the clip of Liza Minnelli and Joel Grey dissolved into the two performers who demonstrated once again why the 1972 film had pulled in eight awards.

It wasn't until Jane Powell and Howard Keel recreated their roles in the 1954 release of *Seven Brides for Seven Brothers* that the latecomer next to Valli leaned over and touched her shoulder.

"Hi, Val. I didn't know you were going to be here."

"Linc?" She kissed his cheek, then pulled away. "What do you mean you didn't know?"

"And Court, too? I think both of you are going to be very surprised tonight."

Michael Douglas and Meryl Streep, with microphones in hand, suddenly appeared in the spotlight at the center of a

golden arch. The orchestra music died away, and the crow
applauded the opening nostalgic numbers from past Oscar
winning movies.

The two entertainers delivered their lines, waited for th
proper laughs, and the ceremonies were underway. Severa
minutes passed before Valli could question Lincoln mor
carefully.

"Linc, what did you mean a minute ago? Didn't you sen
me both an airline ticket and the ticket for the ceremony?"

"Had nothing to do with it. Why did you think I did?"

"A note inside the envelope simply said come, and it wa
signed by you. What else was I to think?"

"Maybe," Lincoln said under his breath, avoiding Valli'
inquiring eyes, "you ought to consider who else might wan
you here."

Valli had been thinking about nothing else for the last few
minutes. Had Rae sent the tickets? Had she arranged the ca
baña for her and Court? What did it mean?

In the darkness, Court's hand slid underneath's Valli's
arm and found her hand. He clasped it tightly, sliding down
in the seat so that he could lean his head closer to hers.

"Did you tell Linc thanks?"

"Linc didn't send the tickets, Court," she whispered. "I
think Rae must have."

"Rae?" The slight tightening of Court's hand was one of
reassurance, and Valli felt herself relax, as much as she could
relax with Court only a warm breath away.

Valli glanced around. From where she sat she saw at least
ten women wearing either a Valli Original gown or one by
Hollywood Classics. One of the nominees for best actress
was wearing a copy of Susan Hayworth's red-satin gown
with the huge ruffled pleat at the neckline.

Valli nodded to one acquaintance after another. In a
strange kind of way this was her element, the tinsel-town
world of a tarnished hero. And she began to feel that telltale
odd sense of power sizzle deep inside that hidden part of
her. This was to be an important night. She smiled to herself
and leaned back in the plush velvet seat.

276

The television viewer watching at home only saw the crowd with rapt attention on the stage. They couldn't see the constant coming and going, nor could they hear the hum of conversation in the beginning. It was only later, when they reached the more important awards, that the crowd quieted.

But it wasn't just the celebrity crowd and the feeling of the importance of the night that caused the insistent flutter in her breathing. Every time Court moved he seemed to be closer to Valli and his fingertips were drawing erotic little pictures in the palm of her hand. She couldn't take much more of this before she would have to excuse herself to powder her nose.

The evening wore on, and Valli's entire body was a mass of nervous energy. What if Rae didn't win the award? Valli had spent most of the evening looking around for some sign of Rae. But she couldn't see her anywhere. Would she make herself known to them?

"And now, to present the award for Best Actress of the Year, please welcome a couple of best actors for every year, Mr. Paul Newman and Ms. Joanne—."

The applause that followed was enthusiastic. Valli squeezed Court's hand, and he nodded.

Joanne slid her finger beneath the flap of the envelope and smiled. "And the winner is...Rae Colton...."

Her final words were lost in the applause as Valli leaned forward to watch a tall, slim figure across the aisle of seats rise and begin making her way up to the stage and into the limelight.

Valli gasped out loud. She couldn't believe what her eyes told her to be true. Rae was wearing a red-satin dress, one that hugged her breasts and cinched her waist just as it had Valli's fifteen years before when she and Steele had won the Academy Award. "How? Where?"

The audience was standing now, not only in tribute to Rae, but in living tribute to her father. She stood in the center of the stage, holding the gold figurine cradled to her breast, and waited. There was a look about her that made

Valli think of the role she'd played in the film, a look of courage and triumph.

Court turned to Valli with a question in his eyes. "Isn't that your dress?" He had seen it on television fifteen years ago and still remembered.

Valli didn't trust herself to speak. The lump in her throat was increasing in size by the second. She nodded.

Finally the crowd hushed, and Rae began to speak. In her lovely deep voice, so like her father's that every person watching felt his presence there, she said, "Ladies and Gentlemen of the Academy, thank you for bestowing your most prestigious award on such a novice as I. I will never again know such a wondrous moment. And I'd like to thank the producer, David Ladd, the writer, my friend Spud—"

Valli looked at Court in shock. "Spud?"

Court grinned. "I'll tell you later."

"...the director, and my leading man, Linc Maxwell, who took a greenhorn little know-it-all and taught me to reach down into myself and become the woman I portrayed on the screen. But above all these, I'd like to say thank you to Court McCambridge who forced me to face life and make the most of it, to my father who showed me the way by leaving me the gift of his great talent, and to my mother, Valli who had the very great wisdom to love both of them. Now with all the love I possess, I want to tell her—thank you for forcing me to be the very best I could be. I love you."

Valli watched as Rae looked straight through the crowd at her and blew her a kiss. The audience finally settled down and Court pulled Valli back to her seat, but the final awards were a blur. She could only see Rae and hear the replay of her words in her mind. And she knew that it had all been worthwhile. Lincoln didn't win Best Actor, but when Valli turned to console him, his seat was vacant.

Court and Valli made their way to the press room and waited outside. More nervous than she could imagine, Valli waited impatiently until she saw Rae making her way toward them. Behind her, his arm possessively on her elbow, was Lincoln. There was a look of something more than simple pride in his eyes, and as they stopped for a moment, Rae lifted her head and whispered into his ear. He smiled and guided Valli's daughter toward her.

Valli simply opened her arms and Rae moved into them while both women began to cry.

They pulled away, looked at each other and tried to speak.

"Mother, I'm sorry. . ."

"Rae, I'm so sorry. . ."

"You got my ticket. . ."

"You sent those tickets. . ."

They clasped each other again, letting their arms and bodies say the words that wouldn't come. Only the persistent flash of the reporters' cameras finally forced them apart.

"I wanted you and Court to be together, to be here with us. . .me, tonight, because I love you both."

"Oh, Rae. I love you too. I always have."

"I must look a mess." Rae wiped away her tears with the back of her hand.

"Not to me. I think you look wonderful. Where did you get that dress?"

They might have been alone in a swirling mass of people who seemed to understand that they needed to be together for that moment.

"Terrance found it at the salon. He said you wore it the night you won your award and Daddy won his. And I don't know, I felt very sentimental. I wanted you to know that I. . .Oh, hell. I liked the dress, and it was cheap."

Valli laughed and linked her arm through Rae's as they made their way to the cars. Their progress was halted time after time as they were stopped by congratulations for Rae and words of genuine welcome for Valli.

When they reached the limo, Rae slid naturally into the seat beside Lincoln and caught his hand in hers. "Oh, Uncle Court. . .this is the most wonderful night of my life."

Court, sitting quietly on the seat opposite Rae, heard the reference to uncle and saw the look on Lincoln's face as he brushed a kiss across Rae's hair. Leaning forward, Court

279

smiled and slid his arm around Valli as she leaned against him, knowing that all the struggle had been worthwhile.

She thought of the words Rae had used tonight. Granny' words from long ago. Even when she hadn't had a glimme of hope, Valli always tried to be the very best. Until now, she hadn't known how wonderful that could be.

She'd left Willacoochee, determined to use whatever tal ent she'd been given to make the world sit up and take notice. Design had been the only thing she knew, and there'd been times when she wondered if the design she'd woven had been wrong. No more. Tonight she saw the fina threads fall into place. Her life had been filled with the bright colors of hope and joy, the deep cutting hues of truth and loyalty, and the sharp inner thread of pain, and now she was adding the beauty of love. From the beginning she'd been the weaver, and the finished product might be nicked and flawed, but she knew that with love, it would endure.

I'LL TAKE MANHATTAN
by JUDITH KRANTZ

Judith Krantz comes home to New York for her lastest
triumph! In I'LL TAKE MANHATTAN, she takes on
the glamour capital of the world, weaving a glittering
tale of power, love, and betrayal in the sophisticated,
high-stakes arena of magazine publishing. Only Judith
Krantz could tell this story of the sensual Maxi, a wilful
hedonist who unexpectedly discovers that her talent for
lust is matched by a hunger for work.

Impudent, raven-haired Maxi Amberville is 29 and has
already discarded three husbands and two continents.
Now Maxi is returning to Manhattan to attend a board
meeting of Amberville Publications and to be reunited
with her mother, Lily, and her daughter Angelica Cipri-
ani. Maxi learns that her widowed mother has married
Maxi's detested Uncle Cutter. She determines to
prevent him from sabotaging her father's life-work – and
selling it to the highest bidder.

Maxi takes over BUTTONS & BOWS, a fashion trade
weekly, and transforms it into B & B, the glitziest, ritz-
iest, most successful fashion magazine in the country.
Her hot-blooded ex-husband, Rocco, and a coterie of
other well-connected friends give their all for B & B –
and for Maxi. What she learns about family, the publishing business, life and especially about love makes this a
can't-wait-to-turn-the-page novel that is truly crême de
la Krantz!

0 553 17242 5

A SELECTED LIST OF NOVELS
AVAILABLE FROM BANTAM BOOKS

THE PRICES SHOWN BELOW WERE CORRECT AT THE TIME OF GOING
TO PRESS. HOWEVER TRANSWORLD PUBLISHERS RESERVE THE
RIGHT TO SHOW NEW RETAIL PRICES ON COVERS WHICH MAY
DIFFER FROM THOSE PREVIOUSLY ADVERTISED IN THE TEXT OR
ELSEWHERE.

☐ 17172 0	WILD SWAN	Celeste de Blasis	£3.95
☐ 17252 2	SWAN'S CHANCE	Celeste de Blasis	£2.95
☐ 17268 9	IMPULSE	Barbara Harrison	£3.50
☐ 17208 5	PASSION'S PRICE	Barbara Harrison	£2.95
☐ 17185 2	THIS CHERISHED DREAM	Barbara Harrison	£2.95
☐ 17207 7	FACES	Johanna Kingsley	£2.95
☐ 17151 8	SCENTS	Johanna Kingsley	£2.95
☐ 17242 5	I'LL TAKE MANHATTAN	Judith Krantz	£3.95
☐ 17174 7	MISTRAL'S DAUGHTER	Judith Krantz	£2.95
☐ 17389 8	PRINCESS DAISY	Judith Krantz	£3.50
☐ 17209 3	THE CLASS	Erich Segal	£2.95
☐ 17192 5	THE ENCHANTRESS	Han Suyin	£2.95
☐ 17150 X	TILL MORNING COMES	Han Suyin	£3.50

*All Corgi/Bantam Books are available at your bookshop or newsagent, or can be ordered from
the following address:*

Corgi/Bantam Books,
Cash Sales Department,
P.O. Box 11, Falmouth, Cornwall TR10 9EN

Please send a cheque or postal order (no currency) and allow 60p for postage and packing for
the first book plus 25p for the second book and 15p for each additional book ordered up to a
maximum charge of £1.90 in UK.

B.F.P.O. customers please allow 60p for the first book, 25p for the second book plus 15p per
copy for the next 7 books, thereafter 9p per book.

Overseas customers, including Eire, please allow £1.25 for postage and packing for the first
book, 75p for the second book, and 28p for each subsequent title ordered.